waiting
for
him

2. Arachnides, Crustacés.

3. Myriapodes, Insectes inférieurs : *Thysanoures, Collemboles, Archiptères* [Éphémères, Libellules, Perles, Psoques, Termites] *Orthoptères, Névroptères, Th*...

waiting
for
him

Copyright 2015
By Todd and LJC Shimoda

Publisher:
Chin Music Press
1501 Pike Place #329
Seattle, WA 98101
www.chinmusicpress.com

First [1] edition

Cover and interior art by LJC Shimoda
Book design by LJC Shimoda
Production by Linda Ronan

All rights reserved

Library of Congress Cataloging-in-Publication Data is available.
ISBN: 978-1-63405-902-2

ALSO BY THE AUTHOR AND ARTIST

Subduction

OH! A Mystery of Mono no Aware

The Fourth Treasure

365 Views of Mt. Fuji

ALSO BY THE ARTIST

Glyphix for Visual Journaling: Drawing Out the Words Within

Application For Investigation

Particulars of request: Ascertain the movements and whereabouts of a missing person
Name: Mizuno Ren
Sex: Male
Age: 29
Marital status: Single
Profession: Entomological illustration specialist, freelance
Comments: The missing man is the applicant's son. He failed to appear at her home for the Festival of the Dead holiday as is his custom. Her attempts to contact her son were not successful. Everything necessary for the investigation will be made available.

I hereby make official application for investigation and enclose herewith the requisite fee. Furthermore, I swear to observe the strictest secrecy concerning all information, to make no disclosures, and to make no abuse of any knowledge obtained.

Signature of applicant
Mizuno Rie

23 August 1987
Zabuton Detective Agency
Chief of Section for the Investigation of Persons

I pressed the brake to slow the car to a crawl. The enclave of old wooden houses was located on a narrow street lined on both sides with power poles, stone and bamboo fences, cars, and delivery trucks, making it difficult to drive while I searched for the particular address. I turned off the air conditioner as if the roar of the fan hindered my ability to distinguish street names and building numbers.

Ahead, not more than twenty meters, an elderly man walked along the side of the street toward a small grocery store. On the store's veranda were stacks of newspapers, boxes of vegetables, and cartons of empty beer bottles. A row of potted plants with yellow leaves indicating they needed a good watering, or perhaps less, marked a boundary between the veranda and three vending machines offering beer and cold sake, cigarettes, and single serving packages of instant noodle soup. A spigot provided hot water for reconstituting the soup. The owner of the machines clearly knew what sells in the neighborhood.

In the contemporary scheme of society, the neighborhood lacked outward significance other than the ground on which it was built. Real estate speculators could easily buy all the houses and commercial buildings, forcing reluctant owners into selling by hiring criminal gangs to overrun the neighborhood. When the properties were purchased, a demolition company would raze the buildings and seemingly overnight they would be replaced with office towers, retail spaces, and condominiums. In terms of functionality, the modernization would exploit the area to a much higher potential. The neighborhood consisted of too much underutilized space, especially too many single-family homes occupying the precious land. Modern space planners design on the principle of a box of one hundred and sixty cubic meters, which is the optimum living space for two people. More volume is not necessary, less can lead to tension and discomfort.

And what of the displaced residents and businesses? The owner of the grocery store would be given the golden opportunity to rent a sleek modern retail space at half the size and four times the cost of the old building. But think of the fluorescent light gleaming off stainless steel shelves, and the protection provided by security cameras. And the local residents could get out from under the maintenance headaches of their ramshackle homes and avoid winter drafts by purchasing new, hermetically-sealed condominiums with low-interest, seventy-five-year mortgages. The secure condominium buildings would have elevators to whisk them up to their units, each with central heating and air conditioning. Not to mention the one-and-a-half dedicated parking spaces. How could the neighborhood residents turn down such progress?

The car rolled closer to the store. The elderly pedestrian's hair was shaved to a salt-and-pepper stubble. He wore a gray overcoat wrapped around him like a quilt—an odd choice of garment given the August heat and thick humidity. Then he turned his head and revealed that he was not a man but a woman of some eighty years in age. Perhaps she was ill enough to cause her hair to fall out. Or she might be a retired Buddhist nun. Do nuns retire? Surely they must, although without much retirement savings.

When the car and woman were even, I rolled down the window and poked my head out. "Hello, excuse me. Could you please direct me to the Mizuno house?"

"Mizuno?" she said. "Which Mizuno?"

"Mizuno Rie," I answered, then gave her the address.

"Ah, the fortuneteller." She shuffled over to the car and peered at me. "You look like a man needing his fortune told. Trouble with women, no doubt. Eh?"

"No doubt."

She cackled then gave me surprisingly elaborate directions: turn right past the store, left at the first alley, park there, walk past a little shrine, and go up a path of stone steps. At the top of the hill, I was to look for a house on the left side. "You will see her fortuneteller's sign."

I thanked her and proceeded to follow her described route; however, finding a place to park in the alley proved impossible. Cars, trucks, and motorbikes occupied all slivers of space, some squeezed in so tightly that they must have been parked by a supernatural valet. I continued past the tiny neighborhood shrine, which was not much more than a rickety gate leading to an open-air altar under a simple peaked roof. A trio of women—I was sure this time of their gender as they were wearing housedresses with aprons and scarves holding back their long hair—cleaned the altar with pink feather dusters and white rags. They gave me, or my car, deep formal bows as I drove past. I returned the greeting with an apologetic nod because sitting in my car I could do no more than that.

Rolling past the shrine, I next came to the workshop of a gravestone carver. Slender yet substantial slabs of cut rock were piled outside the workshop. A few finished stones with names etched in sharp precision were lined up, ready for delivery. I wondered if the gravestone carver ever experienced a pique of interest in the lives represented by the names. Perhaps the first one or two that he carved, but after that? Not a thought, I guessed.

Next to the gravestone supplier was a five-stool, three-table ramen noodle stand not yet open for the day. The narrow stoop leading into the stand was still damp from a recent washing. The interior was in shadow but I could make out the silhouettes of a man and woman going about the mundane duties of chopping onions and stacking bowls.

At the end of the alley was a gas station and auto repair shop. *Minor repairs only,* said the sign. I turned into the station and a young attendant, maybe nineteen, walked up to the car and gave me an expectant look. A smudge of grease above his lip and one on his left ear gave him the impression of a working mechanic.

"Yes, good morning. I have some business back there and thought I might leave my car for fueling and a check of all the fluids. I'll probably be an hour."

The mechanic clucked and took a step back and looked the car over from front to back. "Suppose so."

"Fine," I said. It was unclear what he discovered during his brief inspection. Leaving the keys in the ignition, I stepped out of the car. The mechanic gave me a nod as if assuring me the world would be all right. At least with the car, I hoped.

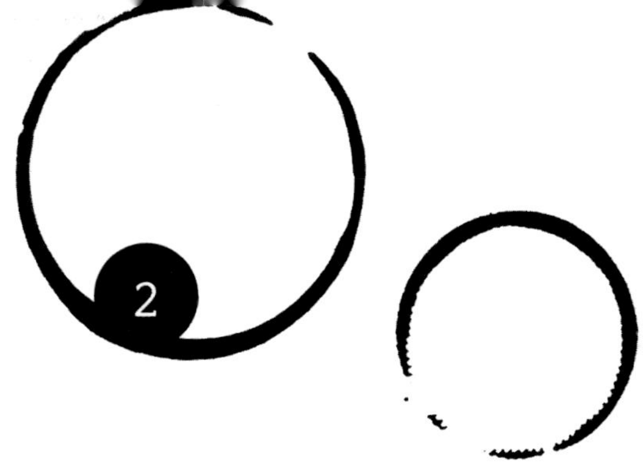

Walking past the noodle stand, I heard a bang of pots and smelled the salty, meaty simmering broth. The stools lined up at the bar were clean but cracked and worn to a point that the white foam padding was exposed along the seams. A man and woman, probably the owners, were getting the stand ready to open. In another five or six steps I came to the gravestone carver. A layer of fine, glittering dust coated the alley. From inside the workshop came the whirring of a rock polisher. Past the carver's shop, I came to the three shrine cleaners who gave me another formal bow. This time I was able to execute one of my own. Whatever I did made them titter. With my briefcase and suit-and-tie apparel, I must have looked like a salesman. Perhaps they had a private joke about salesmen.

Viewed from this plane, that is, walking rather driving, the neighborhood developed only a little more significance. The mechanic revealed himself as an apprentice given responsibility before his time and experience should have allowed. The noodle stand owners were no doubt barely surviving financially. The gravestone carver would likely develop silicosis from inhaling dust particles. These stories of the residents added confirmation to the claim that the neighborhood lacked significance.

But then such significance can only be contextual, a relative comparison. For example, comparing Neighborhood A to Neighborhood B with facts and figures such as population density and socioeconomic status gives us measures that can be analyzed side-by-side. If, however, we are able to observe the internal significance of the neighborhood to the people who live there we can find a different measure, a more subjective degree of significance. Now we have entered the realm of human motivation and desires. The ability to make such observations should be part of being a skilled investigator. Unfortunately, I am not so skilled, and I'm entirely satisfied to make enough to pay my rent and eat.

The path leading up the hill was exactly where the retired nun—I decided to anoint her with that title—said it would be. The path's stones were placed too close for my stride and my steps were mincing. At the top of the hill, really not much more than a rise, were three houses. The one on the left bore the address of the woman whose son was missing. A string of red lanterns signifying the beginning of the ancestor's festival was hung from the door to a pole stuck in the ground a short distance away from the home. The lanterns invited and guided spirits to the home; however, as the festival was now over, they should have been taken down. This indicated a certain state of mind—most likely the woman's concern for her missing son.

The front door was open so I stepped inside the cool entryway. Shoes and slippers were placed haphazardly on the stone floor. A large lantern decorated with the image of a hand, palm-side out, leaned against the opposite wall. "Hello?" I said.

After a moment there was a rustling, like someone putting papers in a box. A woman of some fifty years of age appeared and bowed deeply while apologizing for not meeting me at the door of her messy home—her description not mine. Her hair was white, shockingly so since she was not that much older than me. It was styled to frame her face elegantly, giving her an aura of great intelligence and knowing. That image would be good for her line of work.

"There's no need to apologize," I said. "I didn't realize I had arrived so early." I presented her one of my business cards.

She studied it for precisely three seconds before she said, "No, you're not early. Come in." She selected a pair of house slippers for me to wear. I slipped out of my shoes and wriggled my feet into the slippers at least one size too small. When I looked up, she was studying me, no doubt sizing me up as she would a new client, searching for clues as to personality, profession, and troubles which she could exploit in her vocation.

The fortuneteller hurried ahead into the house. I followed with less speed and passed by the door to a side room containing a table and two chairs. Two lamps cast a dull yellowish glow through their paper shades.

Most likely, the room was where she told her clients' fortunes. The room exuded a coldness. I turned away.

The woman stopped in the main room of the small, dimly-lit house. She whacked a couple of cushions and set them on the floor in front of a low table. After gesturing for me to sit, which I did after putting my briefcase on the table, she scurried into the kitchen before I could tell her I didn't need a refreshment.

A traditional altar for the ancestor's festival was set up in the room. Next to the altar was a cucumber decorated to resemble a horse (giving the spirits a quick ride home) and an eggplant like a cow (to keep the spirits around once they arrived). Both decorated vegetables were splotched with mold. Clearly, her son's failure to visit disrupted her celebration of this year's festival.

A wave of depression flowed through me. The worn-out neighborhood, the residents going about their lives in slow motion, and the fortuneteller's dark home with disintegrating decorations, created the negative energy. It was as if the locality were a black hole from which no signs of life could escape. I reached instinctively for my cigarettes but there were none. I was trying to quit.

I was about to get up to examine the framed pictures on the wall—one was of a man likely to be her missing son as there was a noticeable resemblance—when she returned with a pot of tea and two cups. While she served us, she apologized for living in a place so difficult to find. I said it was not so difficult, although I didn't mention the nun's help.

"Good," she said.

I took a sip of tea and made an appropriate sound of satisfaction, though in fact the tea was too weak for my taste. "Your line of work is interesting," I said, opening with small talk.

"Not too interesting," she demurred. "People hear what they want to hear."

I was surprised by her honesty. The fortunetellers I previously encountered, as few as they were, espoused the occupational line that they possessed mystical gifts allowing them to peer into people's souls and predict their future.

I asked, "Is business good during this time of economic prosperity or do you find people needing your services less because of it?"

"Business is better than ever," she said. "People are consumed by the future. They believe they can become wealthy if they only know which direction to take, or which family to marry into. No one, almost no one, cares about love or happiness."

As she spoke, her gaze darted in seemingly random patterns. Following the path to determine what she might be looking at was impossible. But she was obviously taking in something. I glanced around the room. The walls were spotted with shadows and the longer I stared at a spot the darker and larger it became, increasing my dread of falling into a black hole. The more I stared, the more I was pulled toward the darkness. Well, actually, it was like *half* of me was being pulled; the other half remained securely in place on the cushion. My being was stretching and cleaving apart. Oddly, the phenomenon also generated a calm certitude, as if my own death were coming in a matter of hours and I had fully accepted it.

I looked away and gulped a swallow of tea. Clearing my throat, I opened my briefcase and took out the fortuneteller's application for services, a notebook, and a pen. "How old is your son?"

"Twenty-nine," she said.

To assure her of my professionalism, I made elaborate motions of writing down her answer. "When was the last time you saw or talked with him?

"Last year's ancestor festival."

She answered with a clipped response, implying that it should have been obvious. Of course, she had already given this information to my supervisor. "Mrs. Mizuno, I apologize if you've already answered these questions but I find it necessary to verify information obtained by others. Call it my style."

The fortuneteller's expression didn't change as she focused her gaze fully on me. After a moment a tiny smirk arose at the corners of her mouth and she gave me a little nod. The actions might be patronizing but I couldn't say for sure.

"Where does your son live?" I asked as if nothing had happened.

She recited his ward, block, and apartment number.

"Thank you. What have you done to find him?"

She blinked a couple of times. "Call your company."

"You didn't try to contact him?"

"Of course I tried. But I got nowhere."

"How about the police?"

Her head twitched as if she suddenly remembered something vital. "No police. Besides, they wouldn't give me the time of day."

She was right about the lack of police interest in such a case—it was too soon, too common, for a son nearly thirty years of age to be out of contact with his mother. And she probably didn't want authorities poking around her professional life. Fortunetellers operate on the fringe of legality. Instead I asked, "Who are his closest acquaintances?"

"None whom I know. He's a bit of a loner. He had a few friends in school but they all drifted away. He hasn't mentioned anyone lately." She paused, then added, "Male or female."

"How about enemies?"

"Heavens no. What are you thinking?"

The trouble was, I wasn't thinking. Rather, my questions were routine. The case unfolding before me was premature, lacking substance. Only a few days had passed from when the son should have visited. Nothing yet indicated there was an alarming situation.

"Please forgive me," I said. "I meant nothing. Again, it's simply a matter of routine. How about his work? I understand he is a freelance illustrator of insects."

She got up and pulled a book off a nearby shelf. "The book came in the mail more than two years ago."

It was a book about butterflies and moths, the text in English and Japanese. There were photographs and intricate hand-drawn illustrations. "I assume your son drew these?" I asked her, pointing to one of the illustrations.

"Yes."

"He does beautiful work. May I borrow the book and a picture of your son? I will be sure to get them back to you without damage."

"Of course you will," she said matter-of-factly.

Her statement gave me a start, as if she knew my future.

Not surprisingly, the car wasn't finished when I returned to the service station. The budding mechanic was waiting for me to authorize replacing a part somewhere in the engine. I authorized the work, although I wasn't sure it was necessary. My free parking spot was becoming expensive.

The noodle stand was open with no customers until I sat at one of the counter stools. The proprietress had dark puffy flesh under her eyes and her face was pocked with large pores. She wrote my order on a slip of paper and passed it into the kitchen through a small window, then served me a cup of tea. While I sipped it, I glanced through the butterfly book. On the title page of the book, I found the name of the fortuneteller's son listed as the illustrator. In the preface of the book, the editor noted that the drawings and photographs were made in the field in many locations in Japan, Southeast Asia, and the Americas.

The noodle stand woman brought me a bowl of steaming broth filled with ramen, slices of meat and vegetables, topped with chopped green onion. Her fingernails were chipped and unevenly trimmed.

The son's picture showed the young man holding a sketchbook in a tropical setting of lush greenery. His pose was stiff and his expression anticipatory, nearly grim, as if he were gamely awaiting his execution. A floppy hat shaded most of his face except for the lower part of his chin. Despite the dark mood of the photo, I could see no immediate cause for concern at this point. The son did not show up as was his custom but that could be for countless reasons, some the mother could have thought of but lacked the fortitude to admit because they might reflect poorly on her. Perhaps an argument with her about when he was going to get married and provide her with grandchildren, or his reluctance to visit her more than once a year.

When I settled the tab for the tea and noodles, I used their pay phone to call the publisher of the book—Shinshin Group. After I was bounced through four levels of employees, I was connected with the art director who worked on the book. "I'm investigating the disappearance of Mizuno Ren," I said to the director.

There was a long disconcerting silence before she said, "I don't understand. Disappearance, you said?"

"Yes. Apparently his mother was expecting him for the holiday and he never showed up."

"I'm sorry, I still don't understand," she said with an edge of irritation and suspicion. "You do know he died three years ago."

▸

The noodle stand woman looked at me out of the corner of her eye, quickly glancing away when I saw the direction of her gaze. Her expression softened, as if now that I was a paying customer I had entered a sphere of safety. The pores that were once large had closed up, and the darkness under her eyes had lightened. Either she applied makeup while I was on the telephone or my perception of her changed.

Sitting back on the stool, I asked for another cup of tea. She hesitated as if she were going to ask a question, then opened a tea pot and tossed in two pinches of leaves. Glancing at me, she added a third and filled the pot with hot water from a thermos. While we waited for the tea to steep, I asked her how long she had lived in the neighborhood.

"Not long, I suppose. Let's see . . . my husband and I moved here eight years ago when his parents died. They left us their house." She turned to face the back of the stand where her husband was bent over a counter concentrating on a task. She turned back to me and said, "We started this noodle stand two years ago. He always fancied himself a chef."

"A noodle shop is a good place to start as a chef."

"Not really," she said. "It's a good place to end a career as a chef."

I would have agreed but looking at the husband's back as he patiently worked his knife I felt sorry for him. "I'm sure things will work out," I said. "By the way, I'm in the neighborhood to get my car fixed at the shop and realized an old friend lives near here, or at least used to. Mizuno Ren. Do you know him?"

She shook her head, too quickly to have given my question much thought. She took a rag, lifted a stack of bowls, and wiped the counter underneath them.

"How about his mother? Mizuno Rie?"

Again she shook her head. Now, I was just another nosy customer. The dark circles of loose flesh under her eyes returned, and her pores enlarged. Again, the change may have been due to my perception.

Giving her the benefit of the doubt, I allowed that she didn't know the Mizuno family despite the mother's home being only a few steps away. Perhaps the fortuneteller was never a customer of the stand. Or maybe the noodle stand woman was simply not an observant neighbor, instead too focused on her husband's dream that will wither and die.

▸

The art director at the publishing company hadn't given me anymore information over the phone, despite my persistent questioning. How did Mizuno Ren die? When exactly? Where? She deflected my questions with professional demurs until she broke off our conversation with a quick "Goodbye."

From the noodle stand, I walked back toward the small shrine and the steps to the fortuneteller's home. I would have to confront her with the report of her son's death. However, I lacked confidence in what the art director told me. She may have decided I was not a person she should be talking with about the son, perhaps because she didn't want to be called as a witness in a future legal proceeding. Unfortunately, people thought more and more about such things, making my job increasingly difficult. On the other hand, the change in people's willingness to cooperate could be due to a change in my style of questioning. A brusqueness had crept into my social interactions. The change might be chalked up to middle age, giving me an attitude of having seen too much to let anyone get away with petty, selfish balking.

On the other hand, the change in people could be because as a society becomes more affluent it tends to become more closed. Behavioral scientists studying the phenomenon conclude that financial success, or the hope of financial success, leads to fear of losing those gains. As a society we become hoarders and selfish accumulators bent on the single-minded pursuit of wealth. Of course, what is generally true for a society is not always true for the individual. Some consciously fight the trend of a closed society because they want to be individualistic and antisocial, or rather anti-society. Some are open because they desire acceptance in a given situation, outweighing their need for security. These people are the easiest to get information from, although in many cases they are overeager and will say whatever they believe you want to hear. That reminded me of the fortuneteller's statement about her clients and their willingness to hear what they want to hear.

I reached the shrine at the bottom of the steps leading up to the fortuneteller's house where I stopped and considered what I should do next. When I heard the art director's claim that the missing son was dead, I wanted to confront the applicant immediately. An investigator's time is expensive and should not be wasted. In fact, my section chief at the agency should be informed about the revelation of the son's death. But I rejected that idea—the chief would cancel the assignment, refund the fee other than my hour or two I'd spent on the case. *No time for kooks,* he would say. *We've got real work to do. No time for chasing ghosts.*

I rejected informing the chief because of a strange reaction I was having to the neighborhood and the case. There was a feeling of familiarity, although not déjà vu. It was a similarity to case of some twenty years ago. The old case started in a different neighborhood from the fortuneteller's—one of concrete-and-steel high-rise apartments, sterile grounds, and glaring lights that created artificial shadows. In contrast, the neighborhood of the fortuneteller was older with wooden homes, narrow alleys, and a soft, natural darkness. Also, the client in the old case was a young wife whose husband disappeared, rather than a mother looking for her son.

What the cases shared was an inexorable dread that drew on the energy of the people involved, not only the clients but all those connected directly or peripherally. For example, a couple of scraggly youths with sunglasses and tattoos stared suspiciously as they walked past me and entered the noodle stand. An unmarked van slowly, sinisterly pulled into the service station. Across the street, two women in the alley argued about what I couldn't hear. They gave me a hard stare when they noticed I was trying to eavesdrop.

As I headed to the service station to rescue my car, the neighborhood I had considered insignificant took on the misery of humanity, of rage, of nerves exposed to brine. The noodle stand became a gang hangout where executions were planned, and the garage a drop off point for burglars or smugglers. The two women were embroiled in a turf battle that will erupt into incomprehensible violence.

My car was ready. The mechanic gave me a rundown of the parts and labor but I barely heard. I paid and drove away from the neighborhood having decided to investigate further before confronting the fortuneteller about the death of her missing son.

As I left the neighborhood behind I could not shake the memory of the old case.

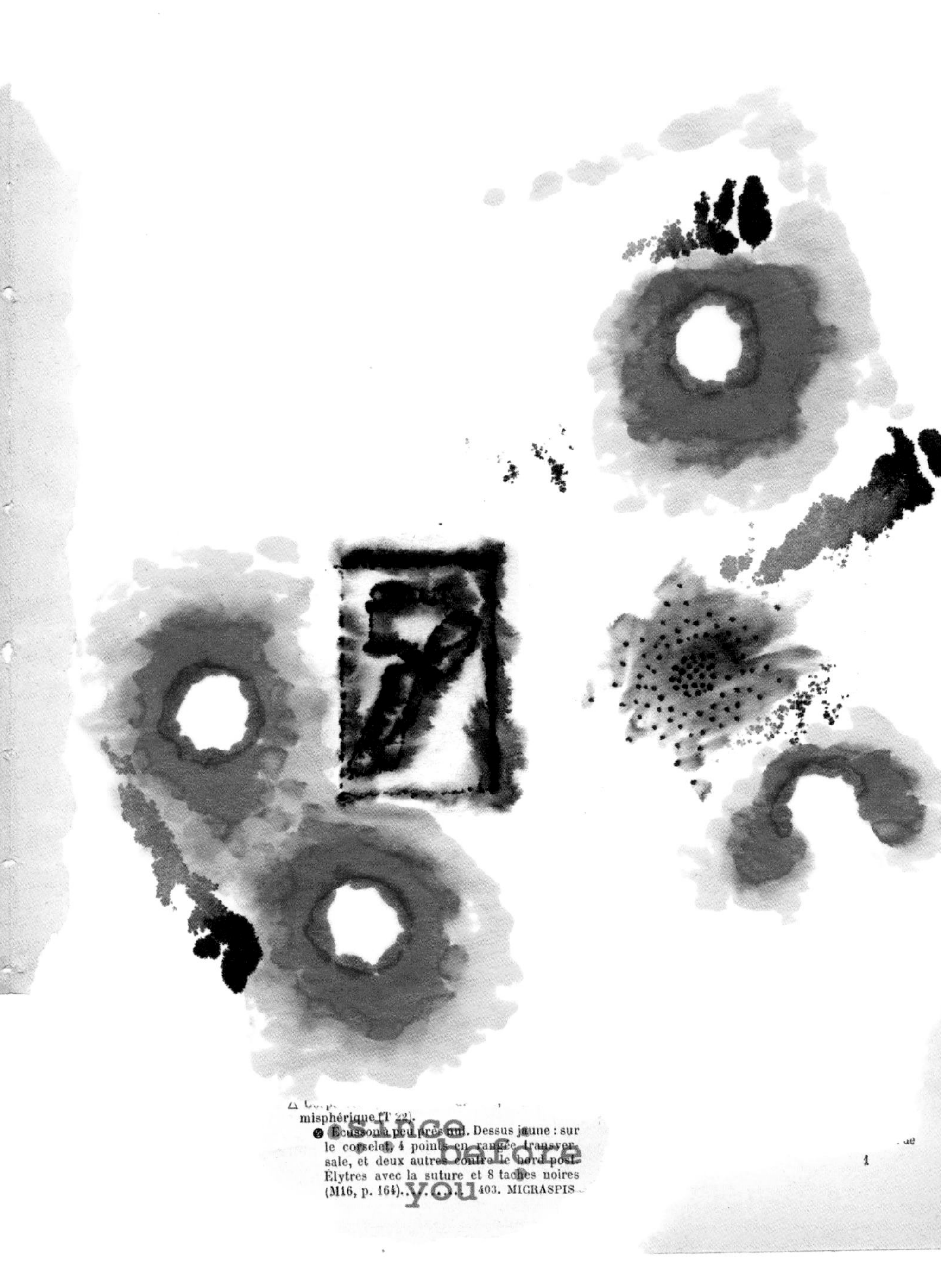
mısphérique (T 22).
Écusson à peu près nul. Dessus jaune : sur le corselet, 4 points en rangée transversale, et deux autres contre le bord post. Élytres avec la suture et 8 taches noires (M16, p. 164)........ 403. MICRASPIS
since
before
you

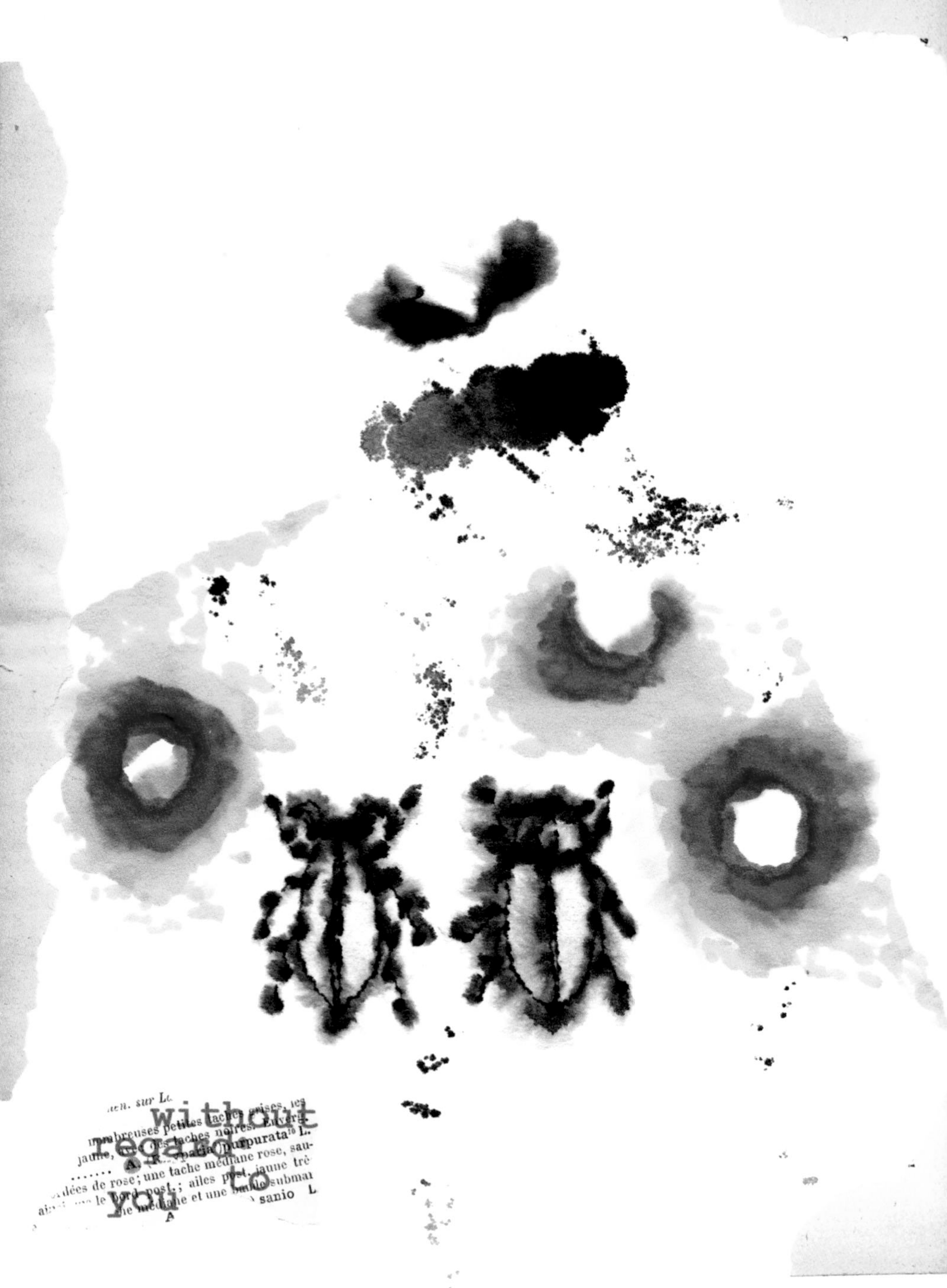
without
regard
to
you

not ever yours

TABLEAU DES FAMILLES DES COLÉOPTÈRES[1]

+[2] *Bouche présentant* 6 palpes, le lobe ... des mâchoires ayant la forme de palpe, en plus du ... toujours ... formes, amincies à l'ext...

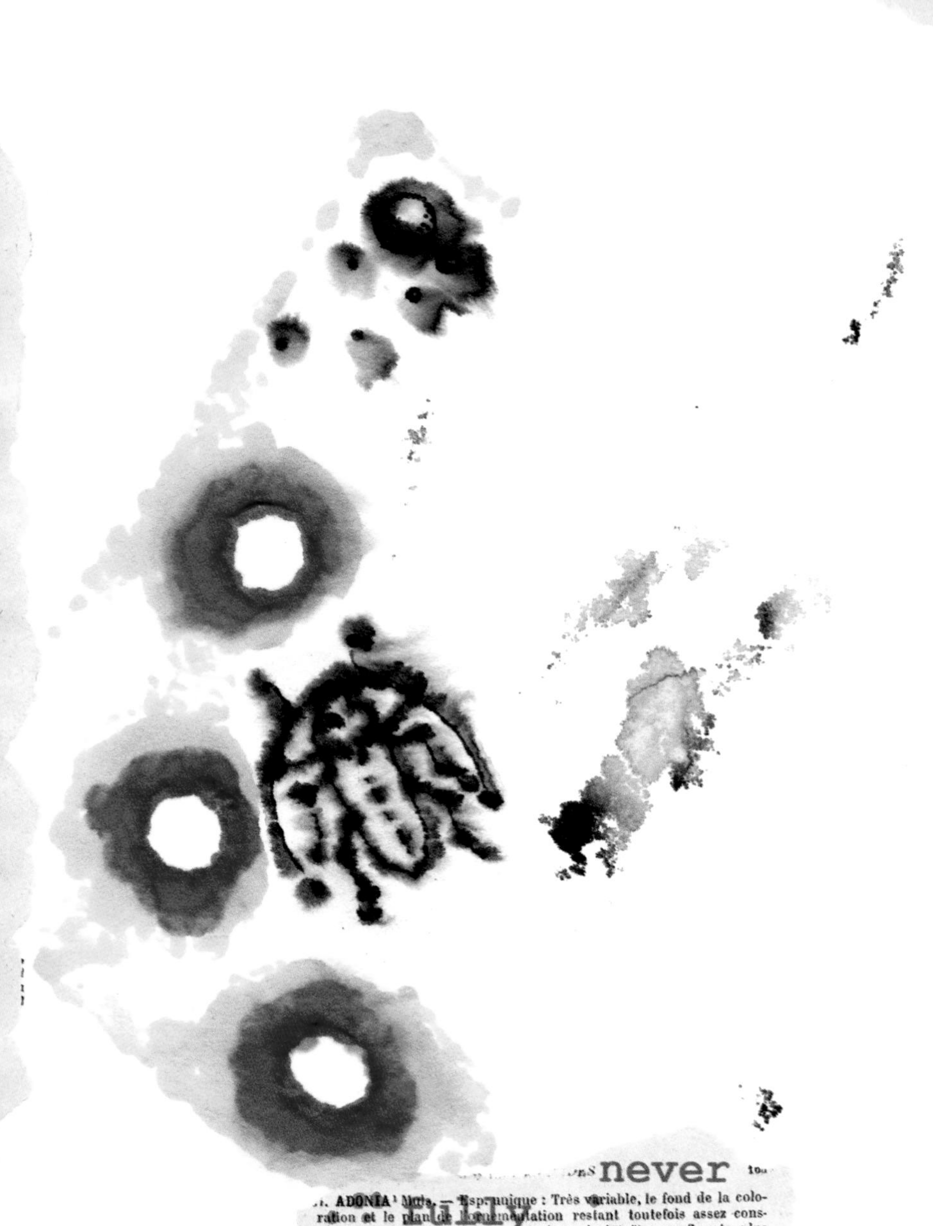

never
fully
be of me

[illegible]. **ADONIA** [1] Muls. — Esp. unique : Très variable, le fond de la coloration et le plan de l'ornementation restant toutefois assez constants. Sur chaque élytre, 6 points (var. de 1 à 5) ± confluents, plus un autre sur l'écusson; de part et d'autre de celui-ci, la base de [illegible] blanchâtre (AV [illegible] 3-5.5 mm .....

my
own self
first
HÉLODIDÉS
Fam. XXXVII. — HÉLODIDÉS
emps réunie à la précédente, renferme
petite taille (au plus 6 mm.), les
autres
M), à tég

6.

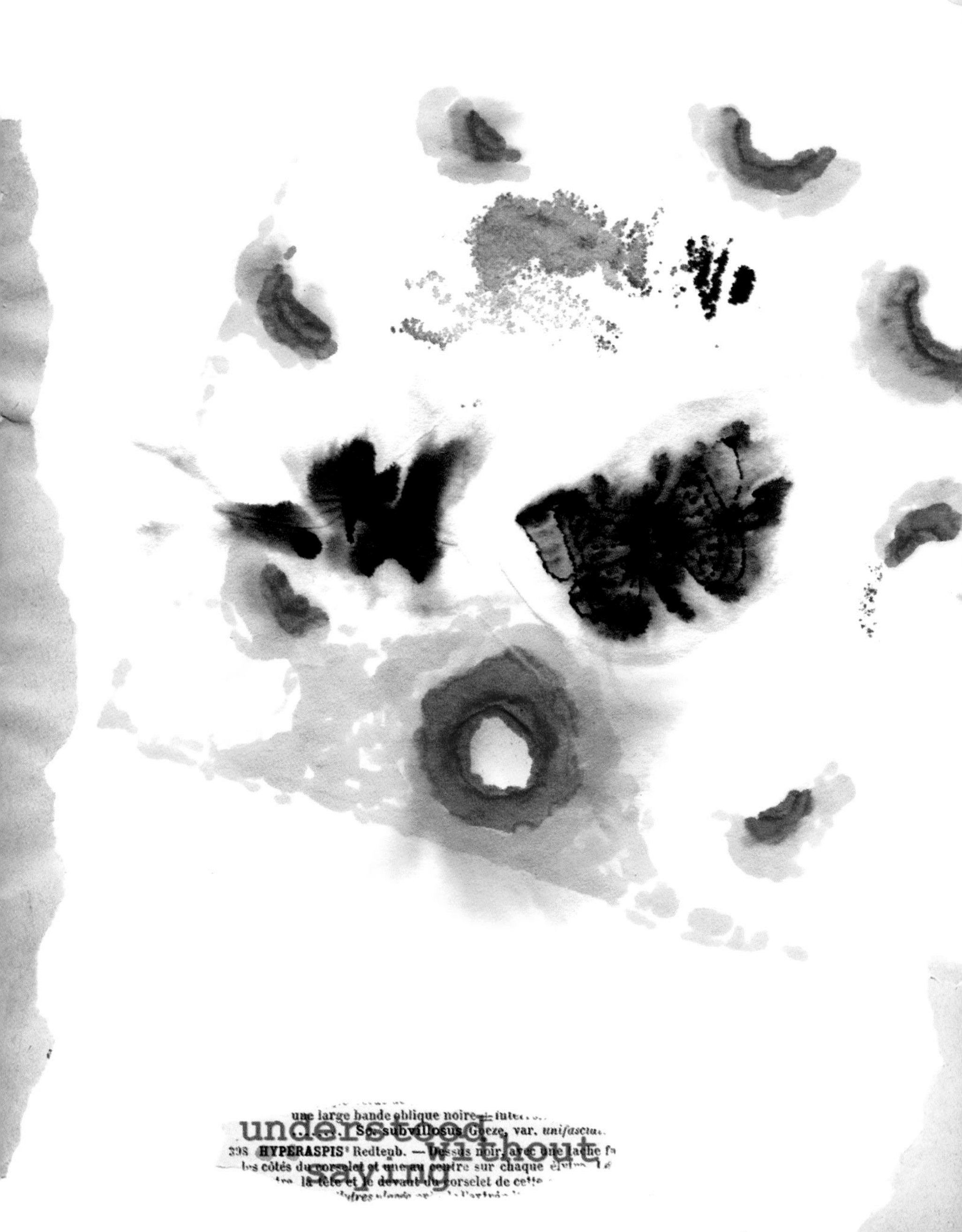

understood without saying
une large bande oblique noire
Sc. subvillosus Goeze, var. unifascia
398 HYPERASPIS Redtenb. — Dessus noir, avec une tache
les côtés du corselet et une au centre sur chaque
la tête et le devant du corselet de cette

7
…, en un bouclier ne présentant plus
dices, et servant de protection aux œufs et a
Divis. 3. Cochenille
fear
of
loss
SOUS-ORDRE I. HÉTÉROPTÈRES
Punaises : Punaises des bois, Pun
vés en organis

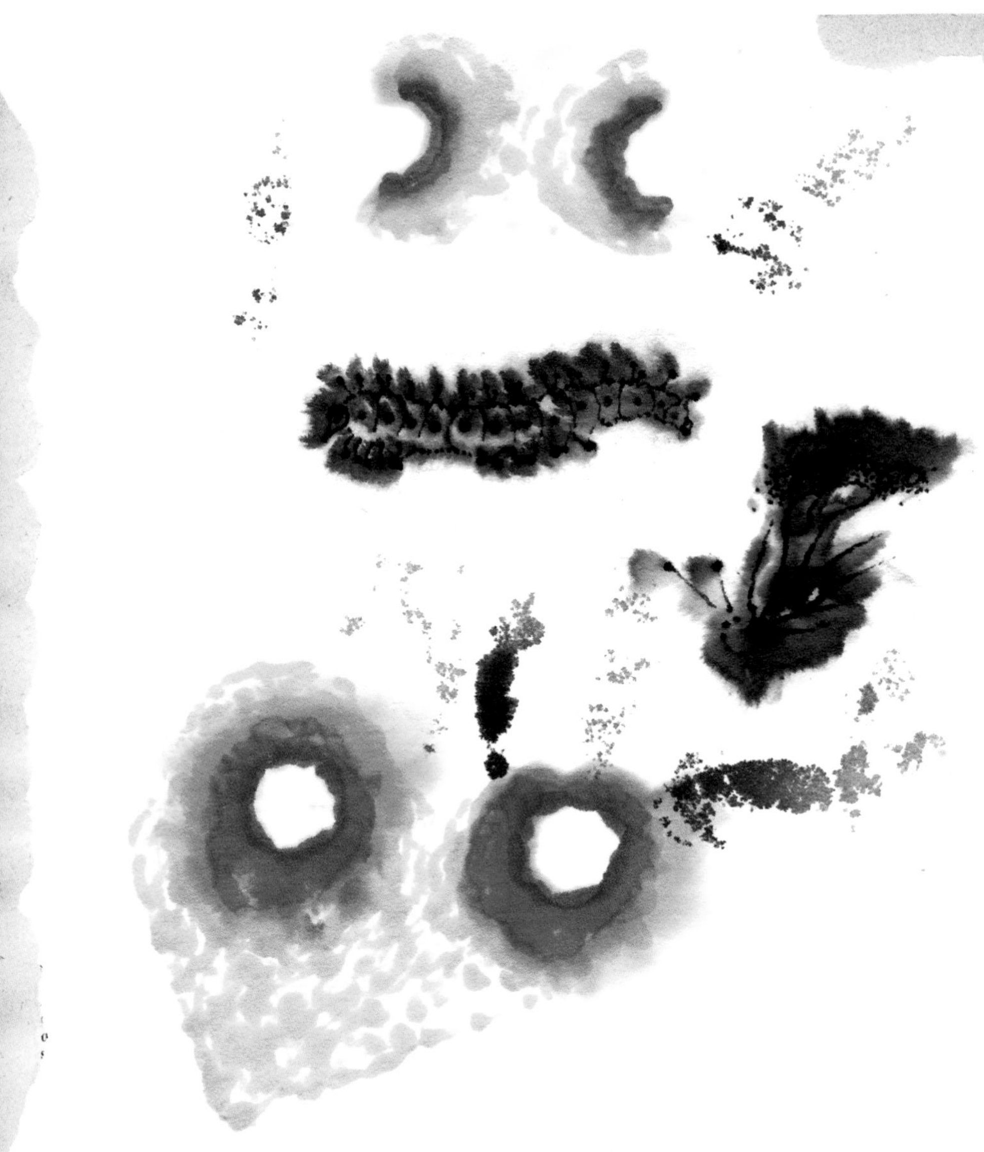

where we came from

…ment vers l'œ… …remité …
…ostre souvent dilatée de chaque côté en forme d'oreilles (*ptérygies*) portant la partie ant. des scrobes (Ot, p. 168)………………………………………… Tribu 1. *Otiorhynchinés* (p. 168).
○ — obliquement vers le bas, passant (eux ou leur prolongem[t]) au-dessous de l'œil (PS, p. 168), leur bord sup. pouvant couper l… bord inf. de l'œil (SG, p. 168). Tribu 2. *Brachydérinés* (p. 16…
Rostre de forme variable, souvent long et cylindrique, et por…
…si les antennes soit vers son milieu, soit dans sa moitié ba…
…ncrure buccale … languette étroite …
…acune une …

The only time I had been told my fortune was twenty years ago, during the case of the missing husband. Over the years, many cases involved missing husbands—the number is surprisingly vast—but this case I never forgot. It ended badly—the wife's brother died violently during the course of the investigation and an innocent suspect in the disappearance committed suicide. The husband was never found (at least not for sure, I had my suspicions about his fate), but it was clear to me that he left simply to leave. The wife was defeated and confused about the course of events, her guilt intense as she believed she was at fault for his disappearance.

Naturally, I had fallen for her.

The fortune I received twenty years ago was printed on a slip of paper that cost me ten yen from a machine. I can't remember the entirety of the fortune; indeed, it was a mishmash of random propositions. Something about luck. That's how it started. I remembered that much. But did it mean that I would have luck, or did it wish me luck because my future would be such a trial that only luck could help me? The years that followed have not been lucky by any reasonable standard. Other than the fact that I was alive and healthy for the most part, things had not gone well. By "things" I mean the mileposts, the memorable events, the gems of existence: love, marriage (to be precise, a good marriage), children, promotions, a decent golf game. None of those occurred. My life was all so much trash floating away on a tsunami of days.

I wish I had kept the fortune. I could have reviewed it, studied it, learned from it. And perhaps understand what went wrong. Instead I lit it on fire and used the flames to chase cockroaches around a table at a grungy sake bar. What a good time. Wait, there was something about radioactivity, and an umbrella. What kind of umbrella protects against radiation? A lead one? Rather impractical, eh? There was something else about a cow or a horse. It was all a hodgepodge of random propositions meant for no one and everyone. Oh, there was something about love, I suddenly remembered, but that's all I could recall. Something about love . . .

▸

The office of fraud complaints was located in a warren of low-rise offices, framed by twin, elegantly sculptured towers occupied by the government finance and policy branches. The architectural disparity made it clear that the government placed a lower priority on consumer affairs than it did policy and finance. As I gazed at the towers, trying to keep both in focus at the same time, the buildings began to vibrate and rapidly change colors. The shimmering was a result, I assumed, of the nerves that control the eyes. Actually, the odd sensation could have been from an inaudible sound created by wind vibrations and the slow oscillation of the two buildings. It's a biological fact that sounds below twenty hertz are detected by the eye. Whatever the reason, it was not unlike the pulling and shearing I experienced at the fortuneteller's home. The shimmering made me dizzy so I closed my eyes for several moments.

The door to the office of fraud complaints was made of thick glass. The sign that announced its purpose was made from cheap, stick-on, black film. One corner of a character had come loose and had been taped down with transparent tape yellowed over time. The pull handle of the door was worn in the middle. A floor ashcan near the door was full of cigarette butts. I resisted the urge to pick out one with some tobacco left and resume my smoking habit.

Inside the office, the quiet astounded me. As hushed as a library, the only sound was the slight hum of a machine, perhaps the photocopier or a small fan. With my handkerchief, I wiped the beads of sweat that bloomed while walking from the subway station to the offices. At the closest desk, I stopped next to a clerk. His white shirt was limp, his tie too large. His belt was snugged too tightly and the loose end flapped away from his waist. On top of that, he had done a sloppy job of shaving—a few hairs longer than stubble poked from the apex of his cheek. He gave me a belligerent glance over the top of his reading glasses and continued working on the form he was hunched over.

"Excuse me," I said. "I'm seeking information about a possible fraud case involving a fortuneteller."

The clerk wrote a few words on the form, then said, "Fortunetelling fraud? That's me all right." He gestured at the chair across from his desk. I sat and waited while he entered a few more words. Finally, he replaced the cap on his pen and put the form in a folder. I started to speak, when he said, "You won't mind if we start this conversation out in the corridor, would you?"

"Need a smoke?" I surmised.

He nodded and headed for the door, a cigarette appeared in his fingers as if by conjuring. The split second we left the office he had it lit. He didn't offer me a cigarette. With a puff of smoke he said, "You don't look like the type to be defrauded by a fortuneteller."

"You don't look like the type to be a civil servant."

Smoke puffed out of his nostrils like a steam engine and his yellow teeth flared at me like a hyena. How he took the comment, which I had intended to be taken as either a compliment or a backhanded insult, was unclear. If he were intelligent enough, he would have grasped the irony of the double meaning.

"Very humorous," he said dryly. "Now tell me what happened."

"I'm sorry, I wasn't very precise with my request. I'm not here to present a complaint but to find out if a certain fortuneteller has ever received a complaint."

The clerk tapped his cigarette over the can but the ash floated around aimlessly and mostly outright missed the target. Investigations were often like that.

"I see," he said. "That puts it in a different light. Are you looking for something specific?"

"I'm researching background on a missing person connected with a fortuneteller."

"Hmm, background, you say. I guess you're an investigator. Private, of course."

"Of course," I said.

"What's it like being a private investigator?" he asked seriously, as if were considering applying for my job.

"A lot like someone in your position. Listening to people with problems, trying to find out what they really want. Discerning what is the truth and what are lies or at least exaggerations. Trying to figure out what they aren't telling you."

"Filling out reports?" he asked.

"More than seems necessary."

The clerk nodded sadly and stubbed out his cigarette which he had smoked almost completely down to the filter in the short time we were in the corridor. "Against my better judgment I'll help you. Let's go back in and see what we have."

▸

The clerk uncovered only a single complaint against Mizuno Rie. "That's abnormal," he said in the matter-of-fact tone of a doctor studying an x-ray.

I waited a few moments. Certainly he'd explain, I thought, but I had to prod him. "Abnormal?"

"One complaint is peculiar because if there is one there are many. None or many is the norm."

That made sense and I let him know with an understanding "Ahh." When I asked to see the file, he sputtered and fumed that such reports were private to protect the complainants.

"Of course," I said. "Perhaps, you need another smoke?"

He laughed. "Such subtlety. Did they teach you that in investigator school or did you acquire the skill through experience?"

While the clerk was out in the corridor, I skimmed the file he left on his desk. The single complaint was registered three years ago by a man named Obushi. He claimed to have been duped of just over one million yen, the amount paid to the fortuneteller for attempting to contacting his wife's ghost. The contact never occurred and, according to the claimant, "was never intended."

A series of notes jotted into official-looking boxes completed the report. In the box labeled RESPONSE, I read this:

Contact with Mizuno Rie was made via phone. She expressed dismay that the complaint was made. She had been working with Mr. Obushi over the course of several months and never claimed that she would be successful in contacting the wife's ghost. In fact, she claimed she told Mr. Obushi several times that there are no guarantees. It was asked of her what types of fortunetelling she conducted, to which she answered primarily *teso*-style palm reading. Contacting spirits was a rare event, used only in very special cases, she said. Less than once a year on average, she estimated when pressed. She added that she was considering no longer accepting clients for that type of work.

ACTION

Because there is no backup documentation or evidence as to what actually occurred between Mr. Obushi and Mrs. Mizuno, and because Mrs. Mizuno has no other recorded complaints, no official action was taken. Mrs. Mizuno was advised to cease her operations in "contacting ghosts," to which she agreed. Mr. Obushi was advised of this outcome and it was suggested he should pursue the matter in civil court if he still wants satisfaction.

Wants satisfaction. Oddly put. Who doesn't want satisfaction yet who ever feels satisfied? Indeed, what is satisfaction? I supposed it is a feeling of completeness, of wholeness, nothing left to act on or desire. In the whole history of the world, of all the billions of people born and dead, there never was a satisfied soul.

Or, maybe it's just me who is so unsatisfied.

The clerk returned apparently satisfied from his cigarette break, his head lolling on his shoulders like a rag doll's. I slid the report file across the desk. "What can you tell me about *teso*?" I asked.

The clerk picked up the file. "Palm reading? What do you want to know?" He put the file back into the cabinet.

"I know the basic idea of palm reading. What I need to know is how it's done, typical fees, how long a session lasts, customer satisfaction. Details."

"All that?" The clerk glanced to the clock behind me and slightly to the left. "How about if I show you in situ?"

"You mean. . . ?"

"Where it's practiced," he said with no small amount of impatience.

"I see. All right. I suppose if that's what you think is best."

The clerk laughed again. I had no idea why.

My car climbed the steep incline to a row of apartment buildings. The automatic transmission smoothly shifted and the tires bit into the roadway, propelling me with one hundred horsepower into the past. Twenty years ago and with eighty horsepower less, my car barely made it up this incline with its grooves spaced at a precise distance designed to channel rainwater away from the pavement. At the top of the incline, as then, the apartment buildings appeared in a line of near infinite perspective.

The wife of the missing husband surely no longer lived in one of the buildings that had not aged gracefully. The window frames were out of square. Roof tiles were askew. The paint had faded. And yet I drove past her building slowly, as if she might still live there and see me. Her expression of determination and incomprehension would compel me to stop.

A young woman with a canvas shopping bag draped over her shoulder appeared from between the two buildings, a leashed dog towing her. Our gazes locked together for the moment it took for our brains to recognize that we had never seen each other before. Of course it was not the wife. I touched the accelerator and the car sped me away from the woman. For unknown reasons, the brief encounter was unpleasant.

After the case ended, I lost my job as an investigator not because I didn't find the husband but for being associated with the suicide victim. The victim was an employee in the husband's company, an innocent subordinate merely taking orders in a complicated scheme to influence government officials. I pushed him hard during the course of the investigation, but the pain in his life was there well before I met him.

More than the mere passing of time, a cloud of regret fogged my memories of the wife. Try as I might, I could not fully form her likeness, conjuring only the gentle curve of her chin, a sensuous droop of an eyelid, a worry crease above her eyebrows, and the freckles under her eyes. I could bring those details to mind but could not put them together. That would be the sum story of my life: *he had a great eye for details but couldn't put them together.*

The regrets piled up during the seemingly endless week during which I investigated the disappearance of the husband. Two deaths, the loss of my job, the realization my own marriage could not be saved. And worst of all, the disillusionment of a human being, referring to the wife. Well, all right, to me as well. I also regretted that I found a disturbing trend in my behavior—a crease of selfishness, or self-centeredness, and a penchant for dwelling on the potential effect my actions. Unfortunately, I discovered the traits were embedded as permanently as reinforcing steel bars in a concrete slab. I could no more extricate them than I could my own skeleton. But I suppose it's better to know one's faults than not.

After the case dwindled to nothing but guilt, I thought of continuing to search for her husband. With enough effort I might have found him. But then what? His wife no longer cared if he was dead or alive.

The twenty years had passed in an instant yet seemed like an eternity in a room with no doors, no windows. I drove away from the neighborhood.

▸

I steered my car to the side of the narrow road where the fraud complainant, Obushi, owned a camera and photographic supply store. This was another similarity to the old case of the missing husband, as amateur pornographic photographs surfaced during the investigation. Along the street barely wide enough for two cars to slip past each other were several businesses including a small hardware store with rows of products lining metal shelving, a liquor store plastered with posters, a beauty salon, a handful of tiny bars and restaurants, various professional offices, and a travel agency. The street was too narrow to provide the proper amount of access and parking for all of the activities suggested by the number of enterprises. Plus, a narrow strip of asphalt delimited with white painted stripes and crosshatches designed for pedestrians now served as a loading lane for delivery trucks. And investigators, since that strip was where I sat in my car.

I turned on my emergency flashers and popped open my trunk to give the appearance I was delivering a package and would only be a minute. I checked my mirror before exiting and was glad I did as a flock of school girls on bicycles swooped past. When the way was clear, I got out of my car and carried my briefcase into the camera store. Occupying most of the shop was a long glass case of camera bodies. Without their lenses they looked like boxy, gape-mouthed, fish heads. There was also a rack of lenses behind the case. The largest lens was monstrous, as big as a good-sized telescope. A row of shelving on the other side of the room held smaller items such as film, paper, chemicals, lens cleaners. In one corner, tripods were stacked and tagged with a price. On the walls were framed photographs, mostly of natural scenery—mountains, waterfalls, flower-filled meadows. A few photographs were of old buildings in Europe, or perhaps Latin America.

A man came from out of a door leading to a back room. "Welcome," he said. "May I help you?" He looked to be forty or so, with a thin, well-tanned face, large eyes, and a softly hooked nose. His hair was on the longish side of well-trimmed but not as long as most artistic types. He wore the casual clothes of a mom-and-pop camera store proprietor, appearing as if he could slip on a photographer's vest, sling a bag of equipment over his shoulder, and in an hour be out in a field snapping photos of moss.

I set my briefcase down and handed him a business card. "I'm looking for Obushi Kenichi."

"An investigator," he said, examining my card. "I assume you're here investigating."

"I assume you're Obushi?"

He nodded and took a stance behind the counter where he leaned on the glass as he might when pointing out the features of a camera. "What's it about?"

"A follow-up investigation, you might say. Do you remember a fortune-teller named Mizuno Rie?"

The camera store owner snorted. "You know I do."

"I'm investigating the disappearance of her son, Ren."

"What's that got to do with me? Look, I'm busy."

I surveyed the legion of customers waiting to be served. Perhaps they were ghosts. “Nothing, directly,” I said. “It’s only a matter of course during an inv—”

“The others sent you, didn’t they? Get out!”

I suddenly felt I was on a treacherous slope, a safety line just out of my reach. If I made an attempt to grab it, I would lose my balance and fall deep into the void below me. My only chance was to leap for the rope and hope to catch it.

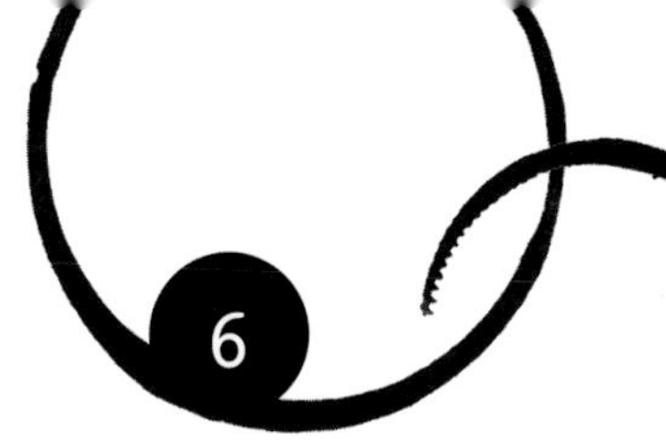

Report

24 August: 11:15 a.m.—I investigated the art director's claim that Mizuno Ren died three years ago by checking the Mizuno family registry at the ward office. There, in the dismal light of the records room, I discovered his death had not been recorded. Of course, this does not necessarily mean that he isn't deceased.

I drove from there to the son's last known address. I encountered a lack of activity at the older, exhausted-looking building of "rabbit hutch" apartments. The neighborhood, however, was undergoing improvement with newer office and retail buildings, as well as construction of a condominium project (starting at prices of 75 million yen per unit!).

No one answered the missing son's apartment door when I rang the bell and knocked. There was no window along the front entrance so I could not see inside. I rang the bell of the apartment next to the son's apartment, but no one answered. As I was about to try another apartment, a man, roughly thirty-years old, with closely cropped hair, dressed in athletic gear (although his doughy physique did not indicate athletic tendencies), came out of the apartment two doors down. I questioned him about the son. He blinked, shook his head, and mumbled he hadn't seen him lately. When

I asked, "How much is lately?" the man shrugged, shaking his head that was the size and shape of a steer's. I offered him a multiple choice response: "One week? One month? One year? Two years?" To which he responded, "Off and on."

I tried another door at the end of the hallway. A woman in her late twenties answered, her eyes puffy as if she had been crying or had just woken up from a fitful sleep. After several moments, she apparently comprehended my question and gave me a response as vague as the one from the man in athletic gear. "Occasionally." When pressed, she said simply, "I can't say for certain. Maybe I haven't seen him at all." At this point, I abandoned further attempts at contacting residents of the building.

expenses:
32-km car expense
¥120 photocopies

Finished writing my report in the stupor of a hangover, which was due to the prior evening drinking with the fraud clerk, I ordered another cup of coffee in the shop where I waited for the next available time for Reiko, a masseuse I visited when I needed revitalization. I rarely drank to the hangover stage, maybe only once or twice a year. The time it took my aging organs to remove alcohol increased each year, to the point now of leaving me incapacitated for at least two days.

I decided not to tell the chief about the art director's claim that the son was dead. The chief was not one to be trifled with, although he could to a degree be manipulated. The line between submission and manipulation was thin but over the years I had managed to keep my position in the company and maintain a degree of independence, an unsatisfactory but tolerable situation. Take the previous night for instance. I did not mention in my report what occurred with the clerk because investigating the applicant is not part of our contract. In short, we can't get paid for it. Anything we can't get paid for is strictly off limits. From a management perspective, it's an understandable policy; however, I deemed my investigation of the applicant critical to my ability to proceed with due diligence. At least that's how I justified it to myself.

I met the clerk on a side street crowded with pedestrians, mostly salarymen on their way to their favorite drinking establishment. The clerk's sloppy appearance had worsened, as if the journey from his office to the bar was rough. His shirttail was partially pulled out from his pants, his hair disheveled. With an elaborate sweep of his arm, he channeled me into a bar, one of ten or twelve on the block. As to how the clerk picked this one I couldn't see an immediate reason.

The owner—a mama-san—greeted the clerk as a regular. Only a couple of other tables in the bar were occupied and we sat at a corner table. The clerk nodded to the mama-san, something related to our order I assumed, then said to me, "The place specializes in *shōchū* drinks. Do you like *shōchū*?"

Despite disliking the grain alcohol usually served sweetened with fruit juice, I said "Depends on the *shōchū*."

The clerk sighed. "You're a sensitive sort, aren't you?"

"Not really."

He ordered plum *shōchū* for us. It was decent enough.

"I did some more research on your fortuneteller," the clerk said, his upper lip damp with alcohol. "It made the afternoon go by quicker than usual."

"But you said there was only one report on Mizuno Rie."

"Only one official file, yes. What I refer to are unofficial records. You see our department functions like an octopus with a competing brain for each tentacle. Sometimes we reach for the same bit of information at the same time only to tear it apart and hoard the torn bits."

"A chaotic situation," I granted him. The clerk obviously wanted to vent about his job for a while, so I let him. The little bar grew dimmer as the night darkened, a strange occurrence because the interior lighting should have increased in relative brightness. Perhaps the drink robbed a part of my vision. While he rambled, I discovered that when I focused on the corner where two walls met, I could see two clerks. The more deeply I stared into the space, the further I projected myself into that alternative universe with two clerks.

The clerk, or rather one of two, said, "The fundamental nature of people is a desire for order, for simple cause and effect, which leads them to unverifiable beliefs. Superstition being one example, fortunetelling another. We can educate people all day long but their fundamental nature will never change because they cannot comprehend chaos. We do not want to believe that things exist or happen due to randomness and coincidence."

The clerk turned out to be an amateur psychologist. "I agree, even though I believe there are instances of direct cause and effect. Now what about the fortuneteller?"

The clerk licked his upper lip. "It turns out that before she was married her name was Kuchi Rie. The Kuchi family is well known in fortunetelling circles. In the past, there have been several fraud complaints against them."

I recalled that the camera store owner, Obushi, said something about "others." I asked one of the clerks about a connection between the Kuchi clan and Obushi.

"Haven't you listened to what I said? Don't look for connections when they aren't there!"

"But," I said, my head aching, "isn't that why you brought up the Kuchi case? Wasn't I supposed to make a connection?"

"If you don't want my information then don't ask me to help. Anyway, you wanted to hear about *teso*." The clerk finished his drink and led me out of the bar.

Down an alleyway, several fortunetellers had set up small tables and signs advertising their specialties. Customers were standing two and three deep waiting for their favorite fortuneteller. While we waited in a line, the clerk gave me a mini-lecture on *teso*, starting with him tracing my lines of fortune and misfortune: life, head, fate, heart, marriage (a stubby, nearly invisible crease below my little finger—no doubt how that would be interpreted).

After I paid two thousand yen to the fortuneteller—a hard-looking woman with short hair dyed a mahogany color and curled in a flip—I sat down and surrendered my left hand to her. She gave it a quick touch. "Please relax," she said.

As I guessed, the fortuneteller immediately pointed out my puny marriage line. "To be honest, there's no hope. Your fate line shows a strong disruption in the past, with a cross indicating a divergence in the future. You need to find a new line of work, something you're more suited for. And at all costs, stay away from love affairs . . ."

I'd had enough.

I didn't mention my evening with the clerk in my report. Not that I could get my head entirely around the experience to make a coherent statement. My memory consisted of scraps around the fuzzy edges of reality. The only thing I recall with clarity was a name: Kuchi. My brain had managed to grasp that one bit of information.

Five minutes before my appointment with Reiko, I finished my cup of coffee and paid my bill with only a quickly dismissed thought of adding it to my expense report. I walked out of the bright coffee shop into a morning that was white hot and bubbling with haze. Inside the Red Lantern Soapland, the cool, softly-lit lobby was scented with citrus. Reiko—a short woman with muscular arms and legs—greeted me. "How are you?"

"I will be fine," I said with a weak smile.

Her room was painted a cheery yellow, a color that made me want to return as often as I could afford the fee of twenty five thousand yen. It was a color that made me melancholy yet feel alive. As I handed each piece of my clothing to her, she folded it with care and placed it in a plastic tub. While I sat in a robe in the tiled room, she ran bathwater warmed to the perfect temperature. When the tub was full, she slipped off my robe and then hers. She scooped a small bucket of water from the tub, splashed it over me, then lathered up a soapy film. Next she helped me onto my back and used each part of her slippery, smooth body on each part of mine. We talked of the weather, how our days were going, which politicians were worth voting for, how long the economic prosperity would last, the upcoming sumo tournament favorites. I both enjoyed and regretted that Reiko's room in the Red Lantern Soapland was the only place of tenderness in my life.

▸

After Rieko's ministrations only a faint tiredness remained of my hangover, although I was still agitated and irritated by the investigation. Of course, that meant I was irritated with me. By investigating the applicant instead of the missing son, I was going down the wrong, although more alluring, path. In the limited time I had been on the case, I arrived at the opinion that the son lacked a regular pattern of activity. As a freelancer, he could pick and choose assignments according to his needs or pleasure. As evidence of this lifestyle, his apartment neighbors could not recall whether they had seen him recently. Furthermore, the art director's belief he was dead supported my hypothesis that the son was hiding out of fear, consistent with missing a scheduled appearance at his mother's home. If I was accurate in my assessment, it would be very difficult to find him. So rather than pursue him, I continued to look into his mother's background.

This reasoning brought me to the Kuchi fortunetellers' gated complex of three large houses constructed in the traditional manner using weathered wood, beige plaster, glazed roof tiles, and eaves extending over the verandas. Between the houses was a garden that would inspire poets.

I pushed the entry bell and after a moment was buzzed inside. As I walked up the stone path toward what looked like a tea house, the dread returned. Deeply embedded in my subconscious, only its vague, tilting effect on my mental stability could be felt, but it was enough to produce disequilibrium. The feeling could have been partly due to my unsure footing in the realm I was entering. In fact, I had little reason to be at the complex, and was there only because of a fraud complaint by a camera store owner, his wariness of "others," and a single name given to me by a screwy clerk who should be dead considering the way he smoked and drank. Three tenuous clues. No, less than tenuous, they were practically imaginary.

Inside the tea house, a dainty structure compared to the sprawling complex of homes, a young woman was seated behind an austere desk. She was dressed in a kimono and had the helpful yet serious air of a corporate receptionist. She looking neither puzzled nor concerned by my appearance, as unscheduled as it was. When I was a few steps away, she glanced at the appointment book open on the desk.

"May I help you?" she asked in a highly professional yet challenging tone.

"Yes, please," I said in a plaintive voice, slumped with the weight of an imagined tragedy. "I was recommended by a friend. You see, I need to contact a person." I gave her a sad frown. "A deceased person."

"Do you have an appointment?" she asked crisply, her lips pressed together in a pout.

"I am sorry, no." I smiled a little, trying to soften the situation and the receptionist. "I know I should have called, but I'm at a real loss, at my wit's end. I was hoping to see someone right away."

"I'm sorry too. But we can help you only by appointment." The receptionist stared at me with her cool gaze, sizing me up for a report to her superiors.

I closed my eyes and slumped forward with my head in my hands as if I was about to start sobbing.

"Please, take a seat," she said, likely concerned that I was going to make a fuss. Clearly, she would not like a fuss.

The receptionist disappeared through a side door. I sat in a plush, velvet-covered Chinese-style chair against the wall, placed for the view of a hanging scroll. The scene painted in black and gray wash showed a ghostly figure emerging from a bamboo forest. I thought of getting up and perusing the appointment book, for what reason I wasn't sure. Perhaps there would be a name I'd recognize, connected to the current case or not. It would also be good to know who was accepting appointments, not just the clients requesting them. Just as I was about to get up, the receptionist returned with a woman dressed in a business suit of skirt and blouse and jacket. As had the receptionist, the woman sized me up. I gave her a grim expression, like a patient about to get a diagnosis of bad news.

"I'm Kuchi," she said, using only her family name. "I'm sorry, I can't see you right now, nor can any of the others. We are booked well into the future."

"It's good to know your future," I said. "Being that you are fortunetellers."

She smiled for a moment at my little joke. "However, if you come with me, we can chat for a minute or two to see if we would be able help you."

We walked into a side conference room. Other than a simple table with four chairs, there was nothing else in the room except for portraits on the wall. One photo was of the Kuchi woman I was with. The others, all women, seven in all, bore a distinguishable similarity with each other—a rounded face with protruding cheekbones, high forehead, although the similarity was somewhat attenuated from the oldest, sepia-toned photo to the latest one of clear, sharp full color. A matriarchal society of fortunetellers, severe in their discipline, defined by strength of traditions and limitations as much as opportunity.

None of them was Mizuno Rie.

"Who is the deceased person?" she asked me pointedly, forgoing any preliminaries. Undoubtedly she was already suspicious of me.

"His name is Mizuno Ren," I said.

After a tiny inhaled breath and a barely-visible rising of her eyebrows, she turned slightly toward the door. I looked that way and noticed a man standing outside the room, his posture as rigid as a sentry's. Instead of a uniform, however, he was dressed in an expensive-looking suit. His impassive expression did not reveal his purpose and I couldn't tell if he was within earshot of our conversation.

"Mizuno Ren," the Kuchi fortuneteller repeated. "And you say he is dead?"

"I didn't have a chance to make myself clear with the receptionist. Actually I don't know for sure. But if he is, I'd like to talk with him."

"You mean his ghost?"

I nodded.

"You don't look like someone who believes in ghosts. What do you really want?"

"Even if I don't believe in ghosts, which I can't say one way or the other, that doesn't preclude me from attempting to make contact, does it? Besides, isn't it more important that *you* believe in ghosts? After all, you would be the one contacting his ghost, not me."

A momentary look of confusion passed across her expression before returning to bland seriousness. "Regardless, we can't fit you in right now. We will have to set up an appointment. If this person is dead then there's no rush, is there?" She smiled and gave me a patronizing look.

"You're right. But as soon as possible, please. In the next day or so?"

"Possibly. The receptionist will give you the forms to fill out."

"Forms?"

"One is an application that tells us exactly what services you want, explains the costs of those services, and asks for particular information about you and the circumstances necessary for us to perform our services. A deposit is required and you must sign a release of liability."

"What does that entail?"

"Obviously we can't be held responsible for any consequences as a result of our services. Using our exclusive procedures and methods, we tell you what we see about your future or past, or in your case when a ghost might communicate. In other words, what you do with the results of the contact is strictly not our responsibility. Now, I must leave." She stood up and ushered me out of the room. The well-dressed bodyguard, if that's what he was, had disappeared from his post.

"Thank you," I said.

With a tilt of her head, she smiled almost sweetly. "Don't thank me yet. It may be bad news."

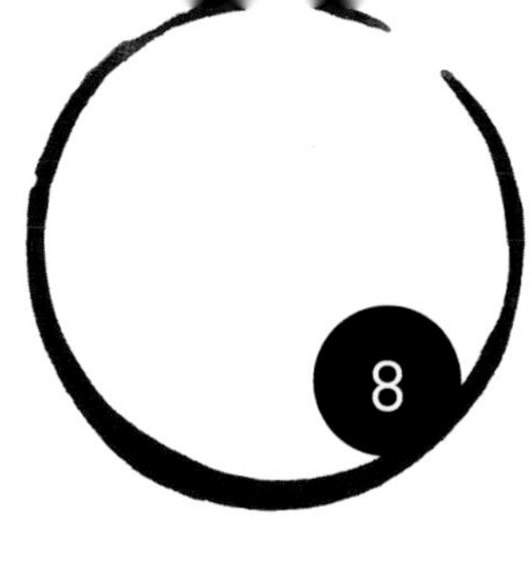

Fiddling with his pen, my section chief looked like a bored cat playing with a nearly-dead mouse. He hadn't said anything for a solid minute, a long time when you are sitting across from someone. As was his style, he needed time to gather his thoughts so the silence didn't bother me, but the pen twirling made me nervous. Would it be poor form to grab the pen away from him? Yes. The boss's face would puff up like a blowfish and turn as red as a pickled plum. He might fire me on the spot.

The chief read my report again. I thought he was going to say something, but the silence entered its second minute. The chief flicked the pen open and made a check mark next to a line in my report. From my perspective, I couldn't see what conclusions or associations he was drawing, so I couldn't prepare a response. Not that my response would have any bearing on his thoughts. He took unwarranted pride in making decisions and sticking to them.

While I waited, I recalled a vivid detail from the old case of the missing husband. The missing husband's co-worker called me early one morning and said something about taking action. I was so tongue-tied in my sleep-deprived state I couldn't ask what he meant. Through the phone came the unreal sound of a chair falling over, a rope tightening, a beam creaking, and a gasp. Then silence. But I doubted I could have heard all that. I must have been inserting it into my memory.

The chief tapped his pen on my report. His crisp collar worked up and down as he pronounced judgment. "Usually, I would withdraw us from a case such as this one. There are too many anomalies in the applicant's statement. Now someone claims that the missing son is dead. We lack verification of this status, although no one knows his recent movements. However, given that this investigation is in the early stage, I can't say that these anomalies will never be worked out. We should go back to the applicant to ask more probing questions."

"Yes, we should." I was glad he hadn't closed the case.

"But keep in close contact," the section chief added. "I'm ready to stop the investigation as soon as we stand the least chance of getting wrapped up in nonsense."

I didn't want to get wrapped up in nonsense either.

▸

My first stop was at the health and disability records office, a very reliable place to find a person's address. I claimed to be working for a life insurance company and requested to verify applicants' medical benefits. Sooner or later the office will catch on to their lax security and tighten their information request procedures.

Unfortunately, there were no records for Mizuno Ren.

However, I was rewarded with an address for the wife of the missing husband. Shortly after the case ended twenty years ago, she had a short stay in a hospital for an illness. Several years of no records followed until four years ago when she received injury treatment and short-term disability payments. The particulars of the injury weren't important, but her address at that time was of interest. On a whim, I tried to find records for her ex-husband. There were no records for him.

I hurried to the nearest train station and managed to get a seat as it was not yet rush hour. Sitting with my eyes closed and swaying with the train's movement was as relaxing as an afternoon on a beach. Luckily, I managed to stay awake and not miss my stop. The station where I disembarked was small but newly renovated. I got into a taxi.

On the narrow, winding roads, the traffic was heavy and all the vehicles were ten or fifteen kilometers per hour above the limit, the taxi being at the high end. We narrowly missed taking the leg off a motorcyclist who got too close to us. He gave us an obscene gesture before he veered and sped away. We flew past a modern shopping center, a business park, a roadside collection of pachinko parlors and family restaurants, another business park. I felt we had been driving for hours, but it had been only several minutes when we drove up a street between a park and a school. A few blocks later, the taxi driver pulled over and pointed to a small house. I asked him to wait.

I walked up to the door through a small garden that could have used some tending. The grass patch was spreading across the walkway. Fallen leaves had turned a crunchy brown and were scattered in the light wind. A tiny pond was half-full of water green with algae blooms.

I stood at the door that had a political flyer stuck in the jamb. I took it out and prepared to give it to whoever answered the door. But no one came. I checked the side to see if anyone was there. When I returned to the front, a woman holding a cleaning brush like a weapon peered at me around the corner of the fence.

"Hello," I said in the friendliest voice I could muster.

The woman maintained her aggressive posture and failed to return my jovial greeting.

"I was looking for an old friend of mine. A woman. This is the last address for her that I have."

"Friend you say? You've come about the accident?"

"There's been an accident?"

"Hit and run. She's in a coma."

The news was a dead weight in my gut.

"You're an old friend you say? I don't think I've seen you here before. Not that I keep track of her visitors."

"I haven't been in touch with her for many years."

A lock of hair had fallen out of the neighbor's head scarf. She pushed it under the fabric and said, "It's strange that you would finally take the time to look her up just when she's had a horrible accident."

"I suppose it does seem coincidental. Do you know what happened?"

The neighbor waved her brush toward the road. "People drive like nuts around here. Especially on the main road where it happened. The poor woman was walking home from the bus stop after her shift. She works at night at a business called Midori." She added in a whisper, "An escort business, you know."

I couldn't believe the wife would be an escort—she would be well into her forties for one thing, but more importantly she didn't have the ability to charm when needed. Maybe she had changed. "Do the doctors believe she will recover?"

"I haven't talked to them. But I do know which hospital she's in." She told me and picked a sprig of flowers for me to give to her neighbor.

I didn't know what to do with the information I received about the wife. Many things came to mind: going to the hospital to see her, finding out what happened in the hit-and-run, tracking down the culprit. But I found my mental and physical inertia too great to overcome. I left the flowers with the taxi driver and took the train to Mizuno Rie's neighborhood. It appeared different from my first visit there only two days ago: more rundown and more crowded yet lacking in activity at the same time. Near the row of vending machines, the potted plants had yellowed further toward death. Our perceptions are colored by mood; mine had deteriorated since the first day of the case.

I dug into my pockets and pulled out a few coins. I sorted through them and found the correct change. The coins plunked heavily when they slid down into the bowels of the vending machine. I selected a can of beer and a pack of peanuts. Very conveniently, a stack of brown paper bags had been provided for the customers' use. I put the beer in a sack and walked to a bench in a pocket park where, like a homeless alcoholic, I sipped the beer and popped nuts into my mouth.

During my surveillance nothing happened related to the case, not that I had expected anything. The sun set and the twilight was deepening when I climbed up the stone path to the fortuneteller's house. A streetlight with a flickering bulb switched on. At the top of the rise, I could see that the fortuneteller had removed the festival string of lanterns. Her fortuneteller's sign was out. I hadn't considered the possibility that she would be open for business and I hoped I wasn't going to intrude on a client. I approached the door quietly and peered into the vestibule. Hearing no voices, I announced my presence with a confident, "Hello."

"Come in, come in," she said, scurrying to greet me.

I followed her into the sitting room where she offered me something to eat. All the signs of the festival had been removed. "Beer or sake? I think I also have some whiskey. Or just tea?"

"Thank you, but I just had something."

We sat in the chairs instead of on the floor cushions. Mizuno Rie looked different too. But instead of deteriorating like the neighborhood, her appearance had improved, perhaps because she was dressed to receive clients. Feeling guilty over my suspicions of her, I found myself smiling.

"Now that I think about it, a beer would be nice," I said. "Would you join me?"

"I couldn't. I might get a customer," she said. She started to turn, then stopped and said, "You know, I think I will join you. Please wait a moment."

When she disappeared into the kitchen, I looked over the room as if fresh on the case. The shadowy wallpaper, the miniature family shrine with a picture of her late husband, a glassed bookcase holding reference books: a dictionary, a multi-volume collection of plants and gardening, several books on palm reading, and one curiously titled: *Why Ghosts Appear.*

She returned with a tray with a large bottle of beer, two small glasses, and a ceramic bowl filled with rice crackers. While she poured the beer and arranged our snack, I asked her how she was holding up. She considered the question for a moment, time passing like the bubbles rising in the beer. "It looks strange, I suppose. I've already gotten on with my life. I'm back at work, the house is clean. It's as if nothing is wrong."

"Now that you mention it, yes, that is what motivated my question. But everyone comes to that point sooner or later. There comes a time to move on."

"Many of my clients never do," she said. She sat down and gestured to the beer glasses. I picked mine up and held it, waiting for her to join me. We murmured a little toast and sipped.

"Your clients want to believe that they can control fate?"

"Exactly."

"Is that what is happening with you?"

She stared at her beer, as if counting bubbles, then glanced up at me with a tilt of her head. I could see a resemblance to the Kuchi women with their round and prominent cheekbones. In the moody lighting, and in my strange disconnectedness, I suddenly found her attractive. Whether it was my mood, or reality, I couldn't tell. As if she could sense my thoughts, she averted her gaze. "What do you mean?" she asked.

I meant to confront her directly about her son, but now I only wanted to be kind, which was not my usual style. I let the moment sink in, to see how quickly it would pass. And when it didn't, I said, "I heard some rather strange news about your son. One of his clients believes he has passed away. She claims it happened three years ago."

The fortuneteller's hand crawled up to her neck and squeezed the skin just above the breastbone, as if she were checking the ripeness of a piece of fruit. "Why would she say that?"

I had no other specific information to offer and I felt badly for bringing it up. "I'm sorry," I said. "That's all I know. She claimed he died three years ago."

"But he's not dead. True, I haven't seen him for a year now, but he's been here twice in the last three years during the holiday week."

"Has anyone else seen him when he visits?"

"No. It's always just the two of us. I know a son visiting his mother only once a year sounds like not many times, but he's busy. He travels a lot, you see."

"It's not that unusual," I said. "Times have changed. We're all busy."

She took a sip of beer and shook her head sadly.

I said, "I have to ask you a question. An indelicate one. I understand you once had a problem with a client who hired you to contact a ghost."

She blinked twice then said defensively, "What does that have to do with my son?"

"I have no answer other than I don't know. But we are in the early stages of our investigation. All possibilities should be considered, otherwise I wouldn't be doing my job."

"You are referring to Obushi? The camera store owner? That was many years ago."

"Only three," I said. The number raised a prickle of a thought. "I'm curious, exactly what were the circumstances with that case?"

"His wife's ghost was trying to contact him, he believed, to tell him about her death."

"How did she die?"

"She died while they were on vacation. Officially an accident, although he implied it was a murder. He was very distraught and I agreed to help him although I rarely do that kind of work. Contacting spirits is ripe for fraud complaints. But he was so desperate, so willing to believe. We tried several times but he was never satisfied and eventually became belligerent. Finally I told him that I couldn't help him. That only made it worse. I offered to give him his money back, but all he wanted was to hear from his wife. From her ghost." The fortuneteller's voice trailed off.

"You don't believe in ghosts?" I asked.

"I do believe in them," she said. "But I don't believe I can contact them. I believe they can contact us, if they have a good reason."

"You didn't mention this before. Is there some reason why?"

She frowned and her cheeks colored. "No reason. I hadn't thought it would have anything to do with Ren."

"Is Obushi connected with your son in some way? Is that how Obushi came to you for help contacting his wife?"

"No, not that I know of," she said.

She may have been telling the truth, or she conveniently forgot about the connection in embarrassment over the fraud complaint. Either way, I lacked enough information to pursue the line of questioning. "Did Obushi go to another fortuneteller after he ended his visits to you?"

"Not that I know of."

"Perhaps the Kuchi fortunetellers? I understand they are known for contacting ghosts."

She covered a shadow of pain with a sip of beer. "I wouldn't know if he contacted anyone else."

More likely she didn't want to tell me anything about the Kuchi clan. "Is your son a ghost?"

Her face turned pale as if she'd seen one. She shook her head.

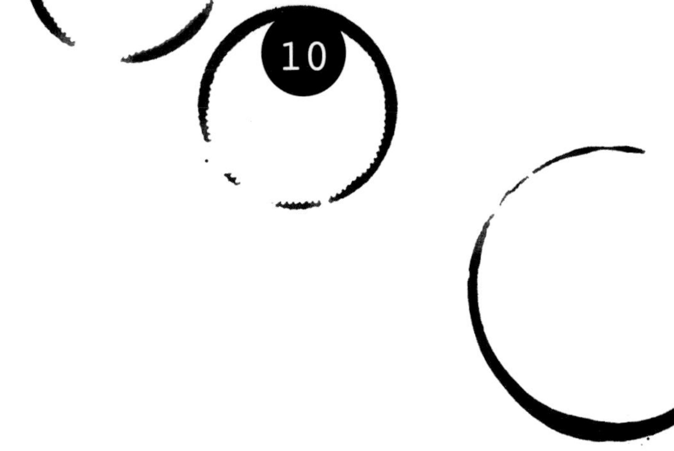

10

A light mist broke up the heat of the night, dampened my raincoat, and moistened my face like a spritz of lavender water at a fancy seaside resort. I walked upright, chin leading the way, maximizing surface area to catch the most water possible. The accumulated runoff dribbled down in waterfalls off my cheeks and ponded at my collar. A trickle ran over my lips, into my mouth.

A car approached me from behind, slowed, then sped up. When it drew even, the car hit a puddle of water and its oily sheen splashed over me.

The fact of the matter: I was not a ghost. How could I say that? Because I perceived the water and grit and oil stuck to me? Because I could feel the pinpricks of water in the air, splattering and adhering to my skin? A ghost has no need for such perceptions. A ghost is only the vaporous manifestation of spirit, of pure energy.

I had no energy, too little to matter. And I was all too real, concretely heavy. My body was old and tired, my mind undisciplined and muddled. This condition likely contributed to my inaction regarding the wife of the missing husband. The realization that I didn't have the courage to see her in a coma, her life slipping away, filled me with a great sadness. Of regret too, because I hadn't tried to find her before. She was not yet a ghost, I felt sure, but she might become one soon.

The son might already be a ghost. He was certainly ethereal—he had no substance I had seen. The more I investigated, the fainter grew his history and trace. I was running out of strategies. My chief should be notified so he could take me off the case. I didn't want to waste the fortuneteller's money.

The thought made me hurry to the apartment building where the son was supposed to live. When I got to the apartment door I listened but heard nothing. I felt along the doorframe expecting the cold wisp of a ghost to slip out. It was chilly, yes, but the draft had the dry, artificial feel of air conditioning. Of course, a ghost wouldn't need air conditioning.

I rapped on the door with a wet knuckle. When no one answered, I knocked again. I grasped the door handle and pushed down. With a satisfying *click* the door opened.

"Hello?" I called out when I entered the apartment. I closed the door and locked it behind me. The apartment was as cold and dry as an upscale department store, the whir of the air conditioning the only sound. There was a light coming from a room, the back bedroom I assumed. The light was a flickering, bluish glare of a television but no audio. I went further inside the apartment, calling out once again, louder.

I turned the corner. A television placed on a nightstand was indeed turned on but no one was in the bedroom to watch it. I touched the volume control and the audio came on. Immediately I muted the sound and watched the images of the late night variety show until I managed to avert my attention. There was a single bed with a spray of wrinkles on the top cover, as if someone had been lying on it. When touched, the spot was not warm.

A small desk was the only other piece of furniture in the bedroom. On top of the desk was a tall pile of books of varied subjects: anatomy texts, field guides, dictionaries, travel books. A small closet built into the wall held only a couple pairs of jeans, three or four shirts, and a sweatshirt. I walked out of the bedroom. The bathroom was clean, nothing on the sink countertop except a bottle of liquid soap and a small hand towel. In the main room of the apartment, two upholstered chairs were gathered around a small table as if huddled in a serious conversation. On the table were a couple of unfolded paper fans, the cheap kind you get as free gifts from a department store. In the kitchen the few dishes were clean and put away neatly on the shelves. There was no perishable food, just odds and ends—soy sauce, ketchup, a few cans of beer, a three-quarters full bottle of whiskey, some oil and mirin, a bag of rice, packages of dried noodles. Not an unexpected pantry for a bachelor who traveled extensively.

The most space in the small apartment was taken up by a drafting table that extended across the entire length of one wall. Attached to the sides were two movable lamps, one on either end. I turned one of them on. On the table were three coffee mugs—one full of pencils, one of pens, and one of colored markers. A few sheets of paper were in two piles, one blank, one of sketches annotated with scrawled shorthand notes. Most of the insects in the sketches I recognized, at least generally, such as beetles, ants, butterflies, and moths. However, some were strange, alien creatures. There were also sketches of buildings, or rather parts of buildings, like a doorway, or an outside corner where two walls came together. I also noted a few sketches of people standing in a street. But the perspective was odd, as if drawn from above. Some of the sketches were details—an ear and shoulder, a hand and a leg. A quick search through all of the sketches revealed no dates or other information written on them.

At least these were concrete signs of existence, proof that the son, the freelance illustrator, had existed at some point. Nothing appeared to be out of the ordinary, but how long had it been this way? Could it have been in for the three years he was supposed to have been dead? No, it was too clean for that—no layer of dust, no dead roaches or flies. Surely the television would have burned out by now, or not. Who knows how long a television lasts.

All in all, the investigation could not have taken a more frustrating turn. The apartment yielded nothing in the end to help, and the fortuneteller's look of horror when asked if her son was a ghost appeared fresh in my mind. As an investigator I was failing miserably. Simply by doing my job, I was digging a hole and finding nothing. My investigation was like looking at cellular life through a powerful microscope: tiny strings of protein making up cells flitting here and there, seemingly without mission, moving with total randomness. How can the chaos, milked of all meaning, create a life? My own life now seemed a pitched fall into a black hole. I was being torn into twos and threes, not parts but wholes, each looking askance, in disgust, at the others.

Then the door opened. A young woman blithely entered the apartment and stopped when she saw me standing frozen like a witless old ram.

"Did you get caught in the rain?" she asked me. "You're soaked."

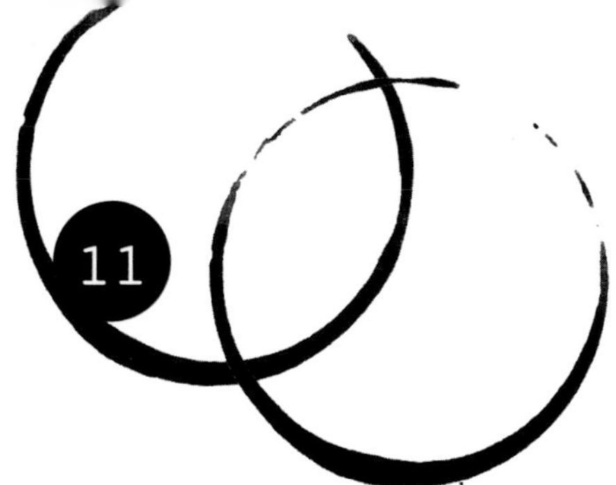

I didn't recognize her at first—she was the young woman who lived in Mizuno Ren's building. Her eyes were no longer puffy and red from lack of sleep or crying; quite the opposite, they were bright and clear. She had applied a touch of makeup subtly and expertly. Her hair looked as if it had been professionally styled that day. Instead of carrying the weight of her life, she was carrying a plastic shopping bag from a convenience store. She went into the kitchen and put the bag on the counter. She walked around me and sat in one of the chairs. I broke out of my catatonic state and sat in the other chair.

"Where's Mizuno Ren?" I asked her in a tone meant to show her I was all business.

"I was going to ask you the same question," she said with a smile of confidence. "When you came by earlier, I was curious, so I came over here." She waved her hands around the air. "No one was home."

"You know him well, don't you?"

She considered the question. "I can't answer because I don't know what you mean by 'well.' If you mean I know his whereabouts at all times, his innermost thoughts, his ultimate goals and aspirations, then I must answer 'no.'"

With a focused effort, I compelled my mind to confront the game she was playing. "But you know him well enough to have a key to his apartment? I assume you let yourself in here with a key," I said, imitating her hand waving.

She smiled again and said nonchalantly, "Would you like a beer?"

I didn't think it was a good idea to share a drink with the woman who had so far presented herself as an adversary. My hesitancy to answer must have seemed an affirmative response, because she got up from the chair and went to the kitchen. I watched as she pulled two cans from the sack and opened them with an expert flip of the tabs.

"Sorry about the can," she said. "I'd rather not use Ren's glassware."

I nodded and we both took a sip. She put down her beer and casually folded her legs underneath her. "Sure, I have a key." She took one out of her pocket and showed it to me, then slipped it back in. Her hand stayed inside her pocket while she looked at me. "That's not unusual is it? Ren gave it to me so I can take care of his place while he's away."

Indeed, that was not unusual, but it suggested they had more than a casual relationship. One person didn't just hand the key to his or her apartment to someone without first establishing trust. I took a sip of beer. She finally drew her hand out of her pocket slowly, making it a deliberate act of sensuality, I believe, or perhaps wanted to believe.

Sounding like an uncle without an emotional thread in his being, I said, "I'm only here out of good intentions. Mizuno's mother is concerned that he didn't show up for the holiday as usual."

She shrugged as if that wasn't important. "I've lived in the building for almost four years," she announced. "Ren moved in a few months after me. I noticed him right off, but he didn't seem interested in me, nothing other saying 'Hi.'"

She delved into the past like a projectionist searching for a particular frame. My own film loop was unraveling while I listened to her, largely because my impression was that she was making up a story, ad-libbing like an actor in an unstructured screen test. Her storytelling was smooth but not practiced, as if she were listening intently to her words, making sure none of her story bore inconsistencies. She was writing a script of falsehoods that had to stand on its own. When I first saw her stroll into the apartment, I thought at last I had something concrete. A real, beating-heart connection to the missing son. Disappointment brings one down from the high of success, or anticipation of such.

She went on with her story: "We finally said more than 'Hi' one rainy night, a night like this one, when the rain was so fierce that walking through it was like swimming. He was coming in from the rain, I was just leaving. We collided at the top of the stairway. He was so sweet . . ."

The limit of my patience was being reached while I waited for her to get to the point. I sipped the beer that tasted more of aluminum than hops. "Excuse me," I said. "I hate to interrupt, but I feel strange, guilty perhaps, sitting here in Mizuno's apartment talking about him as if he is dead. I should be leaving, but I had a few questions before I go."

She unfolded her legs and I couldn't help staring. "Okay. Ask away."

"For one, I asked earlier if you have seen him recently and you gave a rather vague answer."

She switched legs again. "You see, I don't ask him where he goes. I never ask when he will be back. If he tells me, fine. But I'm not the kind to pry. And I'm not his girlfriend."

Girlfriend or not, I believed they had been intimate.

She continued: "Sometimes I don't see him for months but I can often feel he is here. Um, does that make sense?"

Compared to what she said so far, relative to all that I had uncovered in my investigation, it made excruciating sense. My own system of logic—as twisted as it had become—was as irrational and unreliable as the people I encountered. My downfall was trying to make sense of the irrationality I faced: affairs, disappearances, embezzlement, blackmail, and violence. All of the irrational acts occurring for purposes never fully articulated, for if they were, they would sound absurd, outlandish, and with almost no chance of making someone happy. Even if they succeed, the consequences are never what was intended, but then it doesn't matter because the unsociable acts become the goals in and of themselves. Getting away with it, or just getting away, is the measure of success. So the actors come to believe, for rarely do their lives improve with success; they only shift their ultimate demise to another path.

But then perhaps that is all we can really accomplish in life.

"I don't think Ren is dead but maybe he wants to be dead." Her voice grew soft, her gaze went off to the side as if she were delivering a soliloquy. "What does it mean to die anyway? It's more than a loss of a functioning body, it's as if we leave our body behind. This change happens before we actually die, in a physical sense, it can happen a few milliseconds before, or it can be years before."

Again I felt as if my own torturous death were imminent and I had a chance to stop it if I knew how, but I would never reach such a moment of enlightenment. For to reach that moment meant I would already be dead.

Report

26 August: 5:45 p.m.—Shinshin Group is located in their own twelve-story office building near the baseball stadium. I waited for a half-an-hour in the lobby for the art director. When she greeted me, she told me she had only five minutes to spend. "I'm on deadline," she said. An appropriate term but I kept the thought to myself as our company's professional standards require. She was dressed in a blue skirt and white blouse. Her demeanor was stern, all business, clearly wanting to get rid of me as soon as possible. We stood in the lobby like sparring partners waiting in the boxing ring for the bell.

"I'm following up on your claim that Mizuno Ren has passed away," I told her. [NB—I am reporting the exact dialogue in the event she presses charges.]

"It's not a claim; it's a fact."

"Please explain the basis for your claim that it's a fact."

"I have to explain no such thing."

I said nothing, waiting to see if she would change her mind and offer something. Most people get very uncomfortable with silence. She wasn't one of them. "I haven't found any evidence that would indicate Mizuno is dead. Claiming someone to be dead when he or she isn't can be prosecuted as a criminal act."

She grimaced and ushered me into an empty conference room. We sat at a marble-topped table with brushed aluminum legs in swiveling, leather chairs. An office worker followed us into the conference room carrying tea and coffee service, which I declined. [NB—I did so in order to maintain a distant, professional relationship with the art director.]

As soon as we were settled, she said, "You can't bully me. I'm not a person who can be bullied."

"I believe both of those statements," I said, although I wasn't sure if the two propositions she gave really differed at all.

"I want to make one thing clear," she went on, "I'm telling you the truth. I worked with Mizuno Ren on five or six projects and he was always an intelligent and enthusiastic participant. He was never perfunctory with his work as artists can be. Mizuno wanted to know all about the project, who it was intended for, what was the subject matter, who was the book designer, how it was going to be packaged and marketed. It was as if he wanted to know all the details so he could fit them into the art to the best of his ability.

"He was soft-spoken, articulate and knowledgeable without being a know-it-all. He was always interested in you, not only as a client but as a person. He was quite unusual in that regard, a rare trait. I always found myself looking forward to our meetings."

At this point, I wondered to myself if there was some dimension to their relationship other than client and freelancer. But I decided not to inflame her, as her adversarial posturing had begun to soften.

"Of course," she said emphatically, "all that wouldn't matter if his work was inadequate. We will put up with some outrageous personalities to get the highest quality work." Here she paused and shook her head as if recalling some instances. "Ren's work was always outstanding, technically correct, which of course is our highest priority. He also had a way of capturing the essence of the subject. By essence I mean something intangible . . . its life force, its spirit, I suppose. I don't know how better to describe it."

"Sorry," I said. "I don't grasp what you are telling me. Could you give me specific details or examples to illustrate your point? This may be a critical aspect of the investigation."

She sat with a blank expression for a few moments. I assumed she was considering my request or coming up with a strategy to get me out of the office, such as calling security, although other than a vigilant man seated at a desk in a corner in the ground floor lobby, I saw no security force. [NB—If she simply told me to leave, I would have obliged her due to our company policy of not forcing ourselves unduly on people we interrogate except in exceptional circumstances.]

Instead, she told me to wait in the conference room.

While she was gone, I made sure I had enough tape in the recorder hidden in my briefcase. I believe I did, but I put in a fresh tape to be sure. She returned in a minute with a stack of books she placed in front of me. I opened the top one which was a book on urban insect life.

"There," she said, pointing to a technical drawing of a moth, according to the caption a *Pidorus glaucopis atratus Butler,* also known by its Japanese name Hotaruga. Its brownish-greenish wings were ridged, its feelers thick and bushy, giving it a strong appearance, more so than most delicate moths I was familiar with. Two bold white stripes, one on each wing near the end tips, formed a shallow "V." The stripes added to the image of strength, like decorations on a fighter plane or a rugby player's jersey. The moth was drawn on the grid screen of a window, giving it an imprisoned feel. Or maybe it was being kept out of whatever was behind the screen.

The art director said, "Can you feel the power of the moth in his drawing?"

"The technical aspects appear quite outstanding, although I'm not sure of the accuracy as I'm not an entomologist."

"I can assure you that it's accurate. We double-check all of our scientific facts."

"Mizuno appears to be the ideal illustrator for your press. You must miss him a lot."

"We do, of course," she said, with a trace of gentleness that was shocking in its emergence from such a cold shell. "Our only problem with Ren, and this was a small problem, was that he rarely made deadlines. I say a small problem because almost none of our freelance artists make deadlines. We build in a cushion to account for this tendency.

We tell them the deadline is in one month when actually two would be adequate." Here she gave me a conspiratorial glance that I interpreted as her confession being our secret. I gave her a subtle nod. We seemed to have reached a point of common ground.

"How late was Mizuno, typically?" I asked.

"Usually only a week or ten days. I'd give him a gentle reminder, call a day or two after the deadline. He'd be so apologetic. I'd feel badly, but artists might take forever if it weren't for deadlines and reminders."

"How did you first meet him?"

"I saw his work in a magazine, one of those Sunday newspaper supplements. I couldn't wait until the next day when I called the publisher to get his name and phone number. He seemed quite flattered, almost disbelieving, that I would go out of my way to contact him."

I asked her this question: "What was his last project with you?"

From the pile, she pulled out the butterfly book and showed it to me.

"When did he work on this project?"

"Three years ago."

"But you said he died three years ago?"

She frowned and her eyes narrowed in anger. I had lost traction in my interview and felt her pulling away from me.

She said, "I was rounding off. I'd have to look up exact dates in my files and I don't have time to do that."

She stood up and walked to the door. Obviously the interview was over.

"One last question," I attempted as I moved toward her.

She sighed but did not dissuade me.

"Who called you about his death?" I asked.

"I was trying to contact him about another project and left several messages. After a few days, his mother called. I remember her saying, 'Ren has passed away.' She apologized that he couldn't work for us any longer. Then she hung up before I could offer much in the way of condolences."

I choked back a sputter of anger, but it came out anyway. "His mother? That's crazy. She is the one who has claimed him missing. How can I believe anything you've just told me?" After I said this, I realized it could have been someone claiming to be his mother.

Before I could rectify the situation, the art director pointed a finger to the door through which the bank of elevators waited like sentries.

expenses:
14-km car expense
¥950 parking

I arrived at the Kuchi complex a few minutes ahead of my appointed time. I checked in with the receptionist who was entirely professional this time—I was a paying customer after all. She offered me tea which I politely accepted. She went through my paperwork to make sure all was in order. At one minute before the hour, she escorted me into a cozy room. "The fortuneteller will be with you in a moment." She smiled and I smiled. I sat in a deeply-cushioned chair so plush it nearly swallowed me up.

It was only a moment later that I was greeted by the fortuneteller. She wore a dark suit, fitting for our meeting. She took her chair and pronounced she was glad to see me again. "Let's get right down to business. You want to contact a deceased person named Mizuno Ren. What exactly would you like to ask him?"

"I'm not sure I can say precisely. He disappeared so suddenly, like a whiff of smoke."

"Disappeared you say? Are you sure he's dead?"

"I meant disappeared as in 'for good.'"

"How did he die?"

"Now there's a question to ask him," I said. "I would like to know the answer."

"Sorry, but I find it a little strange that you don't know."

"I only recently heard of his death through a third party who didn't know or wouldn't give me any details."

"How did you know Mizuno Ren? As a friend?" Her tone bordered on suspicious.

"More as an acquaintance through his mother."

"You know his mother? Didn't she tell you how he died?"

"She's in denial over the whole thing, I'm afraid," I said. "I do wonder what happened to him, of course, but I'm mainly interested in what he might want to tell me."

"I see . . . that makes it a little more difficult. The more specific the question the better."

"All right. How about these: Are you happy? Is there anything I can pass along to your mother?"

"That's good enough to start with," she said as she set out a dish of cone-shaped incense and lit one of them. The smoke drifted to the ceiling. She turned out the lights except for a single pin light that shot through the smoke and illuminated the particles. "Now relax and think only of Mizuno Ren. Think only of his life, not of his death." Her voice was soothing, like a hypnotist's. After a few moments, she began to whisper, exhorting Mizuno to join us. "Your friend wants to know if you are happy." There was a slight disturbance in the stream of acrid smoke—as if a hand had pushed through it.

"He says 'Yes, I am happy.'" She asked him, "Are you at peace?"

Again the smoke shifted, this time more violently. "He says he is at peace and wants to be left alone."

I glanced down to the table and even in the dark I could see her finger manipulating the dish of incense.

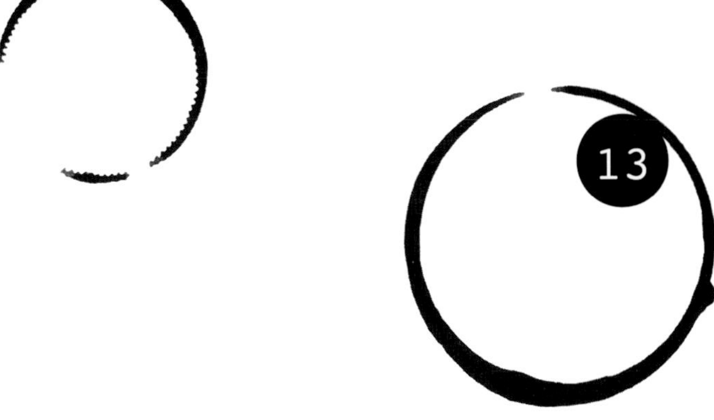

My local pub, if you could call it that, is exactly one hundred paces—a journey of a mere eighty-six meters—from my little shack of a house. At one time, the pub was a portable stall. Every night, Fujii, the owner, dragged the stall from his house and set it up in the space between the two buildings. A few years ago, after a long tiring day, he left the stall overnight. No one complained and it became a permanent fixture. I always count the steps between home and the pub, and then reverse the count from pub to home. Whether we desire to or not, we reach a life steeped in routine by the age of forty. Even if that routine is constant change, it is still routine. The counting prevents me from passing the bar on the way if my mind floats off into another realm of consciousness; while on the way home, especially if I've had too much to drink, I know when I've reached my haven where I can fling my sack of bones and viscera onto my futon.

As I walked my usual path, counting the steps in a daze, my life was projected like a film in a shabby theater, empty except for a lone silhouetted figure in the middle seat of the middle row. The theatergoer's head tilted down, perhaps in boredom, perhaps in fear of what he will see. The film's first scene is a newsstand—four meters wide, twelve deep, with aisles so narrow a customer must turn sideways to negotiate them. Newspapers are stacked near the front of the stand. The first two rows of shelving hold books and slick magazines. The other two rows are filled with manga comics—their thick, pulpy sheaves of pages bound with lurid covers promising fantasies within. The newsstand's owner, standing behind the cash register, is a white-collar dropout. Having lost twenty years of his life to the long hours and stress of his automotive sector job, he is still recovering. Unfortunately, his wife left him when he announced he was leaving his high-paying job to work in a newsstand. Because my wife also left me, the manager and I share a common disappointment and humiliation. In my case, the divorce shined a light on my faults. The manager knows which newspapers and magazines I buy, and keeps books from my favorite authors in stock. His happiness comes from these minuscule interactions during the day and if glued together they would form a rough mosaic of his life. Squint softly at it and an image of meaning and significance comes into focus.

Past the newsstand is a double-sided shop consisting of a fishmonger and a fruit and vegetable stand. The fishmonger is an elderly man, who rarely says a word and communicates by pointing and grunting, nodding and shaking his head. The woman who runs the produce stand never stops talking. The relation between her and the fishmonger is not clear. But there is some connection, as I often catch them in a shared glance. Although it is so furtive, so lacking in definition, I can't begin to guess what it means. Is it conspiratorial, or shared pity?

The next scene played out at a pachinko parlor. The patrons stare at their pinball machines, twisting knobs, feeding coins, oblivious to the carnival of noise. I rarely play, perhaps once a year when I'm truly bored. I'm a rather poor player—pachinko requires practice to play well enough to make a profit. But when I do play, I'm fascinated by the path each ball takes, each seeming to have a deliberate purpose. I know each is bound by the laws of physics in the chaotic randomness of a closed system. Yet as the fraud clerk told me, it's our nature to assign motive and intention to everything.

After the pachinko parlor, the scene shifted to a bakery and pastry shop. I have only been in the bakery a few times. Despite my lack of patronage, the young women employees, some mere teenagers, all wearing bright pink head scarves, always give me a cheery wave when I pass by even when they are occupied with customers.

As the film played on at twenty-four frames per second that night, my counting was disrupted, each step echoed and repeated, doubling the count: sixty/sixty, sixty-one/sixty-one. I looked behind me, suspecting someone was following me, but there was only a trio of young women peering into the bakery. A wave of dizziness made me completely lose count.

Luckily, the bar was only a few more steps and I stumbled in. Fujii greeted me with his usual gusto. He is a few months older than me—we discovered the slight difference one night when I was the only customer and we talked of mundane trivia. A stocky man, bulky with muscle, he looked fit and athletic. He was a star in high school sumo, taking second in the regional tournament his senior year. But he was too short and slight to join the professional sumo. He worked in construction for a while, until he fell and shattered a leg.

The accident and recovery time was depressing and he became a drunk, a worthless human being—his description, not mine. Then one night he ran into the sumo wrestler who defeated him in the regional high school tournament. The rival joined professional sumo for a couple of years before dropping out and was now a restaurant owner. He had a lot of praise for Fujii: the toughest match he ever had, he claimed, was that high school match. The rival must have seen that Fujii was down-and-out and he offered him a job in his restaurant. Starting at the bottom, soon Fujii was able to do anything in the establishment. After a few years, he started out on his own with his portable stand.

Fujii, sporting a fresh headband, served me sake and a plate of appetizers. There were other customers in the place, so Fujii was hopping to keep up. With a couple sips of sake and a few bites of the food, I relaxed until I recalled what the art director told me: Mizuno's mother called and claimed her son was dead. If true, I was being twisted and played with like a child's toy. I wondered how the chief would take the news when he read my report. Then to top off the day, there was the news of the wife in the old case that was haunting me.

A great regret in my life was not finding the woman's husband. Or did I find him? Was he the one behind that wall in the bar? But more than where he disappeared to, I wanted to know why he disappeared. It had to be more than shady business dealings. He was a restless sort, manifested by the number of professional certifications he obtained. The crucial question was: what were the deep-seated reasons for abandoning his wife? He had to know it would hurt her, and he had to know he would suffer pangs of guilt as much as relief. A sudden urge to go to see the wife hot me. I would tell her all would be fine, even if she couldn't hear me in her comatose state. I would bring her flowers, and a fortuneteller to read her palm to show her that she still had a long life ahead, full of happiness and good fortune.

Fujii refilled my sake, replaced my empty plate with a full one, then hurried off to attend to the others, who appeared to be colleagues in the same company. They were boisterous, getting sloppy, but I dissolved their presence from my world with the sake.

Many cases end with as much unresolved as resolved. Answers may be obtained, reports completed and delivered, fees paid. But what remains are the coals of personal destruction, sometimes to flare up, usually to die out slowly. I always wonder what people think will happen when they find what they have search for. It's rarely what they hoped. "I just want to know," they say. But in reality, often it would be better if they didn't.

For instance, my own marriage ended without a clear explanation. Like a car with leaky tires, it rolled along bumpily, sluggishly, until all the air was gone and the car, useless, was abandoned on a desolate beach, corroding and rusting, returning to the elemental minerals and organic matter from which it was created. My ex-wife hadn't run away, hadn't secretly divorced me, hadn't killed me in my sleep. She started a business in a different town, finding that to be more enjoyable than my company. Fine, I didn't want to know anything more.

I downed a cup of sake as if to toast her and was about to refill it when a hand reached from behind me, took up my flask, and filled my cup. "How about a cup for me?" said a familiar voice. I turned to see the fraud clerk grinning at me.

"You didn't detect me, did you?" the fraud clerk asked.

I felt a wave of anxiety, no, call it anxiousness, over the clerk's presence and more so about his question. He must have been following me. But what awful reason could the clerk have for doing that? After all, I was merely walking from home to my local pub as I have done many hundreds of times. I was doing nothing out of the ordinary, unless that was what the clerk was interested in—my routine—although for what reason I couldn't fathom. But worse than his reason for following me was why I hadn't detected him. There were the echoing footsteps but when I turned I saw no one except . . . was he disguised as one of the young women? I nearly laughed.

My change in expression must have made the clerk lose his cheeriness. "So you did detect me?"

"I knew someone was following me. If I hadn't stopped at my destination and continued to walk, it would have taken only a few more steps to make out who it was."

"Oh," the clerk said heavily with disappointment. He pulled a cigarette out of a pack.

Suddenly I realized that not only did I sense the clerk was following me, but when I was viewing my life as a film, the viewer must have been the clerk. That would mean I was tuned into the clerk's mind, or vice versa. Either way, it was disconcerting to say the least. What was it about the clerk that caused the weird mental phenomena—the splitting of my being, the invasion of my consciousness? Who knows what else he might be responsible for?

"Let me buy us another flask of sake. I'm hungry too." The clerk placed his order with Fujii, lit a cigarette, and blew out the first cloud after sucking deeply. "Rather than call your office—which would have been too easy—I found out where you lived by searching the public records I have access to in my position. I watched your house and when you showed up, I thought I'd see what all the fuss is about being a private investigator." The clerk took another drag and looked me over. "To tell you the truth, my work is boring. I got such a thrill finding out where you lived and following you here."

I could do nothing more than grunt. To change the subject, I asked, "What do you have to tell me?"

The clerk looked hurt. Obviously he wanted to talk more about his experience as a fledgling investigator. "It's about Obushi and the Kuchi family."

"Didn't you say we shouldn't imagine connections? You railed against people making cause-and-effect assumptions when there is only randomness and coincidence."

"I further investigated," he said, savoring the word "investigated" like a delicate slice of sashimi. "Obushi filed a subsequent complaint against one of the Kuchi family of fortunetellers."

"Why didn't you find this before? I thought you couldn't find any other complaint on record?"

"That's a good question. You are a master investigator." The clerk took a last draw then stubbed out his cigarette. "The complaint was withdrawn, therefore it was not in the files. We keep inactive complaints in a separate place. A dead-complaint file that gets thrown out after ten years."

"What was the nature of the complaint?"

"There was an intimation of a threat."

"Obushi claimed the Kuchi fortuneteller threatened him?"

"Not by the fortuneteller herself, but a certain party described as a criminal thug allegedly sent by Kuchi. Obushi didn't report exactly what the supposed threat encompassed, he merely stated there was a threat implying physical violence. I believe that is an important piece of the investigation, correct?"

I couldn't deny that, but why he hadn't thought of the inactive file before was a strike against his investigative abilities. "Yes, correct."

"What's next?" the clerk asked, like an enthusiastic puppy.

"Nothing. I'm sitting here enjoying my drink and n strate, I took a bite of the mountain potato dish and washe a swallow of sake.

▸

After the clerk left, bored with my refusal to discuss the case or investigative procedures, I walked to the subway station only a few blocks from my home. With revived interest and energy, my mind worked through the possibilities, the inconsistencies, the connections (yes, in spite of the clerk's claim, not all is coincidence and randomness). I was feeling my old self, whole, singular, contained.

I took the subway to Obushi's shop. It was closed but I could see a light on in the back. I banged on the door. A subtle change in the light and shadows indicated movement. I banged again, louder. Finally, Obushi poked his head out of the back room. He came over to the door and opened it. "What do you want?"

"I'll be quick. I didn't get to explain the last time we met, but I can assure you, I'm not associated in any way with the Kuchi fortunetellers or any other group or individual intending to do you harm. I only want to follow up on the complaint you raised against Mizuno and the Kuchi clan. I believe it might be connected to the case of her missing son."

He sighed, let me in, and locked the front door behind us. We went into a back room lit with a dim low-watt orange bulb. The smell of developing chemicals was sweet and metallic. Obushi worked for a few moments over a tray, and then the light went out and the world was plunged into darkness.

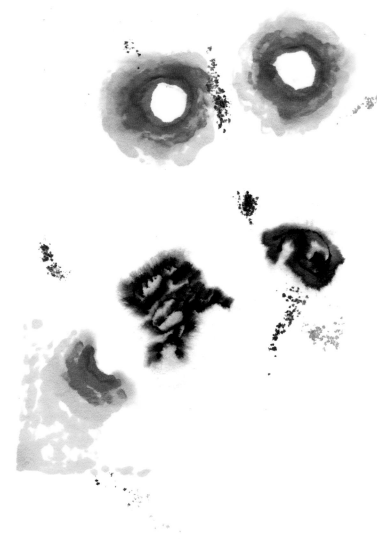

pandues ... près exclusivement exotique, dont les espèces
genre dans toutes les régions chaudes du globe. Un
genre de l'Europe méridionale.
796. **AMORPHOCEPHALUS** Schönherr. — Seule esp. européenne : Brun-
brillant, glabre (AC, P. 151). Lg. 8-12 mm.. ... **A. coronatus** Germ
Midi. Sous les pierres et dans les nids de

untold
as
I travel

– jaunes, … trilobée, la post. transversale, parfois divisée en 2. I. quadriguttata[4] Ol.
Sous les écorces (Chênes, Hêtres, Peupliers). AC.

ready to

Fam. XXVI. — TROGOSITIDÉS

(= PELTIDÉS = OSTOMIDÉS)

give

Insectes de facies très variable, tantôt très allo… aplati… sont de taille moyenne, le… Aucune espèce n'…

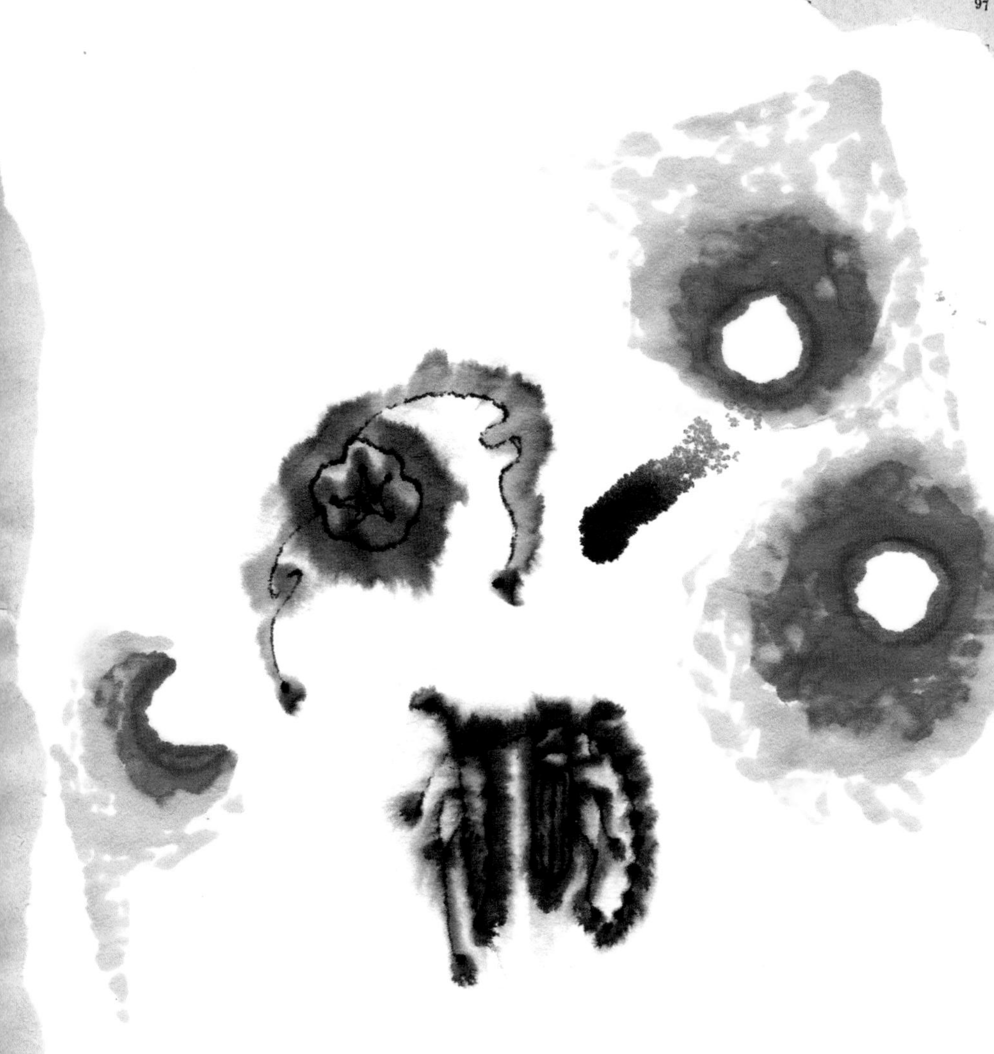

throw my remains away

CÉRAMBYCIDÉS

665. **PURPURICENUS**[1] Fischer.
+ *Extrémité des élytres* tronquée, la troncature limitée par 2 petites dents. Corselet et élytres d'un beau rouge, mais le plus souvent en partie noirs, très variables, le corselet quelquefois tout noir, le élytres, le plus souvent … tache lancéolée commune sur l' …ière (PK), s'étenda… façon à ne lais…

feed
on the
same

commitment
Fam. LXXXIV. — SCOLYTIDÉS (= IPIDÉS)
to
home
Insectes cylindriques, noirs ou bruns, rarement de 2 coul
tête généralement terminée par un museau triangulai
de même largeur que les ély
fois creusées à leur ext

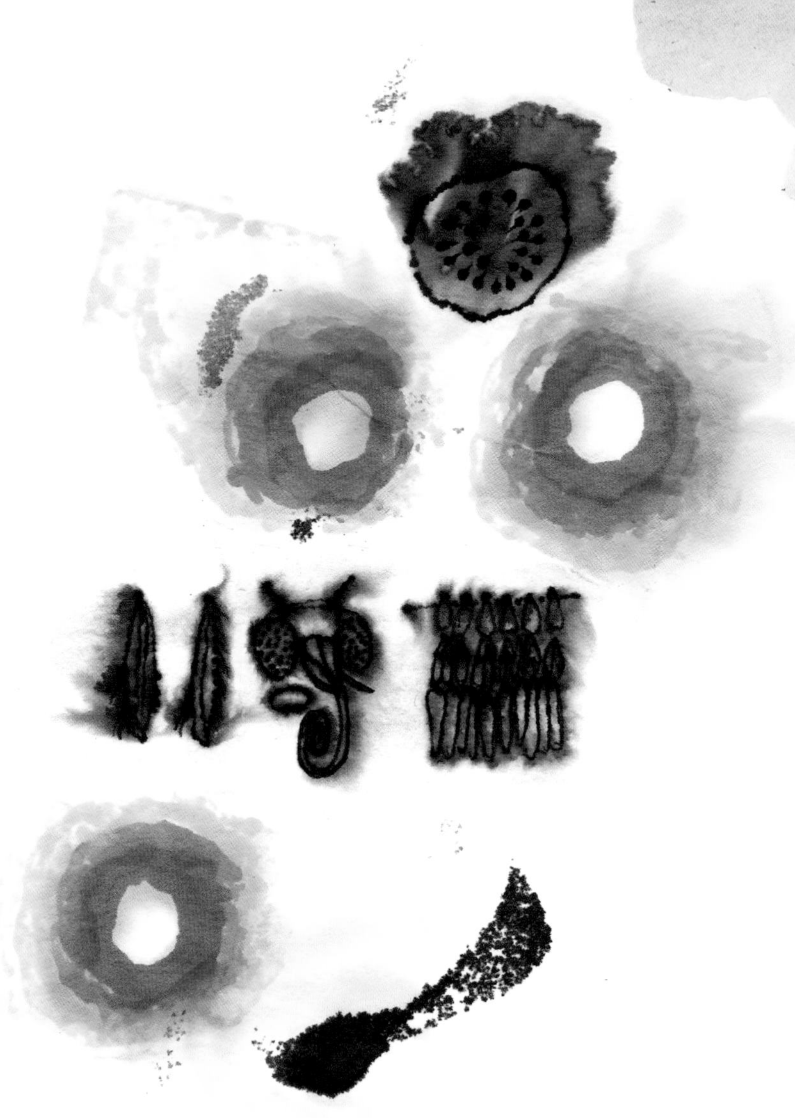

look
past
my
skin

FAUNE DE LA FRANCE

TABLEAU DES GENRES DE SPHINGIDÉS

⊕ *Ailes* en majeure partie dépourvues d'écailles et transparentes.
...ct de Bourdon (HT)........................... 163. HEMARIS.
...èrement écailleuses et opaques.

once I am yours go slow

Sous-famille II. — LAMELLICORNES

416. TROX[1] Fabricius. — *Dans les terrains sablonneux; souvent couverts de terre; se nourrissent de débris animaux : poils, laine, plumes, etc. Sous les cadavres desséchés de Mammifères et d'Oiseaux. Les œufs sont pondus sur place, et les larves se nourrissent, comme les adultes, des débris du cadavre sous lequel elles sont nées et sous lequel elles se sont creusé des galeries verticales.*

+ *Tubercules des élytres portant des poils* noirs ou sans poils (T ♀, p. 167). Antennes et franges du corselet noirs. Lg. 7-10 mm. — AC. *partout*............................ **Tr. perlatus**[2] Goeze.

…unes, ainsi que les franges du corselet.

…usées de p… …rrées et auss

skin
so
full
yet
thin

15

Not moving, straining to listen, I heard a shuffle of rubber soles on the tiled floor. Obushi's footsteps were moving away from me, a relief in one respect, although what he was moving toward was a concern.

A drawer slid open then closed.

It's difficult to prepare to defend oneself without knowing the form of the attack. I steeled myself, raised my arms, and felt the air around me. As suddenly and unexpectedly as the darkness came, a light switched on—this one at full wattage. When my eyes adjusted, Obushi was leaning against an oddly shaped filing cabinet, its drawers narrow and only about ten centimeters high.

He offered no explanation about the light. "Well?"

"It's clear you have a problem," I said. "The Kuchi fortunetellers have been harassing you since you filed your fraud claim."

He slouched against the cabinet as if wracked by sudden abdominal pain. "How do you know about that?"

I took note of several unframed photographs pinned on the walls. They were abstract so it was difficult to determine the exact subject matter. I moved closer to the nearest ones, seeing out of the corner of my eye Obushi stiffen as if I were going to attack him. On further inspection, the abstract photographs were close-ups, some in sharp relief, some out of focus or blurred, capturing the movement of insects, or rather parts of insects—antennae, wings, eyes, legs. Others were photos of people's body parts—a sliver of a face, a close-up of a fingertip. The photos were so intricate, it was as if he had dissected his models with his camera.

"They're experimental," Obushi said.

"You had no purpose in creating them, other than experimenting?"

Obushi raised a hand to his smooth chin and stroked it lightly. "Tell me what you want so I can get back to work." His voice was stern but I could tell it was an act.

"Relax," I said. "This has nothing to do with you, at least not directly. I simply need an explanation of your complaint against Mizuno Rie and the Kuchi fortunetellers."

Obushi sighed and shook his head as if his horse just lost the race. "There's nothing to explain. I thought they had taken me for a fool. Then I realized I was a fool."

An interesting way of putting it. "In what way?"

"I thought they could help me contact my dead wife, but I finally realized that was impossible."

"Why did you want to contact her? Was there anything specifically you needed to hear?"

Obushi winced and again bent over as if hit in the gut. I was about to go over to see if he was ill when he straightened up. "That's none of your business."

"Perhaps not," I said in a soothing tone. "But about the time you made your claim, my client's son apparently died. Or didn't die. In either case, he is now missing, has been for at least for a year, if not longer. But I can't say exactly if there is a connection. I'm merely trying to get background information."

Obushi leaned against the cabinet again. "Look, I want to leave it all behind me. I can't live any longer under all the threats."

"Who is threatening you?"

He gave me a look like I knew, or should know, the answer. I said nothing and waited for him to talk. He seemed undecided whether to answer or remain silent. To push him over the edge, I said, "Perhaps I can help."

His dark, hidden expression softened and he whispered, "My wife died on a trip overseas."

"Please accept my condolences. May I ask what happened?"

He took a deep breath and scrubbed his face with his palms until his cheeks were red. "I was working in Mexico and Makiko came along with me. She didn't usually but we were celebrating an anniversary. Toward the end of our week there, I went on an all day trip to a wilderness area to get some photos. Makiko stayed in town to relax, shop, and treat herself to a nice lunch.

"My trip took longer than expected. The roads were rough, made worse by a recent rain, and we got stuck several times. I got only a couple decent shots, hardly worth the effort. When I got back to the hotel, Makiko wasn't there. I checked at the front desk but they hadn't seen her since she left that morning. I searched the hotel, checked for messages. Nothing.

"I wandered out in the town, checked the places we had been: the café where we ate a late dinner the night before, the plaza where we sat and watched the activity, the street where there were many shops that interested her. Nothing. I went back to the hotel. She wasn't there. But I could feel something as I walked out of our room, down the hallway then down the stairs."

Obushi moved away from the cabinet and sat in one of the chairs. I remained standing so I wouldn't disturb his recall of the events that were taking on quite a sinister tone.

"Finally in the morning, the hotel manager called the police. They took down the information, but were immediately suspicious of my actions. They dragged me to the station and interrogated me for four hours: 'Why did I leave her alone? Where did I go all day? Whom did I go with? Why did I wait until morning to contact them?' All the while I kept saying, 'But she's missing, I don't know where she is, help me.' It was obvious they thought I killed her. I felt that at any moment I was going to jail, never to be seen or heard from again."

He took a deep breath.

"Of course, they never found anything and I finally came back home. A month later I got a visit from the Japanese police. The Mexican authorities found her body in the outskirts of the town. They could not precisely determine cause of death and assumed that she was killed in a fall or a traffic accident."

Obushi stopped, consumed by anguish. With a couple of deep breaths he continued, "I went to Mexico to identify the remains and bring her home. She was kept in the morgue, the little that was left of her. But it's amazing how much you can see of a person even when they are only bone, a little skin and hair, desiccated flesh . . ."

Glancing at the photographs on the wall, his voice deepening a pitch toward anger. "They had no clues as to who did it, and were forthcoming with their pessimism of ever finding the responsible party. Even if they did, the most they could charge him with was leaving the scene of an accident.

"After the funeral, I couldn't come out of my house for weeks, not because I was depressed, which I was, but because of the strange events that began happening. About the end of the first week, I started to hear and see and feel . . . things. Noises, flits of movements, weird moments of warped time. I knew Makiko was trying to contact me. That's why I couldn't leave the house. I didn't want to miss her. I hardly slept, hardly ate.

"But I never could get beyond her simple way of trying to communicate. That's why I eventually made it out of the house, shaving and showering for the first time in weeks. I got something to eat, then contacted the fortuneteller. Mizuno Rie."

"How did you know her?"

He hesitated with a blip of thought before he answered. "I didn't. I just went around asking the fortunetellers in the street. Finally I got her name. But she didn't do any good. She thought I was an easy mark and took advantage of me."

"You then went to the Kuchi clan?"

He nodded. "That was even worse. They drained me, made me get loans from gangsters, then threatened me when I made a complaint."

"They did more than threaten, didn't they?"

His head dropped and shook from side to side as if he were taking slaps or punches to the face. He covered his face with his hands.

"Look," I said, breaking the silence. "If you help me, I'll help you."

He took his hands away from his face and blinked at me, like a frantic rat I once saw floating down the river on a piece of wood.

Obushi's story was pitiable, mired in the unfathomable nature of life and death. He went on to tell me that he'd paid about half the loans and interest, the latter now more than triple the principal. He sold everything he owned except his shop, which was so heavily mortgaged it had negative equity. His inventory was minimal, bought on credit. He was paying interest each week, enough to keep the sharks at bay. Still he lived in fear they'd want more, maybe all of it, and when he couldn't pay they would find places on his body to beat him where he hadn't been beaten before. I was surprised he was putting up with it. Why didn't he just chuck it in, run away, become one of the permanently missing? Or call it a life and hope for better in the next one? The answer to that question was Obushi's wife, her ghost. He was sticking around, putting up with it, because he still believed she was trying to contact him. She would eventually tell him what happened.

I stopped at a red light and looked around the rough area of industrial businesses and rundown apartments, acres of concrete and asphalt, and long stretches of wire fence. When the light changed, I pulled into the drive of an air conditioning contractor's office and warehouse. A few years ago, the owner of the company hired me to track down a client—a failed restaurateur who skipped on a large bill and disappeared. I found him in half a day. The ex-restaurateur wasn't too brilliant, but seemed to be a likable guy. Instead of sitting on the discovery as my company demanded of its investigators (so it wouldn't have to refund any of the week's fee paid upfront), I let the contractor know I'd already found the ex-restaurateur. The contractor seemed honest, not hysterical, so I wanted to give him a break on his fee. Furthermore, instead of the contractor breaking the ex-restaurateur's legs to get his money, I offered to act as a go-between. With some persuasive effort, I convinced the ex-restaurateur there was more to life than hanging onto a few yen.

The contractor was glad to see me when I met him in his office. We shared a cup of tea while we caught up on the last few years. He didn't blink an eye when I asked him if I could borrow one of his vans for the rest of the day.

From there, I drove the van to Obushi's camera shop and parked in a spot down the street. The van blended in with the rest of the delivery trucks. At that moment, there was nothing for me to do but wait. I looked around the van. The contractor's pipe, tubing, fittings, and tools were neatly organized in the racks and bins. Life must be simple being an air conditioning repair and installation tradesman. All is defined and after you've done a few installs or repairs, you've done them all. The possibilities are limited to where to put the compressor, the ducts, and the controls. A clearly-defined beginning and end. A definable outcome.

Less than an hour later, a sporty blue car drove past the van and parked near the camera shop. The driver stepped out—he was the tall well-dressed man I'd seen in the shadows at the Kuchi complex. A plain blue sedan drove up behind the first car. Two men with the squashed, sour expressions of bullies stepped out and the well-dressed man led them to the back door of the shop. He pounded on the door. Obushi opened it and bowed submissively like a puppy afraid of getting whacked with a rolled newspaper.

It was a simple plan: my recording equipment was running inside the shop while Obushi got them to talk, implicating themselves in their criminal enterprise. Ten long minutes passed. Each minute past that mark, my heart sank a little further into the black hole. Its increasing gravity was sucking me in, pulling me to the door to find out what was happening. I got out of the van and ran over to the door. I listened but could hear nothing. I turned the door knob and peered inside. I was momentarily confused by the swinging arms, flying fists, and kicking feet that thudded into the camera shop owner, mashing his flesh and internal organs. My presence disrupted the flow of energy, directed it to me and beyond as I backed out the door, hoping to draw them with me.

Obushi slumped to the floor when the two thugs let him go. He moaned and crawled on his hands and knees. The well-dressed man recognized me—I could tell from the sparkle in his eye, like a raptor spotting its prey. I backed away, drawing him away from the shop, resisting the force of gravity that was pulling me apart. I fought against the increasing power and backed out into the alley. When they took a step toward me, a force sprung me loose and I ran as if my shoes weren't touching the ground. I turned onto the main street, unfortunately and oddly deserted, as if a Western gunfight were about to erupt. Then I heard the mournful lyrics of a warbling folk-song, powered by a cheap sound system.

I ran inside the karaoke bar and waded into the welcoming arms of a drunken crowd of businessmen who took me for one of their own. I accepted their warm, endearing comradeship, as warm as a mother's bosom. One of them thrust a microphone in my face and I sang not in tune but with all my heart.

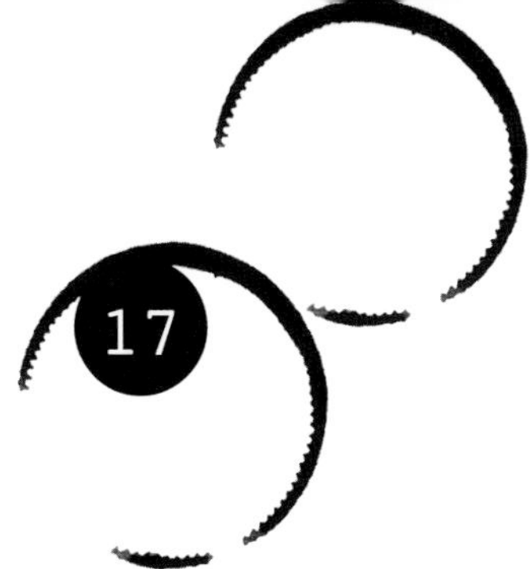

When I was sure the Kuchi thugs had gone, I made my way back to the camera shop. Obushi was slumped against the wall, shivering on the floor and holding his belly. There was a slight swelling along his jaw but no other visible injury.

"I'll take you to the hospital."

He waved his hand—in one gesture declining my offer and motioning me to leave. Lugging my briefcase, I took one last look at him as I moved to the door. I felt sorry for him in his misery, and for his loss from which he will never recover. His guilt was crushing his own spirit as he searched for his dead wife's ghost.

"Lock the door after me," I advised.

Two miscalculations caused the plan to go awry. The first was my estimation of Obushi's resolve. I thought that he wanted to clear up the problem with the Kuchi clan and the money he owed. It was now apparent that he didn't care about the money or what might happen to him. Second, I assumed he would follow my instructions to the letter: he was supposed to offer to pay them off in full in one week if they left him alone. Either that hadn't happened or the thug didn't believe him.

As much as anything, I needed to aim for the center of the investigation, not the peripheral edge even if it might eventually lead me to finding the missing (or dead) son. The chief would soon ask me, "What does Obushi have to do with the missing son?" I had no good answer to that question. I merely had a feeling it would. I considered the possible connections of Obushi to the missing son, and secondarily, the fraud perpetrated first by Mrs. Mizuno and then by the Kuchi clan. If I were to write down the names of those connected with the case—that is, Mizuno Rie, Mizuno

Ren, Obushi and his wife, the Kuchi fortuneteller and the well-dressed man—then draw lines representing links I'd discovered, only one line would be drawn to the son: the one between mother and son. An umbilical cord. Obushi had many more lines, meaning there were more interesting paths of investigation. It was a pity that I couldn't consider Obushi my investigation.

But then I couldn't let go of the potential of a more direct connection from the others to the son. Indirectly, there was the time frame of the son's reported death and Obushi's wife's demise. Both occurred about three years ago. The timing could be nothing more than coincidence, less than coincidence even. A nearly infinite number of events occurred three years ago. A timeline might be more helpful than a diagram of relationships. A nagging feeling at the boundary of my conscious thought and my subconscious demanded a link between Mizuno Ren and Obushi. I mentally drew a dashed line connecting them and labeled it "visual arts," the only possible connection at this time. I recalled Obushi's photographs hanging on the walls in the camera shop, not those in the front but the more abstract works. I tried to recall exactly what they were, how they were constructed, and what they might mean. Parts of insects. . . ?

Mizuno Ren's work also involved insects. Perhaps the two of them belonged to a club of artists and photographers interested in insects and insect parts. There were clubs for all kinds of niche interests these days. Or was I merely searching for connections that in the end were not there? The fraud clerk, my alter ego, would certainly claim that to be the case.

▸

Again, the door to the missing son's apartment was unlocked. I opened it and made my presence known with a "hello?" Like before, no one greeted me and I went inside. Nothing had changed from last time. I set my briefcase on the table, opened it, and rewound the tape in the machine. I opened one of the beers I'd brought with me in anticipation of meeting the woman from down the hall. Teruyo was her given name. Motouchi, her family name. This information I had discovered through the names posted next to the bank of mailboxes. I took a sip of beer as the tape began to play.

At first there was nothing except the shuffling sound of paper, the sliding of drawers. When Obushi was close enough to the microphone, I could hear his raspy breathing. While I waited for something more substantial to happen, I went over to the drafting table. I took a closer look at Mizuno's sketches. The one on top was of a butterfly—a distinct pattern of orange and black, one side of its head and a little piece of its body. I didn't know the technical terms for bug parts . . . thorax? I couldn't tell if the sketch was intended to be finished, or if it was merely practice before he executed a polished work.

Obushi's voice came out of the tape machine, startling me enough to make me turn to see if he had materialized in the room. ". . . never should have stayed away so long . . . I could have made the guide turn around, but all I could think of was getting the shot. The light was so perfect, a bright yet soft, misty kind of light . . . unfiltered."

His tone was quiet, wavering, not so much from emotion, but from walking around the room. He didn't seem to be talking to be heard on the tape. Perhaps he had forgotten about it. He wasn't telling me his story, but talking to himself, as he probably had hundreds of times, going over and over what happened. Telling *her.*

"I thought of you while I was in the forest. The light rays streamed through the trees. The sound of so many butterflies taking wing. If you had been with me, you wouldn't have said anything, only smiled. It would have reminded you of the time we hiked in the mountains on that perfect day the first year after we married . . ."

There was a loud banging sound on the tape, likely the thug pounding on the door. Obushi opened it, and after a grunt, the door slammed shut. In a clear, loud voice, the thug said, "This better be good, Obushi. I've got a hundred other things I'd rather be doing."

Obushi said nothing.

"Spit it out, you wimpy fucking piece of shit, or I'll beat it out of you."

"It's about the money," Obushi said, although I could barely hear him, as he spoke under his breath and on the other side of the room.

"What about the money? Are you finally clearing up your debts?"

"No, not that, I haven't got it."

There was a rustling sound and then a thump, then another, as if a fist was driven into a twenty-kilo bag of rice.

The man's voice said, "That's for dragging me down here for nothing. You want more?"

Obushi groaned. Why didn't he tell them what we had planned? He was supposed to make arrangements for payment, claim that he was coming into an inheritance.

"Not on the face," said the thug.

The pummeling ended after fifteen, twenty blows; it was difficult to count. I turned off the tape as it had become apparent that Obushi *wanted* to be beaten up. He wanted to taste his own bile and blood and feel the rearrangement of his organs because he had to feel one pain to forget about the other.

The door to Mizuno's apartment opened. Teruyo flounced in. "Oh, hi."

"Hi," I said. "I've been expecting you. One of those beers is for you."

She joined me at Ren's worktable as I spread out the sketches. Drinking a beer and standing so close to me, there was a moment of joy and longing that startled me. "No word from our friend the illustrator?" I asked her.

"Not one word. If I knew what you were looking for, I might be able to help." She looked over my shoulder. "What is that?"

"Nothing in particular," I answered honestly. I really didn't know what I was looking for or at. I certainly couldn't tell her of the tenuous connection to Obushi's photos. I took a long look at Teruyo as she looked through the sketches. If I were twenty years younger I would have touched Teruyo's hand softly and said, "That's nice of you to offer. There is something you could do, but not in regards to the case. It's a rather personal matter." And she would guess, smile, blush just enough. She would touch my hand too, and we would walk back to the bedroom.

Before I could make a fool of myself, I imagined how it would really go. She would laugh, giggle really, with her hand in front of her mouth. I would be the older man trying to seduce a younger woman, and she would be reminded of her father, or an uncle. I would smile and shrug and say nonchalantly, "Sorry. Just thought I'd ask. Couldn't hurt."

Instead I asked my routine questions: did she know anything about Mizuno, where he might be, where he was last known to have been? Anything you can think of? She thought for a moment, shook her head. "Nothing really. He's always been like that, off in his own world. Even when he is physically here, he might be drifting over a tropical rain forest in a balloon, or searching for one of his insects to capture and draw."

We finished our beer and she asked if I would like to come to her apartment. I declined, and said I was more than grateful for the offer. As we parted for the night, something she said gnawed at my brain like a mouse on an old, dried corn cob.

18

Report

27 August: 11:30 p.m.—The applicant remains missing from her home. Perhaps I should file a missing person's report, or hire myself as an investigator.

expenses:
¥240 for a pack of blank cassette tapes

My previous report concerning the art director was not well received. "Too long," the chief scolded me. He said nothing about the content which I felt was critical to document. So I made my latest report to the point. "Too short," he will say.

After filing the report, I drove to Mizuno Rie's residence. Luckily a parking spot was available so I didn't have to give the teenage mechanic more of my business which was not eligible for reimbursement. I left my briefcase on the passenger seat after I took out a small notepad and pencil and put them in my suit coat pocket. Most people were more comfortable when talking with a man taking notes, but more importantly, they were likely to be more accurate. I don't know the psychology behind this behavior; perhaps it was because their words were being recorded.

My first stop was the noodle stand, not only to get something to eat but to ask the proprietress follow-up questions. Sometimes, this is a productive investigative technique. People will think about the initial questions I asked, talk to other people, come up with additional information. Sometimes, they tell me they've already answered the questions and to go to hell.

Three of the stools were taken by customers, two men eating together, dressed in ill-fitting suits. They were likely some type of door-to-door salesmen, as they also had briefcases of the type used for carrying samples. The other customer was a young woman, her hair in a ponytail. She was dawdling over her bowl, unlike the men who were slurping up broth-infused noodles as if they were starving. The woman customer ate with the languid pace of someone who had been stood up by her date but decided to eat anyway.

"Hello, again," the noodle stand owner said, somewhat surprised, perhaps even glad to see me. "Same as last time?"

"Yes, please," I said, sitting on a stool. The salesmen gave me the briefest of glances before returning to their lunch.

She slipped the order to her husband, his back to us at the stove, the slump of his shoulders evident. She turned back to me and asked, "Are you still looking for the fortuneteller's son?"

"I am," I said, but added nothing further, hoping she would bring it up on her own.

"No luck then, huh?"

"No luck," I said. She served me a cup of tea. "I don't know much, but I did hear two neighbors talking about a private investigator looking for the fortuneteller's son. They said he is in some kind of trouble."

"What makes them think he is in trouble?" I pulled out my notepad.

She stared at the pad. "Isn't that why a private investigator gets involved? Maybe he is involved in some criminal activity." She shrugged and left to clear the salesmen's bowls. Meanwhile, my meal was delivered by the husband and chef. He had a resigned look on his broad face, as if he was counting the number of bowls he'd have to make before his stand failed.

I slurped up my lunch without getting anything more specific from the noodle stand owner, even with my notepad in plain view. I thanked her, paid, and left.

The noodles sat heavily in my stomach as I walked the neighborhood. Ahead of me I saw the old nun, in about the same place I'd seen her the other day. I ran after her and caught up to her as she stopped in the narrow shade of a street pole. She interrupted me when I started to explain who I was and what I wanted: "You're the one with woman trouble, aren't you?"

"More than you know," I said.

"So the fortuneteller was no help, eh?"

"Not with that particular aspect of my life," I said. "Actually I had an appointment to see her again but I can't seem to find her at home."

"She's not there?"

"Exactly. I think it's rather odd."

She considered my description of the situation. "Can't say if it is or isn't. Are you sure you made an appointment? Fortunetellers can't read minds, you know." She cackled at her joke.

I joined her with a friendly chortle. "She knows I'm trying to see her. That's a fact."

"Maybe you have the wrong day or time?"

"I'm sure I've got it right," I said. "I heard she has a son. Perhaps she's off visiting him?"

"I wouldn't have any idea if she's visiting him. You must be desperate. Your troubles are getting to you, eh?"

"Right, I'm a desperate man. More than you can imagine."

The nun made a "tch" sound and abandoned her thin stripe of shade to resume her trek.

"Thanks," I called after her.

"Good luck," she said, then laughed.

I stopped at a few other places—the grocery store, the gravestone maker, a salon—but got nothing more than supposition and odd comments, differing opinions such as the type of clients the fortuneteller had, what she told neighbors about her son (nothing really, other than he seemed to have existed at some point, although the son was never around as far as they knew). To the question: Did the fortuneteller leave often? I received the most definitive answer of the day from a customer in the salon: "No, not since her husband died. I think the farthest she ever went from the house was here for a cut and style."

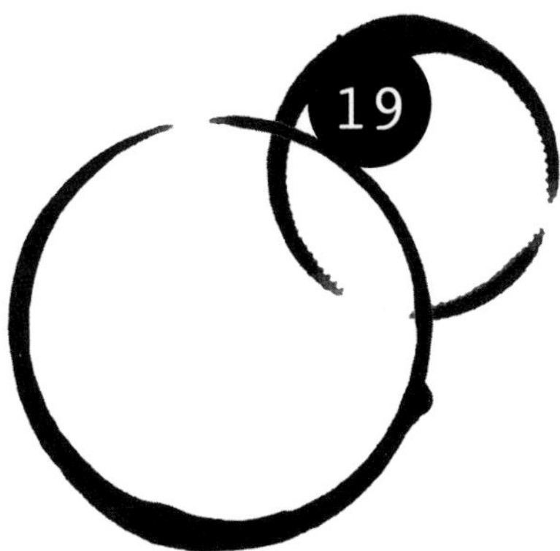

19

Night came slowly to the fortuneteller's neighborhood, likely because I watched each second as the shadows lengthened and consumed everything until the street lights powered up and the house lights blinked on. I contemplated the slow passage of time from the comfort of my car with its upholstered seats and adjustable lumbar support. How does time speed up or slow down? Was it something about the theory of relativity, the warping of space and time? I shrugged to myself.

I received a few glances from people who passed my car. I gripped my steering wheel with one hand and my open notebook with the other, trying to look as if I were engaged in official business.

A pit of futility opened in front of me. The investigation was going nowhere: a missing son who seemed less and less a real person, a rigidly self-important art director, a pitiful widower bent on self-destruction, a violent and apparently paranoid family of fortunetellers and loan sharks, a young woman who seduced older men. Not to mention a missing client and the pesky fraud clerk. The case was not greater than the sum of its parts, but less. Again, it reminded me of the twenty-year-old case, which was going badly as well with the wife in a coma. Maybe to make sense of the cases, I needed to cleave them apart like a diamond cutter making facets in a rough stone. But with my clumsy hands I might reduce the gem to worthless shards.

The pit of futility deepened, threatening to swallow my car whole. Instinctively I pulled the emergency brake. Another display of futility on my part. The Sea of Futility . . . isn't that a feature of the moon? I was nowhere near the Sea of Hope and I had no other course of action but to sit in the car and watch the pit swallow it up with me inside.

▸

Having seen no one go up to the fortuneteller's house, I waited until the sidewalks were empty of pedestrians, then got out of my car and walked up the hill. I assumed the role of a friendly relative coming to pay a visit, leaving my briefcase in the car to reduce my salesman-like appearance. At the front door, I knocked with the quick confidence of someone who has been invited. I expected no one to answer and was rewarded in my belief. That's all we really have: beliefs. We don't have facts or truths; they are subjective, often wrong. We can only believe. Sometimes we are rewarded, sometimes not.

I rapped again. This time with the slower, dull knocks of uncertainty. Immediately, I checked around the vicinity for neighbors. Seeing no one, I slipped my lock jimmy into the doorframe, flicked it, and opened the latch. If I were challenged, my operation would be justifiable as I was hired by the homeowner and was now concerned for her safety. The darkness was complete, enrapturing in a way. So rarely are we in complete darkness. Then, utter silence enveloped me when I closed the door. It was a complete lack of perception, as if I'd finally plunged into the black hole that I'd felt during my first visit to the fortuneteller. The house was musty as all dwelling spaces become when closed up for more than a day, but there were no unusual smells from rotting food, or worse, a decomposing body. Feeling the walls, I found a switch plate and flicked on a light. When my eyes adjusted, I saw the house was different, yet the same, from the first time I sat with Mizuno Rie.

I went into the kitchen first. It was tidy, all things in their place, as if the fortuneteller cleaned before leaving. Living alone, she may have rarely cooked, but she wasn't a bachelor like me who was used to eating most meals away from home. I opened a cabinet and there was proof: the shelves were full of spices and cans of vegetables and bottles of oil and seasonings. Just off the kitchen was a storage room: pots waiting to be filled with soil and plants, boxes of plastic bottles waiting to be used or recycled, and a stack of newspapers—none from recent days.

I checked the two bedrooms, one was obviously hers, the other likely her son's before he moved out. Both were tidy, nothing to indicate a problem. I went in the room where Mizuno Rie told fortunes. It too was in apparent order, furnished with only a round table, two comfortable-looking chairs, and two lamps with simple wood-and-paper shades. Her sign leaned against one wall.

Back in the sitting room, I looked again through the books and picked out the one titled *Why Ghosts Appear.* I skimmed through the first few pages. *Yurei,* I read, are ghosts who haunt a particular person for reasons usually related to revenge or obsession. *Obake* haunt a particular place and are usually the mischievous types that move things around, open and close doors or windows. *Yurei,* on the other hand, are on an altogether more serious mission. They have a strong emotional attachment that will drive them to chase a person to the ends of the earth. Then I came to this line: "Not everyone can become a ghost. It has to be someone who has extra psychological strength."

Other than the picture of the son and the book I was given, I discovered no other evidence. Admittedly it was a casual inspection, a cursory glance at the veneer of life the mother had arranged after her son left home and her husband died. But then most of our lives are that way. My life is so insignificant it could be nothing more than air, or a tiny release of volatile gas, pungent for a moment then gone, dispersed in the atmosphere, its molecules diluted. My life had no impact on anyone, and sitting in the fortuneteller's house in the dark this exaggeration couldn't have seemed more true. I believed it and that's all that mattered.

Conversely, not much in the world had an impact on me. I went through life absorbing little, reacting to a daily routine without much thought considering the continuous flow of sights, sounds, and smells. The event that impacted my life most, I would say if pressed, was the old case of the missing husband. Could I explain why? No, I couldn't, the reason was embedded too deeply in my subconscious. And I didn't want to go poking around because it would be like the fortuneteller's house: a veneer of order hiding something that I would dread finding.

Clearly I lacked the psychological strength to become a ghost.

The chair I was sleeping in was not mine. A dream-like thought about the space-time continuum being disrupted put me in an alien universe. That thought led me to recall my movements in the last few hours and I realized I was in the Mizuno home. While I slept, my head had lolled to the side, pinching a nerve, sending out a pulse of pain with every heartbeat. I stretched the kinked muscles and nerves and tendons, but only succeeded in getting a headache.

Why Ghosts Appear was at my feet, likely slipping out of my hands when I drifted off to sleep in the quiet and darkness. I listened for anyone who might have come into the house while I napped. The silence was pervasive. What a colossal waste of time this was, sleeping like an old man after eating a big meal. What else could I do though? There wasn't anything in the home I'd seen which told why my client had disappeared. I found no travel itineraries, no pages torn from travel magazines, no calendars with dates marked "at Aunt Keiko's" or whatever.

I had to do something to justify my existence as an investigator. I went into the vacant bedroom, which I assumed to be the son's room. Inside was a single bed with a droopy mattress, covered with a light bedspread befitting the weather, likely made up in anticipation of the son coming home for the holiday. Along one side of the room was a row of closet doors. The doors were sticky and I finally slid one open with an extra tug. Inside were the usual items: bedding, pillows, and a stack of towels. I went through those items anyway and found nothing. The top three drawers in the chest also yielded nothing but men's clothes of two distinct styles and sizes, likely the son's and the deceased husband's. There were several packages of handkerchiefs and a shaving kit. The bottom drawer, however, yielded two boxes that I took out and placed on the bed. I was as giddy as a treasure hunter unearthing a lost relic. I opened one of the boxes. It was full of old drawings, no doubt the son's from when he was learning to draw. They were more traditional—*classical* was the better term—than his other works. There were also sketches of human figures, landscapes, even draftsman-like technical works of cars, bicycles, small motors. Most kids, boys at least, capture bugs or take apart things as a hobby. The son drew things, as if fascinated by their surfaces, angles, and shadows.

Then, underneath the last drawing, I found a yellowed newspaper clipping. The headline read: *Factory foreman found dead in car.* The foreman was Mizuno Junichi, forty-four when he died. The car was found behind the machine factory where he worked. The police would not speculate on the cause of death but there were no immediate signs of foul play. Survivors include his wife, Rie, a fortuneteller, and a nine-year-old son, Ren. I put the article and artwork back in the box.

In the second box, the top few drawings were similar to the first box and I almost abandoned looking through it when a different sort of work came to light. The first drawing was a figure of a woman, a nude, again in the classic tradition, as if he'd copied one of the old master's works. I doubted at his age (thirteen according to the date under his name written in the lower right corner) that he would have encountered a Western woman posing nude on a velvet sofa. Even at my age, I had yet to encounter her.

The next drawing was a detailed sketch of the face of a Japanese girl. She may have been one of his classmates. A first love? Her expression was one of deep longing, maybe that's how he wished she might look at him. He must have drawn it from memory or imagination, as I couldn't see a young girl posing in that manner for a junior high school boy. There was no title, nothing to indicate who she might be. No school uniform was visible, for instance.

The young artist in the throes of puberty exhibited a mature eye. His work revealed a critical view of the nature of sexuality and sensuality, well beyond the mere curiosity of raw sex and vulgar eroticism that boys his age—or most men my age—would normally find of interest.

As I inspected the rest of sketches and drawings in this genre, I began to feel something about the son. At last, there was a connection on a deeper level than what I'd achieved thus far. All I'd experienced so far was a superficial glance at him through one photograph, a book that he'd illustrated, and his sterile apartment. Now, I had a sense of connecting with another human being on a subconscious level, going beyond words or even thoughts and into pure existence.

In his works of sensuality, of humanness, there was clear, stark evidence of a strength of character, of insightfulness, of an artistic vision. I now had a grasp of the son's character, of his capacity, perhaps even of his motivation. I could now ask the right questions, interpret the answers in a more focused context. I could delve into the son's world as if it were my own.

Why hadn't the mother given me this box before? It would have saved me a lot of time, wandering down the wrong paths, stirring up unnecessary trouble, although I was not against stirring up trouble when required. Then again I couldn't blame her for not showing me the box, after all, they were old drawings, stuck in a bottom drawer, probably long forgotten. What possibly could they have to do with her son's disappearance? If I were asked that question, I wouldn't have been able to articulate a solid reason; it was instinct or a gut reaction, none of which a professional investigator should trust. But in the end, we listen to those deeply-seated voices, gods in the recesses of the brain, directing silently from their vantage point.

I could have asked her to show me *anything* related to her son. But who knows what that would have brought up? Too many trivial keepsakes that would have done nothing for me, just as the son's earlier classic sketches and drawings had done nothing. It was only when I encountered his genre of figure and portraiture, of expression and sensuality, that I knew I had something tangible, something worth considering. I glanced through them again to confirm my belief. As I did I was overtaken with a wave of tragic loneliness that was not only in the drawings, but in the artist and now in the viewer.

▸

The rain had started again when I walked up the stairs then down the corridor to Teruyo's apartment in Mizuno Ren's building. I wasn't as soaked as I was the first time we met, but I was damp enough that she would likely make a comment. I didn't care, of course. I was only making a prediction.

I hesitated before knocking on her door. What would she think when she saw me? Perhaps she had been secretly relieved when I turned down her invitation. Would she laugh when she saw me? Would she say she wasn't serious? I had no way of knowing. She was a direct person but was also good at keeping her secrets, or any part of her life that she didn't want exposed to critique, locked tightly away.

I gave her door three quick raps and waited. Thankfully, she didn't answer. I walked back down the corridor and down the stairs into the rain.

▸

Midori Elegant Escorts occupied the top floor of a narrow four-story building immediately adjacent to a train station. The first floor was a hostess bar, dark except for the lunar glow of muted blue neon. A sleek, beckoning woman in a well-fitting black dress stood halfway outside the door. I ignored the temptation; regardless, I couldn't afford the exorbitant rates a place like that would charge.

The building had a toy-like elevator—two people could barely squeeze inside the car. Not liking the confined space, I took the stairs which were lit with the glare of naked bulbs. The second floor was closed off and the sign on the door simply said *Tomi Productions.* There was no clue as to what they produced. The third floor was split into two offices, one for a maintenance company, the other a finance company. Neither was open at this time of night.

At last I came to the escort service. The glass door was covered from the inside with a wood and paper screen, the name of the company elegantly painted on the glass. On the wall next to the door, two plastic holders were attached to the wall, each holding copies of glossy flyers advertising the company. I took one of the flyers and pushed open the door and was immediately struck with competing clouds of women's cologne and cigarette smoke. The immediate interior was the size of a small hotel room. Inside, two women were seated at desks, talking on phones. Behind them, a large board hung on the wall with several names—likely pseudonyms—listed down the first column. The next column was labeled IN, the next ON-CALL, and the last was labeled OFF. Apparently the board was magnetic—a picture of each of the escorts was attached to a metal disk and stuck in one of the other columns. Three of the escorts were IN, six were OUT, and two were OFF. From a back room, invisible to me, came the sound of a television variety show. Probably the three IN escorts were wiling away the time until they were ON-CALL.

"May I help you?" said one of the women after she hung up her phone. She was about forty and wore a green dress. The other woman, a few years younger, was talking with a frown even while her voice was lyrically pleasant.

I cleared my throat and then spoke softly to avoid antagonizing the woman in the green dress. She looked like the type to be easily alarmed, like a guard dog on a short leash. "I wonder if I might bother you with some questions about a woman who works here."

She waved dismissively, trying to shoo me out the door. "We don't allow our escorts to have any personal contact with customers outside of the services we offer."

"A wise policy, I'm sure. However, I don't believe this person is one of your escorts."

The woman in the green dress got up from her desk. She tried to steer me to the door but I remained rooted in place. A pained look of frustration and irritation darkened her expression. She pushed on my arm and when I didn't move, she said, "This isn't about the woman who was in the traffic accident, is it?"

"Indeed it is."

"You're not police, that's for sure."

"You're right about that. I'm a friend of hers. I haven't seen her for a number of years but was looking her up when I heard the news about her accident."

The woman on the phone hung up from her call and moved one of the IN pictures to ON-CALL. Then she squeezed past to go to the back room where she called out a name—"Ikumi." A short, thin woman came out of the back. She was maybe twenty-one or twenty-two, and was wearing a pink dress. She took a slip of paper the woman handed to her. The escort glanced at me with indifference and through heavily made-up eyelashes as she walked out the door.

The woman in the green dress stepped between me and the door, blocking me as if she believed I was going to follow the escort. "A friend of hers you say? Why would a friend come here asking about her? It's all very suspicious."

"I'm telling you the truth. My instincts have kicked in telling me something is up with this so-called accident. Her place of employment seemed a good place to start my inquiries."

The woman's eyes narrowed. "Even the police haven't been poking around in our business trying to find something that isn't there. I really don't have anything to say about the accident."

"May I ask someone else then?"

She shook her head. "Can't you see we are working?" As if on cue, the phone rang and she headed to her desk. "You must leave."

I shrugged and, not seeing any other alternative, did as she demanded. I walked down the stairs with my flyer. At the bottom of the stairs I gave the bar hostess a little apologetic smile and stepped onto the street. Soft fingertips grazed the back of my arm—it was the escort who'd just left. She was looking at me but I couldn't see any of the white of her eyes in the darkness and through her lashes.

"I thought you'd be down soon," she said. "You weren't going to get anywhere with Midori. She's very protective of us. But I can't talk now. I'm leaving as soon as the taxi comes."

"But you want to talk, right?"

A taxi slowed in front of the building. "I'll get off work at 2 a.m. There's an all-night coffee shop on the other side of the station. Meet me there." I nodded. She got in the taxi and was whisked away to her appointment.

▸

Ikumi kept her word and spotted me at a table and sat down. "So, what do you want to know?" she asked without any preliminaries. I wondered if she treated her customers that way.

"If anyone wanted to hurt her intentionally."

Ikumi looked me over then scanned the table between us. "You don't smoke?"

"Trying to quit. You want me to buy you a pack?"

"No, never mind," she said with heavy disgust.

"May I get you a cup of coffee?"

"Yes. Lots of sugar."

I flapped my hand at the waitress who curled her lip at me but came over and took Ikumi's order from me. The waitress looked from Ikumi to me, then curled her lip again and left.

"Your friend is okay by me," Ikumi said. "Not a snob who looks down on us. She's never judgmental. It's like she knows who you are just by looking at you, the real you, and she accepts you. Not many people can do that."

"Practically no one, I'd guess."

Ikumi snorted—I guessed in agreement with me, although she seemed like the type never to admit it. "She must have had some tragedy in her life to be so knowing. But she's never mentioned anything like that. She doesn't like to talk about herself. She certainly never mentioned a boyfriend. Or are you an ex-husband?"

"Neither."

"I don't buy your 'old friend' routine. That's nothing more than shit. Midori could see through it too. She can see through shit like it was water."

"Well, then, okay, I'm closer to a boyfriend. An old boyfriend. Definitely not an ex-husband."

The waitress brought Ikumi's coffee. The young escort stirred in three sugar cubes. "She doesn't have any enemies at Midori's if that's what you're implying. Everyone likes her."

"How long has she worked there?"

"Maybe two years, I think. She was there before I started."

"She never said anything about someone bothering her or mention any problems outside work?"

"No. She likes to watch movies, travel. That's about all I know of her personal life. She's never talked about a boyfriend." Ikumi gave me another one of her veiled glances. She was starting to intrigue me.

"It was a long time ago as I said. Where does she like to travel?"

"Hot springs resorts. She'd treat herself to one in Hakone or Izu every few months. When she returns to work, she brings souvenirs for everyone. Nice ones, not junk."

"Did she ever mention any problems during one of the trips?"

Ikumi shook her head and took a slurp of coffee.

"Is she a friend with anyone in particular at Midori's?"

"I did hear that she and Kei—I mean Setsuko—went out for drinks a couple of times. Setsuko's boyfriend was giving her a hard time."

"About what?"

"She wanted to quit the escort business but he didn't want her to. He's a lazy jerk and likes the money she brings in. He got a little rough with her, at least that's what I heard. He's got a temper."

"And my friend was helping Setsuko? Just talking with her? Or maybe giving her money to help her quit?"

Ikumi looked at me like I was a fool. She shrugged.

"Setsuko still works at Midori's?" I asked.

"She quit about a month ago. I haven't heard anything about her."

"Do you know how I can get in touch with Setsuko? Or her boyfriend?"

Ikumi took a long drink of coffee. "Who are you really?"

"I'm a friend . . . she made me happy for the first and only time."

Ikumi looked at me, her eyes wide open, no longer hidden by her plumped lashes. Her mouth opened slightly revealing teeth and the tip of her tongue. It must have been the first time she discovered something important about life.

“Go away?” the fraud clerk screeched incredulously. “Obushi is dead and all you can say is ‘go away’?”

My head was squeezed in a vise. My stomach rebelled against the residual alcohol. Last night, I drank until Fujii lifted me off my stool and shoved me in the direction of my home. Pathetic.

“Go away,” I repeated to the clerk standing outside my door. I finally opened it after he banged on it several times.

“Do you understand what I told you?” the clerk screeched.

I vowed not to drink again . . . or else drink to death. “No, I can’t hear or understand.” Of course I could do both, but I couldn’t deal with his news, couldn’t deal with him being the one bringing the news.

“Are you ill? You look ill. Are you dying too?”

“No doubt I’ve already died. Obushi and I are both dead.”

“Then you did hear me. Don’t you want to know anything about it?”

I heaved a sigh. “You may as well come in before you upset the neighbors.”

The clerk followed me in. I was not accustomed to receiving visitors in my home as it was cramped and filled with stacks of books and magazines. On the other hand, who cared what the clerk thought?

We sat in the small sitting area on thin cushions placed around the worn but comfortable tatami. The clerk leaned and rocked slightly over his crossed legs. I sat as still as possible. I hoped I didn’t start splitting in the presence of the clerk. Just thinking about the sensation made me queasy.

“I was following up on the camera store owner’s complaint—”

“Stop,” I interrupted with a wave of my hand. “Get to the point.” I couldn’t handle anything more than the bare bones of his news.

Again, like a petulant child, the clerk gave me a pouting, hurt look. "I went to Obushi's shop and found an ambulance there. They were just loading him up, a sheet pulled over his head."

I didn't jump to conclusions. A report of a dead person connected with the case did not mean it was Obushi, or that there was even a dead person at all. I'd been given that information before and found it lacking in veracity. The case was a stew of the reported dead and reported missing. An investigator goes about his or her business from a set of beliefs. For instance, the applicant in a missing person case provides the initial beliefs that (A) a person exists and (B) the person is missing. From those two beliefs all others must flow. If they turn out to be false, or at least unreliable, then we are left in a vacuum, a void, and anything is then possible.

"Dead," repeated the clerk, pushing at his cheeks as if they were frostbitten. "That's what the medics told me. They wouldn't tell me what happened, or how he died."

What a pest. Wait, the clerk was a *yurei*. A pesky ghost here to haunt me to my own death. The clerk's presence as a *yurei* would explain his ability to split and get inside my head. I assumed those would be easy tricks for a ghost, even though I know little about the physiology of such entities. Most importantly, if the clerk was a ghost, specifically of the *yurei* species, then I would be able to exploit that knowledge. Conversely, even if the clerk wasn't a ghost, then I could deal with him logically and consistently.

But what I needed most, other than sleep, was to get away from the clerk, who must be a fleshy, chain-smoking *yurei* rattling on about Obushi. I needed to check on his story for myself, but I knew he would want to tag along and continue his quest to learn the secrets of investigators.

The clerk smoked and fumed about my lack of action. Whether a consequence of my hangover or the clerk's ghostly aura, the shimmering in my peripheral vision appeared, a prelude to my splitting or falling into a black hole. The unreality of it struck me as completely ridiculous; however, like telling fortunes or conversing with the dead, there would be no one, scientist or otherwise, who could verify my warped alternate universe. There must be negative consequences of such a warp.

I told the clerk I needed to take an aspirin. In my bedroom, I quietly opened the back door and slipped out.

▸

The front door of Obushi's shop was locked, a tiny *Closed* sign was in the window next to the hours of business. No more business at all, if the clerk was correct. I went around the block and to the back entrance. The door was locked, but with a few pokes and twists with my locksmith's tool, I was in and the door closed behind me. The place was hot, and a chemical taste developed like a photo print in the back of my throat. I recalled Obushi moaning, crying on the tape recording, a man in despair against the world. His plaintive bleating echoed in my head.

I remembered Obushi closing one of his filing drawers. The cabinet in question was narrow, with drawers only a finger's length in height. I opened one and found sheets of contact paper, all blank, unused I assumed, rather than blank photographs. Who would take photos of nothing? Could you even do such a thing? It was impossible to find nothing, because in reality *nothing* cannot exist.

The next drawer contained several developed prints, some of various sites in Spain or a Latin American country, judging by the signs in Spanish. The cracked and peeling stucco exposed stone and brick and wood underneath.

In the third drawer, I found a series of close-up photos of insects and foliage; several that looked familiar. My brain rummaged through some memories and in the recent past came up with the insect book illustrated by Mizuno Ren. Had Obushi been the photographer on the project? I couldn't recall the credits in the book except for Mizuno and the art director (unfortunately).

In the last drawer were photos likely taken for travel brochures: blue waters surrounding tropical islands, sandy beaches, resorts, night life shots of Asian cities. Manila and Bangkok I recognized. And others, again in Latin America, then North America. San Francisco was one of the cities. Below those photos were shots of young women, girls perhaps, leaning in dimly-lit doorways, throwing beckoning gazes yet with distance in their eyes. At the very bottom were several brochures advertising the Moonlight Travel Agency: *Spicy Tours Our Specialty.*

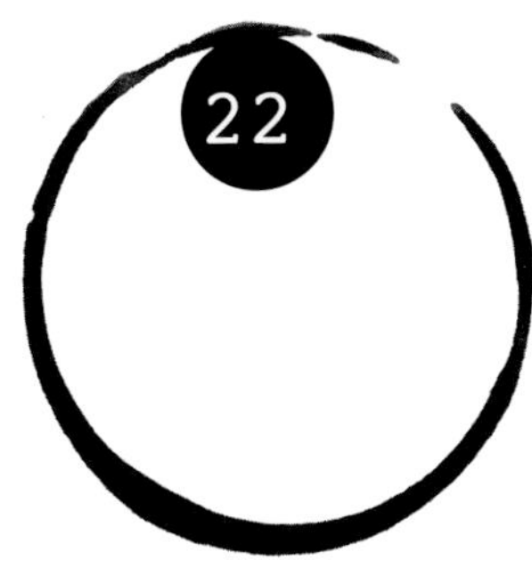

What do people expect when traveling? One thing must be seeing their own lives in relation to the lives of others. This point of view makes them appreciate their corner of the world, or show them what they are missing. That's not something I needed. It was bad enough looking in the mirror each morning and finding a new pouch of subcutaneous fat bulging under an eye. But more than the physical view of self, it's seeing other humans express themselves and satisfy desires in their environment. How does a famished Thai taxi driver decide where to eat for lunch? How does the New York stockbroker cut her steak? For what does the Singaporean executive pray at his temple? How does the Andean father quiet his crying baby? We have a need to see ourselves in a place in our universe, to evaluate our condition. It could just be our brains squirting neurochemicals. More likely, it is far deeper than we can understand.

I didn't have to travel far to reach the offices of the Moonlight Travel Agency—it was on the same block as Obushi's camera shop. I'd noticed the agency when I first visited the camera shop but it didn't register as important, probably because the storefront was characteristic of most agencies and there was no immediate connection between it and the camera store owner. Like a fly buzzing about, following only the odor of rotting flesh, I was oblivious to all but the target.

Inside the agency, I was greeted with a chorus of "welcome" and cigarette smoke overlying an odor of garlic and onions and soy sauce from the remains of a delivered lunch. A pile of dishes was stacked on a low table in the corner. The chorus came from a trio of men, all youngish, seated at desks. On each of the desks were thick catalogues. Each agent had three phones, pads of paper, a roll of pens held together with a rubber band.

One of the agents, the only one not talking on a phone, raised halfway out of his seat and waved me over. A rather casual approach to a customer, it seemed to me. I sat across from him. His nameplate read "Yamaguchi." His hair was of the full, waved cut, gelled style that was the current required look for those concerned with style. He gave me a long stare, assessing me more than seemed necessary for a travel agent. His job was simple enough: ask the client where and when they want to go, what they want to do.

"You're a new customer," he said to me.

I nodded. "Your agency was recommended to me by my friend Obushi."

The agent's expression changed from boredom to anger when I said Obushi's name. The change sent a bolt of anxiety through me, a look that told me I exposed a vein of violent emotion. "Obushi?" he said in a questioning tone that was more accusation than question.

"The camera store owner up the block. He gave me one of these brochures." I flashed him the one in my pocket. "A nice guy, Obushi. He said you could help me out."

"With what?"

I glanced left and right and lowered my voice. "You know."

The agent slumped back in his chair. "It's not a matter of that, it's a coincidence, I suppose."

I didn't understand, but I followed his vague response with one of my own. "A coincidence," I said in drawn-out monotone like a psychotherapist.

"I heard there was trouble at Obushi's store."

"Trouble?"

"Come on, that's why you're here." The agent raised his voice and the other two agents glared at us even as they continued their business.

"Why I'm here?" I asked innocently.

The agent gave an exasperated sigh. "They hauled him away. Now you come around saying you know him. I'm not the kind who puts up with nonsense."

"Clearly not," I said, this time sharply. "But I assure you there is no business other than my previous purport."

"That's a funny way of putting it," the agent said. He flipped open one of his catalogues. "You know as well as I do that something is fishy."

I then knew that I came to the agency too soon after obtaining the clue of the brochures and photographs. I should have researched the travel agency first. Something wasn't right, not that I spent a lot of time in travel agencies. But there should be a certain efficiency, a kind of helpfulness, not suspicions or paranoia about a potential client.

I said, "Perhaps someone broke into his place to rob Obushi. I wouldn't know. This isn't about him. I've come for your travel services."

The agent tapped the catalogue with the tips of his fingers. "If you want a tour then let's set one up. If you're here for something else, then you need to leave."

The other. "A tour, right," I said. "Let's do that."

"What did you have in mind?"

"What Obushi liked."

The agent snapped his fingers at me as if conducting a jazz band. "Again with Obushi. You come in here and expect me to drop everything because of a name? You bum, you parasite. You old fool."

"Bum?" I said. "Parasite? Not even my friends call me that. Old fool . . . not even my enemies call me that."

The agent stood up and took a step toward me. His broad shoulders slumped like a bear's. He was athletic and good looking, like an actor who could confidently appear without a shirt on prime time television dramas. The kind known for their man-about-town suave mannerisms that, while affected, impress most people. I had no idea what set him off, nor was it clear what he wanted to do now, but I guessed it was to pull me up by my lapels and slap me around. I half rose to my feet until I could place my hands on the desk. In that position I braced myself and transferred most of my weight to the foot farthest from him. "There's a misunderstanding here," I said. "No need to take this any further."

A growl came from deep in the agent's throat, like a dog snarling, showing his canines and blood-red gums. The other agents stopped their conversations in mid-sentence. The agent raised his open hand, as if he were about to strike me. My foot instinctively shot out and caught his shin at an angle with the sharp edge of my shoe. I was out the door as his yelp of pain and surprise grew into a bellowing roar. Bone pain is more painful than flesh pain.

I told the clerk about the travel agent's reaction to Obushi's name. When he called me an incompetent imbecile, I responded, "Obushi wouldn't have been in this mess if you had been more responsive in the beginning. He received no satisfaction with his complaint, then he's completely ignored and shoved into some dead complaint file. If that's your standard of competence, then hang me by my ears."

"You don't know what it's like in there," the clerk whined and pointed to his office. "I can't keep track of everything that crosses our door. The paperwork alone is a killer."

"You don't think I have paperwork? Client reports, company memos, expense justifications. That's the dream job you want?"

The clerk shook his head violently and it made mine hurt worse just watching. "That's not the point," he said. "Obushi's dead. If we hadn't started poking around . . ."

So that's it. The clerk felt guilty. At last his motivation was clear. Once a person's motivation is understood then the advantage is yours. "Ahh," I said and nodded sympathetically. "If . . ."

"Yes, if. What shall we do?"

"We can only do one thing. Go to the nearest temple and pray for his soul."

The clerk nodded at my wisdom, finite as it was.

▸

I parked the car in a visitor's spot at the hospital nearest Obushi's shop. An ambulance, I assumed the one that hauled Obushi, was waiting next to the *Emergencies Only* entrance. I walked around to the front entrance and into the lobby. The receptionist at the desk was a middle-aged woman. A corner of her mouth drooped as if she'd had a stroke.

"May I help you?" she asked with a friendly, lopsided smile.

"I'm inquiring about a patient I believe was brought here."

She glanced down to a log book. "Name?"

"Obushi."

Her index finger ran down the page. "Sorry, no one named Obushi was admitted today." She flipped the page back and after a moment said, "Nor yesterday. Would it have been before that?"

"No. Where is the other nearest hospital with an emergency room and ambulance service?"

"Nearest? Hmm," she said, her frown making her mouth symmetrical at last. "That would be Metro. It's a ten or fifteen-minute drive."

Back in my car, I sat wondering if it was worth the trip to the other hospital. My failure to verify Obushi's death wasn't surprising; I was skeptical of the clerk's claim from the start. His power of observation was immature, his objectivity absent, and really, his entire veracity in question. But my enthusiasm was waning as if I'd been on a long, disconcerting trip, seeing too much of the exotic, too much surreal landscape, with red and brown horizons or languid, sensual waters of blues and greens.

▸

I drove out of the center of the city to the suburban hospital where the wife of the missing husband lay in a coma. The going was slow because of the traffic, or my lethargy. Whatever it was, some kind of weird pressure squeezed me from all sides. The case of the missing son was slipping further away from me, diverging into a swamp of unrelated circumstances. Following up on Obushi was turning out to be one of those divergent threads, like a thick chain dragging me down.

I parked in front of the hospital, a colossal structure of five multistory wings radiating out from a center column. Staring at the wing closest to me, I realized the window shades were yellow . . . an odd choice for a hospital. As far as I knew they used white to give at least an illusion of sterility, or at least cleanliness, although viruses and bacteria were colorblind if not out-

and-out blind. Perhaps it was just weird light or an optical effect that caused the blinds to appear yellow.

I knew I should go inside, find her room, kneel at her bedside and pat her arm, grasp her fingers, then softly talk to her. They say people in comas can hear and understand. Their sensory systems could perceive, their memories still recording everything.

Her life was defined by two tragedies. The first was her missing husband, when she discovered life's cruelty. No matter how hard one tries, fairness and truth are rarely encountered. The second tragedy—the hit-and-run accident—occurred as a consequence of the first. There was a causal chain, event A causing event B and so on down to event Z. I was part of that chain. That realization was more than I could bear. Reluctantly, and relieved, I drove away from the gruesome hospital with its yellow curtains, if that's the color they were.

▸

Keina— Setsuko was her ex-escort name—lived in a small apartment complex built between railroad tracks and a freeway ramp. The cars and trains passing created a steady whoosh and rumble, but she didn't seem to notice. The concrete walls of her tiny studio were outlined with an irregular green line of mildew.

She wore a simple T-shirt and jeans on her prematurely fleshy frame. Her feet were bare and she picked at them continuously. "I didn't know about her accident until Ikumi called to warn, I mean, tell me about you. I didn't really know her very well. But she was nice to me when I worked at Midori's."

"Ikumi said she was supportive when you had trouble with your boyfriend."

A little, gurgling yelp came from deep in her throat. "That's. . .wow. I didn't know Ikumi told you that."

"You don't want anyone to know details of your personal life? I suppose that's understandable. Especially me, a complete stranger. I wouldn't want anyone talking about my personal problems either. And believe me I have my share."

Keina failed to smile. "It's not the embarrassment so much, although there is that. The problem is I want to forget about it all. Make it vanish into thin air." She cocked her head like a bird hunting a worm in the grass. "Why do they say that . . . thin air? Is there thick air?"

I didn't know the origin of the phrase nor did I want to think about it. At least not at the time. The noisy apartment was giving me a headache. "I'm here only to help her. Nothing about your personal life will go beyond me. You want to help her, don't you?" Keina's right foot languidly snaked toward me and she focused her efforts on her left foot. Her right foot bore no evidence of being picked so diligently—no loose skin, flecked nails, dark blood vessels. I hoped she didn't want me to massage it.

"Sure, I want to help her. But I don't know what I can tell you. I didn't have anything to do with her accident."

Maybe not directly. "Anything might help. There is little information to go on, nothing as to what happened."

"You sound like a detective."

"Too much TV I guess. What did she say to you the last time you talked with her?"

She rubbed the gap between two toes. "I remember now. We talked about our lives, what it would be like if we were someone else. She said you only get one chance with your life, at least with this life. It's amazing the unnecessary misery we create. If only we were smarter about the time we have." A passing train shook the walls. She switched toes. "Look at me. I'm a perfect example."

"You're young though."

That made her laugh for some reason.

"Ikumi said you wanted to get out of the escort business but your boyfriend didn't want you to. Is that right?"

She switched feet, thrusting her left foot forward. I could smell the slightly pungent odor of it, not horribly bad but undeniably a foot smell. "Tetsuo is a nice boy most of the time. A bit brooding. 'It's a sign of intelligence,' he told me."

She glanced up. I couldn't say for sure, but her look made me feel that she was saying I was brooding as well. She went on, "He has a temper for sure. We used to live here together. He hated it, wanted us to move someplace better . . . bigger, quieter. Of course, he didn't make any money and I wasn't going to get a second job to pay for it. I wanted to quit Midori's as it was. We'd fight about it every day. We'd fight about everything. What to eat, what music to listen to."

"She knew this?" I asked, trying to steer her train of thought.

"She told me to get rid of him. Quit the escort business. She gave me the courage to finally do both."

"What did Tetsuo do?"

She stopped picking her feet and slid her hand to the bottom of her T-shirt. She pulled the shirt up slowly. The bruises were old, yellow-green splotches. She pulled up the shirt higher until her right breast was completely exposed. A set of bruises clearly from teeth marks made her breast look like a rotten apple.

▸

It was useless trying to sit in my car and watch the house where Yamada Tetsuo lived—there was simply nowhere to park unobtrusively. The streetlights were on and people were coming and going as if it were the middle of the day. Not that any of them would have challenged me, but I didn't want to waste my time and scare him off.

Keina told me Yamada lived at his parents' home since moving out of their studio the night he went after her. The abuse she previously experienced with him was nothing compared to what he did to her that night. He said he was going to get the wife of the missing husband too—he found out about their friendship when he followed Keina after work one night. He watched them talk for a while then he confronted them. Before he dragged Keina back home, he screamed at the wife to mind her own business.

I parked my car in a lot down the street a couple of blocks in a multistory parking garage that charged by the minute. I thought about submitting the fee in my next expense report but knew it wouldn't fly. I had only a tenuous hold on my position as it was. I watched the house from the roof of the garage until the car Keina described drove up and parked at the Yamada home. I strolled to the house, walked past and then ducked behind a wall where I could see but not be seen.

The car was a silver Mazda, paid for by his parents, or rather his mother; according to Keina. His father had disowned him. I waited until the street was clear and I went over to the car. I checked the front end on both sides and noticed the body panel behind the headlight on the driver side was dented. The headlight itself looked newer than the other side—the glass was clean and not pocked with collisions with dust or rock chips thrown by tires. I snapped a few photographs.

"What the hell are you doing?"

From Keina's description of Yamada, I knew it was him. His hair was closely cropped. He was stocky and wore black pants and shirt.

"You must be Yamada Tetsuo." I took a picture of him.

He blinked, trying to register if he knew me. I saved him the trouble. "You don't know me, but I've heard of you."

"Huh?"

"I'm with the insurance company and here about the damage to your car." I pointed to the dent.

"I didn't file any claim."

"We have our ways of learning these things, Mr. Yamada. Could I get the details of the accident?"

"My father call you or something?"

"That's not important. Details, please, or I can't proceed with your claim."

"What are you doing working at this time of night? I was just on my way out. Come back in the morning."

"Sorry, this will only take a minute. Did you file a police report? Was there any other damage to the other vehicle?"

His confused look told me I had fired too many questions at him to handle at once. "Let me see some ID," he finally said.

I gave him a look of boredom. "Identification? At this time of night? I'm working overtime without pay and you want identification?"

"Beat it," he said and took a step toward me.

I stood my ground until he flashed his teeth at me and growled like a mad dog.

24

Report

30 August: 3:30 p.m.—When I rechecked the credits for the butterfly book I discovered the photographs were taken by Obushi. I don't remember seeing the name before, or at the least I failed to register it. Of course, this excuse is not meant to justify my actions but to provide a reason for continuing to investigate. In all fairness I would have uncovered the connection at some point, given the way the case has progressed. The difficulties have forced me to use innovative techniques and make connections that are not obvious.

The thread of Obushi leading to the Moonlight Travel Agency is a good example of what I mean. While there is no current connection between the son's disappearance and the agency, other than through the intermediary Obushi, my investigator's reasoning tells me that solving the case might pivot on a connection between the two.

This logic similarly brings me to another line of investigation I will follow—that of the Shinshin Group, the publisher of the butterfly book. I am aware of the damage to our company's reputation that my encounter with the art director might have caused, so I will conduct this phase of the investigation with all due care and professionalism.

```
Indeed, I will avoid contact with the art director at all
costs.

expenses:
none at this time, I will submit car expense with next report
```

My vague report left out big chunks of activities that the chief would see as a waste of time. It also left me wholly unsatisfied, revealing that I had not established any solid leads at this stage of the investigation. In fact, my mind was muddled. Considering all of the possible steps I could take at that time, I chose to focus on Teruyo not merely for my aborted liaison with her but also because of our last conversation about Mizuno Ren. Something she said gave me a start; I couldn't recall the exact words, but in essence she knew more about the son and how he might be in trouble, if not dead.

I ended up again at the son's apartment with my hand on the doorknob, without so much as a light rap, I turned the handle and opened the door. She was sitting in the darkening shadows of early evening. "It's about time," she said. "Where have you been?"

"I got tied up at the office," I said lamely, wondering if we had an appointment I'd forgotten about. "The boss is a needy fellow."

"I suppose you're here now." She got out of the chair and went the few steps to the kitchen that was briefly illuminated from a glaring refrigerator light. She returned with two cans of beer and no glasses. We popped the tops and took satisfying, noisy swigs.

"So?" she said with a gurgle in her throat.

"Yes, so," I replied. "Nothing new."

"Nothing new? I waited hours for that?"

"You haven't waited for hours."

"How do you know?"

"You've waited only about twenty minutes," I guessed, largely on my assumption that she couldn't sit in one place for any longer.

She gave me a playful little smile, a kid caught with her hand in the sweets. "Seemed like hours."

"What about you? Anything new?"

She shrugged. "I didn't know I was supposed to find anything new. You're the one investigating, not me."

"Admit it . . . you're as curious as I am about Mizuno." I took a swig while keeping my eyes on her over the lip of the can.

Her smug expression didn't change. "Why should I be curious? I told you, I'm just a casual acquaintance, not at all tied to him in any way other than as someone watching his apartment. On the contrary, you're the one who keeps busting in."

"Hardly busting. The door is usually unlocked."

"Are you criticizing the way I've been doing my job?"

"Not at all. Quite the opposite, you have a solid grasp on the situation."

She looked away as if distracted. I followed her gaze but saw nothing. I studied her profile. Her forehead slightly rounded to a cusp at the top of her head. Her cheekbone and flesh over it was as oval as an apricot, on top of which was her eye showing a lot of white, even in the increasing darkness. Her nose and lips complemented each other with soft edges, and her chin presented a case for strength and sensuality. All in all she had a pleasant profile, one matching the front-on view, which was not often the case. Most people appear as distinctly different people judged by the two views.

"Enough of that," she said. I was afraid she could read my mind. "Finish your beer and let's go."

I followed her meekly, not sure what was going to happen, trying to keep all the possible negative consequences out of my mind. She led me to the bedroom, her hand in mine, and if that's all that happened, that would have been enough intimacy to hold me for years. But she went further. She undressed me, nibbled at my neck, then trailed the tip of her tongue down my chest and stomach, kissed the tip of my engorged penis, giggled a little when it reflexively twitched. She stood and stroked it lightly and I thought the electrical pulses of pleasure would short-circuit my being. She placed my hands on her breasts, and she moaned when I slipped my hand under her shirt and found them unconstrained. She moaned again when my hand slipped into the waist band of her jeans, and again when I unbuttoned them enough to find her moist below a downy mat.

She took a step back, and I thought all was lost, but she took off her clothes and sat on the edge of the bed, her legs apart, enough for my head to fit, which it did, and she laid back on the bed and slowly rotated her hips, supplying me with the rhythm that I matched until I reached down and checked my erection. Finding it still in the game, I stood up and she lifted her hips and we arrived at a point in space at the same moment in time.

When the struggle could no longer be maintained, I collapsed on top of her, rolling onto my back after a minute of gulping air like a half-drowned swimmer. And, being the great lover that I am, I dozed off.

Luckily I woke up after only a few seconds when she rolled onto her side, her head in her hand supported by her arm bent at a right angle. She had a mole under her left ear. Her pose reminded of Mizuno Ren's nudes and figure drawings. The case became compressed into that one moment and I was hit with a spark of knowing. "Ren has a secret life," I said.

She considered that for a moment then said, "What do you mean?"

At last I had her attention. The first time I had the upper hand in our relationship, if it could be called that. "It's difficult to explain," I said, setting the hook.

She leaned close. I could smell beer on her breath and found it sensual. "Tell me, you . . ." For a moment I thought she was going to call me an *old fool.* My reaction would have been completely different from what I felt at the travel agency when Yamaguchi the agent called me that. It would have made me joyous—pointing out my age in an affectionate way. But she didn't; she left the descriptor like a fill-in-the-blank.

"I found some of his art, in his mother's house," I said. "But never mind, it's nothing really."

She punched me on my shoulder. "What? You have to tell me."

"There are some tropical scenes, some old buildings, like you'd see in Latin America. Some of women, and girls," I told her. "It will lead us to where Mizuno is hiding and what he's doing."

After a moment, she collapsed onto her side. "That's it? That doesn't sound like anything."

And then she said it: "You old fool."

25

Again I was accused of being an old fool. A coincidence, surely, otherwise that would mean the travel agent was connected to Teruyo, and Teruyo to the travel agent. Of course, I saw no evidence (real or imaginary) that Teruyo and the travel agent were in league. If not a direct connection, then who could be an intermediate connection? Mizuno Ren? Obushi? Perhaps it was more complex, maybe a double twisted link.

The insanity of the dead or missing, the missing dead, the dead missing was a crushing weight pressed on my chest. The son, his mother, the camera store owner—was I soon to join them? I supposed that would end the case. All of us dead and missing would be standing in the ethereal mist, having a good laugh at those we left behind. The world would be left to fend for itself, no longer having us to kick around.

I watched Mizuno's apartment after leaving Teruyo when she no longer seemed interested in my presence. Her lust was satisfied, if that's what it was. No, her motive for seducing me wasn't lust—it was strictly curiosity. I was an experience for her. It was more than an interesting experience for me.

A blue sports car drove up to the apartment building and parked. The slick, well-dressed thug from the Kuchi clan got out of the car and walked up to the apartment building in no particular hurry. At last, a connection made, a landmark established. The roads between them were not yet discovered but a faint path was in view. Mizuno Ren => Obushi => Kuchi => Teruyo. The travel agent might be in there somewhere too, in parentheses, or as a tangential path, as was the Shinshin Group publishers who employed both Mizuno and Obushi as freelancers.

I could be making too many assumptions, reminding me of the clerk's admonishment about making connections where there weren't any. I might be making a fundamental error of assuming that the man was at the building to see Teruyo. Yet I had to believe my investigative abilities were sound. If that premise weren't true then all would be mere wishful thinking. Quickly shaking that moment of doubt, I reached for the handle of my door to follow the man, but then I saw him and Teruyo walk down the stairs together.

▸

I bore no ill will against Teruyo, our interlude was fine in the best sense, if not exactly ethical. Of course, I wouldn't mention the encounter in my report. I could berate myself for taking advantage of the situation but not of Teruyo. She knew what she was doing. Her obvious intelligence—a cool and collected intellect—at her age gave me a flush of envy. I had neither, coolness or collectedness, nor much intellect. My way through life, cognitively speaking, was more bulldog-like. Sniff out the bone, grab it and chomp, and hope it digests easily.

Indeed, my feelings went as far as affection, all while knowing hers were neutral at best, affectation at worst. But she was young, dangerously close to half my age, and all youth know is affectation, not affection. There was no hope of anything else.

Gingerly, I let up on the gas to slow the car.

As I could have predicted, she and the well-dressed thug drove in the light late-night traffic heading toward the Mizuno home. I kept far back of his car; there was no need to press too closely. I was so confident of their destination I nearly stopped at a convenience store or a vending machine for a can of green tea and a package of shrimp-flavored rice crackers.

Their steady pace and my intent focus on the taillights of the sports car hypnotized me into a condition where the highway melded with my subconscious, as if it were an asphalt-paved nerve cell. Then my car gradually disappeared until I was flying above the roadway. The world was swallowing me up, my cells stripped of what gave me individuality and my sense of being. I was being returned to the weightlessness of pre-existence, to the innocent fragility of potential, to the hope of a journey where all is restored. A scream came from somewhere; I couldn't tell if it was from me or the world watching me.

▸

He and Teruyo found a place to park next to the shrine at the bottom of the rise. I waited in my car at the intersection. The night was filled with crickets chirping and the occasional dog barking. The distant steady whoosh of cars sounded like a river. And then there was the sweet warbling of a karaoke singer followed by a puff of laughter. I thought about sitting on the park bench and listening to the night sounds until the dawn broke. Finally, Teruyo and the man got out of the car and hurried up the path. I wasn't sure if I should follow them or wait. Curiosity overcame any need to be patient. I closed the car door silently and edged along the buildings to the shrine. I looked up to the house, saw nothing and mincingly ran up the steps, trying to keep my footsteps as quiet as the moon.

Inside the fortuneteller's home, a yellowish light came on, dull as haze. A shadow passed between the source of light and the window creating a ghostly shadow. Was it from a *yurei* or an *obake*?

The house was sided with rough split cedar shakes. A splinter poked me when I walked too close to the house and scraped the back of my hand along its siding. I had no time to deal with it. At an edge of one window I pressed close to the pane of glass, as close as I could without revealing my presence, or so I hoped. I focused all my hearing to the inside of the house, filtering out as much of the night sounds as possible. Only a low mumble of incoherent words was audible. I was about to take a chance and lean further towards the window when a face appeared, filling up the pane.

Life has few moments engraved in mental granite so deeply that only thousands of years would erode them to invisibility. The face at the window was one of those moments. I swallowed my heart that had leapt into my mouth.

The man's face was pinched like a fish's, his eyes small, his nose flat. But the his was focused at too short a distance to be looking at me. When he pushed back a sprig of hair that had fallen over his forehead, I realized he was looking at his own reflection.

If I took a breath, blinked, or twitched my ear, his narcissistic gaze would shift the few centimeters outside the glass and he would see me. At first he might think I was ghost. But only for a moment, then he would recognize me. A spike of adrenalin would propel him to turn and run outside. I was frozen to the spot, so he would easily catch me. Or he could smash his hand through the glass, grab me by my throat and drag me through the jagged glass, slicing my face.

Instead he disappeared, almost too quickly to be human, but he was no ghost, *yurei* or otherwise. I exhaled the air from my lungs that was depleted of oxygen, rotten with carbon dioxide. I slid along the side of the house, across moss-covered rocks and close-cropped grass, crunching leaves from the nearby maple. Gathering my senses, I listened at the front door but heard nothing. Slowly opening the door the voices became distinguishable: the thug's monosyllabic grunting and Teruyo's rapid-fire articulateness. I couldn't yet make out their words.

When the door was open just enough, I slipped into the house. I didn't think much of my chances of getting away undetected, but I ducked into the room where Mizuno Rie told fortunes. I caught my breath enough to slow my racing pulse. In the dim reflected light from deep in the house, the shadows were immense. I peered around the wall, looking for the two intruders, listening for any approach. From their voices I could tell they were in the son's room. I slid across the floor to the bedroom next to Ren's and ducked inside, again catching my breath while I listened.

". . . nothing here," the thug said.

"There's got to be. He told me he saw it."

"He was baiting you."

"He wouldn't lie to me," Teruyo said. "Keep looking. We'll find something."

"Why didn't you ask him exactly where he found it? It would have saved time."

"Don't you think that would have sounded suspicious? I think he was already questioning me."

". . . should have softened him up a little more, then he would have talked." A drawer slammed. Another opened. "Nothing here."

"Hey, maybe this is it," Teruyo said.

After a few moments, the thug said, "A kid's art lessons."

"He was good even then."

"I don't care if he was a child Picasso. It's not what we are looking for."

"I think the investigator tricked me. He's smarter than he looks."

"Smarter than you." A drawer slammed closed. "Mizuno was a momma's boy."

"What do you know about him? I'm the one who spent days with him. He was as gentle and intelligent as you are cruel."

"Shut up." Drawers were opened and slammed closed. The thug said, "If that old fool could dig up something that we can't find then I'm a goat."

Old fool . . . for the third time.

"Nothing in here," the thug said. "You take the kitchen, I'll take the bath."

"Don't know your way around the kitchen?" Teruyo said and the thug grunted.

"Gotta take a leak anyway."

"There's his mother's bedroom too," she added.

"I'll get to it," the thug said.

To the watery splash of the thug relieving himself, I edged out of the bedroom. Her back to me, Teruyo rifled through the cabinets. She was on her tiptoes, peering into the back of a cupboard. I could have told her there was nothing to find. As if she heard me breathe, she turned with a start. Her eyes narrowed with anger. "You."

"Sorry," I said.

"You made it all up, didn't you?"

The thug came out of the toilet, zipping up his fly, saying, "What are you mumbling—" He stopped, stared at me then looked at Teruyo, who raised her hands in supplication. He roared at her: "You got me out at this time of night for a trap?"

I started for the front door but he had the angle to cut me off. I turned away from that path toward the fortunetelling room, hoping I could find another way out, or a weapon to defend myself with. He caught me after I'd taken a step into the room, dragging me by my collar down to the floor. I rolled close to him, trying to smother his fists and kicks. Blows caught me in the ear, the shoulder, the side of the head, my ribs. I wrapped my arms around his legs but managed to hang onto only one. He crouched over me and drove his fist up and down like pistons of some monstrous, organic engine. I rolled into him again, twisting his leg, and he stopped hitting me to regain his balance and get into a better position for killing me. Surely that was his intent.

I took that moment to push myself away from him and roll across the floor. He followed me as I heard Teruyo in the doorway saying something like, "Don't kill him," or maybe that was wishful thinking. The thug was coming at me and, a couple of steps away, he stopped and took aim with a foot. I had enough time to raise one arm. The kick sent a shock wave through my forearm, up my arm and shoulder to my head. The force sent me back and when I thought I should be hitting the wall, I was instead falling into a deep pit of nothing.

Fam. I. — Cicindélidés.

needs back in return

Élytres présentant typiquement (CH, p. 8) 3 taches ivoire dissociées en petites taches arrondies, et variant suivan' ces : une *tache humérale* (*h*), arquée en croissant, sur ext., une *bande médiane* trar· ·rse onduleuse (*m*). "
·le (*t*) en croissant · termi··
·ife

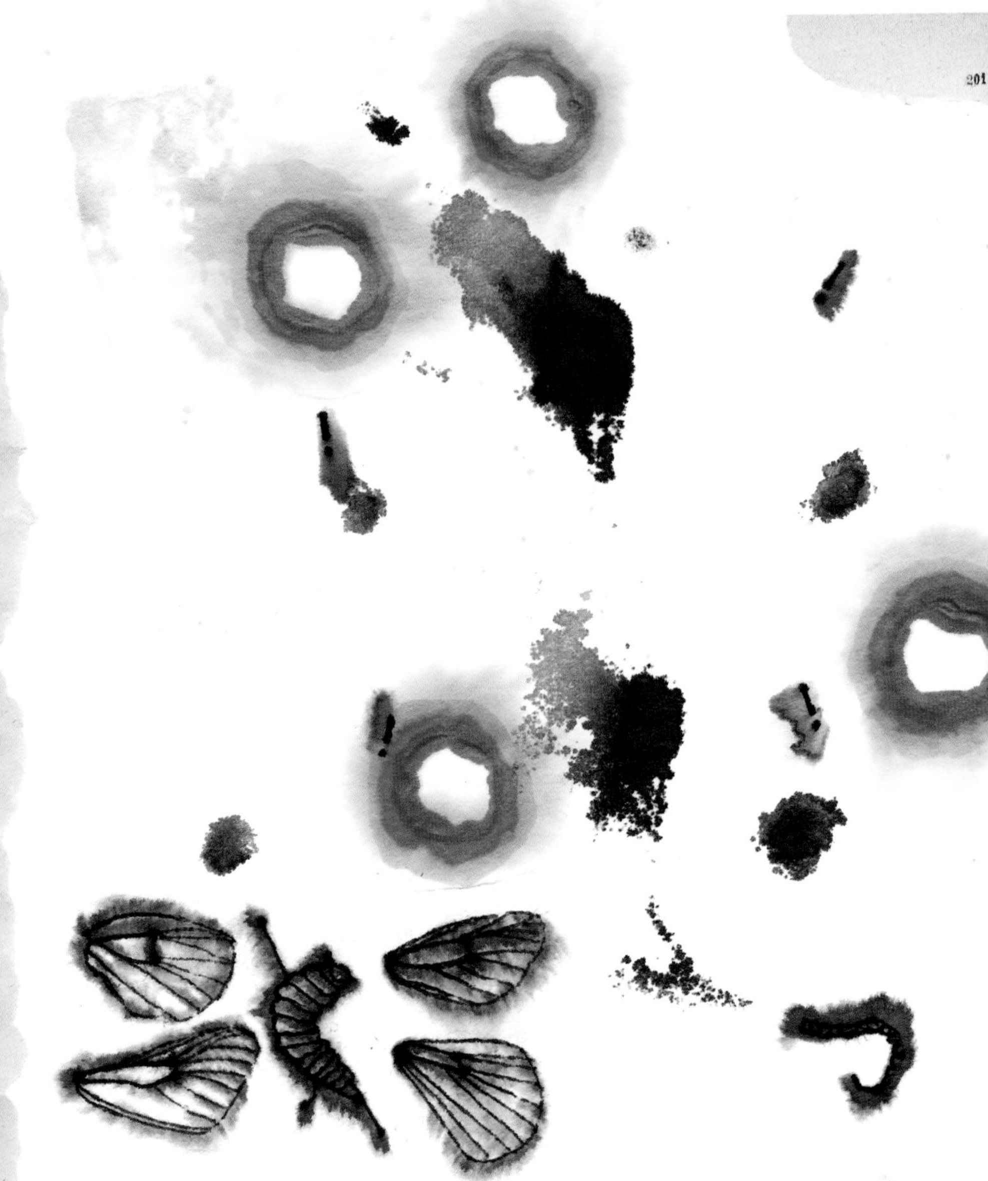

don't ask for it

TABLEAU DES GRANDES DIVISIONS
DES HÉMIPTÈRES

+ *Ailes antérieures* cornées à la base, membraneuses ensuite (hémélytres), en général posées à plat sur le dos, parfois réduites à la base cornée, ou bien très raccourcies, ou même absentes; les postérieures membraneuses, manquant aussi parfois. — Tar... de 3 ou 4 articles.

Rostre n... ...ant de la partie ant. de la têt ....

(n 2.)

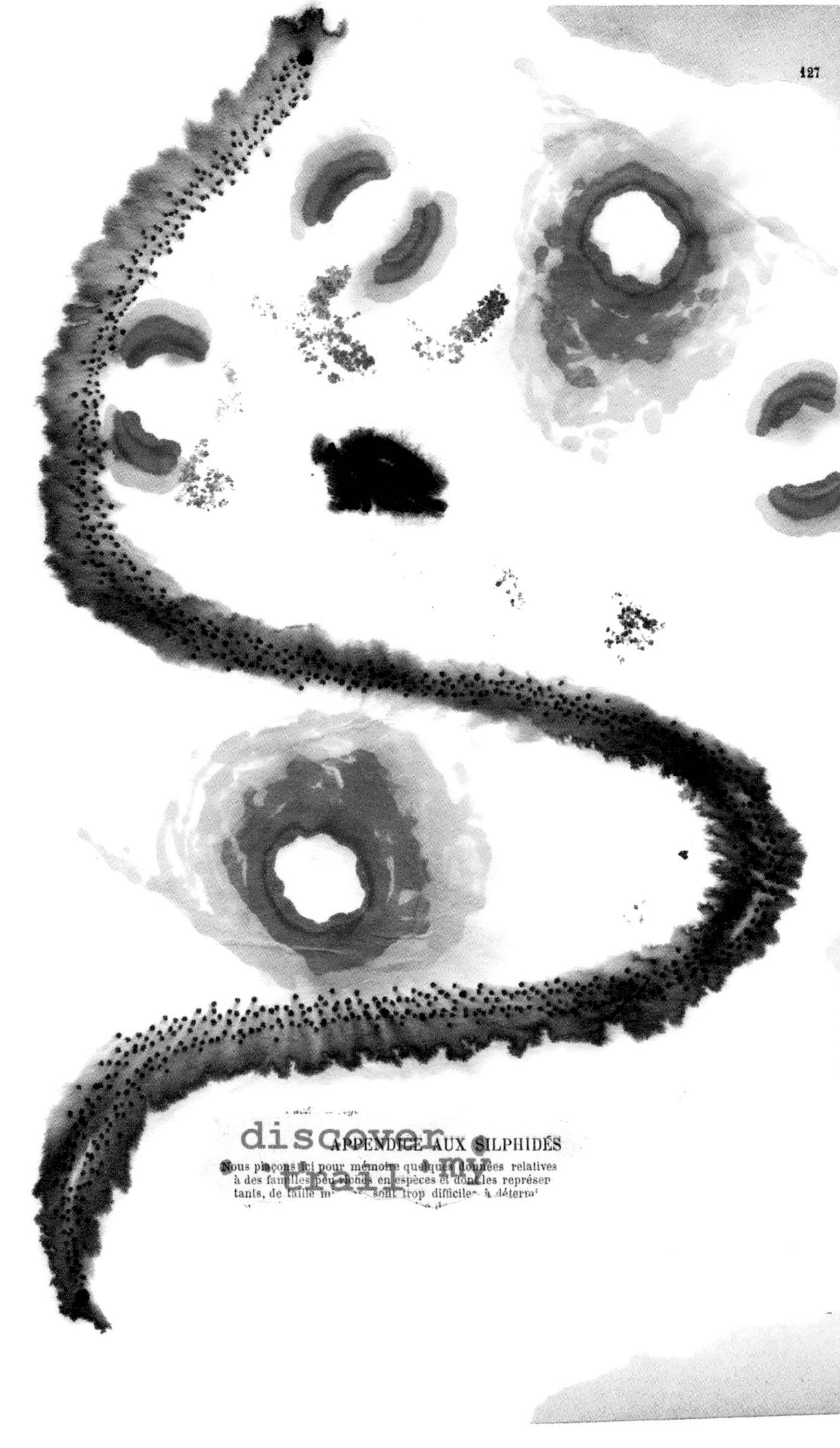

APPENDICE AUX SILPHIDÉS

Nous plaçons ici pour mémoire quelques données relatives à des familles peu riches en espèces et dont les représen tants, de taille m[illegible] sont trop difficile[illegible] à déterm[illegible]

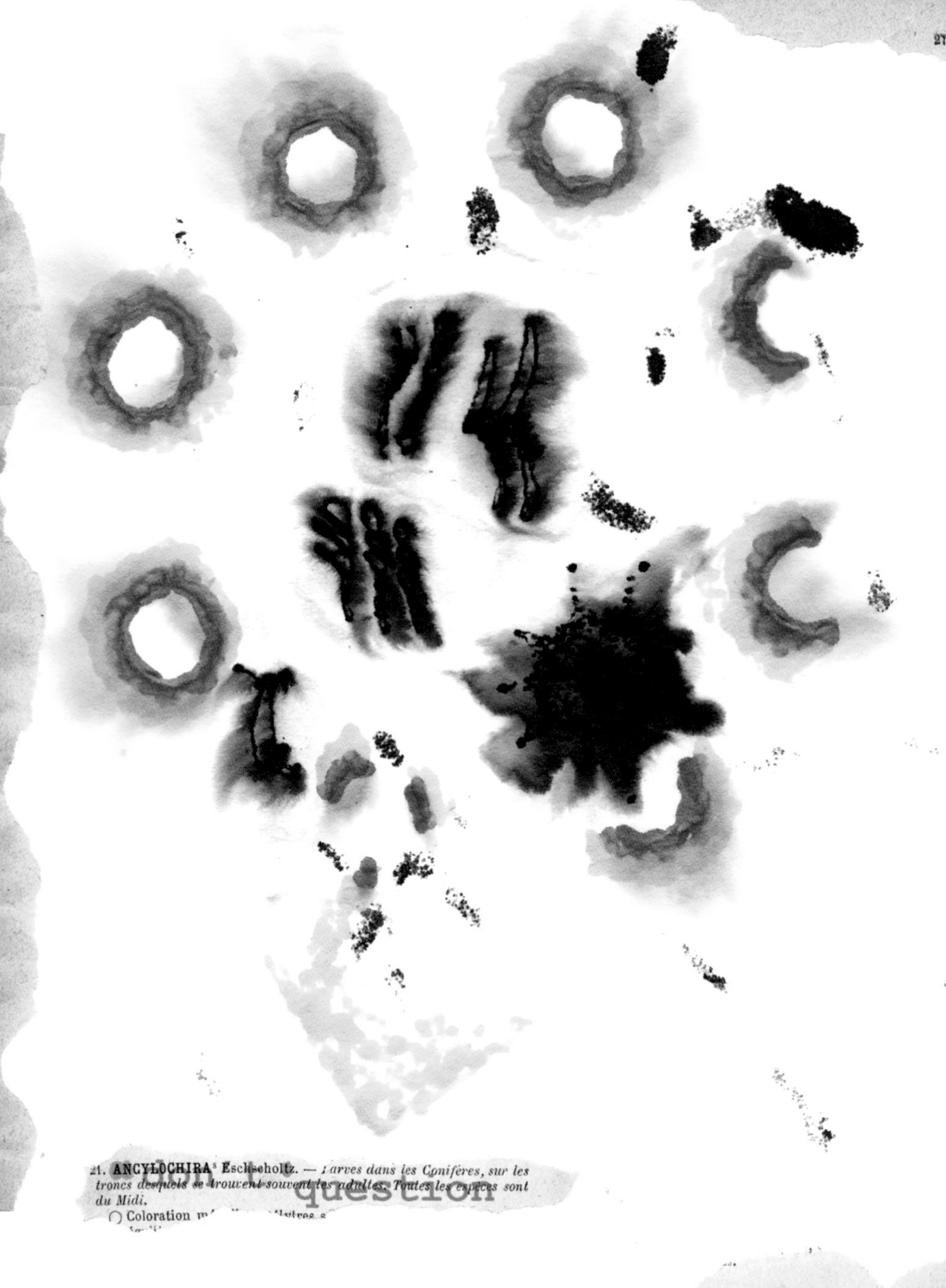

21. **ANCYLOCHIRA**[1] Eschscholtz. — *Larves dans les Conifères, sur les troncs desquels se trouvent souvent les adultes. Toutes les espèces sont du Midi.*

○ Coloration m[illegible]

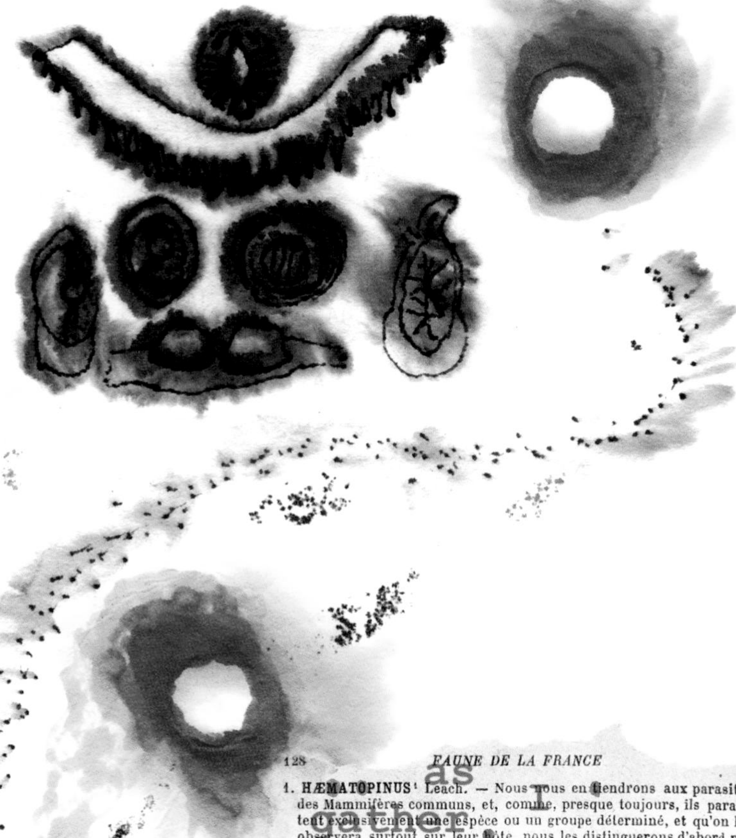

as I gather my dust

128 *FAUNE DE LA FRANCE*

1. **HÆMATOPINUS**[1] Leach. — Nous nous en tiendrons aux parasites des Mammifères communs, et, comme, presque toujours, ils parasitent exclusivement une espèce ou un groupe déterminé, et qu'on les observera surtout sur leur hôte, nous les distinguerons d'abord p[...] leur habitat, une courte description servant de vérification.

△ Parasites du Bœuf.

○ Tête presque aussi large que longue [...] enfoncée dans le th[...]

...ps ovale marg. (NC, p. 68), ressemblant à celui d
Dytiscidé................. XXIII. Naucoridés (p. 7
**. Corps à côtés sensiblement parallèles (CG, p. 68)....
.... XXII. Corixidés (p. 68

but

DIVISION I. — GÉOCORISES[1]

sit

Fam. I. — SCUTELLÉRIDÉS

Espèces surtout abondantes dans le Midi, se distinguant de toutes les autres Punaises par leur écusson recouvrant presque tout l'abdomen, les élytres et les ailes.

still

TABLEAU DES GENRES DE SCUTELLÉRIDÉS[1]

Tarses de 2 articles (Cp); écusson couvrant tout l'abdomen; corps court, très convexe, semi-globuleux (CG), d'un noir brillant; élytr... ...longues que l'abd., se plissant transversalement ... (élytres : Ce et Ce...) ...lobées à leur...

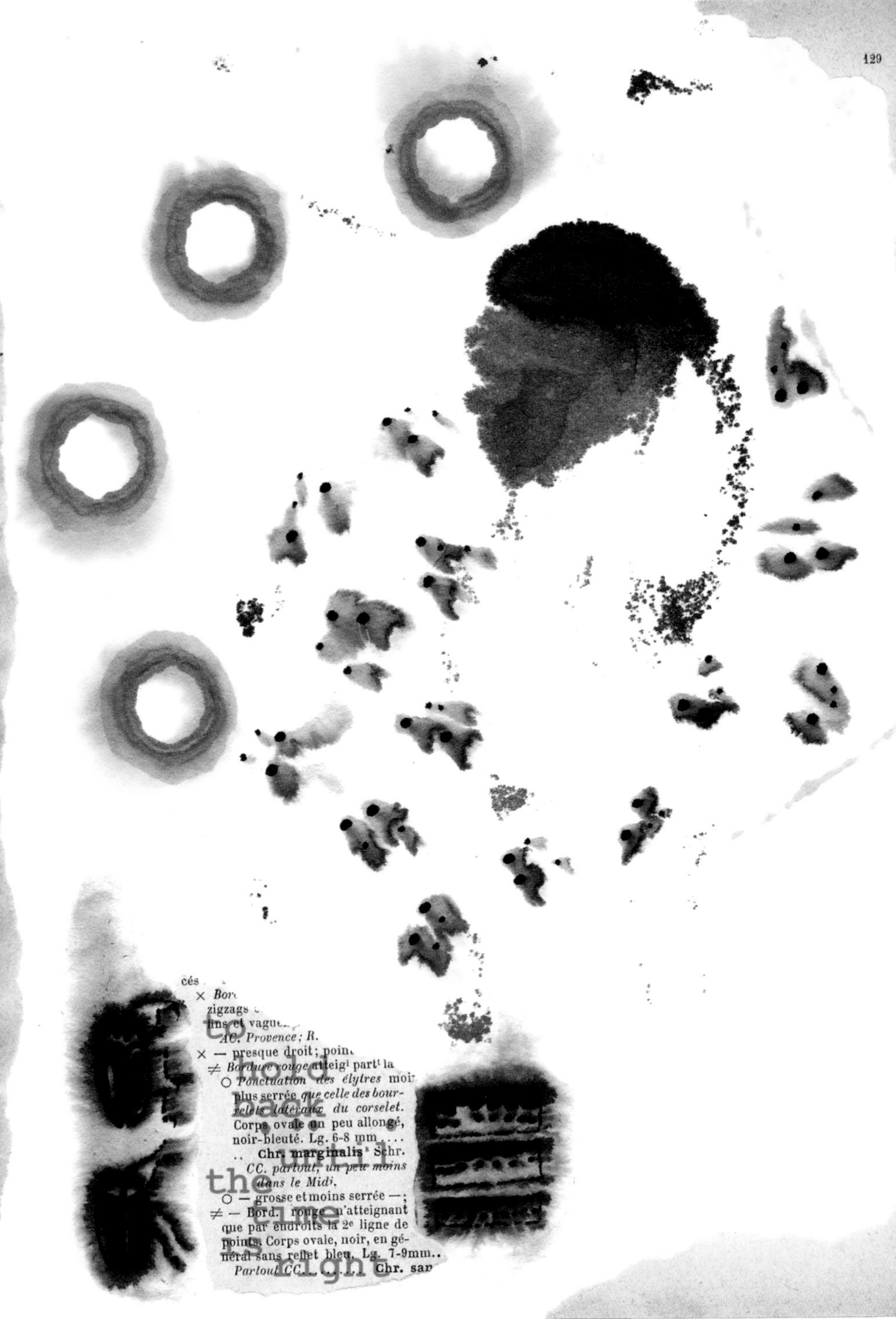

129
cés
× Bor
zigzags
fins et vague
AC. Provence; R.
× — presque droit; poin
≠ Bordure rouge atteig[i] part[t] la
○ Ponctuation des élytres moi
plus serrée que celle des bour-
relets latéraux du corselet.
Corps ovale un peu allongé,
noir-bleuté. Lg. 6-8 mm ....
.. Chr. marginalis[s] Schr.
CC. partout, un peu moins
dans le Midi.
○ — grosse et moins serrée —;
≠ — Bord. rouge n'atteignant
que par endroits la 2e ligne de
points. Corps ovale, noir, en général sans reflet bleu. Lg. 7-9mm..
Partout CC........ Chr. san
to
hold
back
until
the
time
is
right

Brussels,

but
you've
talked
to me
for
years

La FAUNE DE LA FRANCE en tableaux synoptiques illustrés, par Rémy Perrier, comprendra dix fascicules inégaux, qui paraissent sans ordre déterminé :

1 A. Protozoaires (en préparation).

1 B. Cœlentérés, Spongiaires, Échinodermes, Vers, Némathelminthes, etc. (pour paraître prochainement).

2. Arachn…

The hole possessed a life as I fell through it, as if it were filled with an energy more than mere gravity. If pressed to describe the energy, I would have called it a melding of natural and unnatural power, a half-human and half-machine giant.

The end of my fall was abrupt, jarring, and it took away my breath. When I recovered, I found the floor of the hole consisted of dry, fluffy dirt the texture of sawdust. My forearm radiated a sharp pain but I poked the bone gingerly and found no fracture. My other injuries would be colorful bruises in an hour or two.

Surprisingly, the hole wasn't completely dark; there were two distant spots of light. Like dying embers of a fire, they provided a faint illumination. The hole was massive, extending in all directions except immediately behind me where it ended in a wall. The ceiling was low where I was sitting but the floor sloped down and the height of the hole increased as the top maintained a constant elevation. Luckily I fell the shortest vertical distance.

I stood up and listened for the thug or Teruyo, or for that matter any other person in the hole. I heard nothing after a solid minute before I called out a weak "Hello?" that went nowhere, swallowed up and muffled by the hole. No one answered. I wished I hadn't quit smoking, I could light a few matches or use my lighter to check out my surroundings.

Feeling the wall near me, I found a rough texture of dirt and rock, like an old mine shaft dug before concrete reinforcement was available. Yet this was not a mine shaft; as far as I knew there had never been mining in the city. If not a mine shaft, then the hole might have been part of a building foundation. That too was not likely—the hole was too deep, too massive. My speculation on the origin and purpose of the hole didn't solve the more interesting problem of how I got into the hole and why the thug hadn't followed me. His rage had been so unrelenting, I could think of no reason why he didn't jump in after me. I looked up but couldn't see him or anything except the underside of the floor.

I walked slowly toward the two distant points of light. Other than the fluffy dirt the ground had no great dips or rises as one would expect in a naturally occurring cave. There was no sign of human activity either: no pipes, machinery or tools, no discarded food wrappers or drink cans, splotches of oil or grease. I saw no evidence of insects or animals as you'd expect in a cave: no spider webs, insect husks, or rat droppings. It was a clean, well-maintained hole.

Life usually gives us answers if we let it. Rarely do we let it. We prefer to draw our own conclusions, as faulty as they might be. They are what we want to believe. For example, I had no way of knowing which direction I was traveling, but I moved ahead anyway, even though there were no familiar landmarks.

The slope flattened. At the same time I discovered what I assumed was dark shadow was another wall that delimited another end of the hole. This provided me with a sense of comfort, but also gave me a shudder of claustrophobia. I followed the wall, tracing it with my fingertips, and occasionally pushing on spots that might yield a door or opening of some kind. As I walked in the direction of the light that still grew no brighter, the distance between floor and ceiling shortened. I could feel it compressing the air. I stopped.

My fear thickened. If I didn't get out soon, the hole would become an earthen coffin.

Only a few seconds had passed since I fell in the hole, or had it been a lifetime? If a lifetime, how I survived for so many years would have to be explained. At least the coffin didn't seem to be shrinking as I remained still, listening for anything. It wasn't a sound I heard first—it was an odor I smelled. A mix of onion and fatty meat and sweet bone marrow. It had to be the noodle stand's broth simmering in a large, dented pot. I imagined his wife, stacking bowls, making hot water for the thermos, sweeping the floor that would never be completely clean. So much of it was unnecessary but she had to work alongside her husband, sharing every minute of his anguish.

Maybe I was dead and they had already been contracted to cater my funeral wake.

I stood up and banged my head on the ceiling of my shallow grave. Bending over, I moved ahead. Suddenly, there was a whirring noise, then a grinding of a metal blade on rock. Ah, the tombstone carver. The night had already passed. His day began early. There were tombstones to engrave. Mine was one of them, maybe the first one he had to finish. It would take him a couple of hours, I guessed.

There was another smell—a petroleum product—and then a clicking sound of a grease gun. The young mechanic was also at work early, taking care of a rush order. Maybe he was working on my hearse. Not wanting to waste a minute in my bereavement, I was to be buried as soon as possible so I could be forgotten in short order.

My assessment the neighborhood lack significance had turned out to be incorrect. Incredibly, I failed to predict falling into my own grave. I hadn't given the neighborhood the benefit of the doubt. My mistake. Due to my lack of insight, I missed the outward signs of such a possibility that I would die there and become a ghost if I could muster the requisite psychological strength. I would haunt the neighborhood of the fortuneteller from the hole, carrying out pranks without serious consequence.

And yet the smell of cabbage, the whir of a buffer, the clank of a wrench gave me hope that I wasn't dead. I took a chance and walked toward the sounds and smells that grew louder and more pungent as I followed them. The walls became more regular then, perhaps a stone wall from an ancient castle that once stood here. If so, a historical preservation group would have known of its presence and stopped construction. Unless the castle was unknown to the world, and then it would be my duty to alert them.

The wall became even smoother as I progressed. The high-pitched whine of a drill, the bang of a spoon on the lip of the pot, the airy *phhhhhht* of a compressor became louder. I reached a point along the outside walls of the businesses. They were actually, judging by the sound, a little above me. And that's when I saw the point of orange-yellow light coming from a pinprick in the wall that was now as smooth as concrete.

The pinprick was some flaw in construction, a weak point that time had eaten through. I looked through it but couldn't see much except a row of piping, underground utilities of some sort. Probably water, electrical conduit, telephone lines. There was a safety light at the furthest point ahead.

"Hello" I said not too loudly. I found myself embarrassed at the idea of needing help to get out of the hole, my grave. But if there were signs of civilization, then I must be closer to escaping.

"Hello?" I called out louder. My voice fell with a dull thud at my feet. I screamed "Hellooo!" The word sounded like a feeble old man's last moan before he died.

The noodle stand's smells were getting to me. Even if the food was being prepared for my wake, it was making me hungry. So I couldn't be dead. Certainly the dead aren't hungry, not for food anyway. It's also hard to believe that death row prisoners are given their choice for a last meal. If I were about to die for a crime, the last thing I'd want would be a last meal. I'd want maybe to read a last book (a long one), something to give sustenance to my soul, not my gut.

I took a breath. It was time to give escaping another go. My analytical sense of the problem presented one option: keep exploring, even as the hole grew smaller. At least I regained some of my bearings as I had found the noodle stand, gravestone carver, and service station. Using these markers, I turned around and faced the wall that had followed me down the slope.

A sliver of confidence restored, I took a step forward. To my delight, the wall wasn't really a wall, but a solid dark spot. A hole within the hole. It swallowed up all the light from the pinprick. I kept track of my steps, as I knew how to do so well pacing from my house to my local bar and back. I knew the number of steps from the street, up the rise, and to the fortuneteller's house; I must have subconsciously counted them on my visits there. When I reached the number of steps, sixty-eight in all, I stopped and felt around the utter blackness.

Remaining calm in the face of a long torturous death was not my forte. No longer embarrassed, I screamed "help" in my loudest voice. I banged on the dirt until it was dislodged and streamed to the floor, hastening my death, but it was now becoming inevitable. I clawed at stones and they fell onto me, the pain not as bad as the horror of suffocating. Then with one last scream, I must have died. A bright light flooded the hole, and a soft angelic voice called out my name. I shaded my eyes and squinting I saw Mizuno Rie staring at me from above.

▸

Tea never tasted so good. My hair was still wet from a bath. I was wearing one of her son's summer robes while my clothes were drying on a rack in the bright sun. I hadn't wanted her to do all these things, but she insisted.

"It's a hidden door my husband installed when he found out about the space under this hill," she told me. "He thought it might be useful some day."

"How's that?" I asked.

"You know . . . bomb shelter, cool storage, wine cellar."

"Nothing to do with your fortunetelling business? Let me suggest that the hole could be a convenient place for a ghost to live, to be summoned in some session with a gullible client."

She refilled our tea cups but didn't respond to my guess.

"Where have you been?" I asked.

"At my husband's family grave. His ashes are there. Ren cleaned the monument every ancestor's festival. It's a full-day trip and I dislike traveling. But since Ren didn't come home this year, I had to go myself."

"It's unusual," I said. "Applicants usually stay close to home during the investigation. At least they in touch. What if we have a question, or if we find the missing person?"

Mrs. Mizuno frowned and her face sagged. "You're right, I suppose. It would seem strange. It's . . . well, when I hadn't heard anything for a couple of days, I assumed you wouldn't be successful and that depressed me. I had to do something."

She seemed to be telling the truth. Regardless, I had no evidence to the contrary. "How did your husband die?"

She made a little sighing noise. "That was a long time ago. What does that have to do with Ren?"

"A question that should be asked, all right. My answer is that I don't know if it has anything to do with your son's disappearance. I'm filling in gaps of my understanding of your son's disposition and motivations."

My vague answer satisfied her. "Ren's father died of natural causes, a heart attack or stroke. He drove to work like always but died before he could get out of the car."

"They didn't do an autopsy?"

"They found no signs of trauma, so there was no need. Besides, I would have had to pay for it and I didn't want the expense. He simply died."

"I see," I said, not knowing what else to ask about the death. "Besides cleaning the family grave, what else did Ren do during his holiday visit?"

"He'd sleep a lot, eat, watch television. Sketch."

"He didn't talk much?"

She shook her head. "He wanted to come here to relax. There didn't seem to be anything to talk about. Besides, talking takes so much effort."

Indeed it does.

▸

"Have you found something about my son?" she asked after I got into my own clothes.

"There have been developments. I can't say for sure they are related to your son's disappearance. I found out something related to your relatives, the Kuchi family."

Again her expression gave me no clue as to what she was thinking or feeling. "What could they possibly have to do with it?"

"I could ask you the same question."

This time she blinked and looked confused. "I didn't think to tell you before that I'm related to them. They have a fortunetelling empire compared to what I do. We split many years ago when I got married."

"I followed a man whom I saw at the Kuchi complex and a young woman I met at your son's apartment building. They came here and were going through the house when I confronted them. You must have noticed all your things were out of place. The man and I got into a struggle. That's how I happened to fall into the hole."

"That's where you got those bruises? I thought it was from the fall."

"You don't think the Kuchi family would have anything to do with your son's disappearance?"

She shook her head, then turned away.

On the way to my local pub, I stopped at the magazine store to pick up a stack of books the owner set aside for me.

When I was walking out of the store, a voice said, "What books did you get?" Of course, it was the clerk.

"Please," I said. "I'm not in the mood for company."

"I'm not company," he said. He was wearing his office suit, the collar unbuttoned and the tie knot twisted down and to the side. "I'm here strictly for business."

"I'm not in the mood for that either," I said.

"Come on. If it wasn't for me, where would your case be? You'd have nothing."

I didn't have the energy to disagree with him. I walked away from him, clutching my bag of books so he couldn't see what I bought. Not that it was anything important or unusual, I merely wanted my privacy. I kept walking but after two steps said, "All right, you can buy me lunch."

The clerk enjoyed his food and drink with great noisy slurps. I avoided the droplets of spit and broth and bits of green onion he sent flying. When I could get the clerk's attention away from his food, I asked him, "What about Obushi? The nearest hospital had no record of his admittance."

"So they say. That isn't the whole story." Four or five long noodles slithered between the clerk's lips and disappeared with a smack. "He may have started going there, but he didn't end up there. If he was pronounced dead on arrival or during transit, then the ambulance may have taken him away from the hospital to the morgue."

"But that's not proper procedure. The coroner's van should have taken him to the morgue."

"Normally yes, but if the coroner is busy, the ambulance sometimes substitutes for the van."

He had me there. I had to give the clerk his due. "Thanks for that information."

"I just want to do the right thing," the clerk said with one of his grins. "You knew that all along, didn't you? You were just testing me, right?"

I shrugged.

The clerk gave me a nod as if my indifference meant that he was correct. "That's good," he said. "I need testing if I'm going to be as good as you. And I understand the lesson you're teaching me: never let them know what you know."

Or don't know. I drained my sake cup. I didn't need to feign tiredness when I told the clerk I needed to go home to rest. "A long night of surveillance," I said and raised my hands in surrender.

The clerk showed his disappointment; obviously he was hoping for another lesson or two. Or maybe he was enjoying my sterling companionship. But when I told him I would meet him later, he left me alone. When I was sure he was gone, I drove to the neighborhood where the wife of the missing husband lived.

▸

All police stations, even the neighborhood *koban* boxes, have the same unique odor. Or more accurately, especially the *koban* smell of shoe polish, leather, paper, and an underlying but unmistakable whiff of vomit and urine, not from the police, obviously, but their evening clientele who've had too much to drink. The box nearest to the spot where the wife was struck by a car was no exception.

I knew that the last thing the police officers who inhabited the boxes wanted to do was deal with citizens. People were trouble, whether they were troublemakers or not.

"Um, excuse me," I said to the officer on duty.

He gave me a long look, sizing me up, probably hoping I'd go away. "What?"

"A friend of mine was hurt in a hit-and-run accident near here several nights ago. I'm curious if you ever found the driver?"

His dourness lightened; at least I wasn't there to complain about some minor infraction that he'd have to take care of. "I was working that night. Nasty business. Poor woman was moaning in pain before she went unconscious. Gashed up pretty bad too." He sucked in his breath and shook his head.

"Did they catch the driver?"

"Not that I know of. The case was turned over to the district office."

I showed him the pictures I took of Yamada's Mazda. "I happened to hear from one of the victim's friends that she'd been threatened by the boyfriend of a co-worker. And it so happens that he'd damaged his car recently and partially repaired it."

"What is this, a silver Mazda? You've got the wrong car. A witness clearly saw a white Toyota four-door. And a piece of turn signal cover was knocked loose in the collision. I picked it up myself. It was definitely from a Toyota."

My shoulders sagged and I let out a long breath of air that I'd been holding since I was at Yamada's house. "Did the witness see who was driving?"

"Unfortunately no, other than she thought it was a man. Couldn't catch the license plate either." The officer pushed the pictures back across his desk to me.

I picked them up. "Sorry to have taken your time."

The officer shrugged and I left him alone in his box. As I drove past, he was standing on the sidewalk, staring at me and my white Toyota four-door.

▸

The wife's neighbor was mopping the stoop of her home when I drove by and found a place to park not too far away. When I walked up to her, she was waiting for me, holding her mop like a musket.

"How is she?" the neighbor asked.

"Still in a coma," I answered, although of course I didn't know for sure.

"Poor woman. She never raises her voice, always brings me something from the produce stand when she shops there. Drinks a little beer, but that's all right, isn't it?"

"It is all right. Is someone watching her home while she's in the hospital?"

The neighbor glanced next door. "I've been taking care of it. Nothing much to do though. Taking in the mail is about all. She doesn't have any pets or plants. I cleaned out the refrigerator of food that would spoil."

"Very thoughtful of you."

"What do you want?"

"Nothing, except I'm curious about her accident. It could be my imagination but it seems suspicious. Did anything unusual happen in the few days before the hit-and-run?'

The neighbor woman twisted the mop. "Nothing unusual. Not that I can remember. But my memory's not what it used to be."

"She used to be married, still was the last time I saw her. Since she didn't change her married name, I assumed she never remarried."

The neighbor shrugged. "She never talked about a husband."

"How long has she lived here?"

"Let's see . . . several years, maybe seven or eight? She painted it that color the first week."

"An unusual color. Very bright yellow. But it is her favorite color. Say, would you mind if I poked around inside her place? There might be something that would help me find out who ran into her. You can watch me, if you're worried about me being in there."

"I don't know . . . I suppose so."

When she let us into the wife's home, I suddenly felt squashed, a man dropped onto a planet with twice the earth's gravity. I couldn't say why, nothing inside surprised me or was shocking at first glance. It must have been the context of being so close to her. What would happen if I actually came face-to-face with her, even if she couldn't see me or hear me? I couldn't imagine. I was rooted to the spot, unable to overcome the increased gravity. I tried to pick up my left foot and move it, but my leg trembled and shook.

"Excuse me?" the neighbor woman said. "Are you okay?"

I must have appeared to be a madman. "Sorry. I was just thinking. I'll just be a few minutes."

"Maybe I should leave you alone," she said with a slight tremor of nerves.

"I'll lock up after I leave. As I said, I'll only need a few minutes."

When she left, I started my search, for what exactly I didn't know. It was a small house of three rooms, the right size for her. A perfectly-sized volume of space. There were few furnishings in the main room that combined living, dining, and kitchen. I recognized none of the spare, inexpensive pieces of furniture from her apartment of twenty years ago, but that wouldn't be unusual for her to have bought new pieces by now. Her tastes had been unostentatious when I knew her and apparently she hadn't changed.

I went in the bedroom and another pull of extra gravity flattened my internal organs. I wondered what I meant to her . . . probably nothing. She wouldn't have given me another thought after the investigation of her missing husband was complete. Who could blame her? The case was a dismal failure.

The futon was set out—she must have done so before leaving for work. Other than the futon, there was only a lamp and a small dresser in the room. I opened the closet door and found a small cabinet of three drawers. In the top drawer was a plain cardboard box decorated with doodles of leaves. I put the box on the cabinet and opened it. On top of the contents were several brochures from hot springs resorts. Underneath was a bound stack of papers and a folded poster of a cutaway sketch of a car engine. I recognized the sketch as belonging to her husband, as well as the papers being the odd assortment of certifications and licenses that he'd earned—first-class mechanic, electric welder, explosives handler. She'd kept these reminders of her husband, perhaps holding onto hope that he'd return.

The thought killed my faint hope that she had been pining for me.

Underneath the papers was a video cassette. The title printed on the label was *Hot Springs Hot Nights.* There was a television in the main room but I couldn't recall if there was a video tape player. I put away the box, closed the cabinet and closet, and took the tape with me. There was a tape player on a shelf next to the television. I thought about putting it in and watching it, but decided I better leave before the neighbor started to worry. She was the worrying type all right. I slipped the tape into my suit coat pocket.

Something kept me from barging out of the house. I opened the door a crack and peered out. Up the street, the neighbor woman was standing with two police officers; one was the officer in the neighborhood police box where I'd shown the pictures of the Mazda. She was telling them something, likely describing my odd behavior in whispered detail. I carefully closed the door. There was another exit—a door off the kitchen that led to a small garden. I skipped outside and crawled over a short stone wall. I hid there until the police officers left.

▸

As promised, I met the clerk at a coffee shop down the block from the Moonlight Travel Agency. "My mistake," I told him, "was to immediately mention Obushi's name when I visited the agency."

The clerk stirred his black coffee that he had sweetened with two sugar cubes. He slurped it as noisily as his slurped his noodles. "What should you have done instead?" He raised his hand before I could answer. "Let me try. . . . It would seem a good idea to mention Obushi's name because then you would seem like an insider, and the person or persons in the agency might be more forthcoming with information. How am I doing so far?"

I shrugged and took a sip of coffee.

"Okay, well then, um," the clerk sputtered. "You shouldn't have mentioned his name because you were tipping your hand, letting them know you had established a connection between Obushi and the agency. Right?"

I took another sip.

The clerk tapped his forehead as if that helped him think. "Okay . . . You should have waited, checked out the agency before jumping right in. This is an example of the principle I learned last night: never let them know what you know." The clerk smiled and lit a cigarette. "Yes, that's right. I'm ready to go."

The clerk was to act like a customer, I reminded him, nothing more than that. He was not to play detective. I asked the clerk if he could handle his assignment. "Yes," he said and let out a great cloud of smoke that floated over our heads. He stood up and stubbed out his cigarette. I watched him as he walked with his slumped shoulders and thick, unruly hair until he walked into the agency.

The waitress came by and asked if I wanted another refill but I waved her away with a jittery hand. Her smooth youthful face was a mask through which she looked at me with mild disgust. Perhaps I reminded her of her repressive father.

An hour later, at last, the clerk emerged from the agency, strolling casually and holding a piece of paper. He looked like someone who successfully booked a tour or cruise. He crossed the street and walked toward the coffee shop. But then without a glance at me, he passed by.

I watched him continue down the sidewalk, then into the four-level structure where we had parked. I paid the bill. The waitress was no doubt glad to be rid of me. I followed the clerk's path and found him standing by my car. He waited until I was next to him before he handed me the piece of paper and laughed.

Report

31 August: noon—At approximately 8:30 a.m. on 28th of August, the applicant in the referenced case returned to her home. Engaging her in a discussion of her whereabouts during the previous three days yielded a response of "visiting the family gravesite." While this explanation is certainly possible (although I have not investigated the claim as it is outside the investigation), it seems odd that she would leave without letting us know. She should have left contact information. On the other hand, perhaps she was content with the progress of the investigation and didn't feel the need to be present at all times.

In the other aspects of the case, there has been real progress. A connection has been established between the missing son and a photographer who worked with Mizuno on a book about butterflies, and who also had previous contact with the applicant. Also established is a connection between the Kuchi clan of fortunetellers and Obushi. Unfortunately, the photographer has also gone missing at this time. Further investigation on his whereabouts is warranted because he appears to be a key element in the case.

expenses:
58 km car

Yes, I left out a lot in that report, in particular, my interlude with Teruyo, her collaboration with the Kuchi thug, my fight with him and my night in the hole, and of course, the clerk. I will never mention the clerk.

My report was on the boss's desk along with the notepad and pen he always had at hand. "Sit," he commanded.

My inclination was to stand, ready to run out the door. But I obeyed.

"I'm afraid we've received a formal complaint from Shinshin Group. The complaint alleges harassment and trespassing."

"Bad breath and poor posture as well."

The boss allowed me the attempt at humor. "I assume from now on you will stay away from the art director."

"I will certainly avoid any unnecessary contact."

"Unnecessary and inflammatory. Words have consequences."

I wasn't entirely sure what he meant by inflammatory, but I would agree with him that words have consequences. Who wouldn't agree? "I understand," I said.

"Good. Then we understand how to proceed."

"Absolutely."

▸

I wasn't worried about breaking my promise because I wasn't sure what I promised. At this point in the investigation, I wasn't interested in the art director, although perhaps I might be later. I was mainly interested in the Obushi angle, especially what the clerk found in the travel agency, although at first the piece of paper he showed me had nothing much on it: a travel itinerary typical of any you might see. Flight times, hotels, excursions printed on perforated paper in barely legible dot-matrix characters.

"So?" I said to him.

"On the face of it," he said all serious, "one sees nothing, but it's well disguised."

"Huh? What's disguised?"

"The purpose of the trip, while seemingly a visit to a southeast Asian country for shopping, cultural sights, and relaxation, is actually a sex tour."

corporeal entity existed, she was another missing person. Someone should file an application for investigative services:

`Missing person's being, last seen being struck by a hit-and-run driver. Missing person's body resides in Room __, __ Hospital, ___Ward, ___ City. Signed, applicant (me).`

The fortuneteller's son, however, was not actually missing. The term is not accurate. For what does missing mean? The person is never missing in regards to him or herself, that is, a person can never be split away from him or herself. The so-called *missing person* is simply not observing a normal routine in the presence of the usual associates. The missing person has either met with a traumatic event (perhaps death) or has purposefully extricated him or herself from a context—his or her usual situation. The missing person in either case is actually *out of context.*

Mizuno might have simply been remaking his context after rejecting the his existence. His search for a new life led him out of his current context into one with a new environment, new relationships. If we know why an out-of-context person chose the new path, then we can focus on where the new environment exists.

Take the boxman I just passed by. His new context became the box along the river. Working backward through time, the man's motivation could be determined. Perhaps he was forced out of his home. Maybe he lost his job and couldn't find another. He could no longer handle his responsibilities.

I turned and walked back the way I came. The boxman and I exchanged nods when I passed him again.

▸

Meeting at my house, the clerk looked tired, as if he'd been working all night. His eyelids drooped. His two days of facial hair looked like gritty black sand on his pale skin. But I hadn't slept at all, so the clerk's appearance might have been a mirror image of mine.

"I rearranged them according to family name," the clerk told me, sounding brighter than he looked. “Is that the best way? There are many other ways to order a list as I’m sure you know.”

“That’s not important. Did you find any interesting names?”

“I didn’t have enough time to track down all of their identities, only the ones I thought sounded familiar. I found a couple of minor politicians, an actor, and a few criminals I matched from the public records.”

I looked at his list. Nothing jumped out at me.

“What do you think?” the clerk asked.

“Hard to say. We need to find some connection between Mizuno and Obushi. Or the fortunetellers. Any of these names could be a possibility, for example in an instance of blackmail or other extortion, but we would have to spend weeks or months going through them.”

“Extortion or blackmail? Now this is getting interesting.”

“It’s only one hypothesis so don’t get wrapped up in it. There are many others. Keep in mind, we have no idea if this will be fruitful.”

Again, the clerk looked disappointed. “What did you find?”

“Nothing yet. I only had a chance to glance through the list.”

“Let me finish going through the list. I might try to use our office computer.”

“Fine,” I said. “Good idea.”

The clerk stood up and gathered his lists. “Right. I’ll be off then.”

When my house reached a deep, unsettling quiet, I couldn’t believe I was wishing he hadn’t left.

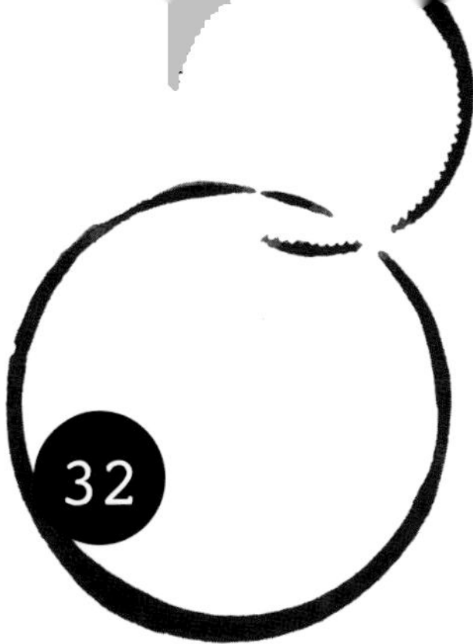

I am no connoisseur of pornography, but I can say confidently that *Hot Springs Hot Nights* was predictable and semi-professional. The plot had barely a pulse; what there was thready. The five vignettes showed guest couples involved in various sexual exploits: spouse swapping, infidelity, voyeurism. The actors were not well trained, not very attractive, and were distracted during the shoot, as if the director was constantly yelling at them. Making it worse, even laughable, the sound track was slightly out of sync with the video. The genitals of the actors were censored with unfocused squares, but sometimes they didn't completely cover the intended target or were incorrectly placed and all was visible.

I saw no particular reason why she would have this particular video, not that she couldn't simply have enjoyed it for its own sake. After all, hot springs resorts were apparently her favorite travel destinations. But nothing specific about the tape was associated with her.

Not until the end of the video when the credits were listed. The last one read:

`A Dreamlike Film in conjunction with Tomi Productions`

The fact that the production company of the video was in the same building as Midori Elegant Escorts might have some meaning. Or none. The production company might give overstock copies to employees in the office building. Midori's might keep them on hand for customers who liked to watch them with an escort. Maybe she found it at a hot springs resort and kept it when she noticed the production company listed in the credits. All were plausible, but there might be a more sinister meaning for having the video, especially considering that she kept it hidden in a box. Whether or not the tape had any significance to the hit-and-run was a more difficult question to answer. Nothing pointed to it. I pushed the rewind button on my tape player.

When the tape was back at the beginning, I punched play and tried to watch it again with a less critical eye and a more investigative view. I decided the video could be used successfully to torture prisoners of war. Halfway into the second vignette—a husband spying on his wife having sex with another guest in one of the baths—the resort manager discovers the husband. The manager peers through a bamboo screen at the action and whispers to the husband, "Nothing on television, eh?"

I paused the pause button of the tape player on the brief close-up of the manager delivering his inane line. It had been twenty years since I'd seen a photograph of the missing husband, but I believed it was him.

There was a bang on the door. Before I could get up, it opened and a troop of police officers burst through.

▸

Prosecutors in Japan have a ninety-eight percent conviction rate. In ninety percent of those convictions the criminals confess. Prison time in Japan is less of a hardship than being interrogated for days by zealous detectives. So when I entered the interview room, I was prepared to spend the rest of my life locked up.

They leave you alone in the room for an hour before starting. In that hour, you imagine the worst. The strong become weak, the weak become jelly, and the innocent become guilty. The seconds ticked as slowly as minutes, the minutes like hours. I was ready to confess. But no . . . I hadn't aimed my car at the wife. Had I? But they had evidence. The neighbor for one. I started snooping around her home shortly after the hit-and-run. Criminals always return to the scene of the crime, so they say. I don't believe it personally. Still, there I was snooping, not only at her home but also at her place of employment. Yes, I'd have to admit I was snooping around. Then there was my car, which was the same type as identified by the eyewitness. The detectives would say I'd done a good job fixing the damage, ask me which repair shop I used. Maybe they had been to the service shop near the fortuneteller's house. They could convince young mechanic he repaired the damage caused by the hit-and-run.

Also, the eyewitness said a man was driving. They would bring in the witness to have a good look at me. *Well,* he'd say, *it was dark, but yes, that's him.*

Of course, if the detectives were worth their salary, they would find out I was involved with the wife twenty years ago when her husband went missing. Perhaps they would go so far as to accuse me of being involved in his disappearance. They had their motive—she rejected me those many years ago and it had eaten at me, every day a kick in the gut of my failure. If I couldn't have her, nobody could.

It was a neat tidy package. I was ready to sign my statement of guilt. Undoubtedly sensing my weakness, one of the detectives came into the room. Before I could ask where to sign, he said, "You're free to go. For now."

It had to be a trick. "What about my car?"

The detective tossed me a large envelope. "Your keys are in there. The car is parked out front."

"Why are you letting me go?"

"You want me to change my mind? Beat it."

▸

Anger swept away the depressing sadness of realizing I was two people, split down the middle because of a rather unremarkable case. At least it was unremarkable on the face of it. I was cleaved in halves, one side sent tumbling down a curve toward negativity, the other arcing positively toward a bright future. At some point in time, the two had slowed, reversed course. We—me and me—now met.

No, my anger was directed at Teruyo, even though I'd played her as much as she'd played me. I felt a little something for her. In that moment, I realized Teruyo reminded me of the wife. More than that, Teruyo tore out my memories of the wife from the hole in my psyche, and showed me that I was not a real person and hadn't been for twenty years. She must have seen the part of me that was twenty years younger, for surely she wouldn't be attracted to me as a middle-aged man, nearing *old.*

I walked up the stairs to Teruyo's apartment. In the light of the yellow security lights posted high on the walls of the corridor, I was overcome with a sense of inevitability, a horrible momentum pushing me to my own destruction. Like matter and antimatter colliding in space creating a new universe.

Reaching her door, I knocked on it. When no one answered, I rapped louder. A door down the hallway opened a crack, I couldn't see a face in the darkness, then the door shut with a slam. Teruyo's door was locked. I hit it once more with my palm, then left. I positioned myself at the end of the corridor and watched for a moment, but no one opened the door.

I sat in my car for an hour, watching the building, but other than four residents who came or went, nothing happened.

▸

In the neighborhood of the Kuchi clan's fortunetelling operation there was a medium-sized shrine. In front of the shrine was an expanse of open space, delimited by a row of plum trees along one side and a row of cherry trees down the other. Between the rows of trees, two rows of vendor stalls offered food, games, good luck charms, paper wishes to be tied on the rope in front of the shrine, and fortunetelling. I found a bench where I could see the action without being involved. My life story to a good degree.

I gained my bearings and noticed a fortuneteller operating a simple stand slightly off the main row of vendors, as if she were an afterthought, or perhaps an unofficial stand operator trying to get in on the action. The fortuneteller had white hair, and her face was smooth and glowed to a burnished copper in the light from a candle burning on her table. Yes, it was the applicant.

I walked toward Mizuno Rie's stand, pausing at a few of the vendors, perusing their wares, feigning interest. As I approached her table, she smiled. "Hello," she said. "Please take a seat."

"I'm not sure you can help me," I said, mainly to see what her response would be.

"I'm not sure I can either, but we won't know until we determine what you need."

She had on a smile that she might give to a new customer. For whatever reason, she did not want to let anyone know she knew me. I glanced around but didn't see anyone within earshot. I sat in the chair and folded my hands meekly in front of me.

"I offer *teso* or *seimeihandan*," she said.

"I know about palm reading, but nothing of the other."

She placed a blank piece of paper and a calligraphy pen in front of me. "Please write your name."

When I followed her instructions she turned the paper and studied it for a moment. "The characters in your name have a total of twenty-four strokes. I can tell you what that means for your fortune."

"How is the fortune correlated with the number of strokes?"

"It's the ancient knowledge of patterns," she said with feigned seriousness. "You wouldn't want me to explain all of the ancient knowledge, would you?"

"No, I wouldn't."

"I didn't think so. You don't really want your fortune told, do you?"

"You are good. No, I don't. But I would be happy to pay for some information."

"An interesting proposition. What kind of information? Or do you want me to divine that as well?" She laughed and I joined her.

"You don't really believe in what you are selling, do you?"

"Of course I believe. Telling fortunes feeds me and puts a roof over my head."

"You're a different kind of fortuneteller. I mean, you are perfectly willing to admit it has no real basis in fact. It might produce a placebo effect in the client, make them do something that changes their life. But they could have done that anyway."

"That's one way of looking at it. Is that the information you are looking for? That I'm a fraud?"

I shifted in my seat to get more comfortable. "I'm interested in the setup here, for one thing. Don't you always do your fortunetelling at your home?"

She looked around the shrine grounds. "You mean, who runs the vendor stalls? The Kuchi family runs them, but the shrine actually owns the land. The Kuchis pay rent to the shrine, and the individual stall owners pay rent to the Kuchis."

"Why are you set up way over here by yourself?"

"I'm just across the property line. I don't pay the Kuchis to be part of the stalls."

"They must not like it."

"When they get sick of me, they send a strong arm or two over to act tough and scare away my customers. I have great patience and come back when they are gone."

"You are here because I mentioned the Kuchi clan in the course of my investigation. And you are one of the Kuchi family, aren't you?"

A frown formed slowly. "I left many years ago, before I married. There really isn't anything left between me and the Kuchis."

"Yet here you are."

She shook her head and went silent.

I dropped the line of questioning and instead I described the Kuchi thug to her. "Have you seen him?"

"If it's who I think it is, he's the Kuchi chief of security and collections. He sometimes does the work himself, sometimes with a couple of hoodlums. It depends on his mood."

"One more question," I said. "Have you seen a young woman with him?" I described Teruyo Motouchi. Her name slipped through my lips with the bitterness of too much familiarity.

She thought for a moment. "That sounds like Namiko, one of the Kuchi granddaughters. Does she talk in a very sophisticated way?"

"I'd say so, yes. She has a mole here." I pointed just under her left ear.

"That sounds like her."

I pulled out a few thousand-yen notes from my wallet and slid them across her table. "No thanks," she said.

"But I have to maintain the appearance of a paying customer."

"I will return it when we are alone."

"No need. I can just add it to my expense account." Not that I actually could.

▸

Outside the grounds of the shrine were several square blocks of restaurants, bars, gambling dens, and businesses with no names nor any immediately obvious purpose. In one of the benign, old-style bars, a grandfatherly type back in the kitchen poked his head out every five minutes, squinted at the customers then ducked back in. Their sake was medium grade and drinkable, the food traditional and bland but edible. There was a warbling folk song blaring over the loudspeakers. As I ate and drank, I wondered why Teruyo/Namiko was so interested in Mizuno Ren. If they were searching for him as much as I was, then he had something they wanted. Perhaps his life. So far, the connections I'd surmised were holding up, strengthened by the fact that Teruyo/Namiko was a Kuchi.

The medium grade sake went quickly to my head and I stopped thinking. At closing time, I walked out to find the nearest taxi stand to treat myself to a ride home instead of running to catch the last train. I was lost in the narrow streets when I heard a disturbance in the otherwise quiet night. Around the next corner, several salarymen were huddled over a prone figure. I thought at first he was one of their group passed out or puking, when I saw one of the salarymen pummeling away with his fists. The others egged him on. When I could see better in the dim light, I saw that the man getting beat looked much younger, maybe even just twenty. His face was bloodied, his hands in front of his face, and he was yelling, "Stop!"

When I shouted "Hey!", they stopped and stumbled away. I helped the young man to his feet. He wiped away the blood, pushed me aside, and ran after the others.

▸

I called Midori Elegant Escorts and asked for Ikumi. The meeting was arranged for an hour later at the coffee shop where I met her before. I got there in plenty of time and ordered coffee with plenty of sugar. While I waited I watched a man who had been following me. He was sitting at a table where he could keep an eye on me. I was sure he was a police detective. He was youngish, maybe thirty, obviously overeager in his job. Perhaps it was his first surveillance job. I'm not sure why he didn't care that I noticed him. All in all, it was worse than being interrogated. Being watched at every turn, with every sip of coffee, made me want to disappear permanently, become a boxman invisible to passersby.

When Ikumi walked into the coffee shop and saw me, she shook her head. "You?"

I slid an envelope toward her.

"What's this?" she asked.

"Your fee."

"Aren't you sure of yourself. What makes you think I will even sit here with you?" Still, she slid the envelope off the table and onto her lap. Where it went after that I couldn't guess. She dropped three sugar cubes at once into her coffee.

"All I have are a few questions," I said.

"Men like you always have questions."

Like me? I avoided the issue and asked her, "What do you know about Tomi Productions? It's on the second floor of your building."

Ikumi snorted out a loud laugh. The detective perked up and stared directly at us. "Of course you'd be involved with them. You like dirty movies."

"Tomi Productions may have something to do with the hit-and-run. She had one of their videos in her home. One of the actors on the video was someone she knows."

Her spoon clinked loudly against the cup. "Who is that?"

"Her ex-husband. I think she may have come to work at Midori's because she saw him on the video."

"That's kind of creepy, seeing your husband, ex or not, act in a dirty movie."

"He wasn't directly involved in any of the, um, sexual acts. Do you know anything about Tomi Productions?"

"Sure, the producer is always bugging us to be in his videos. That's the last thing I want to do."

"Has anyone been in them?"

She shrugged. "Maybe."

"How does he get his actors? Does he advertise?"

"How would I know? You're starting to bug me."

"Sorry."

After a sip of coffee, she said, "I might have seen an ad in *Midnight Blue*."

The slick weekly magazine was dedicated to those looking for any variety of sexual encounters without strings attached. "Thanks," I said.

"That's it?"

"Yep," I said. Surprisingly, she looked disappointed. Or maybe it was my imagination.

▸

I walked slowly toward the train station. The night was unusually quiet. The air was still and muggy. I turned past the station and down a path that was lined with small eating and drinking stalls. At the end of the path, I stopped at a stall occupied with only one other customer. The owner—an older man, maybe seventy—was talking with the customer but greeted me between words. I scanned the menu and ordered a beer and grilled eel. I ate and drank standing up at the counter. When I finished, I went back onto the path and walked toward the station. The detective was sitting on a low wall, smoking. He flicked his cigarette to the ground and stomped on it. As I walked past him I belched.

"Ahh," I said. "That felt good."

The detective pulled my arm, whirling me around. His face was screwed up in anger. "I'm sick of you," he said.

I didn't know what to say to that.

"You ran her down, didn't you. Tell me."

"I'm on my way home. Going straight there in case you lose sight of me."

"You're a real piece of work. Walking around like you own the world. Doing whatever you want. Chatting up young girls. You need to be brought down a peg." He slugged me in the stomach.

I doubled over as all the air was expelled from my lungs. He punched me again and I fell onto my side. He stood over me and lit another cigarette. He took a deep drag. As he let out the smoke he flicked ash on my face.

A thin line of red underlined the white dawn sky. I walked away from my house along the stretch of road that took me toward the edge of my neighborhood. No one saw me, not even a delivery van driver making an early run or the liquor store owner sweeping her storefront. They all failed to notice me. I was an invisible investigator walking toward nothing, away from nothing. The more I walked past stores and service stations and hotels and public baths, I no longer counted steps and my context diminished. If I kept walking toward the red horizon, at some point my context would disappear all together.

Then I would be an out-of-context person.

▸

I met the clerk later that day at his favorite bar. He had puffy dark bags as big as caterpillars under his eyes. He was without a thought in his head other than the list of clients from the Moonlight Travel Agency. It was a list now covered with his notes. He proudly showed it to me.

"This was a lot of work," I said.

The clerk beamed. "I found out at least a little something about two-thirds of the names."

"When did you have time to do your other work?"

"I told my supervisor I was onto a major fraud ring and needed time to work on it."

"He agreed to that? Didn't he ask you what it was about?"

"Not my weak boss. I told him I wasn't sure if it was anything and if it didn't pan out, it would probably be best if he didn't know anything. He agreed."

"You know him well."

"It helps keep him out of my hair."

I started looking at the first page of the list. It was hard to believe he'd done so much work in such a little amount of time. I estimated it would have taken me a week to do this amount of background checking.

I didn't see anything on the first page nor the second. On the third page, next to a name, Tomoguchi Mori, was written: "President, Shinshin Group Publishers."

The clerk must have seen my hesitation. "Something?" he said.

"Something," I said.

The clerk leaned forward. "Which one?"

I shook my head. "I need to be sure before I can say."

Disappointment furrowed the clerk's brow, his woolly eyebrows pushed together. "That's all I get? You saw something."

"Sorry. For now I need to keep it to myself."

"That's very disappointing. I worked hard."

"I appreciate your work, believe me. I couldn't have done such a good job in such a short time. But I want to check this one potential lead before I allow it to become a thread in a case that already has too many."

The clerk brightened. "I see. Another investigative principle. All right then. I'm going home to sleep."

"Sweet dreams."

▸

The possible, maybe even probable, connection established between the travel agency, Obushi, and Mizuno Ren, helped me regain some enthusiasm for the case. The chances of a coincidence were small, although the clerk might have said otherwise. But I needed there to be a connection, or the case would spiral out of control like an airplane without a rudder, a sled with only one runner.

I knocked on the door of Mizuno Rie's home. It opened by itself, as it was not latched shut. I stuck my head inside and said, "Hello?"

I stepped inside the entryway and a rush of dread seized me. I could hear light steps coming toward me. I could feel the hole drawing me into it.

But the fortuneteller appeared from out of the shadows. "Are you all right?" she asked me. "You don't look so good. I'll get some tea. Do you need something to eat?"

I was dizzy but not from lack of food. "No, thanks, I'll be fine with tea."

While she was in the kitchen, I slowed my breathing like a yoga practitioner and kept my focus away from the door leading to the fortunetelling room, away from the wallpaper with its deep, shadowy pockets. There wasn't much else to look at so I read the titles of the books across the room in the shelves. *Why Ghosts Appear . . .*

"Here we go," Mizuno Rie said. "I didn't think I would see you again so soon."

"I didn't either, but a question came up for you."

"Of course." She poured our tea and we sipped the warm, bittersweet liquid.

"To begin, I've made a few connections to your out-of—I mean, missing son. Did Ren ever mention a company president named Tomoguchi Mori?"

She thought for a moment then shook her head. "Ren never mentioned him."

I named the art director, to which she responded with a shake of her head. Then I mentioned the Moonlight Travel Agency.

"Sounds romantic," she said. "But no."

"I was wondering if you know what trips your son took during the last few, say three, years?"

"I don't know. Really I don't keep track of my son in that way. Besides that, he's always off somewhere. Actually, in the last three years, I can't say I know about any specific trips. Before that I did get some postcards. I thought he was too busy to send any more postcards." She looked into her cup.

Reading the tea leaves, I wondered? "Did you happen to save them?"

She blinked up at me. "Yes. I should have thought of them before. I'll get them for you."

She returned and handed me about fifteen postcards from overseas and domestic locations. The cards were wrinkled, faded, blotched with water drops. "They got wet once," she explained, "when I was watering some plants near them."

"May I have them for a while? I'll take care of them and return them."

"Keep them as long as you need. More tea?"

"No, thanks."

She put down the teapot. "We're running out of time, aren't we? Your week is almost up. I can't afford to pay for another week."

"We've made some good progress I feel. We should have a good solid break soon."

She smiled a little then said, "You've spent more time than you should have already, haven't you?"

"I don't punch a time clock. I work on a case as hard as I can without regard to a set number of hours. At least, I don't tell my boss everything I do. I have little else to do with my free time, so it's no hardship." What was all that rambling about? I gulped the tea.

"I feel it's not going to turn out well," she said. "Is there anything else I can help you with?"

I needed help. More than she knew. Then I looked at the fortuneteller with a new perspective. "That's why you went to your family grave, isn't it?"

"To pray to my ancestors for his return? Yes."

His return to his normal context, one should say, but of course that wouldn't help her with the pain. "I'm sorry I haven't found out anything positive at this point in the investigation."

"It's not your fault at all. I know you're trying as hard as you can."

That was just it, I couldn't say I was trying as hard as I could be. Too much else had been going on—real or imagined. My usual linear thinking was fading into twisted logic that wrapped possibilities around each other like tango dancers.

"Sorry," I said. "I wish I could tell you more about your son." I knew I was repeating myself. I was devoid of original thoughts.

"Really, if there is anything . . .," she said.

"Okay, could you tell me more about Kuchi Namiko, also known as Motouchi Teruyo?" I asked. "Specifically, does she know your son?"

"She's one of my cousin's youngest daughters. No, I don't think she and Ren ever met, even as children. I was never close with my cousin. Our side of the family had almost nothing to do with them. A family dispute before I was born." She gathered up the tea set, her hands fluttering.

"What is your cousin's name?"

"Kuchi Noriyo. She is the head of their empire now, at least that's what I hear. I don't know more than that. But if Ren is involved with Namiko, I'm afraid it's bad news."

I watched her sink into her misery.

34

The noodle stand owner smiled when I walked in. The smell of broth reminded me of the hole beneath the stand. "Your usual?" she asked, placing a glass of water in front of me. Despite her inviting smile, she had aged since my last visit. Things must have gotten worse.

While she turned in my order to her husband barely visible in the kitchen, I got out the postcards from my briefcase. I put them into two categories: one domestic, the other foreign. The domestic destinations were as one might expect from an entomological illustrator. A national park in Hokkaido, a forest in Aomori, a wilderness reserve in Kyushu. The note written on the back of each was always the same:

`Looking for the ________ insect. Little luck yet am holding out hope. At least the food here in ________ is good and the air is fresh. Bye for now.`

The woman glanced at the stack of cards as she brought me the pot of tea and poured. "Sending postcards?"

"Looking through some old ones."

"I like to do that too. Reminds me of other places."

"They weren't sent to me. A client. I'm looking for her son," I said.

"The fortuneteller you mentioned?" she asked.

Her husband's face appeared at the small window between the kitchen and the front counter. His eyes were large and with them he looked disapprovingly at his wife. He placed a steaming bowl on the counter. Filmy grease bubbles floated across the top of the broth.

"I didn't mean to be nosy," she said. "After you mentioned the fortuneteller I did a little asking on my own, and I think I saw her. Mid-fifties, strong looking face, slender, white hair."

I nodded.

"She's never been a customer so I didn't know her. You haven't found her son yet?"

As I shook my head, the husband appeared again at the window which seemed to be narrower each time I looked. It reminded me of the hole that was only a few feet below me. It reminded me of the coffee shop I'd spent so many hours chasing clues to the missing husband. Had the person behind that wall, whose hand I'd seen sending food out to the front, been the husband?

▸

The lobby of Shinshin Group was more elegant than I remembered from my first visit. Cambered stainless steel racks displayed copies of their books. Light wood accents softened the modernistic feel. A monstrous chandelier of tiny crystal snowflakes was the only visible light source, although there must have been hundreds of hidden lights. I killed time looking at the display publications while I waited for the art director. As I guessed, the substance behind the glossy book covers did not match the opulence of the lobby. Give me an old dog-eared second-hand book on philosophy or a hardboiled detective story stained with spilled coffee or cheap wine. Coming to the publishers hung my professional life in the balance. I knew that, but I had no choice. Something fragile yet substantive was hanging in the air like the wispy chandelier.

When the art director came down to the lobby, I apologized for my previous unprofessional conduct and requested to ask her a question or two.

"You could have called," she said.

"I tried. But you were always busy and no one would take a message. At least not from me."

"So you thought you'd invade."

"Invade? I must seem quite the brute to you."

"Never mind. I don't have time. Ask me your questions, then I'll hold you to your promise."

"You don't want to do this over a drink after work?"

She grimaced sourly and stood with her arms crossed defiantly. Of course, she was one of the last persons I would like to share a drink with. Suddenly, the lights went dim and the voluminous space began to close in on me. The art director gave me a look of disgust, as if dealing with a homeless man blocking her path simply because he couldn't move quickly enough out of her way. "Something the matter?" she asked.

"No, I mean, yes. Are the lights going out in here?"

She shook her head sadly.

"I'll hurry," I said. "Did Obushi and Mizuno often work together?"

She tapped the fingers of one hand on the opposite arm. "Depends on what you mean by often."

"I know of one book where both are listed in the credits. Would there be others?"

"There is more than one but I couldn't say how many."

"More than one, maybe fewer than ten?"

"Five or six, I'd say off the top of my head."

"I'd really appreciate the titles of those books, so I can buy them at my local newsstand."

"If you really will keep your promise, I'll give you copies. I'll leave them with the receptionist for you. It will take an hour or so."

"Really? That would be perfect."

"One other question," I said, although I wasn't sure she could hear me as my voice squeaked. "Did Mizuno Ren have any contact with the president of your company?"

"Our president?"

"Tomoguchi Mori?" I squeezed the name out of my constricted throat.

"I know our president's name," she said. "Of course not. He doesn't micro-manage. Why would our president have any contact with Mizuno?"

"What about Obushi?"

"Same answer. Anything else?"

A pulsing shimmer appeared in my peripheral vision, reducing the art director to a slender, dancing stick figure. I said, "No, that's all. Thank you."

"You don't look too well. You'd better see a doctor."

Rather than being split, which was like loosening the grip on one's soul, the phenomenon in the publisher's lobby was one of compression. My two selves were pushing on each other with considerable force. I carefully felt my way out of the publisher's building where I leaned against the building, no doubt looking like a man having an attack of some sort. I moved my head left and right trying to make use of what little I could of my visual field.

"Trouble?"

It was the clerk.

"How did you find me?" I asked. Miraculously I was quickly returning to normal. "Following me again?"

"No. I knew you'd be here sooner or later." He gave me his best grin. "I deduced from the page of names that you were looking at which of the names was most likely. Since you are looking for an illustrator, I assumed the publisher was the name of interest."

He was starting to sound like me. A wave of nausea swept over me at the thought. "I need something to drink." We found a nearby tea salon, where the clerk told me he found identities for a few more of the names. I wasn't interested. The connection had already been made. He must have sensed my lack of interest when he asked what I'd found at the publisher's.

"Nothing. And that's the truth."

"What do we do next?" the clerk asked.

"Drink tea and contemplate our misfortune."

The clerk opened his mouth to say something, then closed it and nodded. He closed his eyes and began to contemplate.

I sent the clerk on a benign task—digging up anything on the Shinshin Group president—and settled in with the copies of books I'd retrieved from the receptionist. With my stack of postcards, I was able to establish a timeline of when the books were published and the trips that Ren took.

2/20/1979 => Thailand, postcard 1980 => tropical beetle book
5/14/1980 => Hokkaido, postcard 1981 => wood beetle book
6/20/1982 => Arizona, USA postcard 1983 => spider book

The last postcard from Mexico was dated a little over three years ago. The book on butterflies came out about the correct interval after that, but then nothing. Next to the end of the timelines I added a column for Obushi. There was something at least. Another step, a vital establishment of context, a hope that the investigation would be fruitful in the end. If only I could fill in the gaps in a hurry. Not necessarily for Mrs. Mizuno, who could no longer finance the case, but because the case was slipping away from me. The latest episode at the publisher's left me with some doubt of my abilities.

I arrived at Obushi's camera shop where the *Closed* sign was displayed. I went around back and picked the lock. Inside, it took me only a few minutes in the developing room that still smelled of chemicals to go through his files and archived photos. I added dates and notes to the timeline.

1981 => Thailand, pictures of various insects and habitat, also nightlife scenes, bars, clubs, lights, streetwalkers

1982 => Philippines, pictures of birds and other insects, also nightlife scenes of similar subjects

1983 => Mexico, pictures of butterflies and forest habitat, also scenes of buildings and nightlife, young women in miniskirts

▸

I walked into the Moonlight Travel Agency and the agents began their "Welcome" chorus but ended in mid-phrase. They half-stood, like guard dogs high on their haunches, but sat down when Yamaguchi shook his head at them. I took the empty chair across from Yamaguchi.

"I'm sorry about the other day," I said.

Yamaguchi laughed. "You've got balls coming back. I've still got a bruise on my shin. You think an apology is going to be enough?"

"Nothing would be enough, so honesty won't hurt either. I'm a private investigator working on a case for a client looking for her missing son. Obushi worked with my client's son on a few book projects. I was trying to find out if Obushi knew anything about the missing son. Then Obushi turns up missing, or maybe dead. I found one of your brochures in his office, so I thought he might have taken a trip."

Yamaguchi said, "What was all the secretive stuff last time?"

I shook my head. "Habit. People don't generally open up to me. Most of them don't want to know the truth. A little lie here and there won't hurt, I figure, if it keeps everyone happy."

"You make a lot of assumptions."

"Another bad habit of mine."

"All you want to know is if Obushi is off on some trip?"

I nodded.

"Then the answer is no. At least not one through our agency."

"But he has booked trips with you? I assume that's why he had the brochure."

Yamaguchi hesitated before saying, "A couple of times. But that's important now, is it?"

"I wondered if he went regularly to any particular destination. You don't have any idea where he might be now?"

He shrugged broadly. "I don't know anything about Obushi."

I watched him for any sign he was lying. He stared back. I decided not to ask him about Tomoguchi Mori. "Thank you," I said. "Again, sorry about your shin."

"You've got balls," he repeated. "How about you, do you need a trip? You look like you could use one."

"I'm sure I could. I'll get back to you on that."

"And I bet you could use an extra spicy trip, you old fool."

▸

Most investigations circle in on themselves eventually, as do most of our everyday thoughts. Guided by a subconscious compass, our logic is inexorably circular. So I had no problem about chasing a circular lead for the Mizuno > Kuchi connection. If I could find out why Mizuno Rie fell out with her family, I might also find out if her son was entangled with them, and if that caused his disappearance.

At my office, I found a message from Mizuno Rie. She must be clairvoyant. I called her.

"You asked me if I knew a man named Tomoguchi. I don't know a man named Tomoguchi, but I remembered a woman client I had several years ago named Tomoguchi Yumiko. Tomoguchi Mori could be her husband."

"How did she come to you?"

"That's also interesting. Your question about my husband's death reminded me of her visit. When she called to set the appointment, she told me she read about his death in the newspaper."

"Your occupation was listed in the newspaper story."

"How did you know?"

"A guess. What did Mrs. Mori want?"

"It was a long time ago. But I believe she came three or four times to my house concerning her husband's future success in business as well as her husband's future success in obtaining mistresses. If I remember correctly, her marriage line looked long, and her fate line appeared to have wealth in it. But there was a strong indication of some crisis that would have to be overcome."

36

Report

2 September: 6:15 p.m.—Progress has been made. A timeline has been established documenting the whereabouts of the missing son leading up to nearly the present time. A connection has also been established between the missing son and a photographer who has also gone missing. Particulars are seen in the attached timeline. The connection is further established by a link between the two and an apparent fraud case, although this instance might be a coincidence. Further connections have linked the two missing men and the president of the publishing group who hired both of them and the applicant. It appears that drawing these threads together will result in a resolution of the case.

expenses:
48 km car
¥880 subway
¥900 coffee (in exchange for services rendered)

"What's this?" my boss demanded. He underlined the coffee expense with his pen.

I was tired of paying for the clerk out of my pocket. "A clerk in the metropolitan fraud office has helped me run down the identities of several people on a travel agency list. It allowed me to make the connection I described in my report. It's a cheap price for all his work."

"It's not the cost obviously. Paying a government clerk can lead us into all sorts of problems. Public official malfeasance, that sort of thing."

"Two cups of coffee?"

"It's a sensitive issue. We can't be associated with any kind of corruption. These things have a tendency to spiral out of control, get blown out of proportion. Also, your report is vague and full of supposition. What's this about drawing threads together? It's all quite troubling. Please resubmit your report."

The meeting with the boss left me with a need for a drink. And I satisfied that need at a little drinking place near the office. I rarely went there, preferring not to be anywhere near the office when I drank. My new report read like this:

Met with client at 2:30 p.m. for 45 minutes. She gave me 14 postcards of the following locations listed in the appendix. The last one came three years ago from Mexico.

expenses:
48 km car
¥880 subway
¥900 parking fee

▸

The Tomoguchi home was in a new tract of land carved out of a hillside. In comparison with the average house, theirs was a mansion of two stories with bright blue ceramic roof tiles, stucco finish sparkling in the sun, a gated wall, and precisely trimmed grounds. I rang the buzzer embedded in the wall in a gold plaque. After only a moment came the voice through the tiny speaker, "Yes?"

"Tomoguchi Yumiko?"

"Who is it?" the voice was insistent.

"Sorry to bother you, but I'm searching for a missing person and believe you could help me."

"A missing person? Who?"

"The son of your fortuneteller. It won't take much of your time to answer my questions."

"What? Fortuneteller? . . . Wait there, I'll meet you at the gate."

We sat on a veranda overlooking her garden. She told me it was designed after the garden of a Kyoto temple when I mentioned its beauty. Three landscapers were carefully pruning trees. Her posture was as rigid as a board and she kept one eye on the workers.

"I had no idea Mizuno Rie's son was missing," she said. "But I don't see how I can help. I haven't seen her for many years and I never met her son."

"I'm just asking all the routine questions. Following procedures."

She gave me a nod as if that made sense to her. "I'll do what I can, of course, but . . . well, go ahead."

"Did you know Mizuno Ren did freelance illustration work for your husband's company?"

She laughed. "I'm sorry. My husband knows very little of the details of his company. He told me he likes it that way. He tells me even less, so you can guess how I will have to answer that question. But anyway, shouldn't you ask my husband that question?"

"I've tried to call him. He's out of touch, at least with me."

"He's usually out of touch with me as well. He often travels for business."

"Business," I repeated. "How about for pleasure?"

She hesitated before answering. "I hardly see how that's relevant."

"I understand," I said. "It's just that, well, there seems to be a connection between the son and his travels while working for your husband's company."

"My husband never mentioned it to me, if that answers your question."

"Thank you, yes. It's rather coincidental that the son worked for your husband's company. I'm also curious about your session with Mizuno Rie."

Something caught her eye in the distance. I followed her gaze to one of the gardeners trimming a tortured-looking pine. She stood up and said, "I'm sorry but I must attend to something. Would you be so kind as to show yourself out?"

"I've never been that kind in my life."

She gave me a squinting, confused look then scurried toward the gardener. I felt very sorry for him.

▸

Back in my neighborhood, I picked up a *Midnight Blue* at my local newsstand. The owner didn't lift an eyebrow. "For a case," I let him know anyway. He nodded. I took home the magazine and perused the ads. Nothing tempted me—all the proposed sexual activities sounded too energetic. I found the ad for Tomi Productions in the middle of the ads for "sexual gourmets," the code-filled ads led me to believe they weren't offering anything I'd want.

I called the number and a woman answered. "Tomi Productions. May I help you?"

"I'm inquiring about your advertisement in *Midnight Blue* looking for actors."

"We are looking for experienced actors between twenty and thirty," she said emphatically. She could tell by my voice I was older than her cut-off age.

"To be honest, I'm older than that. But a friend of mine told me you use more mature actors for bit parts. My friend was in *Hot Springs Hot Nights* for instance. I was hoping I might be considered for one of those parts."

"Who was this friend?"

I gave her the name. "Actually I've lost touch with him recently. He isn't by chance still in your stable of actors, is he? He could give you a reference if that's needed."

"I don't know that name, but I could check with the producer."

"Sure, that would be great. He played the husband in the video I mentioned. I'd appreciate it if you could find a way to contact him. I owe him some money, to tell you the truth. I'm sure he'd be glad to get it. I'll give you my phone number if you could call me back."

"I suppose, but I will have to talk with the producer first."

"Of course. Thank you. You've been very helpful, you know."

"You're welcome."

▸

Surprisingly, the employee who answered the phone at Tomi Productions called back. She told me they weren't hiring actors with my characteristics but she did have a contact number for the actor in the video. He was not using his real name, of course. To them, he was known as Hattori. I thanked her profusely again.

I tried the number several times but there was no answer. Using a reverse phone directory, I found Hattori's address. I snuck out the back of my house to avoid my shadow—if he was still following me. I couldn't say for sure, as I hadn't seen him for a day.

It was an hour drive to the neighborhood, a row of rundown homes along the edge of an industrial district. I parked in a narrow space off the side of the road that was streaked with muddy tire tracks. Hattori's house was in the middle of the block, not much more than a shack that looked like it was being held together and kept upright by the two adjacent buildings. I didn't see any activity in the house after a few minutes.

At the door of the house, I listened and heard nothing. I knocked but there was no answer after several seconds. I tried the doorknob and find it locked. I went to a window. It was covered with a curtain and I couldn't see inside.

"Hello?" I heard someone say.

A man had materialized on the street behind me. He was carrying a small plastic sack from a convenience store. "Hello," I said. "Do you live around here?"

The man looked around as if he wasn't sure where he was. "Yep. At the end of the block."

"I'm looking for a friend. Hattori is his name. I thought he lived here, but I don't know for sure. It's been a while since I've seen him. He'd be about my age." I described him.

The man chomped his gums. "Maybe. But people come and go. I can't keep track of everyone. Nobody stays put anymore." With that pronouncement he walked away.

I waited until the street was clear and then tried the window. The latch was set but loose and with a few jiggles it came undone. I looked around again then slid it open and crawled in. The house smelled of unwashed clothes left to sit too long. There wasn't much inside—a small table with two chairs, a television on a cheap stand, and a rickety wardrobe chest. I looked through the wardrobe, found a pile of shirts and pants and underwear, a pair of tennis shoes, and a scuffed pair of black dress shoes.

The small kitchen was barely wide enough to stand with one arm outstretched. There was a tiny sink, an electric two-burner hot plate, and a small fridge, which held only two cans of beer and some takeout containers. I poked around a little more but found nothing of interest, nothing to indicate the identity of the occupant.

I went back to my car and sat in it. The late afternoon sun was hot and I rolled down the windows. I berated myself for not taking the cans of beer. It cooled off immediately when the sun went down, but my throat ached and I was feeling woozy by the time it was dark. An hour into the night, as my stomach growled and my hands were shaking, a figure of a man came up the street and stopped at the door.

The darkness hid his face as he unlocked the door. Before he went inside, he flicked something into the gutter. It exploded in a flash of sparks—a cigarette butt. And then he was gone, and the door shut.

If it was the missing husband, what was I going to do? I suddenly realized I had no plan, barely a motive for tracking him down. I had nothing to say to him, not after all these years. Other than tell him that his wife, his ex-wife, was in a coma, I had nothing to say. He'd have nothing to say to me of course. He didn't even know who I was. He would have no idea that I'd spent a week trying to find him twenty years ago, and still thought about him.

I got out of the car, my heart racing. As I walked across the street, I realized that I wanted to ask him why did he disappear twenty years ago. I banged on the door. I waited several seconds then lifted my hand to knock again. Before I could land the blow, the door burst open, and the force threw me to the ground. When I looked up, the man was running down the middle of the street. He turned briefly and his face was momentarily illuminated in the glare of a security light from the industrial area. His face was drawn together in fear, but the strangest thing, the miraculous thing, was that he looked like me.

For a long minute or two after he disappeared down a side street, I sat on the ground, dampness seeping though my clothes, my mind steeped in turmoil. I got up and brushed off my clothes. I looked in the open door and saw a crumpled piece of paper on the floor that hadn't been there before. I picked it up—it was a flyer for Midori Elegant Escorts. Attached to it was a clipped ad for Tomi Productions from *Midnight Blue*.

I trudged back to my car, cupping the flyer in my hands as if it were an injured bird.

An unexpected call came from the chief. I arrived in the office as several of the company's investigators were leaving for night surveillance, carrying bags of cameras, lenses, and low-light film. I wasn't very good at that kind of technical work. The other investigators gave me a collective nod. They looked exhausted and still had a long night ahead.

The boss was at his desk, a folder open. He gestured me to sit in a chair. I followed his orders and waited for the surge of current that would overload my nervous system and complete my execution. Or would it? I might be permanently split in two, one side a *yurei*, one side an *obake*. I'd haunt my supervisor as a *yurei*, no doubt, but what place would I haunt as an *obake*? Probably my local pub, where I'd hang out for an eternity, or at least an indeterminate amount of time. The oddity of a ghost haunting the pub might increase the number of clientele.

The chief said, "I contacted the applicant in the Mizuno case and she informed me that she could not afford another week of our time. Do you think you can resolve the case tomorrow? If not, perhaps we should consider ending the case now and returning some of her fee. I don't want it to look as if we are taking advantage of her."

He was being uncharacteristically generous. I said, "In my last two reports, I documented my progress. But I can't predict if it will be solved or not. All I can do is try my best."

The boss thumbed through my reports. "I can't say I have much confidence in a resolution in twenty-four hours."

When put in hours, the time did seem daunting, even impossible. But I was not in the mood to give up all that I'd put in so far. But it wasn't up to me so I remained silent.

My boss slowly closed the file. "You have nothing to say?"

"I apologize for the haphazard nature of my reports. I've been quite involved in the case; perhaps this prevents me from being more professional."

"It's never good to become personally entangled in a case. You know that."

"Sometimes it can't be helped."

The boss tapped the folder. "Let's consider the Mizuno case closed. I'll assign you a new case in the morning."

▸

The hospital was closed to visitors by the time I arrived. I missed another chance to visit the wife from the old case. Another missed chance to see the two halves of my life collide at the intersection of the two opposing curves. If I waited too long to connect them, I would remain split, one side winging off one direction, the other in the opposite. Only in another twenty years would the curves intersect.

All of the interactions with the wife folded into a single structure of events like a clever origami. Her bright curtains, her freckles, her beer drinking. So many other memories that I couldn't sort into fantasy or reality. Not that it mattered, I had no way of analyzing my memories objectively. They were like sisal fibers in a rope, twisted together to make a strong single object, each individual fiber now unimportant, giving its identity to the larger identity of a rope.

"Sorry," said the hospital receptionist again. She barely looked at me over a stack of forms. "Visiting hours are over."

"Visiting? It's me who is sorry because I didn't make myself clear. I'm in need of a doctor."

"You need emergency treatment? I thought you said you wanted to visit someone. What are your symptoms?" she asked, pen poised over a form.

"It's as if I'm splitting in two. One part of me goes off and does one thing, another side goes somewhere completely different and does something else."

The woman gave me a long look then wrote my symptoms in a box on the form. "Have a seat."

▸

The doctor took all the usual measurements. "Nothing abnormal," she said. "How long have you been feeling this way?"

"Twenty years."

She shook her head. "Did you say twenty years? Why are you only now coming in for an exam?"

"I didn't realize I was having symptoms until now." I gave her a synopsis of my theory of the opposing curves of my life.

She coughed. Nervously, I thought.

"Are you taking any medications?"

"None."

She made a clucking sound. "Perhaps I should have asked if you have stopped taking prescribed medications?"

"I haven't been prescribed medication."

She checked my pulse, temperature, blood pressure. "Wait here," she said.

After she left, I buttoned my shirt and went out to the corridor. I found a sign that directed me to a wing of patient rooms. I went up a staircase to avoid the elevator.

In the patient wing, I checked the names written on erasable sign boards next to the doors: Shimada Y., Karaki B., Kashigawa R., Abe K., Moto S., Sato R., Hori H., . . . it would have helped if they put them in a more logical order.

"Hey, where are you going?"

It was my doctor.

"I'm feeling much better," I said.

"You can't just walk out of an examination like that." She grabbed my arm and steered me around. "The staff psychiatrist wants to talk with you."

▸

The psychiatrist offered no possible theory to my splitting problem. In fact, he seemed not the least bit interested. I thought my symptoms were unique, and diagnosing me would make him famous. My syndrome would have his name attached to it. Instead he ran me through a battery of tests, psychological profiles, and questionnaires. It was like one of those consumer surveys, like do you own your own home? If so, do you spend more than ten thousand yen a month on kitchen cleaner? If so, do you purchase in bulk?

If he had the least bit of imagination, he would have asked what I was doing wandering around the patient wing. On further probing he would have discovered my obsession with a woman whom I'd met twenty years ago and whom I believed was responsible for my split being. If he was on the ball, he would have asked what I was going to do when I finally saw her again. That would be a good question. Yes, if I found her . . . what would I do? I didn't know, other than to ask her if she had felt anything for me, anything other than indifference. If she had felt something for me, then I would know which curved path to take—the negative one or the positive.

The psychiatrist deemed I wasn't a danger to society, although it wasn't clear how he arrived at that diagnosis. He gave me a mild sedative to take when I returned home.

When I was released, I drove to the shrine near the Kuchi compound. I found a place to park on a side street, off the main arterial that was choked with cars. I felt the pressure of time, which reminded me of the agonizing compression I'd experienced in the publisher's building.

Mizuno Rie was again telling fortunes at the edge of the shrine grounds. She was with two young women, both maybe twenty years old. Each in turn squealed at their fortunes. They bowed several times before they walked arm-in-arm toward their happy lives.

The fortuneteller acknowledged me with a serious nod. I sat in one of her client's chairs, still warm from the body heat of the young woman.

"Two happy customers," I said, hearing them squeal once again.

"For now."

"They won't remain happy?"

She gazed toward them. "Probably not." Looking back at me she said, "Are you here to end the investigation?"

"I still have a few hours." I lied. The case was officially closed.

"Is there anything I can do to help?" she asked.

"I'd like you to tell me my fortune please. *Teso* style." I placed two thousand-yen bills in the plastic basket on the table.

She took my left hand in hers and lightly traced over the lines in the light of her portable lantern.

"It's a nice palm," she said. Her fingertips were soft as cotton swabs. Her touch was sensuous and comforting.

"A long life," she began vaguely. Then she gave me several other highlights: a couple of serious health episodes, no more marriages but another love, never any wealth, a strong heart.

"Something else," she said. "Your life line splits dramatically, in the direction toward the line of creativity, and then toward the eye. A visual artist, maybe a photographer, will open a dual path for you. But it will end badly."

The previous night hung heavily on me even though I hadn't had much to drink. To revitalize myself, I made a soft-boiled egg and put it over a bowl of steaming rice. The egg was almost uncooked with some of the white still transparent, the yolk a viscous orange-yellow lava. On top of that I sprinkled dried seaweed flakes. I sipped coffee from the mug I washed once a week. It was the picture of bachelorhood.

While I ate, I searched through several newspapers for any mention of the death of a camera shop owner named Obushi. There was nothing. But there had to be, according to my fortune. Maybe I took it too seriously. Then again, why should I be so enthralled with what she said? I couldn't explain why I had her tell me my fortune in the first place. I certainly never thought I would take it seriously. My loneliness got to me, perhaps. Paying two thousand yen for twenty minutes of human companionship seemed extravagant yet at the same time a necessary expense. Although it wasn't an expense I could claim, even if I were still on the case of the missing son.

Earlier, I called into the office, told them I was suffering an illness. Then I walked down to the newsstand and bought the stack of newspapers. The newsstand owner was wearing a beret and, when I complimented him on it, he said he was trying to jazz up the joint. Perhaps that's what I needed, a beret. Or a Panama hat. Jazz up my joint too.

I finished my humble breakfast. I didn't know if the fortuneteller was giving me what I wanted to hear, or if she honestly read what she saw. I believed she knew more than she was telling me about Obushi and her son.

But more likely, I was thinking too much. Our brains never shut down completely. In the areas of activity where scientists measure our conscious states, we find only the most obvious of our mental life. Mine had mutated over the years into a black sea at night. Like in an expanding universe, as ours is now believed to be, eventually all the stars will be gone, too far away to be visible.

▸

The metropolitan coroner's office was in a three-story building, just off the expressway. I parked and went inside. The serious odor of official business filled the air in the stark reception area. When I got my bearings, I asked how it might be possible to find out if and how a particular person died. The officer on duty told me to fill out a form and he'd notify me in a week.

"A week? That seems like a long time."

"You know how many people die every day?" he asked wearily.

"I believe it averages five hundred for the metropolitan area."

The officer didn't blink at my guess. He said, "As a matter of fact, it's five hundred twenty six."

I walked out and drove away, wondering if the fraud clerk could help me get a quick answer. But then I'd have to see him. He'd want to know the status of the case and I'd have to tell him I was off it. He'd be disappointed and want to continue on his own. I'd have to explain I didn't want him involved; it was time I worked alone again. I'd gotten myself too deeply into the case and I didn't want to drag the clerk down with me.

I tried to clear my head and think. The number one priority I came up with was answering the question: Why was Obushi missing or dead? His connection to the missing son was established. He was connected to the Kuchi clan, and possibly to the travel agency, which in turn was connected to the president of the publishing house. Find Obushi and find the son—that was my mantra.

Once again I broke into his camera shop looking for any clues. Dust was already beginning to settle on the filing cabinets and display cases. I checked through the files, looked at all of the pieces hanging on the wall, even behind them to see if something else was hidden in the frames. The place had an air of finality. The camera shop owner was never coming back. Even if he were alive.

Obushi had come to a bad end. I could feel it now. It was my fault, at least to some degree. The only reason I came across the lead on the camera shop owner and photographer to begin with was because the art director claimed the son was dead. And since I was skeptical of the applicant's claim that her son was missing, I went to the metropolitan fraud office. A roundabout way of finding the key link to all those involved in the case.

But I had no reason to believe it wasn't a good solid clue. I'd based many investigations on less. Even the case of the missing husband was based on a box of matches from a coffee shop. A simple clue that started me down the chain of events.

I closed up the camera shop, likely for the last time.

A realization struck me, like a clap of a bell calling in the New Year. I drove like a maniac, weaving between lanes, well over the speed limit. I knew where the connection was, or most likely was. It was in Mizuno Ren's apartment. Yes, I'd already been there three times, but obviously I hadn't looked in the right places. Or at the right things. Or at things in the right way. There were too many combinations of reality. It made me dizzy.

I let up on the gas pedal. I had time. I was no longer under the clock for an applicant or the office. The effort I was making, this expenditure of time, was mine to spend. I took a deep breath and let out the stale air of too much thought, of inefficiency, of disappointment. I took a deep breath of the exhaust-tinged air.

Rain started falling when I arrived at the apartment building. It took me several loops around to find a parking spot. My impatience was growing and I almost parked in an illegal loading zone when a spot opened.

I bound up the stairs trying to dodge the rain, not successfully, but not caring. Mizuno's apartment door was unlocked. I opened it enough to peer inside. A single light was on. I ducked in, shut and locked the door. I took quick stock of the apartment—it was sanitized, as if gone over thoroughly before being restored to pristine condition. Someone else had gone through the apartment. That's what Teruyo/Namiko was doing here the first night. How could I have fallen for her excuse of taking care of the place for Mizuno Ren? She fooled me.

I went into the kitchen and looked through the cupboards, found nothing. In the lower cabinets I also found nothing except a cockroach that scurried away into a crack and disappeared. The drawing table had nothing on it or under it, except the pile of sketches I had already inspected. In the bedroom I found nothing new in the drawers nor wrapped up in the bedding. I opened the grate of an air conditioning unit, checked in the bathroom cabinet. Nothing, anywhere. I sat in the chair where I first talked with Teruyo and toyed with the idea of seducing her, if that was what people did anymore. I doubted it. There was never seduction anymore, only a word was necessary: "Sex?" I must have seemed quaintly old-fashioned to her, she knew what I desired, what I needed but I shyly danced around the issue. All the while she was laughing to herself, saying, "Come out with it, you old fool. Say it. Sex!"

I was about to leave when I thought again about what the fortuneteller told me.

What had she said exactly about the fork in my lifeline that would be caused by a visual artist or photographer? Something about a collision of creativity splitting my lifeline. I should have written it down. How could I have forgotten already? A collision . . . that's what happened to the stack of drawings, notes, clips from newspapers, cutouts of photographs. An undone, deconstructed collage. An abstract artist's stained glass window, ready to be assembled.

I got to work, laying everything on the floor.

It turned out to be a mess. No matter how I arranged the pieces, the elements of the collage wouldn't come together clearly. Something must be there, the problem was I couldn't see it. It must have been a crazy idea to begin with. Perhaps there wasn't one big picture, maybe there were a few pictures. Was I was missing some of the pieces?

I went down to my car to retrieve my briefcase. As I was about to go back up to the apartment, there was a knock on my window. It was the clerk. I motioned for him to get in the passenger side. Rain dripped off his hair plastered to his skull.

"Do I need to ask how you found me this time?" I asked.

"How am I supposed to answer that question? How can I know what you're really asking me?"

"That's the correct answer."

"I can't say it was easy. But I did. How's the case going?"

"I'm no longer on the case."

"What?"

I wasn't in the mood for explaining, and there was no reason to explain anything to him. I wanted to be alone with the puzzle. I focused my gaze out the windshield. "See the restaurant down the block?" I said. "I'll meet you there in a few minutes."

The clerk started to say something but I held up my hand. He obediently got out and walked toward the restaurant. I went up to the apartment with my briefcase and spread out the pieces I'd gotten from Obushi's shop. As I fiddled with the bits and pieces of art, sketches, and photographs, a picture gradually emerged. At least what I thought was a picture. I numbered the pieces on the backs to provide a map of how they went together.

I went to the restaurant, which was full of younger singles and couples. Jazz played in the background. The man who seemed to be owner worked behind the bar. He was tall and dressed in a casual pullover shirt and jeans, looking more like a bohemian writer than a bar owner. Maybe he was a world famous novelist. I ordered a beer; the clerk was already working on a glass of plum *shōchū.*

"I can't believe you're off the case," the clerk said.

"I'm not off the case as you put it. My section chief closed the case because there was not enough progress."

"Even after all I did to help?"

"Even after all that."

The clerk gulped from his tall slender cocktail glass. "Then what are you doing out tonight, if not still working on the case?"

"I told you, the case is over." The lie was literal, the case was over. I was working on what used to be the case. "I was there clearing up a few misunderstandings I created, but apparently it wasn't necessary. Look, I'm not telling you a lie. I can't tell you what to do but you need to forget about the case. There are some dangerous people I've run across during the investigation. I don't think that you would want to stay involved. These people might make you disappear. Like Obushi."

"You couldn't find him? Wait, you know he is dead, don't you?"

"Dead or alive, it's the same thing for Obushi."

"This isn't right," the clerk said, pulling a cigarette out of a pack. It was the last one and he crumpled the pack and tossed it onto the table. "We've invested too much."

"It's loss cutting," I said. "My company also wants to avoid potential lawsuits or scandal."

"Weak. Your company is weak." He blew a cloud of smoke and disappointment in my direction.

▸

I cleared a space on the floor of my house where I constructed the collage. It was indeed a scene, one that looked familiar but not necessarily one that I'd seen before. Perhaps my subconscious had been putting together the pieces while I was sleeping. The scene consisted of several elements. The main background was of a street in a Latin American country: buildings of stucco walls, half of which were photographed, half were sketches or drawings. There were faces poking out of the buildings, young women, killing time perhaps. Their faces were thin, eyes large but bored. Further behind the street scene were insects, especially butterflies. A crowd of men congregated in the center of the street. Their faces were hidden due to the angle of the photograph—high above them, as if taken from an upper story window from a nearby building. The handful of men formed a predatory semicircle around a young woman wearing a pink dress. She was folded in on herself as if trying to consume her soul.

Standing on a chair I took several photographs of the collage. Then I disassembled the collage and hid the pieces underneath a chest of drawers in a false bottom.

The rain let up later that night, and I went out in my car to the neighborhood of the Kuchi clan. The air was refreshing but the rain had cleared away most of the customers. The vendors were putting up their stands for the night. I couldn't see the applicant in her usual spot so I looked around the grounds to see if she had moved. I didn't see her anywhere.

I walked over to one of the vendors. "Excuse me," I said. "You wouldn't happen to know where the white-haired fortuneteller might be?"

The woman said, "She got kicked out by the boss, then the rain came, so I guess she gave up for the night."

"The boss? You mean the Kuchi thug?"

The vendor tapped her skull. I guessed the gesture meant I was daft for asking such a stupid question. I didn't have the time to prove otherwise. "Did she go home?"

"Need your fortune told badly, huh?"

"Something like that."

"I don't know. She didn't tell me and I'm not a fortuneteller."

"Okay, thank you," I said.

I headed toward Mizuno Rie's neighborhood. The general store was still open and I stopped there. The family who owned the store also lived there, I could see into them seated around a television, the flickering blue glare gave me the feeling of visiting friends.

"Welcome," a woman said, jumping up and moving behind the counter. She kept one ear cocked to the sound of her television program. I heard a muffled peal of laughter.

I asked her, "Do you know the fortuneteller who lives just up the hill?"

The woman's smile remained frozen on her face but she didn't say anything.

"She has white hair. I'm meeting her and I thought I'd bring her something to drink. Would you happen to know what she prefers?"

The woman nodded and smiled. "Oh, Mizuno. Yes, she likes white wine."

"Then I'll have your best bottle of white wine and two large bottles of beer for me."

Another peal of laughter made the woman hurry to fill my order so she could return to her program.

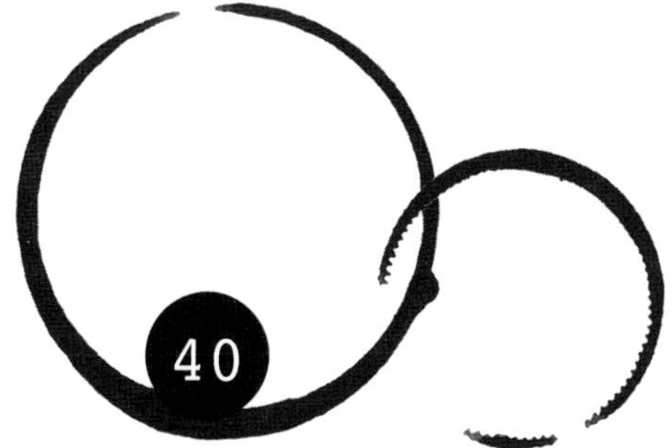

We made ourselves comfortable on cushions in front of the low table.

"You know what I like to drink," she said with a smile. "Impressive."

"Nothing as magical as your fortunetelling, which has helped me make progress finding your son."

"I'm happy to hear I could be of help."

"I'm not interrupting your evening, am I?" I asked.

"Not at all."

Something in the way she said "not at all" caught my attention. The tone made it sound almost as if she had been expecting me. The more I got to know her, the more she radiated layers of a complex personality unlike anyone I had recently encountered. Most people, nearly all I should say, are quite simple. They've developed a routine in life, they exist by four or five rules, have four or five experiences on which they've defined their lives. For example, take a salaryman, the unit of the Japanese post-industrial economy, the most abundant element of the white-collar economy. His routine: work (including maintaining social and professional relationships), home life (just enough to maintain his connection), personal life (make the most of this as the time averages only a few precious minutes per day). His rules: work at the same pace as the others in his level of work (i.e., neither more nor less), maintain a stable home life (i.e., neither above nor below his means economically or emotionally, make sure his two children get into a good college), allow himself one personal pleasure (e.g., fish, watch TV, golf, have a favorite bar hostess). His highlights: getting into college, getting his first job, finding a wife, having a child, losing someone or something precious, experiencing a disappointment and a success.

Not that the human psyche can't handle more. It's not that each person isn't a complex mix of emotions and thoughts and beliefs. But the brain is most comfortable with a minimal mix. If there is a feeling of dissatisfaction, likely it's buried beneath the superficiality of existence. It must be an evolved survival instinct. For if all of us only existed to satisfy internal self-centered desires, society would break down in a few days. Humans cannot exist as pure individuals.

"You were on target with the fortune you told me," I said. "The collision of creativity was in the realm of visual arts as you said. It let me look at what I'd been seeing in a new light. It's a classic case of viewing life through rose-colored glasses."

She said, "That's really what a fortune is, a good fortune anyway. It allows one to change perspective, letting a person focus on a different aspect of a problem. It's the maxim that any change is good. I could have told you anything and it would have helped."

I agreed with her. We sipped our drinks for a while before I asked, "Do you have any other information on the Kuchi clan? For one thing, I'm curious about how they would defraud a client."

She put down her wine glass. "As much as I wanted to sound brave the other night when you asked me about the Kuchi clan, I don't want to become involved in their business."

"Understandable," I said. "You wouldn't be involved. Not directly."

She thought for a few moments. "They have three main ways of working a fraud. The first is to simply take advantage of a particularly gullible person who is desperate for a fortuneteller to give him some particular advice that allows him to do one thing or another. Often he is in dire straits regarding a business or personal crisis. The fortuneteller strings him along with bits and pieces, just enough so that he comes back for more. At an ever increasing fee, of course."

I asked, "Between meetings, what kind of information does the fortuneteller find out about the client?"

"As much as possible. That way the fortuneteller becomes more legitimate in the eyes of the client."

"Adding fuel to the fire. How does the fraud usually end?"

The fortuneteller frowned and shook her head slowly. "When the client has no more money."

"That must be devastating to the client."

"Strangely, clients are not so upset to have spent all their money, but rather they are shocked that the fortuneteller will no longer tell their fortune."

"It's like being a drug addict?"

"I suppose that's an apt comparison."

"Do the clients often seek to have the authorities prosecute the fortuneteller?"

"Rarely. Even if they come to their senses, they are often too mortified and embarrassed to admit they've been victimized."

"And the second?" I asked her.

"During the fortunetelling, the client reveals something that can be held against him or her. Or information about someone the client knows. In short, the fortuneteller blackmails the client."

"Unscrupulous investigators have been known to do that as well."

"Investigators with no scruples? Hard to believe," she said with a smile. "The client falls into a perfect trap, not able to go to the police to press charges against the fortuneteller because then the client's indiscretion or criminal act will also be revealed."

"Despicable," I said. "And the third?"

"It's a bit trickier," she said. "I would call it a kind of brainwashing. Again, the more gullible the client, the better. Unfortunately, there is no shortage of gullible clients. The basic strategy is to have the client do something he wouldn't normally do, embezzle from their company, for instance. The fortuneteller convinces him that this criminal act would be a good thing to resolve their crisis."

"The convincing part sounds difficult. I can't imagine how that would work."

She pointed to the scroll of a Chinese landscape in the alcove. At first glance it seemed conventional. There were common elements of a tree hanging onto a cliff, a waterfall, and a distant forest. But there was also a brooding feeling of imminent disaster. I couldn't say why, perhaps because of the tortured angle of the tree. Or maybe it was the tiny exhausted splash of water falling on rocks. And the forest was so distant it looked as if it could never be reached.

"Let's say this is very valuable and is hanging in the client's company's building. The fortuneteller makes the client believe that it has vital clues to how his crisis could be resolved, or that it is haunted with a ghost of his dead ancestor. The client is convinced his only hope is to steal it and give it to the fortuneteller."

That rang a bell with me. Loudly and clearly.

The rain gave way to a fog-shrouded dawn that enveloped me like a cold damp towel. A few of the neighborhood shops and businesses were preparing to open—owners or employees taking out trash, sweeping the sidewalk, lugging in deliveries, washing windows. I roused myself from the park bench where I had spent the past three or four hours, not really sleeping, too drunk to drive, too late to catch a train, too cheap to get a taxi, even if there were one available at that time of night.

After the fortuneteller and I finished off the wine and beer, she dipped into her own supplies. We talked about all sorts of topics, from baseball to politics, from science to television dramas. But I couldn't keep her lecture on fortunetelling fraud from intruding on my thoughts. I was thinking about the defunct case and how fortunetelling fraud might fit in.

I got up off the bench, my joints stiff, my fingers and toes tingling with blood once again flowing to them. How the homeless could put up with such accommodations every night is a mystery. When I had regained mobility to a sufficient degree, I walked in the direction of my car.

I drove in the heavy traffic to the downtown government offices. The twin towers of public policy and finance again caused shimmering in my peripheral vision. I didn't know what caused the phenomenon, or what it might mean for me, that is, for my health, mental or physical. I parked and hurried into the fraud office where the clerk was writing in his pinched way. My shadow cast over the clerk's desk.

"Yes—" he started to say then tilted his head up. He gave me a rotten-looking frown. "What do you want?" he asked, picking up the cigarette package lying on his desk. He gave a hands-up, surrendering gesture to his supervisor who was eying us, and we walked out of the office and into the corridor.

While he fiddled with his cigarette, I said, "I could use your help, if you have time." He exhaled a great cumulus cloud of smoke. It smelled good today, making me crave one. "What's up?"

"I need some information, something on the Kuchi clan of fortunetellers."

"Anything specific?"

"Whatever you've got."

"Okay, I see."

"And if you can access on your computers any information about the president of the Shinshin Group."

The clerk grinned through another cloud of smoke. "Tomoguchi Mori. I knew it. Sure, I'll check him out as well."

"Good, can you get it by tonight?"

"I'll get as much as I can. Where should I meet you?"

"Here."

He nodded and said, "Say, have you been up all night? You don't look so good."

▸

My appearance did not allow me to easily enter higher echelons of society. I would be the first to admit that I was a person more comfortable in the night, on narrow streets, among people who spoke with a mumbled dialect. Not that I was a reverse snob or an unconfident peasant, I simply belonged in that dark world. Still, I could wash up well, speak in high dialect, and walk with the air of the upper crust. I did my best to achieve this persona in the reception lobby of Shinshin Group.

Of course, I was told that since I didn't have an appointment with the president, Tomoguchi Mori, I couldn't see him. I asked the receptionist to tell him it was about a certain event meaning a great deal to his company. She called someone and when she hung up told me to wait.

I was kept waiting a full hour, during which there was likely a scurry of activity behind the scenes, trying to find out as much as possible about me and my claim. At the end of that hour, a woman met me in the lobby and escorted me up to the top of the building.

"Quite a view," I told her as we exited the elevator and walked past a bank of windows.

She ignored my comment and opened massive double doors. Standing behind a large desk, the president appeared insubstantial, like a bookish accountant. Along the left side of the room was a slender but highly alert man, no doubt his bodyguard. Next to him was the art director. I nodded at her but she ignored me.

"What is it you want?" the president said without prefatory remarks.

"Since you've involved the art director, I assume you know I've been investigating the disappearance, or death, of one of your freelance illustrators."

"You've been disrupting our business. I permitted this meeting so I can personally tell you to never contact anyone in this company again. Not even with whatever information you might think you have."

"All right," I said. "I'm sure I can find someone else interested."

"This is a lowly blackmail attempt, is it? You have nothing that even remotely involves this company."

"Just to warn you," I said, "I know about a certain travel agency."

The president remained unaffected and waved at the bodyguard to escort me out of the building. While doing so, he giving me a bruise on my arm where he squeezed my bicep like it was an overripe peach.

▸

The clerk stepped out into the evening sun colored orange and brown in the haze. He brought with him a folder and his cigarettes. I said, "You got something?"

He nodded and we walked to a nearby bar filled with government office workers in blue suits. We managed to get a small table in the corner. Over beers and boiled soybeans, he showed me his discovery.

"Regarding the Kuchi clan, I found twelve cases of fraud, all resolved due to the fact that the complaint was dropped."

"That's unusual, isn't it?"

"A lot of cases are resolved in this manner. However, twelve for twelve is unusual."

"What kind of fraud?"

"The complainants allege they were duped out of their life savings, sometimes their homes, businesses, and even a pet dog."

"A dog? Strange. When was the last such fraud case?"

"Let's see, eight years ago."

"Nothing after that?"

"Not in our records."

"They must have gotten tired of that kind of fraud."

The clerk popped a soybean from its pod and chewed it once or twice before swallowing. "Meaning they got into some other line of business?"

"Yes," I said, then asked, "Did you find anything regarding the Shinshin Group president?"

"Nothing on him, other than related to his professional life," he said. "Now what?"

"We will drink and eat. When I know more I'll tell you."

"I thought you weren't on the case anymore. I mean, I thought the case was closed."

"Officially I'm no longer on the case. I'm merely satisfying my own curiosity."

"That will get you in trouble," he said. He popped another bean into his red-and-yellow maw.

Report (unofficial)

4 September: 5:40 p.m.—The plan takes shape. Primary goal: flush out the Kuchi fortunetelling clan and the president of the Shinshin Group to expose their role in the missing son's disappearance or death. Secondary goal: determine other persons or other factors that contributed to the disappearance of Obushi. The technique: reverse fraud using the brainwashing technique. The participants (other than this investigator): the fraud clerk and the applicant fortuneteller. Materials needed: photographs of the collage, electronic surveillance equipment.

Specific details to follow.

expenses:
none reimbursable

Working on my own, unfettered by the company's rules and constraints, was freeing but also set me adrift in the sea of possibilities. Habits provide a comfortable existence. I didn't need to write a report, for example, but did so as a good way to crystallize my thoughts. Explaining something to someone else often reveals weakness of logic or beliefs.

I again called the office complaining of a vague illness. This time I talked with the chief. He was suspicious, asked if I'd gone to the doctor. I told him I'd visited a hospital emergency room and that seemed to convince him that I was ill enough to stay away from the office. But he warned me that my pay would be reduced if I didn't have the minimum billable hours for the month. I allowed him that I was prepared for such a possibility. He was silent for a moment before he wished me well and hung up.

Oddly, I was feeling ill, not achy with the flu or rheumy with a cold, but with the unsettled feeling of being split and compressed. Likely it was due to the anxiety of seeing my two lives—one living in the past, one in the future—colliding in the present and wreaking havoc on my psyche.

It could also be the realization I lack the psychological strength to become a ghost. My spirit, whatever was left when the body died, wouldn't be haunting anyone or any place. My ghostly remains would wither to nothing shortly after I died.

But, I rationalized, a ghostly life doesn't sound too exciting—make noise, move things around, creak and groan. It seems once you've frightened someone and got a thrill out of it, doing it over and over again would quickly become a bore.

I couldn't imagine having a reason for haunting anyone or any place. Death should be a release of the grudges, the anger, and the nightmares that accumulate during a life. Death should be a tropical vacation. Or in my case, an afterlife near my magazine stand and local pub.

▸

The car accelerated effortlessly onto the highway. Timing would be an essential part of the success of the plan. That and having good information. In the case of the missing husband, I had neither good timing nor good information. I was always two steps behind the husband or the wife's brother who was killed, or the husband's colleague, who eventually killed himself. I might have prevented one or both had I been sharper and thinking ahead. Sure, you might say something about hindsight, but I was clearly in a reaction, not action, mode. I didn't press the wife to be more forthcoming, even though I was suspicious of her right away. I was too soft on her, no doubt because I was intrigued with her, clouding my judgment. As I became entangled emotionally, my professional skills lagged, even regressed.

Over the years, I began to train myself to be coolly objective and more aggressive in obtaining information, even if it was off-putting for the client. With the case of the missing son, I had broken into the applicant's house and searched it. I entered the son's apartment several times, and illegally entered two businesses. I plied a fortuneteller with wine. While my ethics might have slipped, my efficiency had increased. So be it.

Had I done more in the case of the missing husband, could I have solved it? I assumed he had become involved with an unlicensed contractor scheme, an extortion scam, and a suspicious coffee shop. But none of those provided a satisfactory ending. I had to know what happened; I had to find out from the wife if I had indeed solved the case. Of course, the wife wasn't talking with anyone right now.

A car had been following me since I left my house. It was a white, nondescript two-door sedan, like a million cars. I hadn't seen the driver, who kept well back and out of any light that could illuminate his face. The driver was good at tailing, and kept up with me on the narrow, crowded streets of my backwater neighborhood, before we merged into the incessant flow on the highway. It would have been easy enough to lose the white car, but knowing who was following me might be just as helpful. Unfortunately, I wasn't good at cloak-and-dagger—it took too much concentration. My preferred approach to investigating is largely direct confrontation. *Get it over with* is how I'd sum up my philosophy. I slowed down and took the next exit and the following car did likewise. I pulled into the parking lot of an always open family style restaurant.

The white car slowed then drove off before I could see the driver.

▸

"Thank you for seeing me this late," I said to Mizuno Rie.

"It's all right. I usually work late."

"How are you doing?"

"To tell you the truth, I'm a little depressed. Your company refunded me the rest of the week's fee, which means there is no chance that you can find my son."

Even with all the connections I'd established—some very old, some newer—I'd clearly gotten far from the central issue of the case. Finding her missing son. Obviously, I lacked solid trust in Mizuno Rie. Not trusting a client severely hinders the investigation from the very start. The hypotheses I draw would be worthless, like a termite infested column that looks sturdy but inside is nothing more than dust. All the clues and connections were ghosts haunting me. They were sprites with no purpose but to torment.

"Mrs. Mizuno," I said formally, "despite the fact that the case is officially over as far as my company is concerned, I'd like to tie up a few loose ends if possible. This is on my own time, of course. In other words, I'm not asking for any remuneration, none at all."

"I couldn't ask you to do that, or even go so far as grant you permission to continue." She paused and then said quietly, "It seems a lost cause."

"You don't have to do either. I absolve you of all responsibility in my involvement in the unofficial investigation. I have a few questions about your son, and all you have to do is answer them. Okay?"

She nodded.

"Good. What I'm interested in are your son's mannerisms, such as how he spoke, what words he liked to use. I'm trying to find four or five unique characteristics that would identify him."

As she thought of her son, her face softened gratefully. "I'm not sure what you mean."

"I have a plan," I told her, "and I need your help to make it successful. If you are agreeable." I gave her a photograph of the collage. "I'd like to know your first impression."

"It looks ominous. The girl is about to be attacked by the gang of men and the onlookers won't do anything to stop them. In fact, they might find it amusing. In the background are drawings of insects, mostly butterflies. The main species is the monarch, I believe. The placement gives the scene a surreal quality . . . the people specimens in a jar. Where was it taken?"

"Based on other evidence I've gathered, I believe it's in Mexico. Exactly where and what is going on in the scene I'm not sure, except to say, again based on other evidence, it might be tied to the sex tour trade. In the background, as you correctly determined, are monarch butterflies."

"There are two kinds of work. One is hand drawn, the other photographs. Is that significant?"

"Perhaps it's the collision you mentioned in my fortune."

"Wait, you think my son is involved in the sex tour trade?" A severe look of disbelief crossed her face.

"I'm not sure of his connection to the sex tour business. The photographer has used the travel agency that sets up the tours. The president of the company where they were freelancers ties together the photographer and your missing son."

She thought for a few moments. "You want my help in setting up a fortunetelling fraud involving this collage. That's why you need to know how my son speaks."

"Yes. What you can do now is to help me understand the specifics of how a fraud would take place."

After a few moments, she nodded.

I added forty-some kilometers of unreportable car expense. The white car that followed me earlier had not made an appearance. I was prepared for it. I knew of a parking garage with a tricky back exit. Not wanting to give away my destination in case I was followed, I parked several blocks from Midori Elegant Escorts. Was I the one, after all, who had run down the wife from the old case? Perhaps I had in a moment of unconscious but deliberate violence, hoping to free myself from the cycle of twenty years of two paths of existence.

I walked into Midori's. The police detective was talking with her. Midori pointed at me and said, "It's him."

The detective smiled. "This is convenient."

"Not for me," I said to the detective. Then I spoke to Midori, "I just came to get it sorted out. Did she ever talk about her ex-husband?"

Midori looked from me to the detective. He nodded at her and she said, "She confided to me one night about his disappearance. She'd never gotten completely over it but over the years, she'd gradually moved on. But then out of the blue she thought she saw him. She asked me if she was crazy to try to contact him. I asked her what she needed to say to him. She said she wanted to ask him why."

"Why what? " the detective asked.

I answered for her, "Why he left her twenty years ago. Did she find him?"

"Yes."

"Did she find out why he left?"

Midori's shoulders slumped. "She didn't want to talk about it, not even with me."

The detective asked, "What's this husband's name?"

"Ex-husband," I said and told him. But I didn't tell him his alias, Hattori, and instead asked Midori: "Did she ever mention a private investigator whom she hired to find her husband?"

"Never."

"Was I ever here before her accident?"

She glanced at the detective. "I . . . well, I'm not sure. There was a man here before the accident. I was on the phone so I didn't get a look at him. She talked with him for a minute or so and then he left. She said he was asking about an escort but she was obviously shaken."

I turned to leave and the detective grabbed my arm. "Hey, you can't leave—"

With a quick twist, I escaped his grasp and sprinted out of Midori's.

▸

Having outrun the detective, I waited in my house, in the dark, my own breath as loud as a bellows. My heart pounded heavily, punishing my ribs. The note I slipped under the door at Hattori's house told him that I knew what he'd done and had evidence. But I just wanted to ask him a single question, and left him my address.

He showed up all right, knocking once and stepping inside when the door opened.

"You there?" he asked.

"In here." I could smell alcohol on his breath from across the room.

"What's with the lights out?"

"Sorry." I turned on a lamp with a low-watt bulb. His face was in the dark until he sat down.

I didn't recognize him. He was not the missing husband. Nor was he the other side of the split me. He had a long face, deeply etched wrinkles at the corner of his eyes. He had two or three days of stubble.

"What's all this about? I got this note." He tossed it at my feet.

"You are Hattori?"

"I'm here, aren't I?"

"I'm afraid there might be a misunderstanding. You are not the person I thought you were. But as long as you are here, why was he using your name and phone number?"

"That's a good question. Do you know where he is so I can ask him?"

"Maybe. Are you willing to pay for the information?"

He grunted again. "Give it to me or you will be the one paying."

"Like you made his wife pay?"

Hattori stepped over the low table. "Wife? What are you talking about?" He lunged for me but I rolled out of the way and knocked over the lamp in the same motion. The bulb broke with a *pop* and the house was dark. While Hattori was huffing and struggling to get on his feet, I ran out of the house. After twenty steps down my street, I slipped into the space between the newsstand and the produce shop. Hattori emerged from my house and looked for me. He gave up after only a minute or two and stormed off to his car—a white Toyota four-door.

▸

The next morning, I awoke at home well after the usual time I'd rise for work. I thought about calling in sick but decided it wasn't necessary. I was on my last legs there. It wasn't that I wanted to be fired; the confluence of events and forces was pushing me away from my life as it was. A black hole can repel as much as attract.

I called the clerk and asked him to meet me at an electronics store. He excitedly said he would be there. That made me feel uneasy, not because I was meeting the clerk, but because he was going to be involved in the case to the highest degree. I should have been the one to go inside the Kuchi compound. But they already knew me, due to my blunders and my headstrong bullying in the first few days of the case. Although then I didn't know it was the kind of case that entangles me in its threads as my life is pulled apart.

Why the clerk wanted to get involved in the Mizuno case had to be more than his claim of a dull existence, more than his romantic view of private investigation. Perhaps it was some revenge he wished on the world. Maybe he was the one who made Obushi disappear. After all he was the one who told me about the ambulance and the medics pronouncing him dead. No one else knew anything about it, not the hospital, not the media, not the coroner. If one had a very suspicious mind, one would blame the clerk for all of the trouble the case had caused. If one went even farther down that road, one could suspect him of putting the Moonlight Travel Agency brochure in the camera shop owner's files. Even further, one could believe the clerk set up the situation with the Shinshin Group president. But why would the clerk go to such extremes? I didn't know, but if it were true, I was being taken for a ride on his journey.

Or I was being paranoid.

▸

My electronic surveillance experience was limited to the tape recorder in my briefcase. Old technology. I disliked the tedious details that were required to get the electronics to work properly. I wasn't one for tedium. That's another reason why my chief rarely gave me important jobs that required technology. The clerk on the other hand took to the technology like kid given a new toy.

The clerk adjusted the receiver he installed in the van I again borrowed from the air-conditioning contractor. With a turn of a knob, the picture came into view. It was dark, because the miniature camera was inside the dimly-lit van.

I found a flashlight and turned it on. The light illuminated my face and the image on the receiving screen was a ghoulish me.

"Test it," the clerk said.

"Test, test." A squeal of feedback came through the speakers.

"Sorry. Feedback," the clerk said. "Here's the knob to adjust the volume. And this knob adjusts the antenna. Now remember we only have about an hour of battery power."

"Then it's up to you to get the information in that time. Do you need to go over the script again with the fortuneteller?"

"No, I'm ready."

▸

The fortuneteller and I sat in the back of the van on the rolls of wire. "Sorry about the uncomfortable seating," I said.

"It's fine," she said.

"There he goes," I said, pointing to the screen. The image was grainy and jerky. The people in the image were a man and a woman. "That's the Kuchi security chief and Kuchi Noriyo," the fortuneteller said.

The clerk was barely audible through the earphones. I fiddled with the knob.

". . . straight to the point. What I'm here to offer is a strange proposition. I've come across a haunting and disturbing photograph."

The video image jerked down then up. When it settled, we could see the two Kuchi clan members studying the photograph.

"How did you get this?" the man asked. His voice was sharp and thin through the speakers.

"Actually, I don't know. It simply showed up. Like a ghost. It's been telling me stories."

"What?" the woman said quickly, obviously irritated. "A ghost?"

The clerk sounded anguished. "It's horrible. It's like this " The clerk cleared his throat, speaking the words in a low voice, drawing out each syllable as Mizuno Ren would. "You know what happened. You have the power to bring justice. You can expose those responsible."

The faces of the two Kuchi fortunetellers expanded in amazement, then shrank in fear, as if they had indeed heard a ghost.

44

We raised our glasses and toasted to our success. The clerk wiped a dribble of beer from the corner of his mouth. The fortuneteller sat on the cushion on the matted floor of her home and sipped her wine. I leaned back against the wall and took a gulp of beer. Of course, I couldn't judge how well we succeeded initiating the reverse fraud with brainwashing. I didn't know what was in the minds of the Kuchi clan members, except that they would be a tough pair to convince a ghost was haunting a collage. Whatever the effect, there would be a reaction. Action-reaction. That was the ultimate purpose of this step of the reverse fraud. Whether it played out exactly as hoped was what could not be predicted. But it would not be chaotic; it would be a well-planned and thought-out attack. We had to act fast to keep one step ahead of them.

The clerk was giving us an encore of his imitation of Mizuno Ren. Even the fortuneteller laughed. I did too, for the first time in a long while.

▸

I dropped the clerk off at the nearest subway station. He wanted to drink more at his favorite bar, but I told him I had to take the van back to the air conditioning contractor. Then I said was going straight home to catch up on sleep. He was disappointed but went into the station dutifully.

Instead of driving to the contractor, I went to Mizuno Ren's apartment and parked across the street. There was no certain reason why I should believe that the reaction would be located at the apartment. It was as good a guess as I could make.

The night was sultry, a good night to be enjoying a rooftop beer garden, drinking from immense frosty glass mugs, singing badly but at the top of one's lungs. Not that I'd done that for a few years. There was a time at the company when five or six of us got along well enough and liked nothing better than an evening at a beer garden. But like most things, the group disintegrated: marriages and children, promotions, job changes, bad livers. Like a group of cells in a body reaching the end of their natural life and not able to replicate, the group ceased to exist.

I walked up the stairs and to the door of the missing son's apartment. Again, it was unlocked. I went in and sat in one of the chairs in the sitting area. In the dark and quiet, I wondered what it would be like to be able to draw with the precision and reflective ability as the illustrator obviously could. The light and shadow, the line and space, all coming together with technical precision, making the two dimensions of the image appear to be three dimensions. Fooling the eye, fooling the brain. If I could do what he did with a pencil, my life would have possibility, meaning, a sense of purpose.

A shimmering rose in my peripheral vision. The same shimmering I'd felt before, except this time it gave me a start. It was as if someone was waving at me, trying to get my attention, or maybe warning me away. My body froze to the chair. My mind raced, trying to grasp the meaning of the shimmering, but came up with nothing. No, less than nothing. By trying to understand the son's artistic talent, how it might be understood, I began to feel trapped. Even more, I felt the anguish, the utter helplessness of someone trapped in quicksand, or in a prison cell with no door.

Everything became murky, all the clues smashed together, became indistinguishable. But nothing made sense, as if the elementary particles of meaning no longer existed. Bits and pieces flew out of my core. I tried to hold them all together, put them back in place, but I couldn't. It was simply not possible.

I waited only a few minutes, then left the apartment.

▸

Fujii served me a meal I hardly tasted. I drank beer that might as well have been water. The restaurant stall was slow that night; Fujii chatted about the local scene: a meat supplier raised his wholesale rates, a liquor distributor got in a traffic accident, one of the neighborhood police officers was having an affair with a married woman he stopped for speeding. I barely heard anything except for those headlines.

"What about origin of the universe?" he asked. "Will we ever really understand it?"

I shrugged.

On the way home, feeling none the better, at step count twenty, near the bakery, someone grabbed my arm. I twisted out of the grip and prepared to fight gamely if not valiantly.

"It's me," hissed the clerk. He ducked into the shadows of the bakery storefront. In the window display cases were plastic models of bread and pastries.

"I thought you went home," I said.

"I thought you did too," he said. "They followed me. By 'they' I mean two gangster types. Violent." He looked over his shoulder. "I think they are still up there, around the corner."

"Are you sure they were following you?"

"They weren't playing hide and seek with me."

I walked up the street with the clerk lagging behind. It wasn't likely that he was being followed, probably it was a reaction to the cloak-and-dagger operation that evening. That and too much celebration. The suspicions I had earlier about the clerk made me wonder if he was leading me into a trap. Why would he do that? He might be in league with the Kuchi clan and they had grown weary of my meddling in their affairs.

When we reached the corner, I stopped and turned to the clerk. "I don't see anyone."

He edged around me. "There." He pointed to two figures up the street in the shadows of a building. I couldn't see much more than their casual stance as if waiting for a taxi.

"Let's go see who they are," I said. "They look harmless to me."

"I should warn you," the clerk said. "I'm not much of a fighter."

I chuckled. "I hadn't counted on you to knock them out."

As we approached, the two straightened and began to walk away.

"Hey," I shouted.

One of them turned around and gave us a snarl. He had a face like a guard dog, his canines gleamed in the street light. The two split up, the guard dog ran across the street and disappeared into an alley, the other one, who was nearly a head shorter than his partner, turned into a pedestrian shopping mall.

"You take the one in the alley. I'll take the one in the mall," I said.

"But . . ." the clerk said.

"Okay," I said. "You take the one in the mall."

I took off in a run. When I got to the alley, I made a turn too fast and bumped into a power pole. When I recovered, I had lost the guard dog. In the alley there were a few tiny, dingy, and cheap drinking and food stands. I heard the click of mahjong tiles coming from one of the places. I stuck my head inside, and couldn't see much through the cloud of cigarette smoke other than four men at a table playing the game. One of them grunted when he saw me. I apologized and left them to it.

I checked a few other places, but didn't find the guard dog. I went back to the street. I looked for the clerk, but didn't see him. Only a few stores in the pedestrian mall were still open. A fast food restaurant, a pharmacy, an electronics store. One was a brightly-lit pachinko parlor where I went inside and found the clerk playing one of the machines and smoking a cigarette, his hands trembling.

The clerk stayed at my house, not that it was necessarily any safer than his. Mine was easy enough to find if someone wanted to. I wasn't sure what frightened him so much, the two guys didn't seem to want to harm him. Had they actually been tailing him?

When the sun rose, he began to relax. I poured us another cup of strong coffee. With the clerk around, my splitting disease flared up like malaria, forcing me to concentrate on keeping my mind and body together.

"How are you feeling?" I asked the clerk.

"I'm fine now. It was harrowing last night."

"I can understand if you don't want to continue with your part in the case."

He shook his head, his hair like the bristles of an old, stiff brush. "I'm prepared to go all the way. I lost some nerve last night. I'll admit that. It's lack of experience, I suppose. It was, of course, a simple coincidence that the two gangster-types decided to give me a scare. There was no connection. It was a purely random encounter."

"Exactly," I said.

"What about you? You never seem to lose your nerve."

"Not true," I said. "I do more often than I care to admit."

He made a little grunt of disbelief. It sounded like the croak of a randy frog.

"It's true," I said. "I can run fast if I have to. Anyway, no one wants to bother with me. I'm not worth it. Like you said, those two were having a little joke at your expense. Nothing to do with the case."

"But they seemed so intent on . . . me."

I thought about adding something stronger to his coffee, but I didn't have anything with alcohol other than cough medicine. "If they really wanted to do us damage or even scare us off, they would have. They didn't look like the kind to hesitate. They must have been simply two jokers out for a laugh."

The clerk opened his mouth to say something, but took a gulp of coffee instead. I left him alone and went into the kitchen where I cooked a batch of eggs, fermented soy beans, and rice.

When we finished eating and he gathered up his senses sufficiently to leave, I walked with him to the nearest subway station. "I have a job for you," I said. "I need some more information from the travel agency."

"I can do that," he said without hesitation. "What specifically?"

"Anything on their special trips to Mexico. Let's meet later at your bar."

▸

I rang the buzzer at the gate of the Tomoguchi estate. There was no answer. I tried again. I waited a couple of minutes and was about to try again when a large foreign car came down the drive and pulled up to the gate. A man got out and walked over to me. "What do you want?" he demanded.

He looked like the brother of the bodyguard who'd escorted me out of the Shinshin Group building. I rubbed where my arm was still bruised and sore from his brother's manhandling. "I would like to discuss a personal matter with Mrs. Tomoguchi."

"I am sorry, sir, the lady of the house will not be receiving visitors at this time," he said, using surprisingly formal phrasing.

"But I talked with her before. Surely she wouldn't mind one more question."

"Beat it or I'll beat you," he said, dropping his formality.

"You won't ask her if she will see me?"

The bodyguard stood silently with his glare focused on me.

"I guess not," I said. "Sorry to bother you."

Driving back into the city, I needed some fresh air and stopped at a small, derelict shrine. The bushy vegetation was overgrown, spreading up to the gate. A bamboo grove in the back was impenetrable. A stack of warped and sun-bleached wood slats was piled on one side, as if someone intended to remodel the shrine years ago but never got to it. The shrine appeared to be dedicated to a local deity. A carved image of the deity sat on a post in front of the shrine, but was not recognizable because over the hundred years or more it has existed, shrine goers had rubbed it for good luck. It might be a turtle, I decided. The original meaning was lost by human contact, and only in the mind of the shrine goers did it exist.

I clapped my hands to summon the deity, then rubbed the carving. Only a crow made its presence known with a piercing "caa-caa-caa."

▸

I called on the fortuneteller who was setting out her sign when I walked up the hill to her home. We went inside where I asked her for more details about her fortunetelling sessions with Tomoguchi Yumiko.

"She has accomplished her goal of financial success," I told Mrs. Mizuno.

"Is that so? I only told her what I saw in her palm."

"And what she wanted to hear."

She nodded dejectedly.

"You don't believe it was a good thing for her?" I asked.

"I've thought more about her. I remembered she seemed to have a motive for asking."

"Motives are strong indicators of beliefs," I said.

"It seemed as if she was willing to take her husband's financial success in exchange for his affairs and other philandering. I remember she looked torn in anguish."

I thanked her, wished her well, and drove away. The afternoon sky was purple-gray. Suddenly it occurred to me that the president's wife, Tomoguchi Yumiko, might never be seen again. Whatever I had initiated with my first visit again caused a person to go missing.

When I arrived at the clerk's favorite bar, he was there already and halfway through a *shōchū* with plum. He couldn't wait for a belt of booze to calm his nerves. When I sat down he called the waitress over and ordered us some food and a drink for me. "No one followed you today?" I asked him.

"I don't think so."

While we ate and drank, he showed me his list of Mexico trips. "All special ones?"

"These are all the spicy ones as they call them. That Yamaguchi agent is a slick and nasty fellow. I suppose you have to deal with a lot of those types in this business."

I nodded and glanced through his list. There were eight places. "Good job. Now all we have to do is narrow it down. Are you ready for tonight?"

The clerk raised his glass. I wanted to rub his head like I had rubbed the turtle at the shrine.

The fortuneteller and I again sat on the uncomfortable spools of wire in the contractor's van. Inside the Kuchi clan complex, the clerk was left waiting in a reception area for almost half an hour. On the video screen and over the audio, we could tell he was starting to squirm and sigh.

Kuchi Noriyo appeared and took the clerk into a room. When the door shut, the monitor went dark. I held my breath.

"What happened?" the fortuneteller asked.

"I don't know," I said. "Maybe the battery's already going or there's a loose connection. The room could be protected against transmissions."

"Maybe the room is just dark."

"Hmm, you're probably right."

We waited for a long minute before we saw a flash of movement on the monitor, and heard a hiss of sound from the speakers. We leaned forward to hear better.

". . . Mexico," the clerk said. ". . . I'm sure it . . ."

". . . Mexico . . ."

". . . Mizuno . . ." someone was saying. It was a woman. But it didn't sound like the severe voice of the Kuchi woman. I listened carefully.

". . . we don't want . . . you will give . . . or else you . . . private detective . . ."

Referring to me, I wondered?

Another woman spoke. I recognized the voice of Teruyo/Namiko. But I couldn't understand what she was saying. Had she discovered our reverse fraud? Then there was a scream. It was the clerk, I was sure. It froze my blood, as if I had been dipped in liquid nitrogen. Then he shouted something that I couldn't understand.

It sounded like: "*Ra muraseido.*"

I flung open the door to the van. "Wait here," I told the fortuneteller as I jumped out and shut the door. I sprinted toward the Kuchi complex, my shoes clomping like a horse's hooves. When I neared the complex, I could see that the gate was closed, but two of the guards were standing next to it. One was talking into a walkie-talkie. When I was close to the gate, they pointed to me, or was it behind me? I turned. The security chief had charged out of the complex, running toward the van. He must have figured out what we were up to.

When the security chief saw me running, he yelled into his walkie-talkie. I ran straight at him. He took a step back, and when he did, I veered for the driver's side door. I jerked it open and shut it before he reached the van. As he tried to open the door, I turned the key and pushed the gear shift to drive. "Hang on," I shouted to the fortuneteller in the back of the van. As I floored the gas pedal, the guard smashed his fist against the window. The glass shattered into tiny chunks of glass. The shards sparkled as they tumbled through the air, showering me, flashing in the van with bluish slivers of light.

The van lurched forward and the chief ran with it while grabbing the steering wheel. I fought him for control, his wild stare focused on the steering wheel like a tiger intent on its prey. With his other hand he reached in and pummeled at my head, landing ineffectual blows due to his awkward position, like a kid's first fight. I yanked hard on the wheel and the van turned sharply. The chief lost his grip. His body was thrown against the window frame. The broken glass dug into his arm. He grunted and when I twisted the steering wheel again, the force threw him off the van. With another twist of the wheel, I managed to avoid crashing into a delivery truck coming down the road. I sped past the gate.

Two blocks past the complex, I checked the side view mirror and spotted a car following me. I turned onto an arterial that was choked with traffic, slowing me down. Traffic inched along, the car gaining a little with each block, as the smaller vehicle was better able to negotiate the traffic. When we reached a turn-off to a regional freeway, I turned off and sped along as fast as I could.

"We will shake them now," I hollered.

The car stayed with us and was now only two vehicles behind. I took the exit to a small business park where I'd once visited on a case. Its parking structure was a series of ramps and exits that so confused me I had ended up on the roof instead of the street. I turned into the parking structure then stopped at the automatic gate to take a ticket. The gate opened and I screeched the tires. Behind me the car was stopped by the gate. I made it to the first ramp and I sped up as fast as the tight corners would allow. At the top of the ramp, the van bounced like a small boat in heavy seas.

"Sorry," I shouted.

The squeal of tires behind me indicated that the car was now through the gate. I hit the next ramp, the van's frame complaining with a groan of twisting metal. At the top of the next ramp, I hit the brakes instead of the accelerator. I made a hard turn into the down ramp and stopped behind a concrete wall. I waited until the car sped up the ramp past us, then turned to the ramp going down and to the exit. When I drove the van out of the structure, I glanced up to the roof and saw them looking down on us.

Five kilometers away, when I was sure no one was following us, I exited the regional highway and found a place to pull over. I brushed the glass diamonds off me. I walked around to the back of the van and opened the door. "Sorry about the wild ride," I said.

But no one heard me—the fortuneteller was gone.

▸

Two more people involved in the case had disappeared, had become out-of-context. The clerk had not emerged from the Kuchi complex, the fortuneteller evaporated into thin air. Was I next?

I drove to the fortuneteller's house, to the neighborhood of increasing significance. There were no parking spots so I used the service station again. Luckily it was closed so I didn't have to hire the apprentice mechanic. I ran past the noodle stand where there was a rush of three tables of customers. I caught a glimpse of the woman attending to them, but she didn't see me.

I took the steps up the rise two at a time. I knocked on the door, waited a moment, then knocked again and turned the knob. The door opened. "Hello?"

No one answered and I could feel she wasn't there. When I went inside past the empty fortunetelling room, standing in the middle of the sitting room was the bodyguard from Shinshin Group. Behind him, sitting on a chair as if he owned the place, was Tomoguchi Mori.

"Where is she?" I asked.

Tomoguchi shook his head. "What are you doing here?"

"Are you waiting for her?"

"Don't answer my question with a question."

"You did."

He sighed. "We came to have our fortunes told. There's nothing wrong with that, is there?"

"What did you do to her?"

"There you go again. I'm getting tired of this."

As if the president's statement was a cue, the bodyguard walked around behind me and pulled one arm behind my back as if I was a lifeless puppet. He pulled my wrist until my hand was nearly as high as the back of my neck. My arm didn't want to bend that way.

"Answer the question," he said.

"Which one?" I managed to squeak out.

"The first."

"Why am I here? It's obvious, isn't it? She is the applicant in the case of a missing person. Her son."

"And have you found him?" he asked.

"I can only discuss particulars of the case with her." The bodyguard pulled and twisted my wrist.

I grunted in pain. "Okay. No, I haven't found him."

"There isn't time for you to lie," Tomoguchi said. "I have no patience to play your game."

A muffled cry come from one of the bedrooms. The bodyguard relaxed his grip and I slipped out of it. I ran toward the front door but he had the angle. I veered off into the fortunetelling room. In the dark, I jumped across the floor and collapsed into a ball and rolled through the invisible trap door.

▸

The hole was like an old friend you unexpectedly run across in the grocery store after several years. She would look different but the same. Your shared history would come back in little bits and you'd laugh and feel good about life for a moment or two. I sat where I landed for several minutes, although it might have been only a few seconds. Time in the hole seemed to change with my thoughts. Positive thoughts made time go fast, negative thoughts slowed time.

As with my previous experience with the hole, no one followed me. I stood up and tried to reach the spot where I'd fallen through the invisible door, but couldn't reach it. That didn't worry me too much. As time was changed, so was distance. I walked down to the yellow light. The hole close behind me as it had before, but this time all the dead and missing haunted me.

The noodle stand owners were closing up for the night, banging pots and stacking bowls. I ducked under the row of pipes and conduits and squirmed into the space until I was snuggled into a cocoon. I listened to the muffled sounds coming from above me. After the noodle stand owners finished cleaning up, they sat at the counter and ate their dinner—noodles, of course, I could tell by the slurping sounds. They didn't say a word. What could they possibly have to say after all of the days and nights working side-by-side.

Then there were no sounds, no people. I felt the panic of those buried alive, the utter hopelessness, the fear of dying a slow agonizing death in the dark, with no way of killing one's self to end the misery. I poked around my cocoon, checking for any access doors, or cut-outs in the walls. In one corner, I found an old rusting hatch panel. With a kick, it fell open. I was met with a smell of oil. The hatch opened into the service garage. The concrete floor was spotted with grease and metal shavings.

I found my way out of the garage and looked out through a grimy window into the night. The contractor's van was where I left it in the parking area of the service station. As I neared it, I heard Mori and his bodyguard shouting. I found a back door and slipped into the night.

▸

My feet pounded and slapped the pavement as I ran. The night was sullen, unsympathetic to my cause. People out stared at me like I'd escaped from an institution. I'd gone at least two or three kilometers before I found a taxi. I got in and gave him my address.

While he drove through the streets that seemed unfamiliar, even alien, I thought of the fortuneteller. She'd been wrong about my long lifeline; my life was coming to an end soon.

"Where. . . ?" the taxi driver asked, peering out the windshield.

There was a light on in my house. I never left the light on.

"Keep going!"

"Hey, what's up?" the driver asked, obviously apprehensive over the tone of my voice.

"Turn here."

He did without another question. Several blocks later we reached the riverbank. "Here," I said. "Stop."

"Here?" the driver stopped and opened the back door with his lever. "That's fifteen—hey . . ."

I threw all my coins onto the seat next to him. I got out and sprinted toward the concrete embankment. On the water a barge slowly made its way down the river. I walked past a row of boxmen, all tucked in their cardboard abodes, snoring sounds coming from one or two, cigarette smoke wafting from another. It might not be a good idea to smoke if you lived in a cardboard house. I laughed at my inane concern. Further along the river embankment, I found a pile of rubbish: wooden pallets, sacks of rotting garbage, a bundle of plastic straps, and a large cardboard box that had once held a television.

septembre. Chenille s… … plantes herbacées.

87. **HYPOCRITA** Hübner. = Espèce principale (HJ, p. 182) : Ailes ant. noires avec une bande longitudinale et deux taches rouges ; les postérieures rouges à bordure noire. Enverg. 31-48 mm. — **H. jacobeæ**[1] L. « Carmin, Goutte de sang ». C. Mai-juillet. Chen. sur les Séneçons

… ÉCAILLES. — Abdom…

no other way

leave

TABLE ALPHABÉTIQUE

DES NOMS DE GROUPES ET DE GENRES

for

others

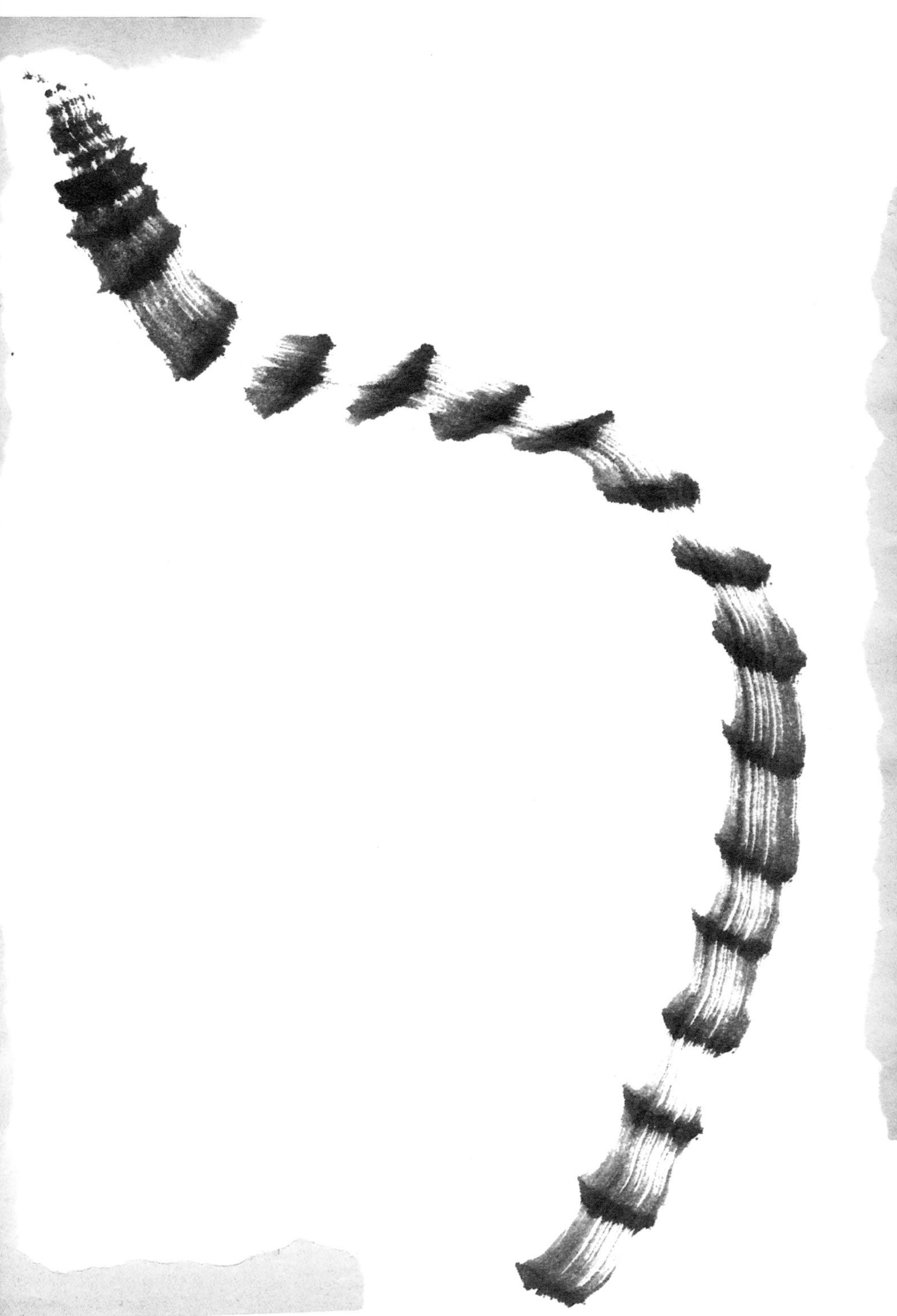

you in see you

Fam. XI. — GÉOMÉTRIDÉS

Les Géométridés ou **Phalènes** (de [illegible], papillon de nuit) sont d'assez grands papillons, nocturnes ou crépusculaires, à corps mince, à ailes délicates, souvent étalées au repos. Quelques-uns volent pendant le jo[illegible] Ils sont déra[illegible]

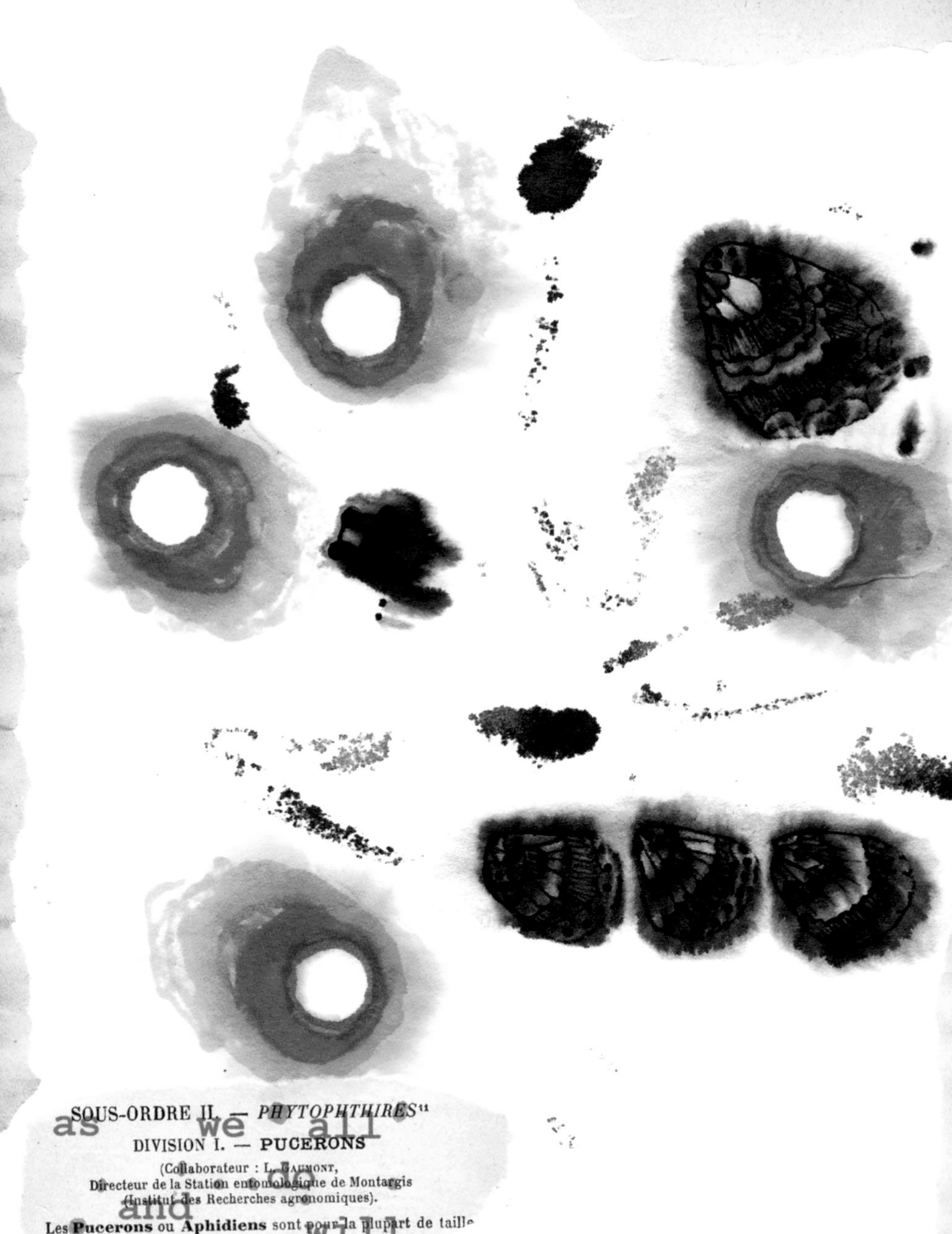

as we all do and will

SOUS-ORDRE II. — *PHYTOPHTHIRES*[11]

DIVISION I. — **PUCERONS**

(Collaborateur : L. Gaumont,
Directeur de la Station entomologique de Montargis
(Institut des Recherches agronomiques).

Les **Pucerons** ou **Aphidiens** sont pour la plupart de taille
très petite, en moyenne de 2 à 4 mm. ([a]), except de 0,5 à 8 m
plantes les plus diverses, en suçant les

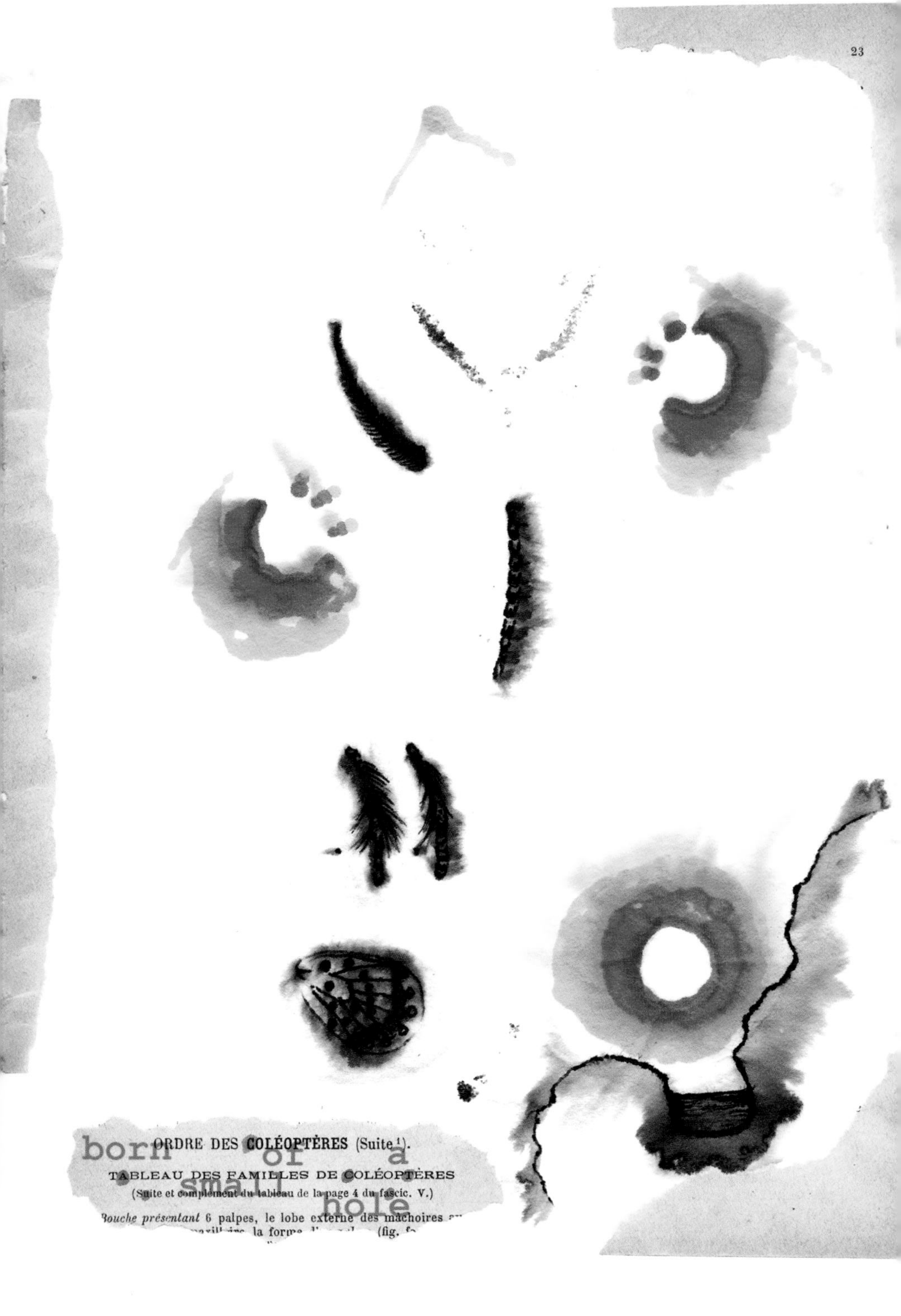

born of a small hole

ORDRE DES COLÉOPTÈRES (Suite[1]).

TABLEAU DES FAMILLES DE COLÉOPTÈRES

(Suite et complément du tableau de la page 4 du fascic. V.)

Bouche présentant 6 palpes, le lobe externe des mâchoires ...
... la forme ... (fig. ...

83
QUE DES GROUPES E
(=Macrocephalus), 155.
(=Macroplea), 121.
Macrotoma, 96.
(=Magdalinus), 212.
Magdalis, 212.
Malachius, 17.
without
MALACODERMES
Malacosoma, 136.
Malthinus, 14.
Malthodes, 14.
Mantura, 145.
tomorrow
Mecynotarsus, 83.
Megapenthes, 34.
Melandrya, 74.
(=Melanimon), 66.
Melanophila, 34.
Melanotus, 47.
Melasis, 43.
Melasoma, 134.
Meloe, 86.
(=Melyris), 21.
Menephilus, 68.
Mesites, 202.
Mesocœlopus, 26.
Mesosa, 113.
Metallites, 182.
Metœcus, 72.
(Metopiorhynchus)
Miarus, 213.
(Miccotrogus), 211.
(Micrapate), 28.
(Micrelus), 207.
Microzoum, 66.
Minyops, 195.
Mnesium, 29.
Mniophila, 143.
Molorchus, 97.
Molytes, 196.
(=Monocha
Monohamn
Monolept
Mord

don't
mind
that
I've
arrived
here

de la « manne », utilisée en médecine p
gatives.

La détermination précise des Cochenilles nécessite microscope; mais les caractères de la ♀ mûre s'obser facilement, et c'est à l'étude de celle-ci, en général très su que nous nous bornerons ici.

Une seule famille : **COCCIDÉS.**

TABLEAU DES GENRES DE COCCIDÉS

+ ♀ sécrétant un *manteau* cireux ± développé, sur lequel sont fixée et restent visibles les deux dépouilles larvaires, formant le *nucléus* la plus petite (correspondant à la 1re mue) étant placée au centre o en avant de la plus grande. Sous le manteau on voit la ♀ libre d'adhérence, et les œufs qu'elle a pondus; un mince plancher, fixé à la surface de la plante parasitée, ferme en dessous l'ovisac (MP, ♀ 3). — ♂ sécrétant un *puparium* de même forme ou de forme différente, ne montrant qu'une seule dépouille larvaire (MP, ♂). — Abd. termi par une large plaque arrondie portant des écailles et des soies les seulement au microscope (AH, AH', p. 125), servant à espèces (Tribu des **Diaspinés**).

culaire, ovale ou elliptique; nucléus
ent marginal.

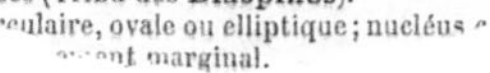

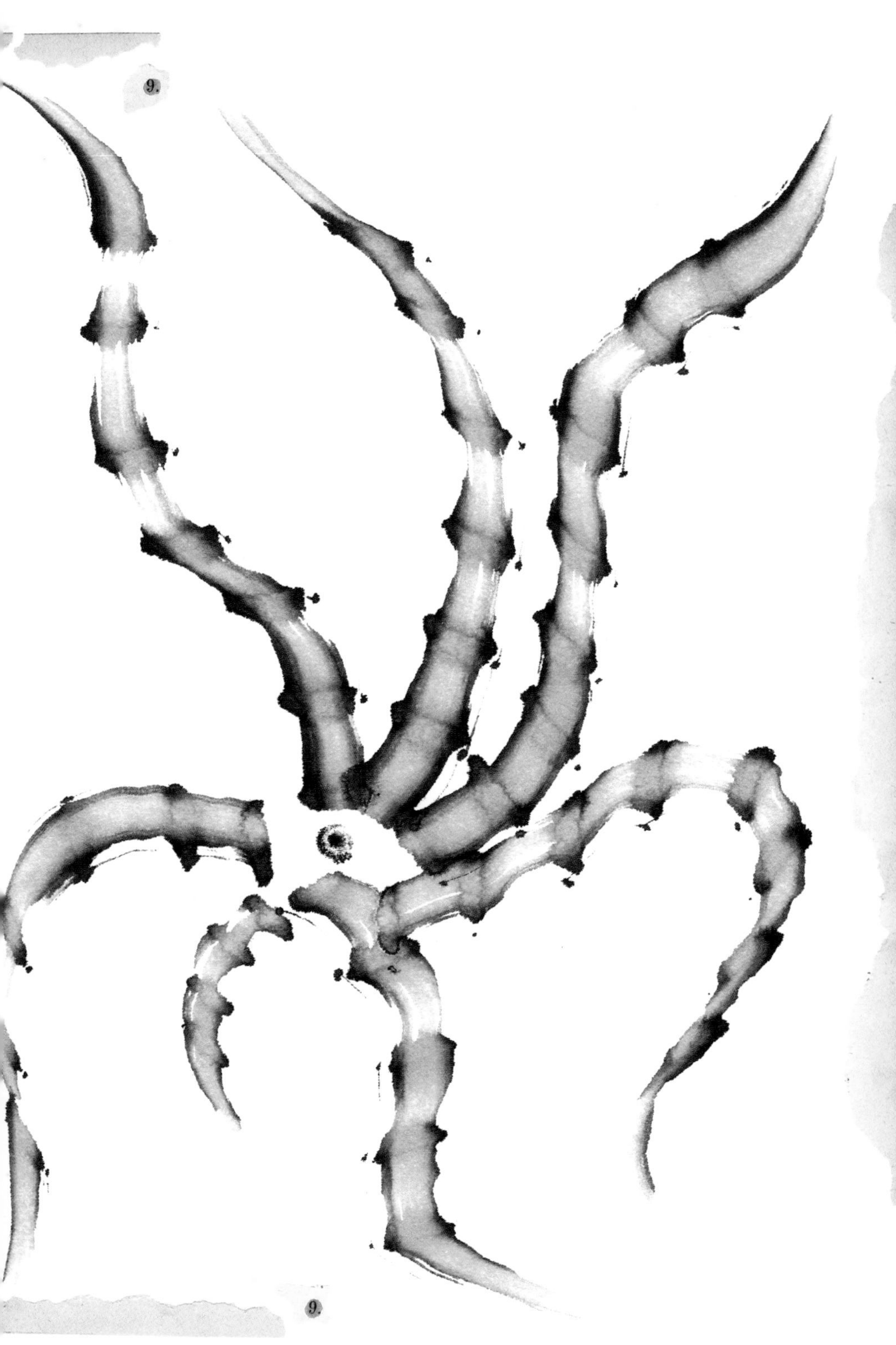
9.
9.

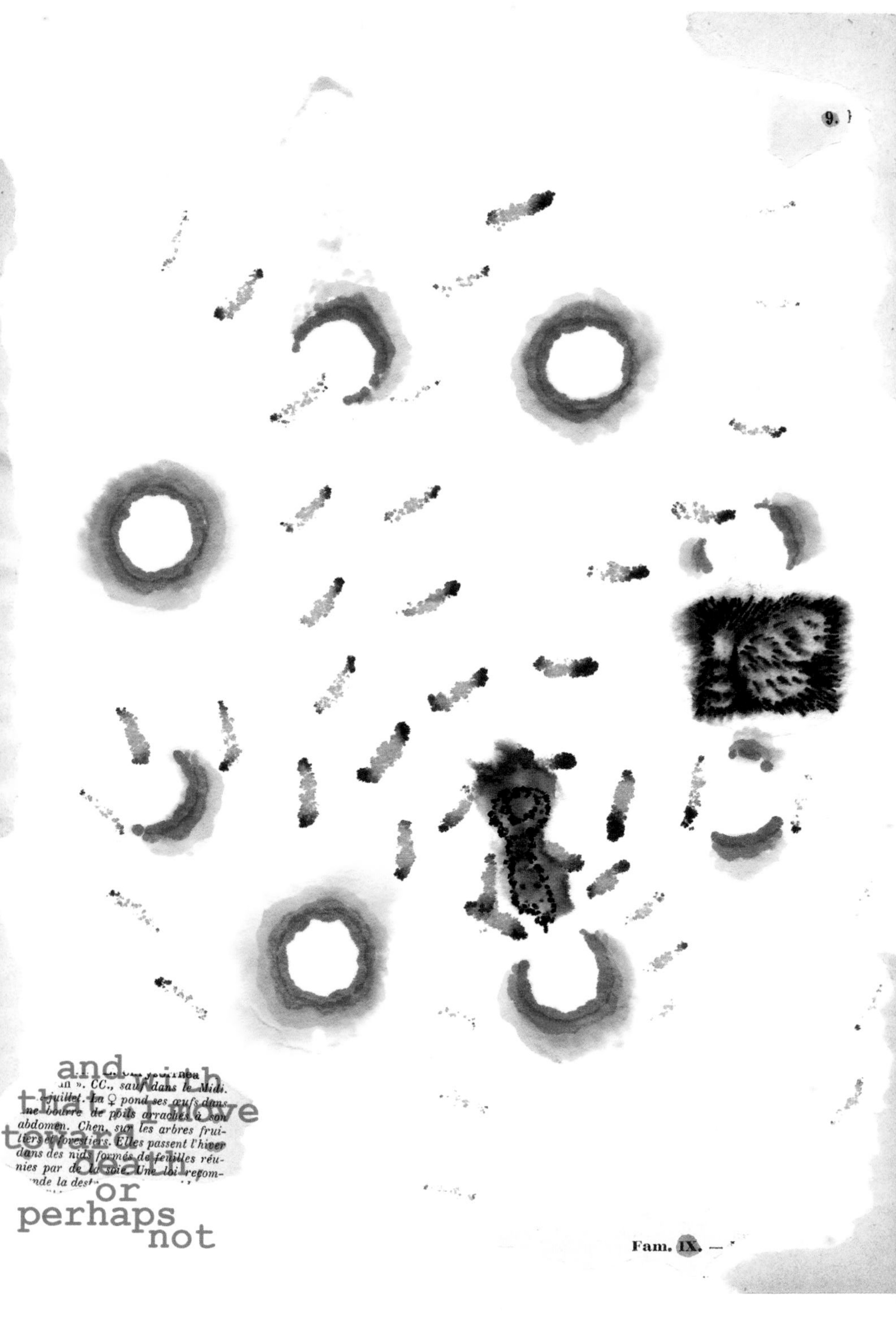
9.
and with
them I move
toward
death
or
perhaps
not
CC., sauf dans le Midi.
juillet. La ♀ pond ses œufs dans
bourre de poils arrachés à son
abdomen. Chen. sur les arbres frui-
tiers et forestiers. Elles passent l'hiver
dans des nids formés de feuilles réu-
nies par de la soie. Une loi recom-
Fam. IX. —

48

Report (provisionary)

Based on the fifty three tick marks I've made inside my box, I believe the date is October 25, 1987.

Nothing new on the defunct case to report.

expenses:
none

The life of a boxman is not entirely horrific. Yes, the box itself defines a living volume less than optimum, but consider the immediate area outside the box. With a scavenged plastic tarp, a covered veranda is created. The embankment itself is a riverside garden with a found potted plant or two. The river itself provides a beautiful view.

The days of a boxman stretch infinitely long, letting him dwell on the minutia of dealing with the increasingly cold and rainy weather, the struggle to gather food. My neighbors had been helpful when they realized I wasn't a threat to their scarce resources. They showed me where a public water spigot allowed them to wash and get a drink, and where the nearest public restrooms were located. A few sympathetic restaurant employees let them to collect leftover food that would be thrown out.

With the rest of my time, I thought about the case of the out-of-context son. Now it was the case of the many out-of-context persons, including myself, although I doubted anyone had filed a missing person report. My life was rather solitary and nontraditional, no one would think twice about my disappearance. At least not for a long while.

During my boxman days, I thought about finding out what happened to the others: the clerk, the fortuneteller, Obushi. But I reached the conclusion that I was not going to do any good, likely I'd make their situation worse. My ponderous investigation caused all the trouble to begin with. Wherever I went, my presence caused violence and pain. If I could have rectified the situation, I would have, but I had no plan, no idea how to resolve the trouble I caused.

I was an out-of-context man to all who knew me. I'd joined the legion of those who walked away from their lives and became a memory, soon to fade. In a sense, I'd become a new person, one with little value. The stares of passersby were the hardest to take. I stopped looking at them, kept my head down, and averted my gaze.

Aches and pains were constant. Only a few days out of the fifty-three were free of some kind of illness like a cold, a headache, or gastrointestinal distress. On this fifty-third day of boxman existence, I was burning with fever and freezing with chills. I made my way across town to a hospital. Not just any hospital, but the one with the wife from the old case. If I was going to die, I wanted to at least see her before I did. I could tell her . . . tell her what?

I staggered down a street in the direction of the hospital. The noon sun came out from behind the clouds and beat me with its radiation. The light blinded me and I felt my way with a hand on the buildings, my fingers filthy with urban grime. I smelled of the cardboard that constantly surrounded me.

When I reached the lobby of the hospital, I collapsed.

▸

When I woke, it was night. A needle attached to a plastic tube was stuck in my arm. I was wearing a hospital gown. My clothes, such as they were, hung from a hook across the room. I was feeling better. No, incredibly lucid. Whatever they were dripping into my veins was a miracle drug.

"Hello?" I called out quietly.

In a few seconds, a nurse appeared. "You're awake," she said.

"How long have I been here?"

"Let's see," she said checking my case record. "You have been here exactly thirty-six hours."

"One and a half ticks," I said.

"Pardon me?"

"Never mind."

"How are you feeling?"

"Very well."

She took my temperature and blood pressure and made several notes on my chart.

"May I leave now?" I asked.

"You seem to have fully recovered, but the resident physician will have to be the one to release you."

"Thank you," I smiled.

She smiled back and I felt human.

The resident came in a few minutes later and flipped through my chart. "You've made a good recovery," he said. "You had an intestinal bacterium and severe dehydration. But it's cleared up already."

"I feel great."

"I shouldn't wonder," he said. "You were very ill when you showed up. You've been living on the street, if you don't mind me saying."

I nodded. "Circumstances."

"You will need to take better care of yourself if you don't want a relapse."

"I don't want that. Say, I wonder if you could help me out. I believe an acquaintance, an old friend, is or was a patient here. She was in a coma."

"Coma patients are in long-term care, that's another wing. It's a big hospital, you know. I treat sometimes fifty patients a day."

He signed my release and left before I could ask another question. I got dressed, my clothes hanging loosely on my frame. There was a mirror in the room and I stood in front of it. An emaciated stranger stared back at me.

I wandered the hospital until I found the long-term care wing. Down the hallway, standing outside one of the rooms, was the police detective who had been following me. He looked my way. I ducked back out of the corridor and hurried out of the hospital.

▸

Walking with renewed energy, almost euphoria, I made it to my neighborhood before dawn. I watched my house from a distance to be sure there was no sign of anyone inside. I saw nothing and hurried across the street and let myself in with a hidden extra key. The smell was strange, foreign. But then I realized it was the smell of me, the pre-boxman me, and I was overwhelmed by a flood of memories.

Some things in the rooms were different. The table on which the television sat was now nearly in the middle of the room, the television on the floor. There was a stack of mail on the table. On top of the mail was a note.

Fujii and I have been taking care of your place. Someone ransacked it and we cleaned it up. Let us know when you get back.

Signed, the newsstand owner.

I checked the rest of the house and found my things in the same dislocated state. But I have nothing anyone would want. Then I remembered.

In my bedroom, I checked the false bottom of the chest of drawers. Inside was the art and photos I'd collected from Mizuno and Obushi.

I showered and changed my clothes for the first time in weeks. I filled a suitcase with clothes, and the art and photos. I grabbed my bank card and passport. After one last look around, I left the house and walked down my street. I slipped a note through the mail slot of the newsstand not yet open.

Thanks to you and Fujii for taking care of my place. I'll be gone for several more days. If I could impose on you for that much longer to look after things, I would be in your debt forever. Please do not tell anyone that I've been around.

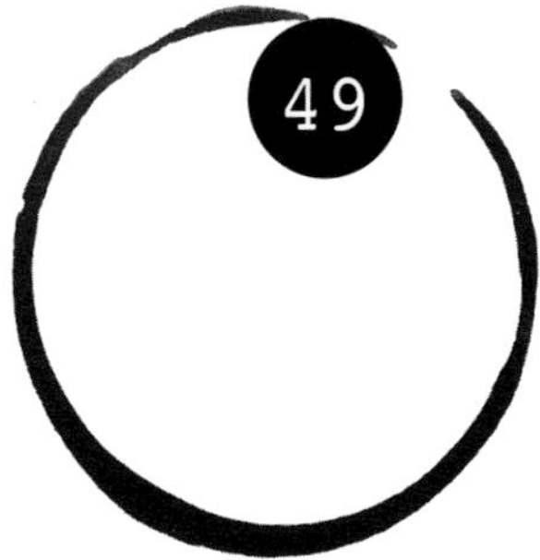

My hotel room on the western outskirts of Mexico City overlooked a small neighborhood plaza. A *zocalo.* The sunlight streamed through the windows in my room at an angle that created severe parallelograms, angular pockets of warmth on the otherwise cool tile floor. With its high ceilings and expansiveness, the hotel room's volume was greater than my entire house. A large bed on posts rising high above the floor had enough room underneath it for four boxman accommodations.

My flight had arrived just after midnight. I took a taxi to the hotel, checked in, then tried to sleep. But I couldn't except for a few minutes. At dawn my jet lag was not unlike being split and compressed. I was really out of context.

A hot shower revived me. I went down to the front desk and with the help of a phrase book made it understood I wanted to hire an interpreter for two or three days. The two employees at the front desk—both young and cheerful—had a lengthy discussion, after which I gathered that it would take them some time to find someone. I told them I'd take a walk, have breakfast, and return. At least that's what I thought I told them.

The sky was a bright, dazzling white, although the sun itself was obscured with a haze of smog that was worse than Tokyo's even on a bad day. The *zocalo* was lively with vendors, newspaper sellers, kids running to school, old men chatting on benches, business people eating at sidewalk cafés making animated gestures, a steady stream of taxis and cars honking and changing lanes without much order. I absorbed the energy, felt my spirits lift.

After a breakfast of eggs cooked in a spicy tomato sauce, slices of mango, and dark, rich coffee unlike anything I'd tasted in Japan, I made my way back to the hotel. In the lobby, the front desk employee saw me and pointed toward a young Mexican woman. She was about thirty I guessed. She introduced herself in Japanese. "I am Cecelia Garza."

"Pleasure to meet you," I said.

"I am happy to translate and humbly show you my country."

Her Japanese was formal, standard dialect and technically fluent. Her accent nearly perfect.

"Thank you for being available at such short notice," I said.

"I am pleased that I can help."

We went into the lobby café where we drank coffee. I was buoyed by the second dose of the strong drink.

"Are you here for the Day of the Dead?" she asked.

"The Day of the Dead?"

"Many tourists come here for the Day of the Dead. During the first two days of November we celebrate our ancestors and those who have died. It's very similar to your country's *o-bon* ancestor festival."

"It does sound similar. Is the Day of the Dead a religious holiday?"

"Let's see . . . it's a little difficult to explain. It's partially Aztec, partially Catholic. The souls of the departed return home to the world of the living from heaven, hell, and purgatory. It's a time to rejoice; we don't cry on the Day of the Dead. The path back to the living world must not be made slippery by tears."

"I like that image very much. By the way, where did you learn your excellent Japanese?"

She smiled. "Thank you very much. I studied at a university here, then I lived two years in Japan."

"Did you enjoy living in Japan?"

"I did for many reasons. But the main one is that Japan is so serene."

"It often is," I said. "But not always."

We left the hotel and strolled along a side street where vendors were selling trinkets, jewelry, clothing. She explained the silver jewelry came from a local artists colony. I admired a bracelet she handed me. I gave her back the bracelet and told the vendor it was exquisite, but not for me. Cecelia translated and the vendor nodded as he placed it on the table and reached over to the end of his spread of jewelry. He handed me a delicate silver butterfly. It was intricate and beautiful.

"It's wonderful," I said. "Surely I can't afford it."

Cecelia asked its price and relayed it to me and said I could bargain with him.

"It's beautiful," I said. "But I just arrived so I'd like to look around first."

Cecelia translated and the vendor took back the butterfly with a soft, knowing frown, much like a fortuneteller's as she divines her client's fate. Further down the row of vendors was a bakery stall. Cookies and candies shaped like skulls were piled high on tables, stacked in pyramidal shapes. Cecelia picked up one of the cookies and a sugary candy.

"*Calavera*—skulls and skeletons—are the main symbol for the Day of the Dead. But we are not frightened because with the laughing skull we see the playfulness of the ghosts."

Like an *obake*?

She bought us a small bag of the candies. "They are given as tokens of friendship and love. You will see them everywhere, on altars and graves, at the favorite places of a dead person. My mother puts them under a tree where my grandmother liked to sit. As my grandmother told her daughters, as my mother told me, 'Bring the sweet bread of the dead for your ancestors, they are hungry. Offer them a sugar skull, so they know you remember them.'"

"How long do the ghosts stay?"

"Only for one day, but on the first day the ghosts of children return, on the second day it's the ghosts of adults. Look," she pointed to vendors selling toy skeletons. There were carved wooden skeletons sporting punk hairstyles and playing in rock bands. Papier-mâché skulls had pink flowers for eyes and green lizards on their brows. Wooden puppet skeletons on rods danced wildly, with arms and legs flailing.

"The *calaveras* sing, dance, laugh. They even ride on merry-go-rounds and drive rickety wooden trucks. The dead are full of life."

"Yes, they are," I said. "Why do the ghosts come back?"

Cecelia thought for a moment. "I don't know. I suppose it's to comfort the living."

▸

We visited a small museum that displayed the local history from pre-Columbian times, through the Spanish conquest, and into the revolutionary era. A minor Aztec ruin was unearthed during a construction project and was partially displayed in the museum. She read the signs that explained the purpose of the stone artifacts and ceremonial trappings.

The warmth of the day, the languid pace of our strolling, my large breakfast still being digested, and the jet lag made me lethargic. I wanted to go back to my room, sleep for days. Sleep for the rest of my life. Wake up just before I die, look around, and say goodbye.

And then we came to a display case with several representations of butterflies carved in stone. "What's this about?" I asked Cecelia.

She translated as she read the sign: "The behaviors of butterflies were studied and worshiped by the ancient peoples of Mexico. The Aztecs believed their ancestors visited relatives in the form of butterflies. Bouquets of flowers were carried and placed in special places to attract the butterflies. On the other hand, many people in Mexico believe that somebody will die when a black butterfly appears."

A tsunami of black butterflies, millions of them, flew at me, taking away all the air, pressing against me, crushing the brittle remains of my life.

"Are you all right?" she asked me.

"Can we sit for a few moments?"

"Of course, she said.

this was made of twenty or twenty-five young women, although some were likely girls. They wore short skirts, skimpy tops, high heels in which they walked around and around inside the arc of the circle. Sometimes they reached out and touched the men on the arms, on their thighs. One of the women walked close to me, not looking at me directly, but I could see her giving me the once over, probably sizing me up for how much I might pay. When she was close enough to touch me, her fingertips traced my groin from one hipbone to the other. I backed away. She looked unconcerned by my rejection and continued her circular journey of seduction.

Rather than desire, I felt revulsion, anger, and disgust, not at the young woman, but the parade of humankind to be had for a few pesos. The men looked disinterested, like customers at a car dealership not expressing too much enthusiasm in fear of raising the price. Occasionally one of the men would peel off from the crowd with one of the women.

When it seemed as if there were too many men to be satisfied, I saw a movement and looked up. In the windows of the narrow buildings that lined the alleyway, many more women were looking down at the parade. I waded back through the crowd. The men closed in around me, but they didn't care about me. Their eyes were focused in only one direction.

One of the women gave me a long look with half-opened eyes, undoubtedly trying to determine my willingness to pay, or my ethnicity, or both. She looked eighteen, nineteen, but I really couldn't tell her age. Her face was full, fresh, with small circles of acne on her cheeks. I nodded at her and she grasped my hand. It was soft, moist. Mine was sweating. She pulled me toward a door, guarded by a pair of men wearing cowboy hats. One of them held the door open while the other stepped inside with us. The woman looked at me, gestured with her head to the man. He said something to me and held out his hand. I dipped into my pocket and took out my roll of pesos. The man laughed and slipped off a few bills from the top.

I followed the woman down a corridor into an open room portioned off with opaque shower curtains. The room was filled with grunts of men, squeals of women, and the smells of sweat and bodily fluids. We went into one of the vinyl-portioned cubicles where there was a single mattress on a rough frame of unfinished wood. She started to take off her thin, transparent blouse, but I grabbed her hand and shook my head. I gave her the rest of my pesos. Her eyes were suddenly open fully, with a look of confusion then fear. There was no telling what she thought I wanted.

All I wanted was for her to get out of there.

I slept only fitfully again. The next morning, Cecelia and I went to a coffee shop and bakery in a historical district of the city to meet a friend. The bakery was ten times as large as the one near my home and was stocked with at least a hundred different pastries and breads. We each picked up a plastic tray and selected two or three pastries. We also got coffee, and we sat a table looking out onto the district's buildings that survived the great earthquake.

There we met Marta Trujillo—a tall, elegant woman who was the director of a social agency that worked with prostitutes and exploited children. We ate and drank for a few minutes before settling into serious conversation. Speaking with authority, Marta's gaze was directly on me while Cecelia translated, as if measuring each word's effect. "The women and girls come from all parts of Mexico. Some are from Central America. They are usually driven here in vans, assigned to a pimp, abused and intimidated to fear their pimp and obey him without question. Then they are thrown to the johns. Sink or swim. If they make it in La Merced, that is, if they make enough money for their pimps, they may be moved to other places with a more exclusive clientele. Like Acapulco, Puerto Vallarta, or to the big cities in the U.S.—Los Angeles, Chicago, Miami, New York."

I nodded that I understood. "What if she doesn't make enough money?"

"If she doesn't respond to being beaten, she's usually turned loose. Of course, she ends up on the streets, trying to make it on her own. She can't go back home. Usually, if she doesn't get help, like from our organization, she will be dead in a year. Killed by a john or a pimp or disease or malnutrition."

We sipped our coffee in silence for several moments.

"I'm here on a mission," I said. "It's rather vague, unfortunately, but if you could help me, I would appreciate it very much."

"I'll try."

What could I tell her? There was so much and so little. I started by showing her a photocopy of the collage.

"Yes, that looks like La Merced," Marta said. She and Cecelia exchanged a few words not translated, glancing at me two or three times while they talked in Spanish. "Go on," Marta finally said.

I told her how the case began, with the fortuneteller's missing son. I showed her the couple of pages from the butterfly book that I'd photocopied and brought with me. I told her about the photographer's wife, dead in this country, but she was a ghost haunting her husband, wanting to tell him something, or was it only in his mind. His delusions created by his guilt.

I explained how I'd found out about the sex tours offered by the Moonlight Travel Agency, one connection leading to another, finally to the president of a publishing group. I told her about the contractor's van and the last words out of the clerk's mouth. *Ra muraseido.* La Merced. Did it make any sense? It didn't to me, so how could it make sense in translation? Cecelia must have worked it into something comprehensible because Marta asked, "What do you want from me?"

But I didn't know. "Help me make sense of it," was all I could think of to say.

Cecelia translated my request and Marta stared at me, her eyes squinted in bewilderment, as if I were a lunatic.

Marta said, "It will never make sense, it's insanity."

▸

Cecelia took me to the Institute of Forest Biology at a university near my hotel. The laboratory of Dr. Rafael Lemos was filled with a musty, slightly sweet odor, like an overripe pumpkin.

"Thank you for seeing us," I said.

"You're welcome, but I have only a few minutes," he said, looking at me over reading glasses. His hair was long and tied in the back in a ponytail. "Sorry, I have a class to teach."

I showed him the sketches and photos of the butterflies and forest scenes. "Is it possible to identify where these might have been drawn and photographed?"

He studied them through his reading glasses. "How precise a location are you interested in?"

"As close as possible."

After he studied them for a minute, he turned around in his chair and pulled a book off his shelves. He opened it on the table and flipped through the pages. "Here," he said, pointing to a map. "Based on the types of trees and geography, I'd say it was the Rosario monarch sanctuary, about one hundred kilometers west of here. The specific location is difficult to see, but it's likely taken from the trail provided to tourists so they can see the butterflies. There's a souvenir stand area just outside the town of Santo Tomas where the trail starts."

The town sounded familiar . . . Was it one of the Mexican towns the clerk found at the travel agency? "Why are there so many butterflies there?"

The professor sat back in his chair. "They are following their instinctual migration. They range over most of North America but only one in four or five generations actually makes it to the Rosario sanctuary."

He waited for the translation to see if I was still interested.

"How do they know where to migrate?" I asked. "They don't learn from others as birds or whales do, if I'm understanding you correctly."

"That's correct," said the scientist. "The sun must have something to do with their ability to navigate. The angle and intensity of light provides the direction. But it's not clear how they adjust their direction from minute to minute as the sun moves across the sky. Perhaps it's tied to some internal circadian clock." He shrugged and added, "No one knows."

"So they migrate to this little part of Mexico because the genes inherited from their ancestors compel them to?"

The professor nodded and smiled at my layperson's understanding. "We don't know for sure if that's the only reason, but of course it must be a part of it."

▸

Cecelia took me to a restaurant near the hotel. I was tired after driving around the city all day, breathing in the smog, trying to explain the investigation. My jet lag and the hangover from my illness and living on the streets for so long had weakened me to the point that I could barely taste the food set in front of me.

"You think the butterflies and the sex trade are connected to the son's disappearance?" Cecelia asked.

Butterflies => prostitution => fortunetellers => ghosts => the Day of the Dead => the Festival of Ancestors. The connections were unraveling in the mush I'd created in my mind. I said, "I don't know how they could be directly related. Perhaps indirectly."

Cecelia said, "It seems to me that you've got some clues that connect them. The collage for one. Let's try to connect them."

"I can't ask you to do anything more. It's become too much."

"But I'm interested. I want to know what happened."

"It's become dangerous before. People have gone missing, some likely killed."

"I can take care of myself."

"I know. It's not that. I don't think I can take care of myself."

"I don't believe that," she said quietly. She patted my hand, instantly warming my cold flesh and bones.

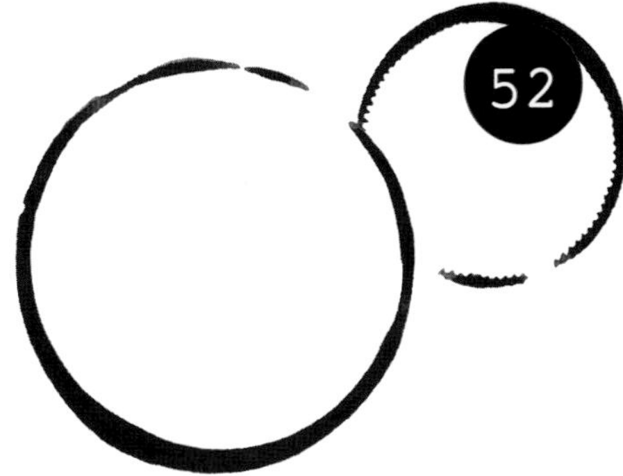

52

Detective Yolanda Profirio-Blanco, a friend of Marta Trujillo, greeted us in front of her office building in central Mexico City. The detective wore her hair pulled back in a bun and her business suit was well tailored. Her expression was somber, somewhat tired-looking. She took us to a nearby café where we sat down for breakfast. I was rapidly gaining back the weight I lost as a boxman.

Detective Blanco said, "Marta told me in general what you were interested in. To tell you the truth, I don't know how much I can help."

"Whatever you can find out would be appreciated," I said. "I know it was a long time ago."

"It's not only that, but you should know that I only agreed to meet you because of Marta. We rarely cooperate with Mexican private investigators, and never with foreigners."

"I appreciate your candor. I will try to make it worth your time."

While Cecelia translated, the police detective pulled out several sheets of paper held together with a clip. She cleared a spot on the table and put the papers there. "In general, I understand you are curious about Japanese tours. We have had relatively few problems; we rarely pick up Japanese tourists in the vice dragnets. They tend to stay in groups, have well-organized tours, and do not venture out much on their own. They tend to stay away from most illegal of activities."

The detective waited for the translation while she gulped some food and coffee.

"Now, during the time period in question, about three years ago. I found a few cases, nothing that sounds related to you. Three cases of Japanese males, two in their thirties, one in his fifties, beaten and robbed by prostitutes. This was probably due to a language problem. In another case a group of younger males in their twenties was picked up for drunkenness and solicitation. They were in a soccer club on tour. The women they tried to solicit were actually university students."

I finished my second cup of coffee. At least my headache was gone, my brain now hyperactive with caffeine and sugar.

The detective turned to a new page. "Now in the case of the Japanese woman who died, Obushi Makiko, I found nothing in our jurisdiction. I tried to get something, but the local police have yet to get back to me. I doubt they will. The locals avoid dealing with federal agents as much as possible. The only thing I can find at the national level was an appeal for information filed by the Japanese embassy."

She dug through her papers. "Ah, here. It says that the woman's case was resolved as being a traffic accident. A hit-and-run without witnesses and no suspects ever found."

"And that was the end of the case?" I asked.

"That's all I could find."

"Where did this happen?" I asked her.

"Santo Tomas, a small town in the state of Michoacán."

Cecelia asked the detective a question and when she got the answer, she told me it was indeed the same Santo Tomas mentioned by the butterfly biologist.

▸

"You need to go to Santo Thomas, don't you?" Cecelia asked. We were in the hotel bar, sitting outside on the patio, watching the sun turn fiery red as it set. The color was caused by smog particulates in the air refracting and spreading the light.

"Yes. But I can't ask you to go there."

After a sip of the tart-sweet tequila drinks she ordered for us, she said, "I want to go."

"Why? It's not your problem."

"What's that got to do with it? I'm intrigued. I want to help. Besides, you need a translator, don't you?"

"I can get by."

"As I said yesterday, I can take care of myself. I won't charge you."

"It's definitely not a question of that."

"Then what is it?"

"You're a good person. You have a lot to offer the world. You should stay here and do what you do best. I'm only here because of deep-seated guilt. A purely selfish need to resolve my failures."

We sat in silence for a while, the sun had set and it was getting cool. Cecelia said, "Why are you so wrapped up in this case? It seems personal for you."

"It has become so, but I would find it difficult to explain why."

"You don't have to explain. Do you think you'll find your answer in Santo Tomas?"

I shrugged. "I've given up on the idea of an answer. But something happened there. I feel something will happen there again."

Cecelia got up. "All right. Then let's go. I'll pick you up first thing in the morning."

"But . . ."

She shook her head and patted me on the shoulder. "In the morning."

I watched her walk out of the bar, leaving me to finish my drink. I declined the bartender's offer of a second one. Instead I ordered a beer. The bar was crowded, and all I wanted to do was sit and listen to the conversations that I couldn't understand and didn't want to. My instinct was to leave without Cecelia. Her presence was potential for trouble. What had happened so far in the defunct case of the missing son could happen again. But maybe with effort it wouldn't. With concentration and focus, I could keep from losing another person.

"Another beer?" the bartender asked me, pointing to my empty glass. His brow was furrowed. No doubt he was questioning if this tourist staring into space should have anything stronger than water. I declined and paid my tab and walked up to my room wishing I weren't alone.

As we neared Santo Tomas, the air became fresher, drier, and clearer. The town started in a flat plain near a river flowing from a mountain valley. Along the road were pockets of shacks. The roofs were scavenged tin and the walls were made from discarded plastic and posts from road signs.

The town's *zocalo* was dominated at one end by a gothic-style church. The town was less impoverished in the center district, with a ring of shops and cafés and a steady flow of cars and trucks. Our small hotel was just off the *zocalo*. When we pulled up to the lobby entrance, a doorman helped us with our bags and a valet parked our car. After we checked in our adjacent rooms, we went back down to the *zocalo*. There were a few tourists going to the cafés and shopping, but most of the town's residents were busy setting up for the Day of the Dead, putting up skeletons, devils, and other ghostly figures everywhere. A few monarch butterflies floated on the air currents around the trees in the plaza. They seemed weary, as if just waking up from hibernation only to find it still winter.

Cecelia left me sitting on a green wrought-iron bench while she went to look for information on going to the forest reserve. A clump of dark clouds massed overhead enough to block out the sun and chill the air. I wished I'd brought a heavier coat. I spotted a clothing store across the *zocalo*.

When I emerged with a jacket that smelled too new but was much warmer than my suit coat, Cecelia was talking with a police officer. He wore a tan uniform with gold shoulder braids making it look like a costume. A large handgun in a holster was strapped to his hip. His mustache was thick and bushy. Something I couldn't grow in a hundred years.

"This is Captain Sanchez," Cecelia told me.

We shook hands. His grip strong and fleshy.

"Welcome to Santo Tomas," he said. "Ms. Garza tells me that you are interested in a case from several years ago."

"Three years to be precise."

The captain laughed deeply. He grinned while Cecelia translated the captain's philosophical discourse on the meaning of three years. "Three years in Santo Tomas is both a lifetime and a few moments. It's a lifetime if you consider what can happen in three years. It's a few moments if you consider the hundreds of generations of people who have lived here."

"The case would have been unusual," I said. "A Japanese woman named Obushi Makiko died here. I imagine a case like that would be fresh in your mind."

Captain Sanchez stopped grinning. "Of course, I remember. It was resolved. An accident."

"I'm trying to find out if her death is connected to a case I'm investigating in Japan. It's concerning a missing person who was connected to the victim through her husband."

"We have no reports of a missing Japanese national."

"He may not have disappeared here. But he was here about the same time when the woman died."

"What questions do you have?" the captain asked.

"Could you tell me details of how the Japanese woman died? I'm also interested in her movements the night she died. Were there any witnesses to her death I can talk to?"

The captain crossed his arms as he listened to the translation. He spoke angrily to Cecelia and without looking at me, walked away. When he had disappeared behind a building, Cecelia said, "The captain warns me to keep your nose out of his business or it will get cut off."

"He's serious, I suppose," I said. "How did you find him in the first place?"

"I went to the local police station. The captain seemed friendly and helpful at first."

"I must have asked the wrong questions."

She got up and said, "Let's explore the town."

▸

The afternoon sun never made an appearance. In the gloom, Cecelia and I wandered the town, looking at the shops, eating a late lunch, then going back to the hotel to rest. We hadn't said anything else about Captain Sanchez or the case. In my room, I drifted off to sleep and when I woke it was dark. I rapped lightly on her door, but she didn't answer. I went down to the hotel front desk and tried some Spanish, asking, I hoped, if they had seen Cecelia. They told me no, she must still be in her room. I thanked them and went outside.

The night was cold and I was glad I had my new jacket. I walked to the *zocalo* that was lively with people listening to a band playing in one corner, or buying Day of the Dead goods from the wooden stalls. A procession of teenage boys and girls eying each other circled the plaza in opposite directions.

I walked around the plaza a couple of times, checking out the food stalls, sampling bits here and there, trying to understand what people said, but didn't care when I couldn't. I enjoyed being caught up in the festive mood, despite my not understanding exactly what was going on. In the crowd I was alone with my thoughts.

I tried to remember what Obushi told me about his wife's last night in Mexico. He was gone and she went off on her own. Where would she have gone, and what had she seen before she was killed? I turned off the street that went around the *zocalo*. There were residences behind high-walled fences. Through the gated entrances I could see into lit courtyards. From inside came music, conversation, laughter, and the smells of dinners cooking.

After two or three blocks, I turned again and came to a block where there were several noisy bars. I slowed when two men came out of one of the bars, each holding the other vertical, both laughing like drunks who think everything is hilarious. They walked past me, said something in Spanish, and started laughing louder.

I went into one of the establishments. The men were standing three or four deep at the bar, seemingly talking all at once, slapping each other on the back, waving at the bartender for drinks. I managed to catch the bartender's eye and ordered a beer. He rattled off some Spanish. I shook my head and cupped my right hand behind my right ear. The bartender showed me a bottle of beer. I nodded.

The beer was cold and tasted good. I slunk to the back of the bar and leaned against a wall. A jukebox blared Mexican music dominated by an accordion. The crowd was fluid, mostly men going in and out, greeting those inside or slapping a back when leaving.

It was not a staid Japanese drinking establishment.

I quickly finished the bottle of beer. Outside, I continued past the block and turned down another side street. An odd feeling of familiarity made me stop and survey the immediate surroundings. But I couldn't see any reason why I felt that I'd been there before. The buildings were old and rundown residences and businesses.

In the near distance, I heard music. I headed in that direction, making a few turns down dark streets to an industrial area. There were an auto parts supplier, a machine shop, a warehouse for construction materials, among others I couldn't tell what they were. At the end of the block I made another turn and saw an arc of men standing around a small makeshift stage of plywood on bricks where music was playing from a radio.

I stepped up onto the delivery ramp of a closed warehouse. Under the lights of a streetlight, in front of the stage, a circle of young women who appeared to be in their teens paraded as they had in La Merced. The men were clapping and dancing to the music, occasionally reaching out to grab one of the women who would giggle and scoot away. One of the men would follow her and she'd run, but not too fast, into the shadows away from the streetlight.

There was a tug on the sleeve of my jacket. I looked down to a young woman, maybe eighteen or nineteen, smiling at me, looking at me out of the corner of her eyes like the woman in La Merced. She was thin and wore a midriff-baring, pullover top with no shoulders. Her breasts were small, her nipples erect in the cold.

She gave me a long stare and said, "*Japonés?*" Surprised she guessed my ethnicity, I smiled and said, "*Sí, Japonés.*" She laughed then said something in Spanish while rubbing my thigh. I shook my head. The smile left her face, and she tugged insistently on my sleeve. When I told her no, she spat on the concrete ramp near my feet then moved on to the next man. I heard a familiar laugh and I looked out into the crowd.

In the middle of the sea of men, Captain Sanchez was clinging to two young women. They snuggled up to him, one on each arm, trying to pull him in opposite directions.

Report (makeshift)

31 October: exact time not noted—The defunct case of the missing son has hinged on a connection among all of the clues. Perhaps that isn't reality. The several persons I'd met during the investigation simply may not have had a direct association with Mizuno Ren. In essence, what I may have stumbled across was a manifestation of the unpredictability of cause-and-effect, of action-and-reaction. In dealing with the irrationality of humankind, the effect that follows an initiating cause, the reaction that follows an action, may not always be the logical conclusion. In short, my failures in the case were attributable to my overreaching for a solution. The clerk would say, "I told you so."

My failures might also be due to an arrogance that allows me to assume I would be able to easily resolve the Mizuno case using my experience and skills as an investigator. I am of no superior intellect, of no great reasoning powers. Unmistakably, I lack the ability to understand the world beyond my feeble perceptions.

The case itself was pulling me along in its vortex, rather than through a deliberative and rational investigation on my part. Since the first day of the case, I have been spinning rapidly, only seeing one small arc of the curve at a time, unable to get a clear picture of the entire situation, not understanding the context. Without that overview, that frame, I'm doomed to failure. On the other hand, there is no way out of the vortex. I have to go along for the ride.

expenses:
none reimbursable

As the night grew colder and the shadows grew darker, I watched the police captain and the other men touching the women, the women touching back. The music drove the wriggling, shaking, pulsing of the crowd with a rhythm of lust oblivious to the rest of the world, escalating to the point of frenzy. Despite its similarities to La Merced in Mexico City, the mood in Santo Tomas was perversely festive instead of dismal and lecherous. But what did that matter? The result would be the same.

It must have been nearing midnight of the first of the Day of the Dead holidays. The shivering of the dead coming back to visit, their cold dark whispers on my neck, announced their appearance. But they weren't frightening, in fact they spoke to me of spirit and beauty, of strength and power. Beauty is a ghost, a spirit that exists to haunt, to make mischief, to expose the essence of truth before it disappears into the netherworld of the human mind. Ugliness, the ghosts told me, only reveals itself when beauty dies. I wanted to know more, but the ghosts were as fleeting as a butterfly winging past before disappearing in a puff of air. The ghosts must have been dying by the legion watching the girls enticing the men.

The captain grabbed one of the women by the wrist. I recognized her as the one who'd tugged on my sleeve then spat near my shoes. She sidled up to him and they began to move, dance, his bulk jiggling like an ungainly bear, her lithe body wriggling like a snake's. The captain moved her slowly to the edge of the crowd, and when they reached it, they walked off. As if my raw skin was exposed to fiery heat or deadly cold, my reflexes sparked muscles into motion, propelling me forward. A woman, then another, grabbed at me, but I ignored them. They seemed unconcerned as they danced to the next potential customer. I pushed my way through the hopping and flailing and twisting men, but they didn't notice me, their eyes were dilated and focused on the women. I kept my gaze on the captain—he was a good head taller than most of the men so I had little chance of losing him.

Another woman reached out for me, raking her fingers across my groin. She laughed when I turned away. My own mortality was exposed. Suddenly I wondered if this is what Mizuno Ren experienced. Is this when the son disappeared? Is this when he gained the psychological strength to become a ghost? A ghost that visited his mother during the Festival of the Dead? Or was I imagining too much?

The captain and the woman escaped the crowd of dancing men and girls. I waited at the edge of the crowd until they were at the end of the block. I burst through the crowd and followed them. At the end of the next block, they disappeared into a building. I ran up the street, keeping in the shadows, until I stopped at the edge of the adjacent building. I peered around the edge of the exposed brick wall where ancient stucco had flaked off like dead skin. The building the captain and the woman went into looked like an abandoned hotel. I edged into the entryway lit with a low-wattage yellow bulb. Painted in faded lettering on the portico above the door was the hotel's name. "La Merced."

Ra Muraseido.

▸

The hotel lobby was stripped bare of chairs, tables, potted plants, any of the usual trappings of a lobby. Splintered wood and chunks of plaster were all that remained of the front desk. Muddy footprints tracked through the dust covering the wood floors. On the walls were rectangles of bright paint where framed works of art had once hung. A few slips of paper that looked like blank receipts or invoices were scattered on the floor.

A naked light bulb burned at the top of the abandoned hotel's stairway casting knife-blade shadows. I walked up the stairs, the sound of my shoes on the wood steps echoed harshly against the walls, each footfall a step toward the executioner waiting for the condemned. There was a beer bottle on the landing, shards of glass crunched under my shoes. The smell of stale beer and spilled tequila was pungent. At the top of the stairs, the first floor of rooms went in two directions, each consisting of four or six rooms. I looked in one of the rooms, its door missing, the interior dimly lit from the bulb in the stairwell. The room had no furniture except a stained mattress. There was a pile of garbage: beer bottles, rags, stray pieces of clothing, used condoms.

Down the corridor, I heard the grunts of men, the phony pleasure from the women. Their sounds reverberating in the corridors like a ghost's haunting cries. A man came out of a room, buckling his belt. It wasn't the captain. His cowboy boots clunked on the floor as he passed by me with only a glance, then hurried down the corridor to the stairs. A woman came out of the room adjusting her worn, short skirt. In one hand she clutched a few bills. She saw me and stuffed the bills into a pocket in her skirt. She smiled. I shook my head and she shrugged and said something that likely denigrated my virility.

I climbed the stairs to the top floor of the five-story building. From the lack of sounds, the rooms on the floor were vacant. I went to the end of the corridor where there was a large gap in the wall that used to be a balcony. Standing as close as I could without falling, I looked down onto the street and up the block to where the unearthly dance of men and women continued. From that point of view, the scene was identical to the one sketched by Mizuno Ren, the scene reconstructed in the collage.

The shimmering in my peripheral vision raised the hairs on my neck. With a whip of my head, I turned and braced myself against the wall, expecting to be pushed through the jagged gap. But there was no one in the dark corridor.

It was the first of the Day of the Dead, the one reserved for the children who died, the *angelitos.* The *zocalo* and surrounding streets were already buzzing with people buying candles, flowers, costumes, toys, candies, *pan de muerto*—breads and pastries in the shape of skulls. Amid the festivities, Cecelia and I ate breakfast at a square table in the circular patio of our hotel's café. We were having some of the *pan de muerto,* fruit, and coffee. Cecelia pointed out a person carrying bags of flowers with thick and curling yellow-orange petals. "The souls of the dead follow the fragrant trail of the *cempasúchil* petals to return to earth." She took a small dictionary from her bag. "Marigolds."

"The dead, the ghosts, can smell?" I asked.

Cecelia nodded. "The petals provide a road for them to walk on. The altars use the colors of orange, purple, and white because they signify the dead. The altars must have dirt or earth because we live on the earth. There must be some ash because when you die you become ash. The altars also have water and some type of food because the dead are very thirsty and hungry, since they haven't had a drink or something to eat for a year."

"In Japan, we do something similar with our altars. We leave oranges, rice, and sake."

"I remember seeing that in some of the homes I visited. They also burned incense. We light candles for the dead, representing the light inside each person."

"Wouldn't you rather be at home for the holiday?" I asked her. "Your family must have plans."

"It's all right. They know I'm working. I want to be here."

We started on another pot of coffee. The clouds gathered and bunched, then loosened, allowing the sun to show through before they bunched again. When the sun was behind the clouds, the air was instantly cold. Cecelia wrapped her hands around her coffee mug. She was wearing a thick sweater made of brilliant blue, white, and yellow yarn. She seemed tired, as if she hadn't slept well. I hadn't slept at all, other than a few fitful minutes. My mind wouldn't stop reliving the time I spent in the Hotel La Merced. After standing in the corridor of the top floor for several minutes, catching my breath, watching the dance below, I wanted to find the captain, pull him off the woman who spat at my shoes. But I knew it would be useless to interfere. I'd be dead if I stepped one foot into the room.

"What do we do next?" Cecelia asked.

I hadn't told her about the Hotel La Merced. I didn't know if it was the key to what I was looking for. If it was, it had to be me alone who pursued that line of investigation. I had to be careful, much more careful than I had been. Cecelia glanced at me and noticed something that must have distressed her because she looked away quickly then stared at her coffee mug. She might have seen in my eyes the horror of the street dance and the transactions in the Hotel La Merced. I gazed to the bottom of the patio's short wall where it met the tiled floor. I felt the shimmering and then the compression dragging me into the angled edge. I shook them off.

From my pocket, I took out one of the photographic prints of the collage and pointed to the butterflies in the background. "I'd like to go to the butterfly sanctuary. It must be where the missing son visited to capture his images."

"Okay," Cecelia said. "I'll find a guide for us."

I showed her the print and pointed to the row of artist stalls in the background. "And this place."

"Shouldn't that be back in Mexico City?" Cecelia asked. "Near the La Merced District?"

"I'm thinking it might be somewhere near here."

Cecelia studied the print. "It looks like a typical artisan marketplace. There is might be one here."

I pointed to a stall in the print that seemed to be the focus. "This place, I think, was important to Mizuno Ren."

She nodded and took the photograph from me. "You finish the coffee while I make some calls about a guide to the butterfly sanctuary. And I'll ask the hotel staff if there is a marketplace like the one in the photo."

▸

When Cecelia returned, we walked away from the main plaza, down streets that were filled with Day of the Dead celebrations. People were dressed as skeletons, the devil, ghouls, and ghosts. Bands and portable stereos created impromptu dance floors. Marigold petals floated among the monarch butterflies drifting leisurely toward the mountains. Doors to homes were wide open, so the dead could find the altars dedicated to them.

After we walked several blocks, we came to a dead-end side street with a small park where a soccer game was being played on the scruffy grass. The kids playing ranged from six to sixteen years old, I guessed. The goalposts were made from mismatched poles and sticks held up with a pile of rocks and broken chunks of concrete. Along the other side of the street was a row of artisan stands selling woven blankets, pottery, jewelry, paintings. A few tourists were walking slowly along the stalls, but no one seemed too interested in buying or selling. The area didn't seem to be on the main tourist route. Maybe the prices were lower here than those able to secure spots near the *zocalo.*

We walked up and down the street holding up the photo in front of us.

"There," Cecelia said.

"I think you're right," I said, looking at one of the artisan's stalls. It was built out of wide rough hewn boards, and painted colorfully with purples and reds and gold. It reminded me of the murals we'd seen at Teotihuacan. We stepped closer and the artist watched us from her chair. Inside, there were sketches and paintings on the wall, mostly abstract visions of flames, clouds, or a living, colorful mist.

We walked up casually as if we were only mildly interested in her work. The artist smiled and nodded. She was probably sixty years old with highlights of gray-white in otherwise deeply black hair. Her face was strongly presented with high cheekbones and a sharp arch to her eyebrows. Cecelia engaged the artist in a long conversation. As they talked I inspected the paintings more closely. When I changed my focus from intense to soft, as if trying to split, I could make out familiar patterns within the mass of brushstrokes, seemingly random lines, and splashes of color. The patterns were organic and inorganic images of leaves, buildings, animals, people, flowers, cars. But then it might have been my imagination, like watching clouds and spotting recognizable forms.

The more I gazed, the more the images in the paintings became recognizable and the more animated they became. The leaves changed color, the flowers dropped their petals, the animals ran, people died. Emotions collided deeply inside me: profound horror, ethereal happiness. The paintings were a manifestation of the opposing curves that defined my life. There was no reason for simple paintings to contain so much meaning. Her work was merely interesting, clever, nothing more than that. I wanted it to be nothing more than that. Too much of the case of the missing son had been imagined, conjured up from what I wanted to believe.

When their conversation ended the artist's gaze rested softly on me, and suddenly I was reminded of the fortuneteller. In a strange, whispered voice, Cecelia said, "She claims she paints a person's spirit, the ghost that the person will become."

The artist said, "When I was a girl, maybe ten or so, I started painting. Other artists start with representational art like figures, landscapes, still life. I started out simply painting my feelings, what I felt in my heart. Sounds, tastes, words have color for me."

After Cecelia finished translating, I showed the picture of Mizuno Ren to the artist. "I wonder if you remember a Japanese man who was here about three years ago. I think he was looking at your stand here; I don't know if he actually came in or if you met him. He is, or was, an illustrator of insects. Most likely he was here to work with the butterflies."

She handed back the photograph. "Yes, I do remember him. Very well. He was interested in my work."

"Did he believe in your work?" I asked her.

"He didn't say one way or the other. He was disturbed about something. I could feel that strongly. I finally understood he was seeking something within himself. Whether you would call it a spirit, a ghost, a soul, an essence of energy, it doesn't matter."

As she spoke, I felt the dread I'd felt at the Mizuno home when I first visited. The black hole of negative energy began sucking me in. I gripped the edge of the artist's table and forced a question from my drowning lungs. "What did he experience here?"

"He spoke little," she said, shrugging. "Not because his Spanish wasn't good. It was actually very good. He didn't have the words, not in any language. But I could feel he had indeed experienced something."

"Was he alone?" I asked after a thought.

"Alone? He was when he came to my stall. I don't know if he had come alone to Santo Tomas."

"I ask because it was about the time that a Japanese woman died in Santo Tomas."

"I remember the Japanese woman dying. An accident, wasn't it?"

"Officially, yes. Did Mizuno talk about her or anything to do with prostitution?"

"Nothing like that." The artist thought for a moment. "He experienced something, is all I can say. And like all who experience life, rather than merely going through daily existence, he felt the weight, the gravity of life." She gazed at me softly but intensely at the same time. Then suddenly she looked away from me. It was as if she had torn away a chunk of my consciousness, as if she ripped away my soul and tossed it to the dogs that roamed Santo Tomas.

The artist and Cecelia spoke for two or three minutes before Cecelia said, "She wants to paint you. You won't fully understand until you've experienced it. I need to leave you alone with her."

I nodded.

"I'll be at the hotel," Cecelia said.

Behind a blanket drawn across her stall doorway, I sat as still as possible, breathing slowly, regularly, as if in meditation. After a few minutes, my mind began to slow, dispensing with unnecessary thoughts, blocking out the sounds of the Day of the Dead celebration.

The scratching of the brush across her canvas sounded like fingernails on a coffin lid. I let the feeling of dread wash over me like a cold wave. I had to sacrifice myself, my "self," for understanding. The cold grew worse—the cold of death. Was the artist sucking life from me? The little bit of warmth left? But what was the essence of life, simply the little bit of warmth? But it wasn't my coldness I was feeling—it was the cold of the missing son. The cold of Mizuno's realization of the inhumanity in him, in all of us. We are one step away, one thought, one desire, one second of self-preservation, from unspeakable horror. The splitting of our soul, our spirit, whatever it was that allowed us to have the psychological strength to become a ghost.

The son at last found his strength.

The last spark of warmth left me. I felt weaker and weaker until I nearly passed out. Then it was over and the light flooded back into the artist's stall. She turned her drawing so I could see. I shivered in the cold, and all I could see were white and black waves and where they crossed they created little spots of gray. It looked like a pool of dark, dirty water filled with brown leaves.

I thanked her and paid and left with the drawing of my miserable ghost.

▸

The guide Cecelia found picked us up at our hotel. Jorge Mendoza, a forester and biologist, had a thick, unruly mass of hair and yellow teeth. In that regard, he reminded me of the clerk, and a pang of regret stabbed at me. Jorge helped us climb into his jeep, me in front, Cecelia on the back seat. We drove slowly through the streets, as many of the townspeople were out for the festival.

"Thank you for helping us on a holiday," I said to our guide.

Cecelia leaned over the backseat and translated my thanks to him. Jorge responded in Japanese: "No problem."

"You speak Japanese," I said. "I'm sorry I don't know a word of Spanish."

"No problem," he said. Then he said something in Spanish to Cecelia.

She laughed. "All he knows how to say in Japanese is 'No problem.' Helps with Japanese tour groups."

I said in Japanese, "No problem."

We drove several minutes, first through the town then past small farms, patches of dirt really, with a few heads of livestock. In the distance was a cloud of smoke adding to the low clouds.

"Someone is clearing land," he shouted over the roar of the engine. "Slash and burn. It's why we need the government to dedicate more land to the reserve system. We need to protect the habitat, or the butterflies will not have the biosphere they need to survive when they migrate here."

"Will it be successful?"

"Only time will tell," he said.

We drove slowly through the increasingly dense swarms of monarchs.

"It's getting thick," Cecelia whispered, as they butterflies scattered in front of us.

We drove a little further and when we reached a ridge we stopped. Jorge got out of the jeep with a pair of binoculars. Cecelia and I stood beside him. I couldn't see what he was looking at except a small cloud of dust being raised in the distance. "Illegal logging," Jorge said.

He handed me the binoculars. I looked through them and saw a big truck and flatbed trailer loaded with cut and trimmed trees of considerable girth. I handed the binoculars to Cecelia. She translated as she looked through them.

Jorge said, "They're taking advantage of the holiday. All of the forestry marshals have the day off. I could radio in the sighting, but no one would answer. At least not in time."

We got back in the jeep and drove a few more minutes until we came to a sign announcing the limits of the reserve. Just past the sign, we parked by a row of souvenir stands: butterfly t-shirts, postcards, cookies, kites. Butterflies encased in acrylic. There weren't many tourists, as they must have been down in town at the festival. We walked past the stalls then to a trailhead. There were signs in several languages. I read the Japanese:

`Please stay on the trails. Do not disturb the butterflies when they are resting or engaged in mating.`

"I'd never disturb anything engaged in mating," I said. Cecelia laughed and Jorge did too after she translated.

Other displays described the butterflies' migratory patterns and other information about the butterflies that Professor Lemos in Mexico City had explained.

I asked Jorge: "Do you give many tours to Japanese tourists?"

"Not many. Only two since I've been here."

"Would you have been a guide for an artist who was here to draw the butterflies? It was about three years ago. His name was Mizuno Ren." I showed him the photograph. "He may also have been here with a photographer, also Japanese. His wife was killed in a hit-and-run traffic accident. Obushi was their name."

"Three years ago? Wouldn't have been me. I was just transferred here two years ago. But I will check with my colleagues. Most of them were here then."

After we finished reading the signs, we began to walk up the trail. Jorge led us with a quick pace, soon I was breathing heavily. But the exercise felt good and warmed me. When we stopped at a small clearing in the forest overlooking a dense stand of trees, several butterflies flitted by my ear. I could hear their wings beating, the sound like a silk robe sliding from a body.

Jorge said, "They are flying a little slow. Must be the cold."

"Is the cold weather unusual?" I asked.

"This cold is very unusual," Jorge said, then pointed. "Here."

We turned down a side path off the main trail, and then hiked down a slope until we came to a glen. The space was about the size of a soccer field. It was filled with the fluttering, dancing, flitting, orange-and-black soup of millions of butterflies. I turned to Cecelia and she smiled and wrapped her arm around mine.

57

When we drove into town, church bells were chiming. Cecelia told me that it was another Day of the Dead tradition. At six p.m., the bells begin to ring, summoning the deceased. In the town's cemeteries, families gather around the graves of their departed relatives. They bring baskets of food and drink, musical instruments, and heaps of marigold petals. The families stand vigil throughout the night, ensuring they will be recognized when the ghosts arrive for the feast offered them. The following day, after the spirits have had their fill, what's left is consumed as part of an elaborate picnic.

Jorge dropped us off at a restaurant lively with locals. The forestry biologist had to go to his family, so we couldn't persuade him to have dinner with us. Cecelia and I had to wait for a table in the restaurant's bar where there was a fire burning in a large stone hearth.

"You didn't tell me about your drawing, the one the artist made for you," Cecelia said.

"There isn't much to say because I didn't understand what she said to me. I can show you the drawing." I took it out of the folder I'd been keeping in my carry bag, and handed it to her.

"Wow. I don't know what to make of it either," she said. "You must have a colorful spirit." I looked at it from across the table. The whites and blacks, and browns and grays I'd seen before were splatters and shapes of so many colors that their chaotic patterns made me dizzy.

I put it away when the waiter brought our drinks and the appetizers we ordered. Cecelia said, "Are you any closer to solving your case?"

I didn't know. "Maybe a little," I said.

Cecelia smiled cheerfully. "Good. I'm glad." Then she laughed. "You know, you remind me of someone I met in Japan. That's one reason I wanted to come with you."

"I feel sorry for anyone who reminds you of me."

She shook her head. "He was a teacher at the school where I was studying. You hear of teacher-student affairs of course. I never thought I'd be the type to be involved in such a thing. But it happened."

"Was it good or bad?"

"The sex?"

"I hadn't meant that in particular, but if you wish to indulge an old man's fantasies."

"You're not old. The sex was, well, nice. No, very nice." She smiled again, perhaps in reminiscence.

"But that's not why you brought up your affair, is it?"

"No. When he was a boy, I think he was eight or nine, his mother disappeared. He came home from school one day and she wasn't there. Still, he wasn't too alarmed, she might have been at the store or a neighbor's. He went about his business, homework, playing. When dinnertime came around, he grew a little concerned. He sat in the kitchen, now getting very worried, but not knowing what to do, and feeling guilty that he might have been the reason she was gone.

"When his father came home and saw his son sitting in the dark, he yelled at him, calling him stupid for not doing anything, for not making his own dinner. Of course, it seemed strange even to the young boy that his father would say those things, instead of being concerned for his mother's whereabouts.

"His father made them instant noodles. He still remembered that. The two of them ate in silence until they finished and then the father told his son to go to bed. He did, but couldn't sleep waiting for his mother to come home. She never did. His father never left the kitchen that night, he just sat there in the glare of the overhead light. The empty bowls were on the table, the pan in the sink.

"He finally went to sleep. When he woke up the next morning, his father had cleaned the kitchen and made breakfast like nothing was wrong. His father took him to the bus stop and told him to come home after school and do his homework. And make his own dinner.

"And so it went like that for days. There was never a word spoken about his mother. He asked his father two or three times about her. His father told him that she was away, and to stop asking about her. Whenever he would cry, his father would walk away from him. Not surprisingly, he grew aloof from his schoolmates. His other relatives told him nothing. Aunts and uncles visited a few times and had secret conferences with his father. Once a police officer called and asked for his father, who grabbed the phone and shooed him away.

"But over the years, it gradually seemed that nothing had happened, as if he'd never had a mother. When he graduated from university and got a job, he was suddenly overwhelmed with her memory and began to search for her. He spent most of his free time chasing leads, making visits to police stations, posting flyers. Needless to say, he wasn't a great boyfriend and we gradually slipped apart. He never found her as far as I know."

▸

Cecelia went to her room after giving me a hug. Of course I wanted to follow her into her room, but I'd be taking advantage of the melancholy brought on by her story. I almost volunteered to contact her boyfriend when I made it back to Japan to see if he ever found his mother. If he hadn't I could offer to help him. But I thought that would be the wrong gesture. She wanted her story to end the way it had.

I couldn't face the loneliness pervading my room. I walked out of the hotel and down to the *zocalo*, quieter than it had been, probably because most people were in the cemeteries or in their homes for the evening's activities. Winding through the streets, I followed the sound of the bells until I came to a cemetery. A cacophony of music came from portable stereos as well as musicians. Children screeched and ran around the gravestones playing games that I didn't understand. Adults talked and laughed, leaning on gravestones. Blankets were spread out and plates of food were arranged.

I reoriented myself and headed toward the street of the Hotel La Merced. As I walked I decided it was coming down to this: Mizuno Ren walked these streets at the same time Obushi had, likely at the same time as Obushi's wife had been killed. Assuming that Obushi's wife was not accidentally killed, the question was why had she been murdered. Whatever the reason, it was clear that Mizuno Ren and Obushi were involved somehow in the prostitution business.

Obushi was more involved than Mizuno, based on the number of his works that I'd found devoted to the subject. Wherever he went on business, he took photographs of the natural environment, likely the intended subject of the visit. He also photographed scenes from nightlife, particularly of the young prostitutes frequented by the sex tours. But the photographs weren't lascivious or erotic. They were more documentary, but not academically so, they were almost sensual, definitely artistic. They were meant to stir sympathy and empathy, not lust.

Mizuno's sketches and drawings stuck to the business of his trips: insects. Mizuno and Obushi had obviously collaborated, working so closely together that their works overlapped the same scenes. The artist's contributions had deep moods and feelings painted or drawn in them, like the earlier figure works I'd seen in the bottom of the box at his mother's home.

How did Obushi's wife fit into the collaboration? Maybe not at all. Obushi's wife perhaps stumbled on her husband's hobby and, as innocent as it was, she might have taken it wrong. But that would lead to the conclusion that Obushi killed his wife. That made no sense. All of his troubles happened while he tried desperately to contact his wife's ghost. He was genuinely distressed by her death. No, she must have seen something, or someone, that got her in trouble. Perhaps she was suspicious of her husband and followed him where she stumbled onto something she shouldn't have.

As I neared the Hotel La Merced, I slowed my pace, checking out the target. It was a quiet night, the music wasn't playing as it had been the other night. And the lights were out.

There were still two elements to the case that needed to be integrated: the Kuchi clan and the Shinshin Group president. Perhaps they were separate from what happened to Obushi's wife. But the president was involved in sex tours, that seemed certain. He could have come to Mexico supposedly to research the butterfly book. If he was here at the same time, then his presence might have been what caused the death of Obushi's wife. Maybe Mizuno or Obushi or his wife saw the Shinshin president taking a woman, or a girl, to the Hotel La Merced.

That might be cause and effect.

The Kuchi clan came in later, involved only when Obushi had begun his quest to communicate with his wife's ghost. They had bled him for more than money, as he didn't have much. They may have bled him for information. Perhaps he knew about the Shinshin president's participation in the unsavory business. But where was the proof of any of this? I needed to find out if my reasoning was on track. I had to find someone who was around then, who might have seen all or part of it. Then I remembered her, the young prostitute who knew I was Japanese, who tugged on my sleeve, rubbed my thigh, and spat at my shoes.

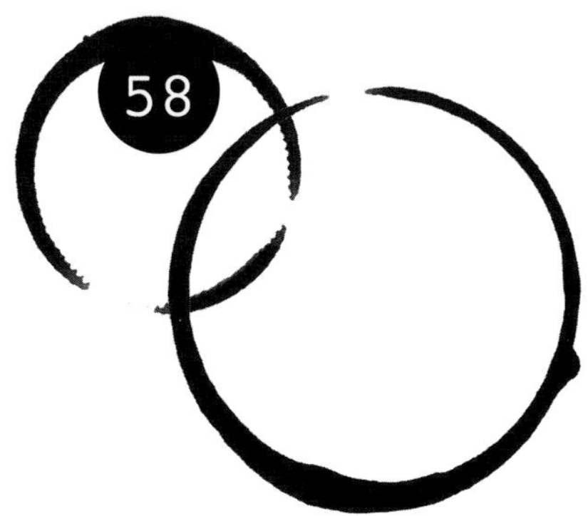

There were a few stragglers near the Hotel La Merced. The men hung out along the street and leaned up against the buildings as if they had accidentally come upon the scene and were killing time. The women and girls were not in as festive a mood as last night, and were giving the men the hard sell. No seductive smiles or touches or whispered words. I strolled into the intersection like a lost tourist. A couple of the women spotted me and came over my way. I was a fresh prospect. I gave them a goofy smile that in the garish light probably was off-putting as much as innocently inviting. They sidled up to me and said something in Spanish, one pushing the other one away, then the two argued.

A man wearing denim pants, a denim jacket, and a bandanna wrapped around his head, appeared out of the shadows of a building. He pushed the women apart and glared at me. He said something in Spanish and when I shook my head, he said a few words in bad Japanese, something like: "Hey, Japanese, you want a girlfriend?"

I tried a few words I hoped described the woman I'd seen last night. He shook his head, so I gestured at him to watch. I spit on the ground. He gave me a look of disgust, then laughed and gestured for me to wait. He disappeared into the buildings again and in a moment came back out with her. With a shove he pushed her in front of me, close enough for me to smell her earthiness not yet completely covered by a man's cologne, or countless different colognes. She was wearing her skimpy costume and her skin prickled in the cold. She crossed her arms to get warm, but the pimp slapped her on the hands and she let her arms fall to her side, and she thrust her chest out toward me. The pimp and I negotiated a price and as soon as I handed him the money, the woman took off toward the Hotel La Merced. I followed her and caught up to her side. She said a few words in Spanish. I told her in bad Spanish the obvious, "I don't speak Spanish."

She shrugged and mumbled something, then walked faster, crossing her arms in defense against the cold.

The hotel wasn't warmer than the open air, in fact, it was colder. We climbed the stairs to the first floor and she went down the corridor to the fourth room. The room was in marginally better shape than the other ones I'd seen. She motioned for me to sit on the mattress while she started to take off her skirt. Instead of complying, I reached for my pocket dictionary and money.

What I tried to get across was that I needed help to find out what happened to a friend. "Three years ago," I kept saying.

She stared at me bewildered. She shook her head. Her skirt was off and she reached for the bottom of the skimpy t-shirt she was wearing.

"No," I said in a pleading voice. "Talk only."

That stopped her. "Talk?"

"Yes," I said, first in Japanese then Spanish from my pocket dictionary. "Another Japanese man here . . . three years ago."

She put on her skirt then grabbed my hand. Hers was small but plump. She pulled me out of the room and we climbed the stairs to the top floor. We turned down the corridor where there was the gap in the wall looking down onto the street. I knew she was going to push me out of the hole. Instead we turned into a room at the end of the corridor.

In the dark I could see there were drawings tacked on the walls. When she turned on the light I knew they were done by Mizuno Ren—insects, mostly butterflies, but also caterpillars, moths, beetles, and spiders, practically his entire etymological illustration vitae in one room. Besides the insects, there were figure drawings like the ones in the collage of young women and girls with pained flirtations on their faces. Looking closely and touching the art lightly, it was obvious that the work wasn't fresh. It was faded, dry, smudged. I stood back and then I saw that in the middle of the wall, as if all the drawings emanated from it, Mizuno had created the ghosts that people will become.

▸

Cecelia threw on some clothes while Monica, the name she gave us, got comfortable in one of the chairs in Cecelia's room. I started a pot of coffee. Through the bathroom door, I asked Cecelia, "Is it all right if I let Monica wear your sweater?"

There was a pause before she said, "Okay."

I didn't think Cecelia was too happy that I'd woken her up in the middle of the night with a young prostitute in tow. But I had reached the limit of my ability to communicate with her, other than offering her double her normal rate for coming with me. She seemed reluctant, obviously not sure what her pimp would do to her if he found out. But she must have decided to take a chance. I gave Cecelia's colorful sweater to Monica, and she put it on without saying a word. Cecelia came out and finished making coffee with chocolate. She gave Monica a mug.

"How long have you been working there?" I asked after she'd taken a couple of drinks.

"Four years," she said. "I only do it sometimes, when we need money."

Cecelia translated slowly, as if still half asleep, or perhaps judging the veracity of Monica's response.

"You mean your family?"

"Yes. I have a daughter."

"How old are you?"

"Almost twenty."

"You remember the Japanese man who drew on the walls in the room you showed me?" I asked.

"Yes, he wanted to draw us too. We let him for money. Never sex, just drawing." She took a gulp.

"You remember what happened to him?"

She shrugged again. "No," she said quietly.

"It's okay," I said, "we aren't here to do anything to you. We just need to know." She stared for a while into the mug, then said, looking at Cecelia. "There was trouble one night. A Japanese woman came to the street, got into an argument with another Japanese man. A couple of the pimps dragged them away. Only the older man came back."

"You remember what he looked like?" I asked.

"A few years older than you, taller and thinner. He wore glasses. Kind of looked like a teacher, I thought."

Tomoguchi Mori? I asked her, "What happened to the Japanese artist after that?"

"He hid in that room for a few days then he disappeared."

▸

After Monica left wearing Cecelia's sweater, there was a knock on my door. Captain Sanchez came in and said something rapidly in Spanish. Cecelia responded rapidly and heatedly. "He says you need to go with him to answer some questions. He says you were seen at a building frequented by prostitutes."

I stared at him as I said, "I did nothing."

He yelled something. I could understand the meaning well enough, if not the exact words. The captain made a motion with his head for me to get out. Cecelia started to come with us, but he shoved her back into the room, pulling the door shut. He pushed me down the hall.

"You like young girls, don't you?"

He cuffed me in the back of the head. Behind him, Cecelia yelled, "Look out!" I turned to see the police captain looking back at her. I knocked his legs from under him. He landed with a grunt and I ran down the stairs two at a time.

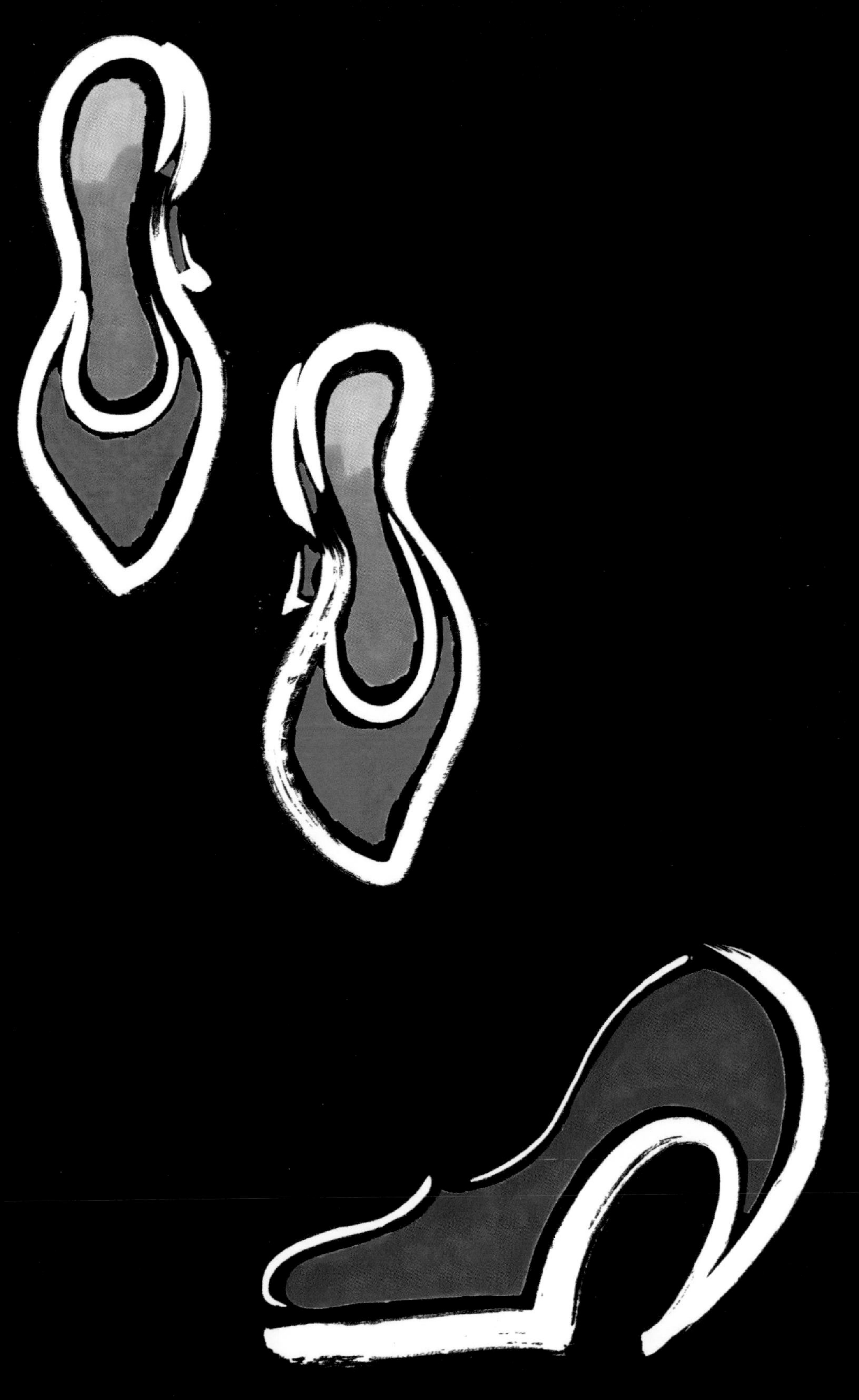

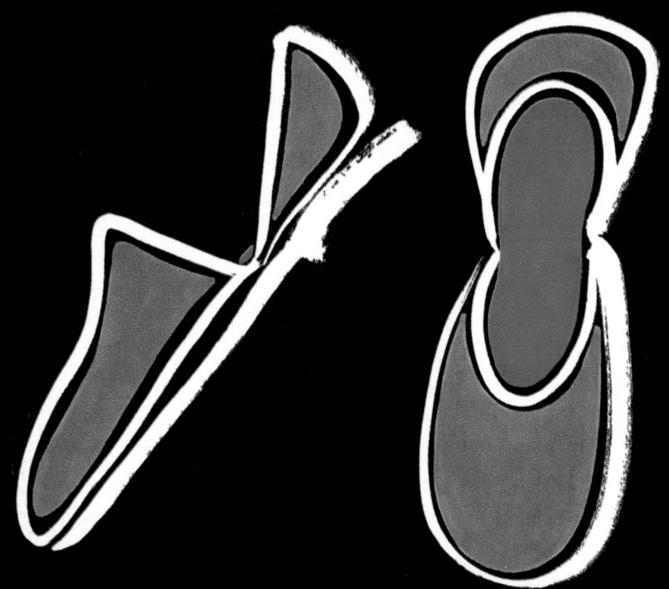

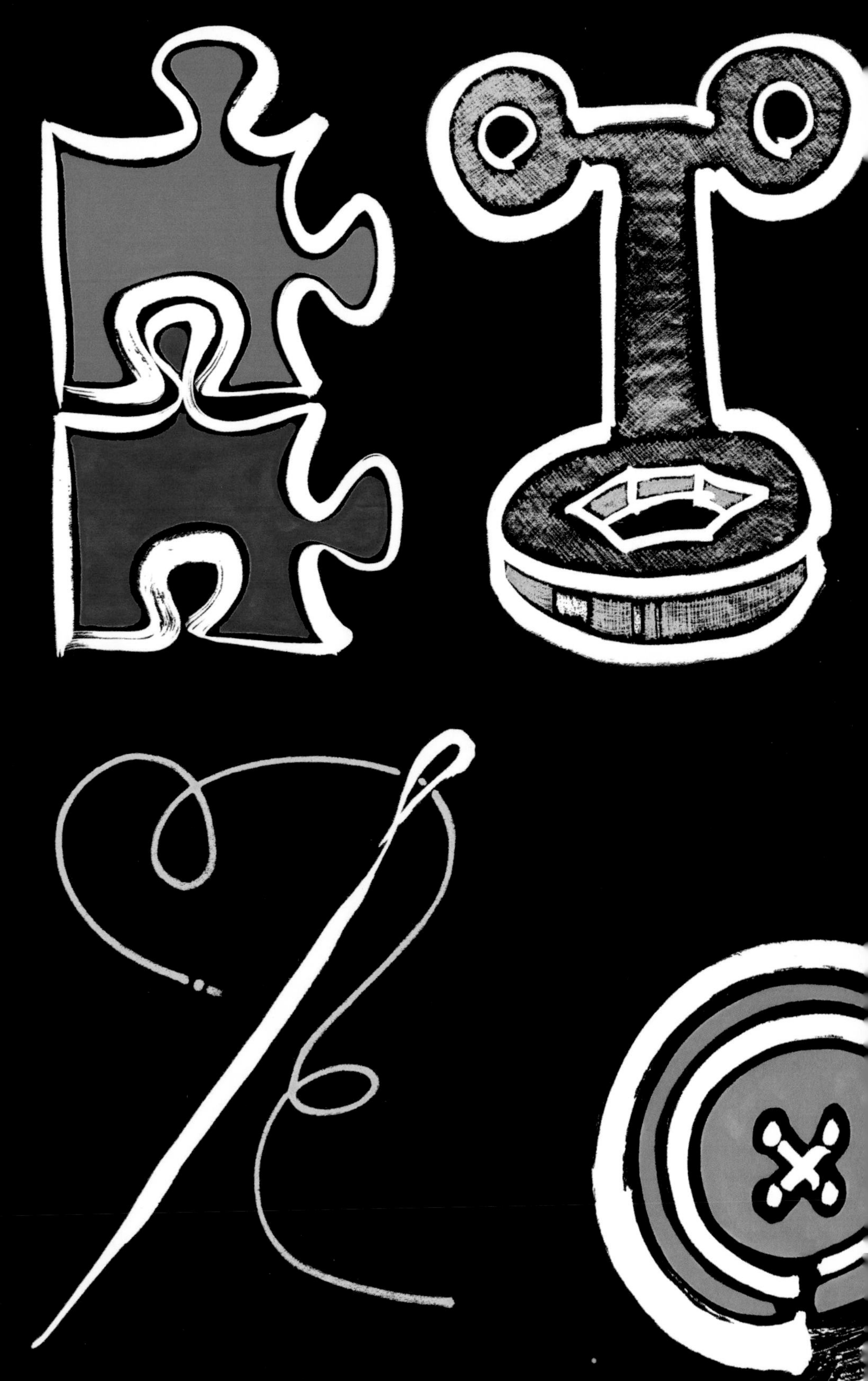

5
6
4
2
3
1

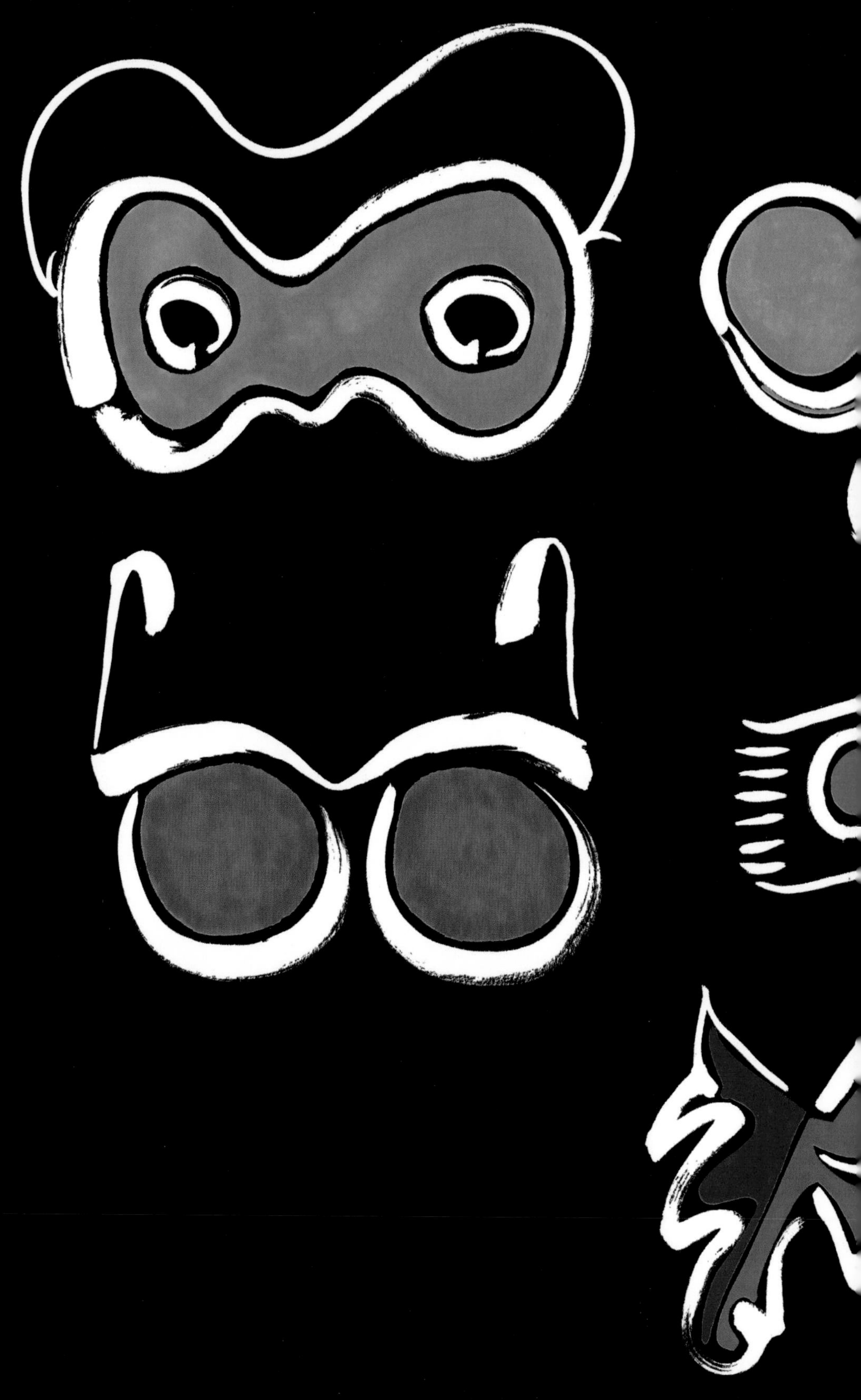

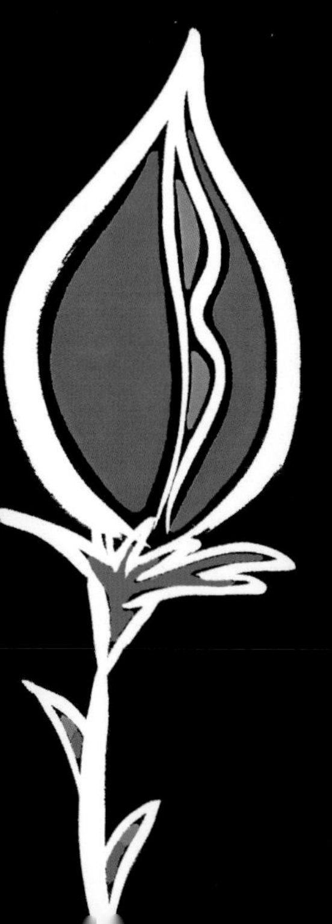

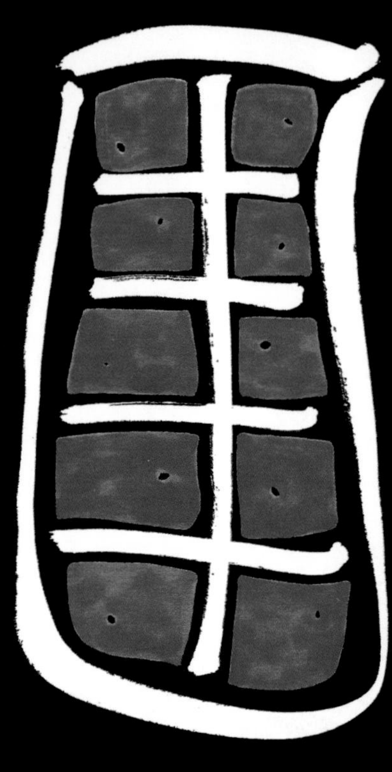
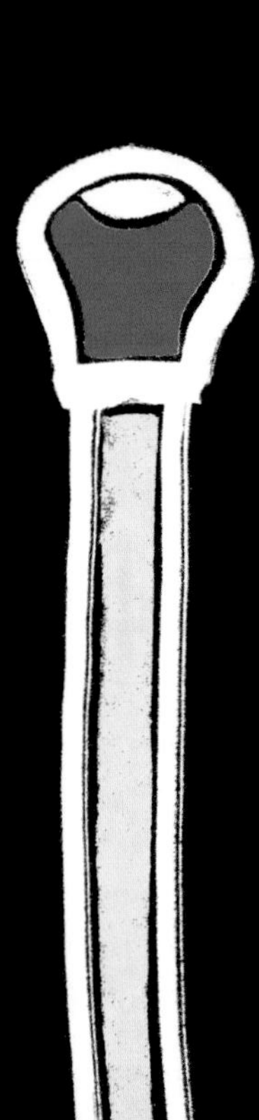

59

Two police officers were standing in the lobby. One of them pointed at me and grunted something in Spanish. I assumed it meant: "That's him, the old fool."

The police officers started after me, but I was already running out of the hotel.

I had no idea where I was going to go but I had to go there fast. Without a plan, without a map, I ran through the town. After a few blocks, I realized I was following the route Jorge had taken earlier in the day to the butterfly sanctuary. With an objective, I settled into a pace that I could sustain.

A car approached from the end of the block and I ducked between buildings and then behind a stone wall. The Day of the Dead celebrations were winding down as the cold night grew even colder. The exertion warmed me—I'd left without my coat. Adrenaline coursed through me like hot oil and when the car passed, I began to run. Then, not too far away, a siren screamed in the night. I turned off the main road and slid into the shadows of the side streets. The siren was going away from me and I started running again.

Cecelia and Monica would be safe, I hoped. She had taken a risk distracting the police captain. I'd taken a risk with Monica, but it had paid off. I found where Mizuno Ren painted the ghosts haunting him.

After an hour of running and walking I made it to the butterfly sanctuary. The souvenir stands were closed and in the dark they looked insubstantial and decrepit. I hurried past them and searched for the trailhead leading into the sanctuary. Finding it, I made my way up the trail as well as I could in the dark. In addition to my labored breathing, there were tree limbs creaking in the wind, owls hooting, and dogs howling in the distance.

WHY GHOSTS APPEAR

When I looked closely I could see butterflies at rest, huddled in the trees, under the limbs, clustered together. Occasionally a clump of them moved in a breath of light wind and there was the rustling of wings.

After I'd hiked far into the sanctuary, I sat down on a flat rock. When my breathing slowed, my body began to cool and the blood stopped rushing and pounding in my ears like an ocean's surf. But the slower my breathing became, the more I felt I was dying, like a match burning itself out. The dread that had dogged me since the first day of the investigation was becoming all encompassing, filling the voids in the universe.

It grew colder, and my breath came out in great clouds of vapor, the last animated energy in my body. The vapor covered me in a fog that condensed, coating me with frost. I was being dragged into the pit of gravity where any sliver of strength that I could use to become a ghost was destructing, tearing itself apart. The dread, the negative energy, the splitting and compression I'd experienced since the beginning of the case was not an external force, it was inside of me.

I was imploding.

It was clear to me now that the missing son had not only the psychological strength to become a ghost, but had enough to appear at his mother's house as a human being. What an incredible feat that must be for a ghost. But at this year's Festival of the Dead, he didn't appear. For whatever reason his bodily existence had been snuffed out, most plausibly because he finished the task he had to complete as a ghost. I guessed that it was to see that his mother was safe from the destructive forces that had wrenched him from life. And that's why ghosts appear—to clean up unfinished business.

I shivered in the cold. The ghosts of the others—the fortuneteller, the clerk, Obushi and his wife—came to visit, treading on the cold waves of energy permeating the forest sanctuary. They touched me with their vaporous wisps of tendril-like fingers, whispering that they wished me a quick and painless death.

▸

When the rising sun turned the sky a muddy gray, a cold mist began to fall. I was now shivering uncontrollably, violently, pulling me apart fiber by fiber. I drew my arms around my chest, hugging myself to keep every last bit of body heat from escaping. I tried to stand but my legs were frozen in place. I released my grip, exposing myself to the cold, and rubbed my knees and muscles.

The mist began to freeze into tiny pellets of ice. The icy mist stuck to the trees, the rocks and dark soil, then to me.

I pushed myself up and wobbled a few steps. The butterflies in the trees fluttered their wings trying to shake off the irritant. Their wings now coated with the ice, the butterflies began dropping from their perches. They struggled one last time on the ground. I tried to catch them, warm them in my freezing hands. I gently blew on one that floated onto my outstretched hand and it flapped its wings trying to fly. But the ice weighed it down. I put it next to my heart, holding it softly to my shirt. It fluttered there for a moment then stopped. I put it on the ground with the others.

I walked around their inert and spongy bodies, a carpet of orange and black, to the glen. There monarchs were falling from the sky and from the trees, hitting me like huge snowflakes in a blizzard of orange and yellow and black. I squinted just enough to see the opening in the trees. The glen was as big and open as a soccer stadium, now a makeshift morgue for a million butterflies. I was no longer cold, instead filled with a warmth, as if the energy of their deaths, of their last migration, resolved itself in me.

▸

Cecelia and Jorge found me, standing in utter awe, in shock, in disbelief. Butterflies had piled up to my ankles.

Cecelia draped her coat over me and put her arms around my shoulders. That gesture and the warmth of her body was unreal, unlike anything I'd ever felt. It was like ten thousand people staring at me at the same time, making me painfully aware of my own existence.

Then I heard a moan.

It had come from Jorge, his face miserable in terrible incredulity as he stooped over the deepening piles. He dipped his hands and held them as if scooping water from a stream. He held the butterflies close to his cheek before returning them to the ground.

"How did you find me?" I asked Cecelia.

"I didn't know what to do when I heard you got away from the police captain, so I called Detective Blanco. She told me the best thing to do was to get out of town. If the police captain was corrupt, it wouldn't be safe. So I called Jorge and he drove me to the places you and I had been. This was one of them. We need to get you away from here, go back to Mexico City. I've got your bags in Jorge's truck."

"There's one thing I need to do first," I said. "Monica showed me Mizuno's art in a room at the Hotel La Merced. I need to get it."

"That's not a good place to go," Cecelia said.

"It's not, but it's the best thing I've found in the investigation that gives meaning to his life. I have to have something to bring back for his mother. I know my way around the hotel. I'll be careful."

We took one last look around the glen then walked back to the jeep. While Jorge drove us back into the town, I asked him if the freezing was unusual.

"I've never heard of such a massive die-off," he said.

"It's tragic," Cecelia said. "Will they ever recover?"

"That's hard to say. Luckily not all of them are here yet. But it might be years before we see them in these numbers."

As we neared town, we encountered a stream of cars and trucks heading toward the sanctuary. Jorge said, "They must have heard the news about the butterflies."

The street in front of Hotel La Merced was empty. Jorge stopped in front of the hotel and I ran inside. I bounded up the stairs, my footfalls echoing loudly in the stairwell. I turned at the top of the stairs and found the room where Mizuno had hidden and worked.

The first thing I noticed was that another piece of art had been added to the mural, stuck on the wall like an artist's pallet: it was Cecelia's sweater. Why had Monica left it there? As a gift to Mizuno? I didn't have the time to find her and ask.

I removed the sweater to return to Cecelia. When I detached Mizuno's ghost drawings from the wall, the shimmering in my peripheral vision returned. The vibrations were stronger than ever, a vise pressing directly on my brain. I couldn't move, my muscles were rigid, and there was a deep pulsating roar in my ears. It was the collective scream of all the ghosts coming home on the wings of butterflies, only to die in the freezing mist.

All the way from Mexico I carried the burden of the millions of weightless ghosts whose hopes died on the wings of butterflies. The freezing mist followed me home, coating trees and power lines with frost. I stood outside an unfamiliar house in an unremarkable neighborhood. It was like dimly recalling a memory of a memory. But it was my house, I was sure of that when I stepped inside. The house with its low ceiling was a cold dark shack compared to the voluminous and sunlit hotel room in Mexico.

The house was quiet, and there were no ghosts, no fraud clerk *yurei* haunting me, following me to the ends of the earth. So if he were dead, and that was my belief, then he must be an *obake* haunting a particular place, probably the place where he died. If I could find that place I might help him rest at last.

Fujii and the newsstand owner had again taken care of my home; I owed them much but they would have to wait. I dropped my bag and found my winter coat in a musty closet. Out into the unusually early cold snap I went, merging into the flow of workers mindlessly seeking their place of employment. I, of course, had none.

I drove into the heart of the city and ducked into the coffee shop across from the Shinshin Group building. In a few minutes I was sipping weak and watery coffee compared to that in Mexico. Still, the warm liquid was welcoming and the quiet well-lit shop appealed to a part of my being. Unfortunately, it also illuminated a festering corner of my heart that needed to be lanced and bled. Using a pay phone I called the Shinshin Group and asked to speak with Tomoguchi Mori. When his secretary said he was in meetings all day and asked me to leave a message, I said, "No, thanks."

I went into that opulent building with its pumped-in, filtered, warmed, and scented "fresh" air. I gave a confident nod to the receptionist and strode up to the bank of elevators and pushed the button. A car came and the doors opened; it was empty and I got in and was whooshed up to the top floor. I was intercepted as soon as the elevator reached the top floor and the door opened. The bodyguard gripped my arm above my elbow and steered me out and to the side of the waiting area. He barked into his radio. "Got him."

"Yes, you do," I said. "But if you want to keep your job, you better tell your boss that I'm here to see him. If I don't get to see him, then I will be glad to leave and go to the nearest newspaper office." That seemed to be too much information for him to digest at once and on his own. He repeated my request into his radio and after several moments during which he didn't take his dull gaze off of me, he heard something in his earpiece that made him growl. He shoved me in the direction of a small conference room where he shut me in and stood outside the door.

After several minutes cooling off to distant piped-in classical music, the Shinshin Group president came into the room alone. "This is the last time I will see you," he said. "One way or the other. What do you want now?"

"I just got back from Mexico."

Tomoguchi adjusted his glasses. "You've come to show me photos of your vacation?"

"I didn't have time to take any. To get to the point, I've come to tell you a story about a hotel called La Merced in a little town in Mexico called Santo Tomas."

The president showed no emotion when I paused.

"The story is about a publishing group president who indulges in a certain illegal recreational activity illegal. Although it is overlooked by the local authorities. You can fill in the details. Anyway, the president was seen during his activities and as a result was involved directly or indirectly in making several people disappear and, at least one, murdered. I have returned with evidence of all of this and will use it to bring down this person."

Tomoguchi glared at me over the frames of his glasses. "Are you crazy? You come in here wasting my time with a fantasy, no doubt to blackmail me. If I snap my fingers, you'll be tossed off the roof like a sack of garbage."

I didn't like that prospect even though I knew he wouldn't blemish his company's reputation with a grisly murder in broad daylight. "You misunderstand my purpose in coming here. I am no blackmailer, well, not the typical one. I'm here to request your help finding three people who have gone missing as a direct result of the story I told you."

That made him think for a moment. "I'm not one to be blackmailed in whatever form you call it. But for the sake of discussion, what do you propose?"

"Specifically, I need your assistance with the Kuchi clan of fortunetellers."

▸

A curtain of malaise draped over the Kuchi complex, although it was likely my mood and not an intrinsic quality of the location. I slowly drove past the gated entry and I had a wild thought of driving my car through the fence and inside the building. My pulse picked up at the idea. "Where is the clerk?" I would demand, before the well-dressed thug pulled me from the car and attacked me. I drove away.

Mizuno Rie welcomed me into her home. Clearly whatever disappointment or anger she might have experienced because of me had not lingered. She told me she jumped out of the van at the beginning of the fracas at the Kuchi complex before I drove away. "When I got home," she said. "I called the police. Of course, they said they couldn't do anything merely on the basis of my claim. There were no apparent victims of a crime. You were gone and the clerk couldn't speak for himself. What happened to you?"

So much had happened that I couldn't begin to explicate the tangle of events. I mumbled something about it being a long involved tale requiring more than one bottle of wine. "It's not that I don't want to tell you, I do and will, provided you don't turn me out when I ask one more favor."

"Life's been a little monotonous since you went missing. Count me in."

"I hope it goes more smoothly than our last plan," I said.

After I explained what I needed, I left the fortuneteller's home. I met Tomoguchi in the old couple's restaurant where I'd eaten months ago. The wife kept up her unremitting pace serving us as she had during my first visit. Tomoguchi watched her anxiously as if she might accidentally spill a drop of soy sauce or beer on him. His bodyguard sat at a table near the door where he could watch us and anyone coming into the restaurant.

Tomoguchi asked, “Did you bring your so-called evidence?”

“It’s not on me. But you’ll be given the location as soon as this is over.”

Tomoguchi sucked in air and let out a breath that smelled of mint. “This isn’t starting well.”

“It’s starting fine, but how it ends is up to you.”

Tomoguchi tapped the table a few times. “Don’t push me to drag you out of here and make good on my threat.”

“You would have done that already if you had decided to,” I said. “It’s time. Let’s go.”

Tomoguchi and his guard followed me out of the restaurant, through the maze of alleys toward the Kuchi complex. As we walked, I pulled my collar out of my coat, ripped a button off my shirt, ruffled my hair. At the door to the Kuchi complex, Tomoguchi and his bodyguard stood on either side of me, squeezing me between them like a piece of meat needing to be tenderized.

The door opened without any of us pushing the intercom button. The Kuchi security chief was there along with his two subordinates. Behind them were Kuchi Noriyo and Teruyo/Namiko. She and I gave each other a vague look, as if we thought we recognized each other but weren’t sure. The Kuchi thug stepped aside and nodded toward me, and the two guards grabbed me by the arms. We went into the conference room where I’d been interviewed during my first visit to the complex. Kuchi Noriyo spoke first to Tomoguchi. “What makes you think we care about him?” Meaning me.

Tomoguchi said, “I know you want to clean up this mess. As do I.” He took off his glasses and said in voice an octave deeper than usual. “I want you off my back. I want this over with.”

The security chief said, “Don’t talk to her in that tone of voice.”

Tomoguchi’s bodyguard made a barking sound.

The security chief took a step toward the bodyguard.

The head of the Kuchi clan raised her hand and the chief stopped. She said, “I’m not going to listen to all this posturing. Let’s make the deal and get it over with.”

“You’ve got my offer,” Tomoguchi said. “I brought in the nosy investigator. You will give me an assurance that you will stop blackmailing me, and I will keep quiet about the fraud clerk that you did away with. I know where you left him."

Teruyo/Namiko said to me, "You found out, didn't you?"

She had more faith in my abilities than I did. It was all a bluff. I said nothing, setting my jaw in defiance. She said, "Then you must know about Mizuno Ren and the photographer's dead wife."

I said nothing and turned slowly away from Namiko. She was definitely no longer any part Teruyo. For some reason, I laughed. Everyone stared at me. Then the meeting quickly deteriorated into chaos—the Kuchi guards grabbed me as I stood up and shoved me against the wall. The security chief barged between me and Tomoguchi's bodyguard while the head of the Kuchi clan was yelling, "It's over."

I was pulled out of the room, pushed down the hall and into a garage where I was shoved into the backseat of a car. One of the guards got in beside me and the other in the driver's seat. The Kuchi thug walked into the garage a few minutes later and got into his sports car. We drove out of the garage.

It wasn't a pleasant ride—the bully kept jabbing me in the ribs with his bony elbow, laughing at some inside joke with the other bully. Other than bruised ribs, I was feeling surprisingly well and calm. It was as if I knew nothing about the world, nothing of the motives of men who are bullheaded and self-centered. The calmness was because the two opposing curves of my being were at last drawing close, intersecting with a universal power. I understood but couldn't explain.

We got on a freeway closely following the sports car. I guess he didn't want any of us soiling his leather seats so he drove alone. It was dark when we turned off the freeway and drove a few minutes into a construction project, dust particles kicking up in front of us like moths in the headlights. The end of the gravel road led to a gated fence. We stopped and the Kuchi bully driving the car got out and unlocked it. He drove through the open gate and stopped at the edge of an old gravel pit filled with water.

The guards pulled me out of the car and pushed me to the ground. My head bounced off the dirt and a sharp headache spread over my forehead. There was an unnerving feeling of someone watching me groveling at the feet of the security chief and the guards. But I could see nothing but the dirt illuminated by the harsh headlights. The presence had to be the ghosts of the clerk, of Obushi, of Mizuno Ren. They had become *obake*, howling silently in the night, staying close to their bodies at the bottom of the murky water in the gravel pit. They were waiting for me to find and release them. Or join them.

A chain of thick metal links clanked next to my head in a puff of dust. As one of the guards yanked my arms behind my back, a car's horn blared. I rolled into their legs and lunged up. The guard lost his balance and collapsed onto the other. The chief yelled at them to get me but I was already running back to the gate, running through it, running back to the gravel road where the fortuneteller waited in a car.

▸

I gave the fortuneteller her son's last drawings. She looked at them slowly, as if trying to read a message in each. Then I gave her the drawing made by the artist in Santo Tomas. As best as I could, I explained that it represented the ghost that her son would become. When she understood what I was trying to say, she inhaled sharply, as if her son suddenly materialized in front of her. She gazed at it for several minutes. As I left, I told her I hoped that her son would return to visit during the next Festival of the Dead holiday.

As I was leaving I saw a shimmering in the shadows on the wall, but when I looked closely, there was nothing.

I'd seen enough.

▸

I asked Reiko, the Red Lantern Soapland masseuse, to live with me. But she declined. What would be better, she asked, independence and working at the Red Lantern or living with me in utter dependence? Besides, she won't be working there too much longer. Nearing forty, she was losing customers who wanted younger attendants to service them. Besides, she told me that she had saved a small fortune.

▸

Before I left Mexico, I asked Cecelia Garza how much I owed her for her translation services. She smiled and shook her head. "I owe you for giving me an interesting experience, so I think we are even." I wasn't sure I would call it an interesting experience but agreed to her terms. When I am employed again I will send her a plane ticket so she can visit Japan. Maybe she will have an interesting experience here.

▸

Hattori left his house at seven in the morning. I was waiting in my car down the block and watched him enter a parking garage. In a minute, he drove out in his car. I followed him for about ten minutes when he turned into the graveled lot of a construction site. I kept driving until I could turn around. I drove back to his house and parked.

The man who lived up the street walked past, carrying his plastic shopping bag. I didn't wave at him when he gave me a look. He continued on his trip. I made myself comfortable. The day stretched out through hours as long as a lifetime. When night fell, I yawned and stretched my legs as best I could. I started my engine to make sure it was ready. Then I turned it off and waited.

Only a few minutes later, the white Toyota pulled into the garage. I started the engine and shifted the transmission into "drive" while stepping on the brake. Hattori came out of the garage. I eased the pressure on the brake and the car crept forward. I was rolling faster and faster when I stepped on the gas pedal and the car lurched ahead. With my hands gripping the steering wheel I veered toward him. I flipped on the headlamps so I could see his face lit in fear as I drove toward him.

But it wasn't Hattori—again, it was me.

I pulled the wheel at the last moment and careened down the street like a drunk driver. My mind kept redrawing the image of my face in the headlights. I fought to believe it couldn't be me. Surely my subconscious was merely projecting my own fears onto the face of another.

I reached the end of the industrial area and turned at the main street leading to the freeway. I got on the crowded but flowing roadway and drove for an hour without thinking about where I was going. Finally I took an exit and stopped at a pay phone. I called the detective who had been following me. "It's Hattori," I said. "He ran down the woman." I told him where the car was parked and Hattori's address.

"Why should I believe you? Where are you?"

I hung up the phone. There was nothing left to say.

▸

I spent a night parked in my car across from the hospital looking at her window covered with the yellow curtains. Of course, my eyes likely saw white curtains, but my mind wanted me to see yellow. A memory from twenty years ago was superimposed on reality.

My view of the world, of myself, had changed twenty years ago. The wife of the missing husband had been the catalyst. I had become a dimensional being then, not merely a person existing in the random nature of the world. It also became clear that my memory of her was itself a ghost, appearing not to haunt me or play tricks on me but to show me that no matter what happened, she had the psychological strength to become a ghost. At last the two opposing curves of my existence were finally in sync. The old case had set the two halves of me going in opposite directions but now they finally had met and rejoined.

As I drove away from the hospital, I smiled.

▸

Report (final)

31 December: 10:30 p.m.—It's been enough time that I should have found the words to explain what happened in the Mizuno case. But there will never be enough time, and in fact, time is already blurring the meaning of what I'd discovered and not discovered. Still, the facts are clear: the Shinshin Group publishing company collapsed under the excesses of its president and under the weight of the extortion by